Praise for the Novels of Iris Johansen

"Action-packed!"
—*Publishers Weekly* on *Eight Days to Live*

"With an imaginative plot and gut-wrenching action . . . this novel packs a wallop and is impossible to put down."
—*Tucson Citizen* on *Eight Days to Live*

"You'll want to keep the lights on while reading!"
—*Romantic Times BOOKreviews* on *Blood Game*

"Johansen is becoming a master of the macabre and paranormal thriller, and her latest riveting Eve Duncan tale has it all, from ghosts and secret cults to supernatural avengers."
—*Booklist* on *Blood Game*

"Readers won't soon forget either the enigmatic hero or the monstrous villain. This one's chilling to the bone!"
—*Romantic Times BOOKreviews* on *Deadlock*

"Johansen's knack for delivering robust action and commanding characters kicks into high gear."
—*Booklist* on *Dark Summer*

"Action-packed, adrenaline-fueled . . . will keep [you] eagerly turning the pages."
ksand

RE...

"Keeping the tension high and the pace relentless, prolific and compelling Johansen adds depth to her popular characters as she continues this suspenseful series."
—*Booklist* on *Quicksand*

"Bestselling author Johansen captivates readers with her latest suspense thriller . . . the suspense escalates toward an explosive conclusion."
—*Library Journal* on *Pandora's Daughter*

"An exhilarating thriller . . . suspense that will keep readers on the edge of their seats."
—*Booklist* on *Pandora's Daughter*

"A fast-paced, non-stop, clever plot in which Johansen mixes political intrigue, murder, and suspense."
—*USA Today* on *The Face of Deception*

"[A] thrill ride . . . Action, romance, castles, bomb plots, and a booby-trapped hideaway in snowbound Idaho—what more could Johansen fans want?"
—*Publishers Weekly* on *Countdown*

"Intriguing suspense . . . her new tale will please both fans and new converts."
—*Booklist* on *Blind Alley*

"Thoroughly gripping and with a number of shocking plot twists . . . packed all the right elements into this latest work: intriguing characters; creepy, crazy villain; a variety of exotic locations."
—*New York Post* on *The Search*

TITLES BY IRIS JOHANSEN

EVE

IRIS JOHANSEN

St. Martin's Paperbacks

NOTE: If you purchased this book without a cover you should be aware that this book is stolen property. It was reported as "unsold and destroyed" to the publisher, and neither the author nor the publisher has received any payment for this "stripped book."

This is a work of fiction. All of the characters, organizations, and events portrayed in this novel are either products of the author's imagination or are used fictitiously.

Published in the United States by St. Martin's Paperbacks, an imprint of St. Martin's Publishing Group

EVE

Copyright © 2011 by Johansen Publishing LLLP.
Excerpt from *Quinn* copyright © 2011 by Johansen Publishing LLLP.

All rights reserved.

For information, address St. Martin's Publishing Group, 120 Broadway, New York, NY 10271.

www.stmartins.com

Library of Congress Catalog Card Number: 2010046789

ISBN: 978-1-250-78580-0

Our books may be purchased in bulk for promotional, educational, or business use. Please contact your local bookseller or the Macmillan Corporate and Premium Sales Department at 1-800-221-7945, ext. 5442, or by email at MacmillanSpecialMarkets@macmillan.com.

Printed in the United States of America

St. Martin's Press hardcover edition / April 2011
St. Martin's Paperbacks edition / October 2011

10 9 8 7 6 5 4 3 2 1

CHAPTER

1

Two minutes.

The explosive was in place beneath the back veranda of the house. The charge set.

Agent Art Benkman slid behind the garden wall that surrounded the pool and house and waited.

No mistakes this time. His superior wouldn't tolerate another near miss. It had been made clear that Black must be destroyed. He was a monster who knew too much.

No, he'd seen Paul Black go into the house an hour ago. It was the best time for the kill. Only one person in the house besides that son of a bitch. A housekeeper who occupied the end bedroom of the rambling bungalow. He'd seen her light go out two hours ago. She'd be asleep by now.

Good night.

And good-bye.

No one would survive this blast. He'd had to be sure. One minute.

The flames from the blast would probably reach the top of those palm trees hovering over the roof.

"I've got you, Black," he murmured. "Burn in—"

Pain.

He was flipped over and was looking up at the man who had sent the needle-sharp stiletto deep into his back.

Black. But it couldn't be Paul Black. He was in the house.

No, he was here. That dark, devil's face . . .

"Who sent you?" Black asked. "Who told you I was here?" He was searching in Benkman's pockets, pulling out his wallet and the e-mail that he'd received two days ago. He glanced at it and smiled. "Very explicit. And you obeyed blindly like a good agent? Never mind. You don't have to answer. I don't need you now."

"Kill you . . ." Benkman whispered. "I have to—"

"Die," Black supplied as he picked up Benkman as if he were a child. "That's all you have to do." He was carrying him over to the house. "How do you feel about cremation?"

"No!" He started to struggle as panic overcame pain. "Don't leave me here. It's going to—"

"Blow?" Black dropped him on the floor of the great room. "In about forty seconds." He looked down at him. "Why don't you see if you can make it through the French doors and out onto the terrace? You might survive then." He turned and strolled out of the house.

Bastard.

Benkman rolled over and started to crawl toward the French doors.

Pain.

The blood was pouring out of the wound as he moved.

Weak.

The blood was slippery . . .

He was dying.

No, he'd be okay. He was always okay. He just had to get out of this damn house.

So slow. He was moving so slow.

He reached the French doors. Now crawl out onto the veranda. He was almost there . . .

And then he saw Black standing by the garden wall and watching him. He was smiling.

He tapped his watch.

Too late, Benkman realized frantically. He was too late. Time had run out.

"Don't leave me!" he howled. "Get me out of—"

The house exploded and became an inferno.

"Here's the report, sir. Shall I call Atlanta and give it to her?"

Venable scowled as he looked down at the report that Agent David Harley had put in front of him. This inquiry was shaping up to be a king-size headache. Why had he become involved in this mess?

He knew the answer. He liked Joe Quinn and Eve Duncan, and they had helped the CIA on many occasions. When Catherine Ling had asked him to pull strings and get this report concerning the death of

Eve's daughter, he'd thought it might be a way to pay back.

He wasn't sure that would be true any longer. Eve Duncan was very fragile where anything connected to her murdered daughter, Bonnie, was concerned.

"Is anything wrong?" Agent Harley asked. "I used three sources. It all checked out. And Catherine Ling is usually very accurate."

And Harley would be careful, Venable thought. He was new, but he was eager and conscientious.

"No, I'm sure you verified it correctly." He shrugged. "I can just see a blowup looming on the horizon."

"But Catherine Ling's e-mail said that—"

"I know." Venable held up his hand to stop him. Harley had met Catherine Ling only once, but he had been dazzled by her. Most men had the same response to Catherine. She was not only a top CIA agent, but she was part Caucasian, part Asian, and was one of the most gorgeous and exotic women Venable had ever met. "Catherine may be accurate, but that doesn't mean she might not trigger an explosion. She's ramming her way through every source I have to get that information, and she's not going to stop."

"Eve Duncan," Harley repeated tentatively, glancing at the report. "I've heard of her. I saw some photos. Skulls and stuff. She's a forensic sculptor, isn't she?"

"Have a little respect. She's *the* forensic sculptor," Venable said. "She's probably the best forensic sculptor in the world. Every police department in the country is standing in line to get her to work on their cold cases involving skeletal remains. Totally dedicated."

"Not totally." Harley smiled. "I read that report. She's been living with her lover police detective, Joe Quinn, for a number of years. In real life, she obviously prefers a warm body to those skeletons."

"He's a good guy," Venable said. "And tough as hell. He's an ex-SEAL. As I said, have a little respect, or you might regret it. He's been with Eve since her daughter Bonnie was kidnapped by a serial killer years ago. The kid was only seven years old, and it nearly destroyed Eve."

"I can see how it might be traumatic. Was she murdered?"

"Almost certainly. Though Bonnie's body was never recovered and the real killer never arrested. That's why Eve went back to school to become a forensic sculptor, to help bring other lost children home. But Eve's been on the hunt for Bonnie's killer all these years."

"My wife's pregnant and should be delivering my son any day," Harley said. "I don't know what I'd do if anything happened to him."

"Go on the hunt," Venable said. "As Eve Duncan is doing. As Joe Quinn is doing."

"What about you, Agent Venable? Do you have any children?"

Venable shook his head. "Divorced. No kids. I have a job. A family would get in the way." He tapped the report. "And Eve Duncan is a prime example of why I should stay that way. Finding her daughter's killer has become an obsession that's dominating everything and everyone around her. Including me." He swore beneath his breath. "Catherine Ling should have stayed out of

it. But no, she thinks that she can straighten out the entire world if she puts her mind to it."

"She's very clever," Harley said. "It could happen,
sir."

"Are we expecting any more info?"

Harley shook his head. "Those are the only sources
you asked me to tap."

And the sources Catherine Ling had asked Venable
to tap. She had known exactly what she'd wanted. He'd
asked her to wait for these reports before she went to
Eve Duncan with the information, but he couldn't be
sure that she'd do it. Catherine marched to her own
drummer and had been so on edge that she'd wanted to
get the confrontation over. That was always Catherine's
way. Bold, up-front, on the attack.

That had been Eve's method of handling problems,
too. It was one reason why the two women had become
close friends.

"I'll be glad to call Agent Ling and give her the information on this report for you," Harley offered.

"I bet you would," Venable murmured. "But I think
I'd better handle this myself. You can't expect a straightforward response from Catherine on this particular
matter."

"It seems pretty cut-and-dried to me."

"Does it?" He was tempted to let Harley contact
Catherine and have her interrogate him. If he thought
she would become his new best friend, he was going to
be sadly disappointed. She was going to want every detail so that she could mull the pros and cons, and she
would be firing questions like a machine gun. It wasn't

often that Catherine formed a friendship with anyone, but she genuinely liked Eve Duncan, and she wanted every detail to be absolutely correct. "No, I'll talk to her."

Harley looked disappointed, but he shrugged and left the office.

All right, Catherine. Venable took out his phone. Here's your ammunition to blow Eve out of the water. You may mean well, but it could go either way. I hope to hell both you and Eve manage to survive it.

There was something wrong with Eve.

Joe Quinn had glanced casually up to the porch from where he was standing at the barbecue grill near the lake. Eve had been sitting on the porch swing, but was now standing beside Catherine Ling, and Joe could tell that every muscle of her body was taut with tension.

What the hell?

Maybe he was mistaken. The sun was going down, and it was almost dark. Perhaps those nuances of unrest he thought he was seeing weren't really there. Catherine Ling had become a good friend to Eve, and there was no way that she would deliberately upset her.

Dammit, he *wasn't* mistaken.

He had lived with Eve so long that he knew every mood, every flex of her body as if it were his own. Whatever Catherine was saying to Eve, it was disturbing her. He'd better go up to the porch and—

His cell phone rang, and he glanced at the ID.

Venable. CIA.

Joe was tempted to let it go to voice mail and call back later. No, Catherine Ling was also CIA. Joe had an idea it might be a good idea to take the call before he barged up those stairs in protective mode.

"What do you want, Venable?" he asked as he pressed the button.

"Is Catherine Ling there? She's not answering her phone."

"She's here. She's been here all afternoon. Maybe she doesn't want to talk to you. The jobs you send Catherine on aren't always pleasant. It could be that she wants a vacation."

"Catherine?" He added testily, "I told her to take a vacation after Russia, but she dove right into this inquiry and pulled me in with her."

"What investigation?"

"Just an inquiry. Tell Catherine I need her to call me. I have the final report."

"Venable, what's this all about?"

"Ask Catherine. I'm supposed to be discreet. You'd think that she was *my* superior." He hung up.

Joe gazed up at the porch. It was fully dark, and they hadn't turned on the porch light. He could barely discern the two women standing by the rail. But what he couldn't see, he could feel. His instincts toward Eve had been honed to sharpness, and he could sense the emotional disturbance that was swirling about her.

Ask Catherine.

There was no doubt that he'd ask Catherine. He didn't like any of this. He felt closed out.

He started toward the porch, then stopped.

What could he do? His instinct was to join them, become part of whatever was going on between them. But Eve wouldn't appreciate his interfering. She was an independent woman. It wasn't as if Catherine was a threat. She was Eve's friend.

But even a friend could become a threat if circumstances warranted.

Not Catherine. He trusted Catherine.

He slowly turned and went back to the barbecue pit.

Keep cool. Eve would tell him what was going on eventually.

Ignore that uneasiness.

Until he couldn't stand it any longer.

Eve asked Catherine, "But why not leave in the morning?"

". . . I don't want to inconvenience you any more than I have to. You've done enough for me, Eve." Catherine's gaze was on Joe standing below them at the barbecue pit. "We've done nothing but talk about my problems. Let's talk about you and Joe. Is everything all right between you?"

"Why do you ask?"

"I just thought I caught some vibes from him today." Her gaze was still on Joe. "You're very lucky, you know. He's pretty fantastic."

"Yes, he is." Eve added, "And I know you think he's special. You've told me."

"Yes, I've always been honest with you." She paused. "I always will be." She turned to face her. "I'm no threat to you, Eve."

"You could be if you wanted to be. You're an incredibly magnetic woman, Catherine." She gazed steadily at her. "But in the end, the threat would come only from Joe. He's the only one who can hurt me."

"I'd never hurt you." Catherine's voice was passionate. "I've never had a friend like you before. At first, I was only concerned about what you could do for me, but that changed. You changed my life. I felt . . . close to you."

"And I feel close to you." Eve smiled. "So stop agonizing about it, Catherine."

"I don't want to hurt you."

Eve's smile faded. "Are we still talking about Joe?"

"No. Yes. I guess in a way we are."

"Speak up. It's not like you to be inarticulate."

Catherine turned back to look down at Joe. "Did you finish the reconstruction on Cindy?"

Cindy was the reconstruction that Eve had been working on weeks ago before she had gone to Russia at Catherine's request. It had been very difficult, and Catherine had been a great help. "Of course, she was done a week after I came home from Russia. It wasn't that difficult." She smiled. "Not after I had a little help from my friends during the initial prep work."

"Was she a pretty little girl?"

"Yes."

"Like your Bonnie?"

A tiny disturbance rippled through Eve. She didn't look at all like Bonnie. "Why are you talking about Bonnie, Catherine?"

"Because I think Joe is jealous of your obsession with Bonnie. Not of your daughter. Just of your feelings for her. He'd have to be a saint not to feel a little put in the shade by the way you feel. Isn't that true?"

She didn't speak for a moment. "Yes. But friend or not, I don't want to discuss this with you, Catherine."

"I have to discuss it with you. Do you think I want to do it? I was even thinking of walking away and forgetting about it. But I can't do that, Eve."

Eve frowned. "What are you talking about?"

"You and Joe have a giant problem, and I don't want to make it any bigger."

"How could you do that?"

"Easily." Her lips twisted. "I'm good at what I do. I'm an expert. I just set my mind to it and cause the sky to fall."

Eve slowly rose from the swing and went to stand beside Catherine. "Talk to me."

Catherine looked away from her again. "I told you I'd pay you back, remember? I was so grateful I wanted to give you what you wanted most in the world."

Eve gazed at her with exasperation. No matter how she tried, she couldn't convince Catherine to accept what Eve had done as a gesture of friendship and let it go. Catherine had come to her to ask her to do an age progression on her son Luke, who had been kidnapped when he was two and had been missing for nine years.

Eve had been inevitably drawn into the search for Luke that had culminated in a deadly race to save him from his kidnapper in Russia. "And I told you to forget it."

"That's not in my makeup." She was silent for a minute. "What you want most in the world is to bring your Bonnie home. To do that you have to find her killer. When I came home from Hong Kong, I had lots of time to concentrate on thinking about your problem. I tried to look at the crime from an objective and fresh point of view. Then I started to dig. I used every contact and information-gathering unit I had at my disposal and at Venable's disposal. We even tapped the NSA."

Eve could feel her chest tightening. Don't hope. The search had gone on too long for Catherine to just step in and perform a miracle. "Joe was FBI at the time Bonnie was taken. We didn't exactly stop at local law enforcement."

"But all the information wasn't available then."

"I know that. My friend, Montalvo, recently gave me a list of three new suspects. Two didn't pan out, but I still have the third one to investigate. Paul Black. Is that the name you ran across?"

"His name popped up."

Eve's gaze narrowed on Catherine's face. "But?"

"I was more interested in someone else."

"Who?"

"He had opportunity. He might have had motive." She was speaking quickly, tersely. "In this type of crime, there's ample precedent for this kind of perpetrator."

"Dammit. Why are you being so evasive?"

"Joe. I can see you have to walk very carefully where he's concerned. He's very emotional about your obsession with Bonnie. He's nuts about you." Her hands tightened on the porch rail. "And he doesn't need to come face-to-face with this for it to tear him apart. Hell, it might tear you both apart."

"Catherine."

"Okay." She drew a deep breath. "Joe has been thinking about you as being totally his own since the moment you met. It's been the saving grace when he had to come to terms with your obsession with Bonnie. It would disturb the hell out of him to lose that security."

"There's no way he would lose it."

"No? You're very cool, very controlled, but it wasn't like that always. There was a time when you lost your head and spun out of control over a man."

Eve was beginning to see where Catherine was going. No, it couldn't be. It was impossible. She asked hoarsely, "Catherine, who killed my Bonnie?"

"I didn't say I was certain."

Eve was shaking. "Tell me. Tell me the name."

"You want a name?" Catherine drew a deep breath. "The name you didn't even see fit to put on the birth certificate, Eve," she said gently. "Bonnie's father, John Gallo."

Eve had been expecting it, but the name struck her, stunned her. She couldn't breathe. She could barely speak, "No . . . it's not true. You don't understand. It's not true."

But if Catherine thought it true, then somehow it might be.

No, it was impossible.

"Eve, I wouldn't have just pulled his name—"

"No!" She had to get out of here. She had to be alone. She whirled and was across the porch, fumbling at the screen door. "You're wrong, Catherine. You couldn't be more wrong. It's not—" She slammed the door behind her and leaned back against it, staring into the darkness.

Cool and controlled, Catherine had called her. Where was that coolness now? She felt as vulnerable and emotional as she had when she was that sixteen-year-old kid who had given birth to Bonnie. So angry, so defiant, so passionate.

John Gallo.

Catherine's words had sent her spiraling back to that sixteen-year-old girl.

Back to John Gallo . . .

CHAPTER

2

I need a little money, Eve." Sandra Duncan's soft, Southern tone was coaxing. "You got paid last night, didn't you? A ten spot will do me." Her hand fluttered to her short red-brown hair. "I need to get my hair tinted so that I can go look for a job. I've got to look my best."

Her mother was stoned again, Eve realized in despair. Eyes a little unfocused, movements slow and uncoordinated. And the ten spot she wanted might go for crack or marijuana instead of hair tint. Yet what the hell could she do? Sandra hadn't had a job in four months, and they needed any money that her mother could bring in. The rent at their apartment was a month behind, and Eve barely made enough working part-time at Mac's Diner to pay the utilities. "I can give you five, Mother. Can you go to that beauty college in College Park and get it any cheaper?"

"How many times do I have to tell you to call me

Sandra?" her mother said. "Everyone tells me I'm much too young to have a grown daughter of sixteen. Why, I'm just a little over thirty myself." She reached over and patted Eve's cheek. "I had you when I was only fifteen. I could have had an abortion, but I decided to keep you. It wasn't easy for me. You owe me, don't you, honey? Ten?"

Sandra always brought up how much Eve owed her when she needed something, Eve thought with annoyance. When she was younger, it had hurt her. But then she'd realized that her mother used it to get what she wanted, and that big sacrifice was probably because Sandra had been too far along to safely get an abortion. She reached into her wallet and brought out a ten-dollar bill. "Okay. But I want you to show me how pretty you look tomorrow after you get your hair done."

"Do you think I'm pretty?" Sandra looked in the mirror. "You never say so." She patted her hair again. "You're not exactly pretty, Eve, but you have my hair. Everyone says that my hair is very unusual." She picked up her handbag. "That's why I have to keep it looking nice." She headed for the door. "Do you know, I bet that manager at Mac's Diner would give you a full-time job if you asked him nicely."

It wasn't the first time Sandra had made that suggestion. Her mother always conveniently forgot what she didn't want to remember. "I'm not going to ask him. I haven't graduated from high school yet, Sandra. And Mr. Kimble has already said he'll keep me on and work around my hours when I go to college."

"College?" Sandra smiled with genuine amusement.

"People like us don't go to college, honey. You'll be much happier if you get that thought right out of your head."

"Would I?" She tried to smother the anger, but it burst free. "And are you happy jumping from job to job, Sandra? Are you happy sniffing coke to make you think everything is what it should be?" She looked around the shabby apartment. She tried to keep it clean, but everything about it was worn, drab, and depressing. "Are you happy living here? Well, I'm not, and I'm not going to stop thinking of ways to get away from here."

Sandra was looking at her in bewilderment. "Don't be ugly. There's nothing wrong with smoking a joint or sniffing a little coke now and then. It's not as if I'm one of those drug addicts on Peachtree Street."

"No? Have you tried to kick it lately?"

"Why should I?" She opened the door. "You're just too intense about most everything. You seem to be mad at me every time you see me. You work or read all the time. You don't even have a boyfriend. Sometimes I don't understand you, Eve." She slammed the door behind her.

Sandra had never understood her, Eve thought. Even when she'd been a child, her mother had often looked at her as if she were some strange creature from another planet.

But then Sandra had been revolving in her own solar system ever since Eve could remember. Marijuana, crack, coke, acid.

Don't think about it. Sandra wouldn't listen to her, and she had her own battles to fight. She couldn't help her mother, but she could help herself. She had grown up in the streets and learned every trick in the book to fight those battles.

She glanced at the clock. It was almost six. She had to get to work, or she'd be late. She'd hoped to finish her geometry before she had to leave, but Sandra had been home, and that usually meant a delay. She closed her geometry book and stuck it in her canvas book bag. Maybe she'd get a chance to finish on her break.

She locked the door and ran down the four flights of cement stairs that led to the front entrance of the housing development. The stink was overwhelming. Someone had thrown a sack of garbage on the third landing. All they'd had to do was take it down two flights more to the garbage cans, but that was too much trouble.

Don't look at the garbage, the iron banister rails, the scrawled graffiti on the dirty gray walls. She had control of their apartment, but all she could do was ignore everything outside their apartment door.

She threw open the worn oak door of the front entrance. Two silver-haired black ladies were slowly approaching, and she waited to hold the door for them.

Then she was quickly outside, drawing a deep breath.

Fresh air. Sunlight. The smell of garbage was less down here.

"Hello, Eve, aren't you late?" Rosa Desprando was sitting in the sun on the green bench outside the building with her year-old little boy beside her. She spent a lot of time outside; her father was always yelling at her because the baby was too noisy.

"A little." Rosa was her own age, sixteen, and had

been in her homeroom at school before she had gotten pregnant and dropped out. Eve had always liked her. She was a little slow, but that didn't matter. She had a good heart and was always smiling, something that wasn't common in Eve's world. In fact, she had too good a heart. She'd been a target for every guy in school because they could con her into anything. Including getting pregnant with adorable Manuel, who she loved more than anything in the world.

Eve stopped by the bench and stroked the baby's dark curls. "Hey, hot stuff," she said softly. "How you doing?"

Manuel was gurgling and batting his long eyelashes at her. She had once told Rosa that he should be doing commercials for mascara. He was a plump, rosy-cheeked child, and completely enchanting.

Eve chuckled. "I think he's doing fine. Is he still keeping you awake teething?"

"Yes, it doesn't matter," Rosa said as she adjusted the baby's Braves baseball shirt. "He's worth it. Doesn't he look cute in this shirt you bought for him? Say thank you, Manuel."

"No big deal. It only cost me fifty cents at Goodwill."

"But he's so cute in it. Like a real baseball player. I'm trying to teach him to say thank you. He said it yesterday."

Manuel beamed up at Eve. "Mama."

"I don't think so," Eve said.

"He calls everyone mama," Rosa said. "Even my papa."

"He'll get it straight soon." She dropped a kiss on his head and opened the gate. "See you, Rosa."

Rosa nodded. "I saw your mama a few minutes ago. She looked real pretty."

"Sandra always looks nice," Eve said as she started the four-block walk to the bus stop.

"Eve."

"What?" Eve glanced back over her shoulder.

"Watch out." Rosa's gaze was fixed on the alley at the end of the block. "I saw Rick Larazo and Frank Martinelli and some of their gang around earlier this evening. Rick looked . . . wild. I think he's on something bad."

"I always watch out," Eve said. "You keep away from them, Rosa."

"They don't do anything but call me bad names." Rosa cuddled her baby closer. "They can't hurt me, but I don't like them talking like that about Manuel. He didn't do nothin'. It was all my fault."

"It wasn't your fault." That wasn't true. It was Rosa's fault for trusting and believing and for being born in a world that victimized the innocent and the weak. "It was just something that happened. It can work out. You take good care of Manuel and look through that GED pamphlet I gave you. You'll get your diploma, then you can get a good job."

She shook her head. "I'm not smart like you, Eve."

"You don't have to be smart. You just have to want it enough. Look, Rosa, we don't have to be like our parents, living hand to mouth, falling into the same traps, making the same mistakes. We can dig ourselves out of here." She could never understand why that desire wasn't there in the people around her. It had always been a burning passion with her. But she didn't have time to argue with Rosa at that moment. "Study for that GED. I'll talk to you later. See you."

Her pace quickened as she kept a wary eye on the dark cavity of the alley as she passed it. She had been attacked more than once by scum hiding in that cluttered dimness.

This time she was lucky.

Evidently Rick Larazo and his gang had moved on and she didn't have—

A scream.

Rosa.

Eve whirled.

Dear God.

Rick Larazo, Frank Martinelli, and two other boys were in front of the housing development.

Rick had taken the baby away from Rosa and was holding Manuel over his head. She was trying desperately to jump up and reach him. Frank Martinelli was laughing and backing away. "Throw him, Rick. He thinks he's a baseball player, let him play."

"No!"

Rosa screamed as the baby was thrown up in the air and across the yard.

Eve stared in horror.

It was almost like watching slow motion. Manuel's plump little legs flailing in the air, Rosa whirling and reaching out, the boys laughing and calling out.

"Don't worry, Rosa. I've got him." Frank Martinelli stepped forward, pretended to catch the baby, then deliberately stepped back and let the baby fall to the ground.

Damn them. Damn them. Damn them.

Eve raced back toward the development.

Rosa was crying, trying to get to her baby, but Rick was holding her back.

The baby was lying still, crumpled on the ground.

"Let her *go*!" Eve tackled Rick Larazo, her hand grabbing for his penis and twisting.

He howled, falling, and released Rosa.

"Get Manuel inside, Rosa," Eve yelled, and jumped on top of Rick. She wouldn't be able to hold him long. He was big, strong, and his eyes were as wild as Rosa had said. His dirty straw-colored hair was scraggly, with pink-dyed streaks, and he looked like some weird cartoon character. Only there was nothing funny about him. She was surprised he'd even been able to feel the pain through the drugs.

Rosa snatched up the baby and ran up the stairs and into the building.

Good.

Now to try to get away herself.

Too late.

Frank Martinelli grabbed her hair from behind and jerked backward.

Rick punched her in the stomach and pushed her off him and to the ground.

"Bitch. Interfering bitch." He was kneeling over her and his fist lashed out and connected with her cheek. "Come on, guys, it's party time."

Pain.

Darkness.

Don't give in to it.

She wouldn't be raped by these bastards.

She shook her head to clear it, then her teeth sank into Frank Martinelli's hand, the one that was holding her hair. He screamed and released it. She butted her head as hard as she could against Larazo's chest.

She rolled sidewise and reached for the strap of her book bag. She slung it with all her force at Larazo's head. She jumped to her feet and ran toward the front entrance.

Her way was blocked by the two other boys, who had been watching with wide grins.

"Get her," Larazo said. "Don't let her inside. Frank, go watch the street. I'm gonna make her scream. I want to—" His voice suddenly cut off into a gurgle. "Shit!"

Eve glanced over her shoulder. Someone, a dark-haired man, was standing behind Larazo, his arm around the boy's neck. As she watched, he jerked Larazo's head sidewise, lifted the edge of his hand, and brought it down in a karate chop.

He let Larazo drop to the ground and turned to Frank Martinelli. "Come on," he said softly. "I haven't had enough."

Frank Martinelli hesitated and lunged forward, reaching for his switchblade. He barely got it out when he was whirled around, his arm twisted behind his back. He shrieked as his arm was pushed up higher and higher.

Eve heard the bone snap.

The other two boys who were blocking Eve's path

parted like the Red Sea and ran, leaving Larazo and Martinelli on the ground.

Martinelli was moaning and trying to crawl toward the street, but Larazo was still slumped, silent.

"Did you kill him?" Eve whispered. "You'd better go quickly. The people who live here never come out to help, but they do call the police. The cops don't care who's to blame; they take everyone in and book them."

"I know. He's not dead. I wouldn't let a bastard like that ruin my life. I've got plans. He should be coming around in a few minutes." The dark-haired man who had taken down Larazo and Martinelli came toward her. "You okay?"

She felt dazed, and her head was still spinning. "Yes."

He was younger than she had thought at first glance. She had thought he might be in his twenties. He was tall and powerfully built, but was probably no more than eighteen or nineteen. Olive skin, dark hair, dark eyes, full lips, and an indentation in his chin that made him look vaguely exotic. He was wearing a blue-and-white jacket, jeans, and black T-shirt. "Who are you? I've never seen you around the neighborhood."

"John Gallo. My uncle just moved into the project two blocks down two days ago." He was close to her, and his hand reached out to touch her cheek. "Bad bruise."

She instinctively moved away, and his hand dropped.

She hadn't wanted to move away, she realized in surprise. Why . . .

"I'm fine." Then the shock left her as she remembered Rosa and the baby. Manuel had been lying so still . . . "But Rosa's little boy may not be fine." She whirled and was hurrying up the steps. "Did you see what they—"

"I saw everything." John Gallo was behind her on the steps. "It might be okay. The kid could just have been stunned."

"Yeah." But babies were so fragile. It hurt her to think of how easily they could be hurt.

Bastards.

Rosa was sitting on the landing, holding Manuel, and rocking back and forth. "He's dead." Tears were pouring down her cheeks. "He won't wake up, Eve."

"Shh." She looked down at the baby. He was pale. Those impossibly long lashes were lying on pallid cheeks. She bent her head close to his lips. "I think he's breathing."

"Really?" Rosa's face was suddenly luminous. "I couldn't tell."

"Stop rocking him. I've heard if he's hurt, you're not supposed to move him." But it was probably too late. The damage would have already been done. They'd had to get Manuel inside and away from those scumbags, and afterward, who could blame Rosa for holding and rocking him in her agony. "I'll go use the public phone downstairs to call for an ambulance."

"No, I'll do it." John Gallo ran down the dozen steps to the first floor, picked up the receiver of the phone on the wall, and deposited a coin in the slot. "I'll make sure you have help coming, then I'll take off. I don't want to have to answer questions if I don't have to. They'll probably take him to Grady Hospital. Are you going with her?"

"Please, Eve," Rosa whispered.

She should go on to work. She'd probably lose her job. Then she looked at Rosa and nodded resignedly. If Mr. Kimble fired her, she'd find another job. "I'll go with her. What else can I do?"

John Gallo smiled. "That's how I felt when I saw them hurting you. What else could I do? Sometimes you just have to do what you feel is right."

And right for him had been breaking bones and coming close to killing Larazo.

And saving her from being raped and maybe murdered.

"Thanks," she said awkwardly. She knew she should be grateful, but she wasn't accustomed to anyone stepping in to help her. "You didn't have to do that for me. I'd have found a way out."

"I bet you would. You were really something. Hell, maybe you wouldn't have needed me at all." He started to dial the phone. "That's what I kept telling myself while I was watching you take them all on. Don't get caught up in this mess. It's not your business. She might be okay. You'll end up in jail or the hospital." He looked over the phone at her, and his eyes held hers. "It didn't do any good. I had to do it anyway." He began to speak into the phone as the operator answered.

She gazed at him while he spoke, watching the play of expressions on his face. Why couldn't she take her eyes off him? He was just a guy. Yeah, good-looking and kind of . . . different, but that shouldn't matter.

Why couldn't she stop looking at him?

GRADY HOSPITAL
THREE HOURS LATER

"They say Manuel is going to be all right, Eve." Rosa's face was wreathed in smiles as she hurried down the corridor to the waiting room, where she'd left Eve. "They said it was a minor bump, a possible concussion or something, but he's going to be fine."

"Great. When can we take him home?"

"When my papa comes. They won't let him go with me. They say they need to ask him questions." Her expression clouded. "He's going to be mad at me. He said I could only keep the baby if he didn't cause trouble." She frowned. "And those doctors were asking me all kinds of funny questions. If I ever shook Manuel or maybe threw him in his bed when I got mad at him for crying."

"You told him about Larazo and the others?"

She nodded. "But none of them were still there when the ambulance came. The police said none of the neighbors had seen anything."

Of course they hadn't, Eve thought bitterly. It would make them targets of Larazo and his gang. "Well, your papa will tell them how well you treat Manuel."

"He's never home. He works all the time. He might tell them he doesn't know." She moistened her lips. "And he doesn't really want me to keep Manuel. He doesn't like babies. They cry too much. But I know after Manuel gets a little older, he'll like him much more."

Providing Rosa got to keep her son, Eve thought.

DEFACS sometimes yanked a kid at the first sign of abuse. Though she'd seen them give the child back with equal speed if their budget was cut.

But Rosa didn't deserve this kind of hassle. She was a good mother and loved that baby. "Talk to your papa as soon as he gets here. Tell him what happened."

Rosa nodded doubtfully. "But how can I prove it? They won't believe me. They'll say I made it up."

"Tell them to ask me."

"But you're my friend." She paused. "And you're the same age as me. They won't believe you, either."

Eve knew that was true. Not only was she sixteen, but a check would show that her mother was on drugs. She'd be tarred with the same brush. "Then we'll find another way to convince them. I'll go to every apartment in the development and talk to the tenants. Someone will be willing to tell the cops the truth."

"Will you do that?" Rosa's face lit like a sunrise. "You'll keep them from taking my baby?"

Eve gazed at her helplessly. Simple question from a simple, loving girl. But nothing was simple in the slums where they had been born and raised. Sometimes the people who were trying to help blundered and managed to destroy every chance of happiness. "I promise, they won't take Manuel. If they do, we'll get him back."

Rosa gave her a hug and whirled. "I've got to go back to Manuel. They won't let me stay in the same room with him without a nurse being there, but they said I could watch him through the window."

Eve watched her running down the corridor. What

were they afraid she'd do to her baby? Smother him? Anyone could see that she adored Manuel. It was a crazy world.

"Hi." John Gallo was coming toward her from the direction of the elevators. "How's the kid?"

"He'll be okay," she said curtly. "It's a miracle. They could have killed him."

"You look like you're unraveling." He went to the coffee machine. "Coffee? Or maybe, a Coke?"

She nodded. "Coffee. Black." She sat back down. "And I'm not unraveling. What are you doing here?"

"I got to thinking about the kid." He handed her the coffee. Then he went to the soft-drink machine and got a Coke for himself. "I don't know how anyone drinks black coffee. It tastes like tar to me."

"It was all my mother kept in the house when I was a kid."

"You're not much more than a kid now."

"Sixteen."

"That's what I was afraid of. I was hoping for a little older." He sat down beside her. "Eve, Rosa called you. Eve what?"

"Eve Duncan." She took a drink of the coffee. It was strong and generally foul-tasting. She didn't care. It was hot. "And why do you care how old I am? Are you making a pass at me?"

"No, you'll know when I do." He lifted his cup to his lips. "Just a comment. You're still in high school?"

"I graduate next year. You?"

"I graduated over a year ago. I've been moving

around the country and raising a little hell with a couple of buddies for the last year. Sort of a last hurrah before I go into the service."

"You're joining the Army?"

He nodded. "My parents are dead, and I don't have money for college. I thought it was my best bet to get more education and move up in the world. The Army's not a bad deal." His lips tightened. "And I won't be caught in the same trap that choked my folks to death. Minimum-wage jobs and kids they never wanted. You think that housing development you live in is bad? I moved down here from Milwaukee, and the place I lived was called the Bricks. We had a killing nearly every two months, and the cops never came near it without a backup."

"Is that where you learned to— You broke Frank Martinelli's arm."

He shrugged. "I learned a little self-defense from living at the Bricks. But my uncle was a Ranger in the Army, and he taught me everything he knew. Uncle Ted is the reason I'm down here. He's got a back problem, and he moved down here because the VA Hospital has some specialists in Atlanta. I wanted to get him settled before I checked in for basic training."

"Self-defense?" Eve's brows rose. "It didn't look like self-defense to me. They didn't have a chance."

He smiled. "If I'd let them move first, it would have been self-defense. It's all how you look at it." His smile faded. "And they made me mad. I didn't like what they were doing to you."

"Neither did I." She leaned back in the seat. "I was scared."

"But you went running in after them anyway."

"They were hurting the baby." She lifted her hand and rubbed her neck. "No one has a right to hurt the helpless. Most of us can take care of ourselves. But you have to do something about it if they go after babies or animals or—"

"Is your neck hurting?"

"Aching. That bastard was jerking me backward by my hair."

"I can help." He put his Coke down and stood up. "Lean forward a little."

She looked at him warily. "What?"

"I won't hurt you." He stood a little behind her. "My uncle taught me this, too. It helped when I got whiplash from an accident." His hands were on the back of her neck. "It's all in the thumbs . . ." His thumbs were digging into her neck in deep massage. "Relax."

She couldn't relax. Her flesh felt hot beneath his touch, and that heat was spreading out in waves throughout her body. The muscles of her stomach were clenching, and her breasts . . .

What the hell was happening to her?

She knew what was happening. She wasn't ignorant. It just had never happened to her.

"You're not relaxing," he said softly.

"No." But she didn't want him to stop. "You're not . . . helping me."

"I'm not helping myself much, either." His fingers never stopped moving, digging, pressing. "But I want to keep on touching you no matter how much it hurts." He drew a deep breath, and his hands fell away from her.

"I didn't mean it to happen this way. I didn't mean it to happen at all. Hell yes, I wanted to get my hands on you. I've wanted that ever since I saw you sitting on those steps at—" He dropped down in the chair next to her. "Sorry. I didn't know you would—"

He didn't know that she'd respond as she had done. She hadn't known it would happen, either. That flash of sensuality had come like a bolt of lightning. Searing, melting, overpowering. She instinctively pushed the knowledge of that response away from her. "It's okay. I'm . . . it's not as if—nothing happened."

"The hell it didn't." He wasn't looking at her. "But I'm trying to work it out in my head and decide what's going on. Look, I'm no saint, but I don't jump every girl I run across. The whole damn night has been crazy. I don't usually interfere with— But I couldn't let them hurt you. And then later on the stairs, I couldn't keep from looking at you."

And she hadn't been able to stop looking at him. She still couldn't. He was staring straight ahead, but her gaze was drawn to him like a magnet. Her gaze fell to his hand, lying on the wood arm of the chair.

His nails were short and clean, and the thumbs, which had dug into her muscles, looked long and strong.

They had been strong. She felt as if she could still feel the imprint on her flesh. Her chest was tightening, and her heartbeat was suddenly faster.

His gaze shifted to her face. "Oh, shit." His cheeks were flushed, and his dark eyes were narrowing on her throat, then wandering to her breasts.

She had to stop this. She hunted wildly for something to break the web of sensuality that was tightening around her.

Rosa. The reason she was here. Talk about Rosa.

She jerked her eyes away from his. "Rosa's afraid they're going to try to take her baby away."

"I don't want to talk about Rosa right now." His voice was soft and with a note in it that sent a shiver through her. She hadn't realized that a shiver could be hot as well as cold. Then he paused. "But you need to back away from me, don't you? Okay, I'll try not to think about— but it won't be easy." He combed his fingers through his thick, dark hair. "What did you say? Oh, yeah. Why do they want to take the kid away from her?"

"They think she might be the one who hurt Manuel. It's nuts. She loves that baby."

He nodded. "I could tell."

"None of the neighbors will talk to the police about what Rick Larazo and the rest of the gang did. And the guys were gone by the time the ambulance came. They're not going to believe me, either. I'm too young." She added in disgust, "They never believe anyone under thirty."

"And you're just a little over halfway there." He grimaced. "Dammit."

"I'll get around it." She finished her coffee. "I promised Rosa I'd go talk to some of the neighbors and try to persuade them to tell the truth about what they saw."

"You really want to help her, don't you?"

"Of course I do. Any way I can."

"Then, if you can't find someone to tell the truth because Larazo's got them scared, get one of the pot-heads in the place to lie and say they saw it. It shouldn't be hard. Just slip them a joint. There are addicts in half the apartments in the building."

"I don't deal drugs," she said sharply.

"Whew." His eyes narrowed on her face. "Did I hit a nerve?"

She ignored the question. "Do you deal?"

He shook his head. "But if it came to a choice of pay-ing someone a few joints to help your friend keep her kid, I'd do it in a heartbeat. It's a shitty world, and you have to pick both the weapons and the battles."

"Not drugs."

He nodded. "Whatever you say." He was silent a mo-ment. "But you have to know that I'm not like you. I won't lie. I'm not what you'd call a good guy. I do what-ever I have to do to survive and get what I want." He paused. "It's not always safe to trust me."

She couldn't look away from him. He was telling her the truth. She could see it in the intensity of his eyes, the tautness of his lips. "It doesn't matter. I don't have to trust you." With an effort she managed to pull her gaze away. "You're nothing to me."

He chuckled. "Liar. Telling the truth should go both ways, Eve." His smiled faded. "But maybe I'm asking too much. This is hard for you, isn't it? Sometimes I think you're tough as nails, then you surprise me." He reached out and touched the soft hair at her temple. "How many guys have you made out with, Eve?"

His fingers were warm against the sensitive skin of her temple and were causing her pulse to leap as if to reach out to that touch.

He muttered a curse. "Dammit to hell."

She could feel the heat rise to her face. "I don't want to talk about this. It makes me feel . . . It's none of your business." She moved her head so that he was no longer touching her. She jumped to her feet. "I'm going to go back to the development and ring some doorbells."

"I've got wheels. I'll take you."

"No." She shook her head. "I don't want to go with you. I don't want this. It's not a good idea."

He rose slowly to his feet. "Maybe not. Probably not. But I'm not going to stop. I need it too much. I told you I wasn't a good guy." His eyes were suddenly glittering recklessly. "What the hell. If I wasn't the first, someone else would be. I don't know what's happened to me, but I'm going to go on until we're both drunk and dizzy with each other."

Drunk and dizzy. Eve felt that way already, and it was scaring her. "You listen to me," she said fiercely. "You've been telling me all the things you want to do with your life. That's fine, go do them. I'm not going to be a play toy for anyone. You think I don't want to get out of the slums and make something of myself? I've worked at all kinds of jobs since I was twelve years old, and nothing is going to keep me down." She started down the hall toward the bank of elevators. "Not my mother, not you, not anyone."

"I wouldn't keep you down. I'd help you fly, Eve." He

held her gaze as he added softly as she got on the elevator, "We'd both fly. It might not be for long, but how we'd soar."

He was the last thing she saw as the elevator doors closed.

He stood with legs slightly parted, worn, faded jeans hugging his muscular thighs. He was tall, strong, but there was nothing bulky about that strength. He looked graceful, yet . . . tight. Sensual and wired and completely in tune with his body. Like a powerful machine, tensed and ready to move.

Ready to perform.

And heat was tingling through her as she stared at him. She wanted the door to close and block out the sight of him.

Yet when it did, she felt as if he was still with her. She didn't want to feel like this. It bewildered her. It wasn't as if she wasn't familiar with sex. Sex was everywhere. She had seen sex on street corners, on the landings of the development, heard the sounds in the next room when Sandra brought home one of her men. Sex was what had drawn all those boys to Rosa and given her a child to raise. But it had never affected Eve. She hadn't understood it.

She understood it now. It had a name.

John Gallo.

CHAPTER

3

I didn't see nothin'." Mrs. Smythe scowled. "I told the cops. Leave me alone." She slammed the door in Eve's face.

Eve drew a deep breath. It was the ninth door that she'd knocked on. Two of the occupants had been too stoned to even understand what she was talking about. The others had been either indifferent or clearly afraid. All of them were very annoyed to be disturbed in the middle of the night.

Too bad. If she'd waited for morning, the hospital might have already made a decision to turn the baby over to DEFACS. She had to get Manuel away from them right away.

She turned away. Don't get discouraged. She still had other doors to try, other people to try to persuade. All it would take was one person, one witness, and Rosa would be safe.

"Eve!"

She turned to see Rosa running up the stairs. Her face was glowing and she was carrying a sleeping Manuel in her arms.

"They let you take him?" Eve smiled jubilantly. "That's wonderful. Did your papa convince them what a great mom you are?"

She shook her head. "He signed the release papers and left." She was stroking the baby's silky hair as she balanced him against her shoulder. "But I prayed and prayed, and God must have heard me."

"Those doctors changed their minds?"

"They had to do it when the police called them." Her brown eyes were dancing with happiness. "They couldn't keep my baby."

"Police?" She shook her head. "Slowly, Rosa. Why did the police call the hospital?"

"Because God answered my prayer."

"How?"

"Rick Larazo went into the Third Street Police Station and told them that he was the one who threw my baby on the ground."

"What?" Eve shook her head. "No way, Rosa. He wouldn't have done that in a million years."

"I know," she said simply. "That's why it had to be God who made him do it."

"I don't want to shake your faith in God, but I think there has to be some other explanation. I don't think he would bother to deal—"

"But you can't give me any other reason." Her smile

was brilliant. "God must just love my Manuel and knew he'd be happy with me."

Give up. It was as good a reason as any other that she could think of, and it was making Rosa happy. "Who wouldn't love your baby?" she asked gently. "I'm glad he decided to intercede." Her tone hardened. "And I hope he used his influence to throw Rick Larazo into the hoosegow for the next twenty years."

Rosa giggled and started up the next flight of stairs to her apartment. "I'll pray, Eve. Maybe it will happen. He's listening to me right now."

As she heard Rosa's door close behind her, Eve sank down on the bottom step. Lord, she was tired, and she had only a few hours before she had to shower and get ready for school.

It had been a strange and terrible night. But the ending had not been as bad as the beginning. Rosa would be able to keep her Manuel, and if God continued to be good to her, then maybe she'd soften her father's heart enough to accept the little boy.

He answered my prayers.

Maybe he had, but by what means? Rick Larazo was an addict, and he'd been wild tonight. Even if he'd come down off whatever he was on, he wouldn't have waltzed into a police station to confess. He would have known that they'd book him. Being locked away from drugs was a nightmare he wouldn't have risked. He would have had to have been more afraid of what was outside than what awaited him inside that jail. What would that be?

I'm not a good guy.

I'd do whatever I had to do to survive and get what I want.

You really want to help her, don't you?

John Gallo?

He had handled Larazo as if he were nothing, and it had taken him no time at all to knock him unconscious.

How long would it have taken, what terrible punishment would he have handed out, to force Larazo to actually go into that police station and confess?

And would he have done it if she hadn't said that she wanted to help Rosa any way she could?

If not, then his act bound her to him in a dark, breathless intimacy.

It was all guesswork. John Gallo might not have been involved at all.

She got to her feet and started up the flights of stairs. She'd probably be able to go straight to bed. She doubted if Sandra would be home. She spent the nights with "friends" most of the time. She only showed up at the apartment once or twice a week.

No, she couldn't go to bed yet. She hadn't done her geometry. It seemed forever ago that she'd tossed that book in her book bag and taken off from the apartment. She'd have to do her homework before she could go to sleep.

Just as well. She was still wide-awake. She didn't want to lie awake in her bed. She wouldn't mind if she lay there and thought about Rosa and the baby.

But that wasn't what she'd be thinking about. She'd

be remembering how she'd felt when John Gallo had touched her.

And she'd be remembering that last glimpse of him before the elevator closed . . .

It was five to eleven the next evening when John Gallo walked into Mac's Diner, where she worked.

"Hi." He stood at the counter. "You get off in five minutes, don't you?"

She tensed, then tried to say casually, "Fifteen, I have to do the setup for tomorrow." She wiped the counter with her cloth. "What are you doing here?"

"It looks like rain. I thought I'd take you home."

She shook her head. "I can take the bus."

"I know what you can do." He smiled. "And I know what I want you to do. But what are you going to do, Eve? Why should you take a bus when we're both going to the same place?"

Because she didn't know if she wanted to get in a car with him. Just standing here a few feet away, she was too physically aware of him. "I'm not sugar. I won't melt in a little rain."

He chuckled. "No, you're not sugar sweet. That's what I like about you. You strike sparks. I can't forget how you tackled Larazo." His smile faded. "But you should have had a weapon. You weren't strong enough to handle him."

"Maybe I should ask your uncle to give me lessons."

"That's a thought. Or maybe I can teach you." Then

he shook his head. "No, lots of body contact. It wouldn't work. I'd forget what I was doing."

And so might she. Why did every reference come back to the physical? No, she shouldn't let him take her home.

He was studying her face. "Take a chance. I'm not going to do anything you don't want me to do. We'll talk." He thought about it. "Maybe." Then he grinned. "It's hard to be honest when I'm trying my best to convince you I'm no threat."

He couldn't convince her. He was a threat to her. No, it was her own emotions that were the threat.

"You have to leave. I have to finish my shift."

He didn't speak for a moment. "I'll wait for you outside. I'm parked across the street. Old beat-up tan Chevy. It's not pretty, but it's transportation." He didn't wait for her to answer as he strode toward the door. "And it will keep the rain off you."

He was gone before she could reply.

She stared after him, her hand clenched on the cloth.

"Who is *that*?" Teresa Maddel had come out of the kitchen and was standing, gazing out the window at John Gallo as he ran across the street. "Hot, very hot, Eve." She made a mocking gesture of fanning herself. "I don't think you can handle him. You should leave him to me."

Eve didn't think she could handle him, either. Just those few minutes had made her feel uncertain.

"His name is John Gallo." She began to fill up the saltshaker. "And you're welcome to him."

"I'll take him." Teresa was only half-kidding. "You

don't run across sexy guys like that every day of the
week. Introduce me the next time he comes in." She
wandered back toward the kitchen. "And I'll do the rest."

Yes, Teresa would give him anything he wanted and
ask for more. She was almost twenty, and some of the
stories she told Eve were very graphic. Eve had a mental image of a naked Teresa moving beneath him and
Gallo driving hard, fast, and—

Only the naked girl had suddenly become Eve, not
Teresa. And the muscles of her stomach were tensing as
he entered her and—

Don't think of it.

Ready to perform.

She had thought that about John Gallo at the hospital. Tight, sensual, ready to perform.

She had spilled the salt. Her hand was shaking.

Stupid. She wasn't this weak. It was only a crazy
physical yen. She should be able to control it.

But Teresa had evidently experienced that same reaction and she was not going to control it. Maybe she had
the right idea. Take any pleasure that came your way.

But she wasn't like Teresa. She knew that sex had
consequences that eventually caught up with you. Look
at her mother, look at Rosa. She wouldn't be caught in
that trap.

She wasn't that weak.

It had started to rain when she left the restaurant.
The tan Chevy was parked across the street.
She stopped, staring at it.

John Gallo got out of the car and stood in the rain, holding the passenger door open for her. "Come on. Hurry."

The rain was pouring down his face, and his shirt was already starting to cling to his body. He didn't look as if he even felt it.

He smiled and repeated softly, "Hurry. I can't wait."

Neither could she. She was running across the street. "You're an idiot." She jumped into the car. "Look at you. You're drenched." She leaned back in the seat. "Now get in the car and drive me home."

"Not such an idiot." He was in the driver's seat and starting the car. "I needed something to help you make up your mind." He slanted a glance at her. "And I don't melt either, Eve. At least not in the rain."

"I should have left you standing there in the downpour," Eve said. "And I will next time. Or I'll send out Teresa, one of the girls I work with. She wants to meet you."

"Not interested." He smiled. "And you wouldn't leave me out in the rain."

"Why not?"

"I might rust. I'm going to be too valuable to you for you to take the chance. You're going to like the way I move."

"Stop it." She drew a deep breath. "You said we could talk. This isn't talk. This is some kind of game I don't know how to play."

"I know how to play it. And it's all I can think about." He stared straight ahead, watching the windshield wipers brush away the rain. "Okay. Talk. How is Manuel?"

"Fine. It's as if last night never happened." She paused. "What did you do to Rick Larazo?"

"Who said I did anything?"

"What did you do?"

He didn't answer for a moment. "You don't want to know. It took a little persuasion to make him see that confession was good for the soul."

"Why did you do it?"

"It was easier for me to remove Rosa's problem than it was for you to do it." He paused. "And you told me you wanted it."

"As if that would make a difference."

"It made a difference. I wanted to please you."

"Why?"

"Why do you think? Because I wanted you to please me. I thought there might be a return on the investment."

"You thought I'd screw you if you did that for Rosa?"

He sighed. "If you want to put it bluntly."

"I do. I hate people who beat around the bush. And I didn't tell you to go after Larazo." She added grudgingly, "Though I might have done it if I'd thought it would work. He deserved to be punished."

"Oh, he was."

"But I wouldn't screw you as some kind of reward. That would be nuts."

"It wouldn't if it turned out to be a mutual reward. I was just hoping to sway you a little in my direction." He lifted his brow. "Are you swayed?"

"No."

"Then I'll have to keep on trying." They had reached the housing development, and he pulled the car over to the curb across the street from the project. "I've only just begun."

The rain was pounding on the roof of the car and enveloping them in a rhythmic sound that had its own intimacy.

Intimacy. That was what Eve had been trying to avoid, and all of a sudden it was there, surrounding her.

"Thanks for the lift." She reached for the handle of the door. "Good night."

"It's still pouring. Stay a minute until it lets up."

"I have to get to bed. I have school tomorrow."

"No mother waiting anxiously for her little girl?"

"No."

"You were all bent out of shape when I mentioned drugs. You took it personally. Is she the user?"

She didn't answer directly. "I hate what they do to you."

He nodded. "She's the user. I don't like them, either. My uncle was on prescription drugs for a while, and it turned him into another person. Does she make it rough on you?"

"You mean, does she beat me? No, she's not like that even when she's on the stuff. She just wants everything pretty, and it looks that way to her when she sees it through a veil of crack. She doesn't see that everything is really falling to pieces around her."

"Not a good life for you."

"I manage," she said tersely. "Keep your pity, I don't need it."

"I don't pity you." He smiled. "I wouldn't let myself.

It might get in the way of getting what I want. I told you that was my main objective."

"Why?" She looked straight ahead. "Why me? I'm not drop-dead gorgeous. I'm not even particularly pretty."

"No, you're not." His smile vanished. "You're too thin, and your face doesn't look like some movie star's. But I don't want to stop looking at it. Do you know what I thought when I first got a good look at you when you were sitting on those stairs? You burn, Eve. Your hair was shining more red than brown under those lights, and your whole being was focused on Rosa and her baby. You were so alive and intense, I felt as if I'd scorch my fingers if I touched you." He added softly, "And I couldn't wait to feel the burn."

She was feeling that burn, with every breath she took. She swallowed and pulled her gaze away. "That's crazy. I don't want this. Why are you bothering? Why don't you go screw Teresa or someone else? When you get down to it, isn't one girl as good as another to a guy? That's what I've always heard."

"That's what I've always heard, too." His lips twisted. "Hell, that's what I've always believed. Sex is sex. Why not take it wherever you can?"

"So?"

"But it's not working right now. There's some kind of wild chemistry going on between us. I've heard about that happening, but I thought it was a bunch of bull. But I felt it the minute I saw you, and I think you felt it, too. I don't want anyone else. It has to be you, Eve."

"No, it doesn't. Not if I don't want it." She said shakily, "And I don't. It would get in my way. My mother had me when she was fifteen. I've seen girls my own age having babies and being left to raise them by themselves. And then they're stuck in a rut that they can never climb out of. That's not going to happen to me."

"I'd protect you. I don't want kids, either. I'm going to basic training in four weeks. Do you think I want to leave a kid behind? I have to be on my own."

She shook her head. "Why are we even talking about this?"

"You started it." His hands clenched on the steering wheel. "And I'm glad you did. I wanted to have everything aboveboard. I don't want to hurt you, Eve. We can take what we need without hurting each other. Let me show you."

"No." She jumped out of the car. It was still raining, and she was wet in seconds. "You won't hurt me because I won't let you." She started across the street. "I take care of myself."

"I'll pick you up at work tomorrow night, Eve."

"Haven't you been listening to me?"

"Every word. And you've been listening to me. That means progress." He started the car. "I'll see you tomorrow night."

She slammed the heavy door of the entrance behind her.

Close him out. Close out the thoughts his words had brought rushing to the surface.

She couldn't do it.

Every word he'd said was still with her. She was wet

and should have been chilled, but she felt as if she had a fever.

Yes, that was it. That was exactly what John Gallo was.

A fever that would leave her if she didn't let it take over her mind as well as her body.

It was clear that he'd had a lot of experience in sexual encounters. His interest in her was probably fleeting and would go away soon. Then she would not have to deal with these bizarre and disturbing feelings again.

All she had to do was hold on.

"Hello, Eve." He walked up to the counter at ten forty the next evening. "I came a little early. I thought I might need to do a little repair work."

"Repair work?"

"Haven't you been trying to tear down everything that I tried to do last night?" He chuckled. "Don't answer."

She didn't intend to answer. "I don't need a ride home. You might as well leave."

He shook his head. "I'll stick around. You might change your mind."

"I won't."

"Let me help you fill up those saltshakers, Eve." Teresa was suddenly beside her, her gaze fixed on John Gallo. "Hi, I'm Teresa Maddel. Are you a friend of Eve's?"

"I'm trying to be." He smiled at Teresa. "John Gallo. Nice to meet you, Teresa."

Teresa's smile was brilliant. "Me, too. You wouldn't

have any trouble being friends with me. Eve has other fish to fry. She's so serious, she even spends her breaks doing homework. Can you imagine that?"

"I can imagine." His gaze was on Eve. "I can imagine all kinds of things about her."

Eve could feel that now-familiar heat moving through her. She abruptly turned away. "You two get to know each other. I'll go clean the soda machine." She disappeared into the kitchen, and she kept busy doing preps for the next twenty minutes. She was aware of Teresa's laughter and John's voice, but avoided looking at them. It was only when she saw John leaving the restaurant that she came back out front to finish the counter fill-ups.

"Thanks for giving me my chance with him." Teresa's gaze was on John moving across the street toward his Chevy. "Damn, he's sexy. Will you look at that tight butt?"

Eve automatically glanced at John, then hastily averted her eyes. She didn't need Teresa drawing her attention to anything about him. "Did you make any progress?"

"Maybe. I gave him my telephone number." She was still staring at him as he got in the car. "Of course, he wouldn't make a move on me since he was here to see you. He said he'd wait outside for you."

"Why don't you go out to the car and talk to him? It's eleven now. Clock out, and I'll finish your side work."

Teresa's brows rose. "Are you kidding? Are you trying to get rid of him?"

"Yes."

Teresa stared at her in disbelief. "You've got to be crazy. I knew the minute I saw him that he was a good time walking. He could give a girl a really good ride."

"Then go have your good time." Eve didn't look at her as she finished filling the pepper. "Like you said, I'm too serious for him."

"Well, I'm not." Teresa clocked out and was heading for the door. "Thanks, Eve."

Eve put the cap on the shaker. Don't look out the window and see whether Teresa had been welcomed by John. Of course, she would be. She was pretty and sexy and very willing. Eve had done the right thing. Soon she wouldn't have to worry about—

"Eve." It was Mr. Kimble, frowning as he called her from the kitchen. "Phone call for you. It's your mother. I've told you all that there are rules about receiving calls here unless it is an emergency."

"Sorry." She moved quickly toward the phone on the wall. "You know I've never gotten one before, Mr. Kimble. There must be some mistake."

He turned away. "See that it doesn't happen again."

"Yes, sir." She picked up the phone. "Sandra, I can't talk now. Why did you call me here?"

"He hurt me." Sandra was sobbing. "I thought Jimmy was such a nice man. We had such a good time. But he hurt me. I'm bleeding, Eve."

Bleeding?

Eve stiffened. "How did he hurt you, Sandra?"

"He slapped me and cut my lip. And then he punched

me in the stomach. Why would he hurt me like that? It wasn't as if I wasn't going to let him—but a woman has to be treated with respect."

"Where are you?"

"A hotel room at the Marriott."

"Is he still there?"

"No, he said he was going to go out and find a dealer and score some heroin. He said I needed to be sweetened up a little." She paused. "I'm scared of heroin, Eve. I take other stuff, but I'm scared of heroin."

"Sandra, why are you calling me? Why don't you just walk out of there?"

"He locked the door from the outside."

"How did he do that? Never mind. Call downstairs to the front desk and have them send someone up to let you out."

"I can't do that. That would make a fuss, and those security people would be on the lookout for me if I ever came back into the hotel."

"Then don't go back."

"That would be . . . awkward. There are a lot of nice little get-togethers at these hotels. It would be easier if you just came and got me out."

"And how am I supposed to do that?"

"How do I know?" Sandra was crying again. "You're smart. You're always thinking. Think of a way to get me out of here before he comes back. I don't like to be hurt. I don't want to take that heroin, but if he says he's going to hurt me . . . Fix it. You owe me, Eve. Find a way to help me."

Anger and fear were racing through Eve, and she

tried to suppress both so that she could think. All Sandra had to do was call the front desk, but she wasn't about to do it. Typical. She'd rather take a chance on everything working out so that she could have it all.

"I really am bleeding, Eve," Sandra said. "He didn't care. He's not a nice man."

And if Sandra didn't get out of there, she was going to risk either a brutal beating or an overdose. "How long has he been gone?"

"I don't know . . . it seems like a long time."

If Sandra was on crack, that could mean anything. Two minutes or two hours.

"What's your room number?"

"It's 2012."

"I'll come after you. Go to the bathroom and wash your face and try to stop the bleeding."

"I will. You'll hurry?"

"I'll hurry." She hung up the receiver, and leaned her head against the phone for a moment. She tried to think. Dammit, Sandra, why wouldn't you just call the desk? But Sandra wasn't going to do it, so that meant the ball was in Eve's court.

So get it done.

She whirled and strode toward the front entrance. "I have to go, Mr. Kimble. Emergency . . ."

A moment later she was running across the street toward John's car. Teresa was leaning with her elbows on the open window of the passenger door talking to John. She glanced at Eve in surprise as Eve nudged her aside.

"Get out of my way. I'm in a hurry." Eve jumped in

the passenger seat and turned to John. "Take me to the Marriott Hotel."

"A hotel? That's too good to be true." He was studying her expression. "Yes, I'm right, it is too good." He started the car. "Bye, Teresa, nice talking to you."

"Yeah." Teresa was still in the street watching as the Chevy pulled away from the curb.

"Why the Marriott?" John asked as he stopped at the red light on the corner.

"Sandra . . . my mother is in trouble. Someone beat her up and locked her in the hotel room. I have to get there as quickly as possible."

"And I had a car."

"The Marriott is ten or twelve blocks away. Just drop me off, and I'll take it from there."

"I know where it is. That fancy downtown Marriott." He glanced at her. "How badly is she hurt?"

"I don't know. She wasn't too coherent. She said she's bleeding." She shook her head. "I don't think that she's too bad. She wasn't scared enough to call downstairs to the front desk." Her lips tightened. "She'd rather have me rescue her again."

"How many times has it happened?"

"Two or three times. Not like this. Once was at the apartment, a couple times in bars. She's not a good judge of men. Anyone who has the stuff and is willing to sweet-talk her is enough."

"You're angry with her."

"Yes, this is so stupid. I'm angry and I'm worried and I want her to *stop*. She's only a little over thirty. At this rate, she won't live to forty. She's selfish and vain and doesn't care for anyone but herself." She crossed her arms across her chest, her hands tightly gripping her upper arms to keep from shaking. "I try to hate her, but I can't do it." She repeated through set teeth, "I *can't* do it."

"Easy." John's hand was on her thigh. "We'll get her out of this."

"This time," Eve said. "What about next time?"

"You can't keep doing it. You're not the mother, she is."

"That doesn't seem to make any difference," she said shakily. "And it won't, until I find a way to hate her. I'm not sure I ever will."

"Then we'll just worry about this time." He pulled up the ramp of the Marriott and parked at the far end. "Leave everything to me. Stay behind me. You look too upset. We don't want security thinking I'm dragging in an underage girl for sex."

She got out of the car. "I can handle this myself, John."

"Stay behind me." He got out of the car and moved toward the doorman. "We're just going to run inside and pick up my girlfriend's mother. Would you keep an eye on my car?"

The doorman frowned as he looked at the shabby vehicle. "You can't leave that thing parked out here for long."

"Ten minutes." John smiled. "I don't want to make her mother walk far. She had an accident last week." He was pushing Eve through the revolving doors. "Thanks a lot, buddy."

He moved Eve quickly through the glittering lobby to the elevators. "Casual," he said in a low tone. "Smile."

She smiled with an effort as she got into the elevator. "It's 2012."

He pressed the button. "Right."

"I thought I'd try to find a housekeeping maid to let me into the room."

"That's one way." The elevator stopped, and he nudged her out of the elevator. "It might take time to find one that we can con into unlocking the door. But, you know, I don't understand how he could lock her in." He stopped in front of 2012. "At any rate, let's try my way first." He bent over the lock. "You're sure this is the right room? Otherwise, it could prove embarrassing."

"She said 2012. But no, I'm not sure. I'm never sure with Sandra. What are you doing?"

"Picking the lock."

"Something your uncle taught you?"

"No, something I learned when I was running with a gang when I was fourteen. I told you I wasn't a good guy." He frowned. "Oh, that's how he did it." He pulled on the knob, and it came off in his hand. "He smashed the knob off." His gaze narrowed on the lock and then he took out his pocketknife and started to work on the tumblers. "And then he stuck in something metal to jam the lock and put the knob back. I don't think this is the first time that he did something like this. Your mom should be more careful with her friends." He worked for a minute and straightened. "That should do it." He pushed and the door swung open. "There we go."

"Sandra?" Eve pushed ahead of John into the room. "It's Eve. Are you—"

"Eve!" Sandra came running out of the bathroom. Her

hair was mussed, her pink dress torn, her face bruised and washed clean of makeup. "I knew you'd find a way, honey." She gave Eve a hug. "It's been positively terrible for me. Men like him should be arrested."

"Then stay away from men like him." Eve pushed her back and looked at her. Yeah, she was definitely on something, but Eve didn't know how deep. Deep enough for her not to realize that she'd been beaten worse than she'd thought. Four bruises marked her fair skin, she had a black eye, and her lip was cut. "He worked you over, Sandra."

"I told you he wasn't nice to me." She lifted her hand to her lips. "See my cut? He didn't have to do that." Her gaze wandered to John Gallo. "Who is this, honey?"

"John Gallo," John said. "I'm a friend of Eve's." He looked around the room. "We should get out of here. Do you have anything you need to take with you?"

"My purse." She gestured vaguely. "On the bed." She was studying John as he got her purse and handed it to her. "What a good-looking young man. Have you been keeping him from me, Eve? And he's so polite. I wouldn't mind you having a young man like him. A woman needs a man to take care of her needs. You've never seemed to understand that."

"We have to go, Sandra." She took Sandra's elbow and pushed her toward the door. "Try to walk straight. When we get to the lobby, you have to move fast if you don't want to attract attention."

She nodded. "Mustn't do that. Hotel people are so suspicious . . ." She looked back at them over her shoulder. "How did you get in the door? I didn't ask—"

"What's this?" A big, muscular man in a tan sport coat was standing in the doorway. "Where do you think you're going, Sandra?"

She stopped. "Hello, Jimmy." She moistened her lips. "I'm going now."

"The hell you are. You promised me a party."

"Party's over." Eve took Sandra's arm and pushed her forward. "And parties don't usually start with assault and battery. She's leaving."

"This is my daughter, Eve," Sandra said. "And she's right, you didn't treat me right. I didn't like you—"

The man she'd called Jimmy grabbed Eve's arm as she passed with Sandra. "You can stay. I've never had a mother and daughter together before. But you don't take her anywhere."

"Yes, she does." John was suddenly between them. He grabbed the hand that was grasping Eve's arm. His thumb was pressing into Jimmy's wrist. "Let her go."

Jimmy gasped with pain, his hand releasing Eve's arm.

"Get your mother out of here," John said. "I'll be right with you."

Eve grabbed Sandra's arm and hustled her out of the room and down the hall.

"Should we leave him?" Sandra asked. "I don't want Jimmy to—"

"I don't think you have to worry about John Gallo." Eve punched the elevator button. But she didn't like the idea of leaving him, either. The situation was her responsibility. When the elevator door opened, she pushed Sandra inside and hit the lobby button. "Go outside and get in the tan Chevy at the far end of the driveway."

"But I want you to come with—" The door closed on her protest.

Eve was running back down the hall to the hotel room.

The door was still open. The big man in the tan sport coat was lying on the floor unconscious.

She hoped he was unconscious. Jimmy was lying very still. As she drew closer, she saw his face. His jaw and left eye were already starting to swell, his nose was smashed, and his lips were cut and bloody.

John turned to face her. He didn't have a mark on him, she realized in astonishment. "I told you to take off."

"He's not dead?"

"He'll be okay." He shrugged. "I bloodied him up a little. I don't like guys beating up women. I thought he should see how it feels." He took her arm and led her out the door. "It's been a frustrating night. I thought I deserved to enjoy myself."

"And doing that to him made you enjoy yourself?"

He glanced sidewise at her. "Are you surprised?" His smile was chilling. "Oh, yes, I enjoyed the hell out of what I did to him."

CHAPTER

4

Sandra wasn't going to be able to climb the four flights of stairs at the development, Eve realized, after her mother almost fell twice on the first few steps. She moved to stand on the step beside her and put Sandra's arm around her shoulders. "Hold on to the banister and lean on me. We can make it."

"Sure we can," Sandra said. "I just feel a little wobbly . . ."

"I'll do it." John was suddenly beside them, pushing Eve aside. "It will take you half the night to get up those stairs. What floor?"

"Four."

"Go on upstairs and unlock the door." He was picking Sandra up in his arms and starting up the stairs. "Come on, Ms. Duncan. This will be much easier for you."

"Call me Sandra." Sandra smiled. "Like I said, nice

and polite, Eve. A real Sir Galahad, like I saw in that movie."

"Wrong." John smiled down at her. "But I make a good packhorse." He was moving quickly up the stairs. "We'll get you into your place in no time."

Eve had the door unlocked and thrown wide by the time he reached the fourth floor. "Take her to her bedroom. It's the door on the right."

She went to the bathroom and got a damp washcloth and some salve.

John was looking down at Sandra lying on the bed. "I think she's fading fast. Do you want me to help you undress her?"

"No, it won't be the first time she's slept in her clothes." She turned on the lamp by the bed. "When I was younger, there was no way I could manage to help her." She carefully bathed the cuts and bruises on Sandra's face. "Bastard. Why would he want to hurt her like this? All he'd have to do is treat her nice, and she'd do anything he wanted."

"He'll think twice about doing it again."

Yes, the beating John had given him had been brutal and merciless. She had been a little shocked at how merciless at first. She wasn't shocked after getting a closer look at Sandra's face. "Do you think he'll call the police?"

"No chance. Not if he had heroin in his pocket. He'll just cut his losses and get out of Dodge."

"Good." She was gently rubbing salve on Sandra's cut lip. "I just hope he doesn't try to look up Sandra again."

"I'll be around for a while. Let me know if there's a problem."

"I'll handle it. She's my mother."

"Hurts, Eve . . ." Sandra was opening her eyes. "What are you doing, honey?"

"Just putting some salve on your lip. Go to sleep, Sandra."

"I was bleeding . . . and there were bruises."

"Yes, but they'll go away."

"I'll be just as pretty as ever?"

Eve nodded. "In a week or so."

"That's good." She was gazing drowsily up at Eve. "You have a bruise, too." She reached up and touched the purple mark on Eve's cheek. "Did Jimmy do that to you?"

"No, someone else. A couple days ago. I'm okay."

"Poor Eve." She gently patted Eve's face. "Poor little girl. Like mother, like daughter." Her eyes closed. "Like mother, like daughter . . ."

Eve stiffened as if Sandra had struck her.

She threw the salve on the nightstand and got to her feet. Her voice was shaking when she said, "She'll be okay for the night." She turned and strode out of the room. "Turn out her lamp."

An instant later, the light went out, and John came out of the bedroom.

"Thank you for helping with her." She was standing at the window with her back to him, looking down at the street. "Though I didn't give you much choice, did I?"

"I had a choice." He paused. "And you're not like your

mother, Eve. She's not a bad woman, but she's weak. There's nothing about you that's weak."

"I know that," she said. "But when I see her like that, I have to keep reminding myself. And how can I be sure that she wasn't stronger when she was my age? Was she like me? Can life beat me down and turn me into what she's become?"

"Not if you don't let it."

She drew a deep breath. "That's right. I'm not thinking straight right now." She turned around to face him. "Sometimes I get scared, but it doesn't last long. Do you ever get scared, John?"

"Now and then. Usually it's about being trapped somewhere and not able to get out."

"And that's why you're going to join the Army and see the world. You're going to avoid all the traps," she said. "I don't have to see the world. I'm going to make my own world."

He smiled. "And what a world it will be. I'd like to stay around and see it."

And she would like him to be there to see what she could accomplish, she realized. He would give life an edge, an excitement.

What was she thinking? That edge and excitement were what was most dangerous to her. She needed steadiness and focus to reach her goals.

He was looking around the room. "Very clean, very neat. It looks like you."

"It's the only way I can stand it. I taught myself to keep house, but I'm still a lousy cook. Strictly TV dinners."

"I like to cook. It relaxes me."

"Another thing your uncle taught you?"

He nodded. "He never got married. He had to do for himself. I'd like you to meet him someday." His gaze was on the wall beside the window. "That's a nice sketch on the wall. It's Manuel, isn't it?"

"Yeah, I did it when I sat with him while Rosa went to the store. I'm going to give it to her when she starts her GED study. It's sort of a bribe."

"It's good. Is that what you're going to study?"

"Art? No way. I've heard too much about starving artists. And people who starve end up in places like this. I'm going to study engineering. That's solid."

"You have something there." His gaze was still wandering. "One bedroom. Where do you sleep?"

"On the couch. It's pretty comfortable."

His gaze went to the paisley-covered couch across the room. "Cushy. Yeah, I can see you lying on it." His eyes shifted back to her. "I'm glad I'll be able to picture you there."

Heat again. Out of nowhere. Just a few words, and that tingling tension was back.

"You'd better leave."

"I'm going. I knew I said the wrong thing. I was making headway. We've gotten to know more about each other. You're not thinking of me as a threat to you any longer. I should have let it go at that, but I couldn't do it." He added, "But I didn't want to let you forget what's going to be important to us." He turned toward the door. "I'll pick you up tomorrow night."

"Don't you ever give up?"

"If I'd taken you at your word tonight and left you when you handed me my walking papers, then it would have been a hell of a lot more difficult for you." He opened the door. "You can never tell when I might come in handy."

"One-in-a-thousand chance."

"When it comes, I'll be there." He looked back over his shoulder. "Do you know how I'm going to be thinking of you lying on that couch?" he said softly. "Naked, Eve. Naked and moving."

He shut the door.

Damn him.

A wild kind of chemistry.

Searing hunger, mindless need. She was feeling all of those emotions that very moment.

Her hands were clenched as she stared at the door. The hell he was no longer a threat. Yes, they had gotten to know more about each other. Though he had become more knowledgeable about her than she was of him. He had caught her at a susceptible time, and she had revealed a vulnerability that she had shown no one before.

All she had learned about him was that he could be even more brutal and dangerous than he had shown her with that encounter with Larazo. That he had effortlessly made himself a necessity to Sandra and her during this hellish night. That he had read her mind and emotions with a cleverness and sensitivity that made her uneasy. That he had a patience that was almost intimidating. That his worst fear was of being trapped.

And that he was able, with one look or sentence, to make her body respond.

Naked and moving.

She knew as she lay on the couch trying to sleep to-night that she would be thinking, feeling, imagining John Gallo's vision of her . . . and of him.

Damn him.

She took an hour off from work the next day so that she'd be gone when he reached the restaurant.

The next night he showed up at the restaurant three hours early.

"I was worried that you weren't here," he said as he sat down on the chair. "Until Teresa told me that you'd left early. Is Sandra okay?"

"I guess so. She only stayed at home one day. When I got home from school today, she was gone."

"Then it wasn't trouble at home. You were running away from me." He added quietly, "You shouldn't do that, Eve. I know you can't afford to miss any hours."

"I wasn't running from you. I had homework."

He looked at her skeptically.

"What's wrong? Didn't Teresa entertain you?"

He shook his head. "You keep pushing her at me. If I wanted a substitute, I'd choose my own." He studied her. "And you're changing the subject. You must have had a reason to panic."

"I didn't panic."

"Too strong a word? Maybe just a couple of really bad nights?"

She didn't answer.

"I had them, too." He got up from the stool, and said

curtly, "And it's time you brought this to an end. I'll be waiting outside every night until you decide to either call the cops on me or give me my shot at convincing you that I'm not going to do anything to hurt you."

He walked out the door.

And he would do exactly what he said, she realized. She had already gotten a taste of that patience. He was right. She would have to settle this in some other way because he wouldn't be avoided.

And she wouldn't run away from him again.

"Let's go." She opened the passenger door and got into John's Chevy. "I'm tired of the people I'm working with thinking I'm being stalked."

"I guess you could say they're right. Except stalking implies violence, and there's no way I'd be violent with you." As he started the car, he said, "Unless you wanted it. You don't have the experience, and I'd shy away from it. But we could try it if you—"

"Shut up." That heat was rising within her again. She only had to be near him, and it started. "I don't want to try it. I don't want to try anything." She moistened her lips. "You said we had to put an end to this. That's why I'm here. You helped me twice in some really bad situations, and I'm grateful. But now I want you to go away. You make me feel . . . I don't like to feel like this."

"Yes, you do. Or you would, if you'd let yourself. It's the sport that makes the world go round. You're feeling what I'm feeling, and there's nothing more exciting.

You're just scared of the consequences. There wouldn't be consequences, Eve. I'd take care of you."

"And you think I'd trust you?"

"I think we're going to have to trust each other. We need it too much to do anything else."

"I don't . . . need it."

"The *hell* you don't." He drew a deep breath. "And I can't talk right now, or I'll end up wrecking this car. Give me a few minutes to get you home."

He didn't speak again until they were parked across the street from the housing development. His hands were clenched on the steering wheel, and he was looking straight ahead. "You may not need me, but you want me." He turned and slid across the seat until he was touching her thigh-to-thigh. "Do you think I can't feel it? I know damn well you can feel me. We're both sending out signals that are basic as hell."

She couldn't breathe. Her hand reached out for the door handle.

"No, stay." His hand was suddenly covering hers. "Let me show you just a little of what we'd have. I'll stop whenever you say." His hand moved slowly up her wrist to her upper arm. "You feel so good . . . Silky, and yet every muscle tense and ready." His hand moved up to cup her throat. "And your heartbeat . . ."

Her heart was jumping out of her chest. The instant he'd touched her, she'd felt as if every nerve in her body had been electrified. She could feel the crispness of his shirt against her body and breathed in the scent of him. Spice or something else that was making her dizzy.

No, it was Gallo who was making her dizzy. His mouth was on hers, his tongue probing, playing.

She made a sound deep in her throat and moved closer.

"Yes." His hands had slid down to undo the buttons of her shirt. "That's right. Give me your tongue. I want the taste of you . . ."

She arched with a cry as his hands cupped her breasts. They were swelling, the nipples hardening, peaking.

Then they were free; he'd unfastened her bra, and his fingers were pressing, pinching, squeezing.

His mouth was on her breast, his tongue . . . his teeth . . .

Heat. Tingling between her thighs as his hand reached down to cup, rub. She shuddered as the tingling became a burning hunger.

"Not here. Let me take you someplace," he said hoarsely. "I'll make it good . . ."

She didn't want to go anywhere. She didn't care. She wanted to stay there and let him do whatever he wanted to her. Fill her, stop the burning, the hunger . . .

Hunger. The world was full of hunger that could have only one satiation. His face, sensual, lips full, his breath hot, his hands . . .

"Eve, I don't want to make it with you in the back of this car." His breath was hot on her breasts as he spoke. "If you don't want to go up to your place, I know a motel near the airport. But we have to hurry."

She looked up at him dazedly. What was he talking about?

"Eve?"

A motel. The backseat of the car.

What was she doing? A quick hump in the back of the car? She was behaving like an animal in heat. Oh, she was in heat. She was mindless and wanting only one thing, one act.

But she didn't have to act like that animal.

She sat up straight and pushed him away. She was panting, her voice uneven. "No."

His arms tightened for a moment. "What?"

"No." She had to get out of this car. Or she wouldn't go at all. "I said no. You proved your point. But it's not much of a triumph for you, is it? I don't know enough about this to fight it."

"Triumph? What the hell are you talking about? I'm not trying to—" He drew a deep, ragged breath. "I just wanted to show you what we'd be missing. But then I couldn't stop. I don't think I'd ever be the one who can stop."

"You showed me." She was trying to button her shirt. Damn, her hands were shaking. "Are you satisfied?"

"Hell, no, and neither are you."

"I'll get over it." She was opening the car door. "I'd never set eyes on you until a few days ago. Now I'm supposed to jump in bed with you?"

"If that's what we both want." He leaned forward, his face lean, hard, intense in the dashboard lights. "Why not, Eve? What difference does it make? We need it, we want it. Let's take it. We can have a hell of a good time for the next few weeks. Then you'll be rid of me. No strings."

She got out of the car. "Good-bye."

"No way. I'm not giving up. Why should I? You're on my side." He said softly, "Think about it. Think about how it felt. How it could feel. It's going to happen sometime. Why not with me? I'll protect you. No responsibilities. All you'll know is the pleasure. I'll show you a real good time. Okay?"

She didn't answer. She was hurrying across the street to the development. Almost running.

Because she wanted to turn around and get back into that car.

She glanced back over her shoulder as she reached the front entrance. He was still sitting there, watching her.

She slammed the door and ran up the stairs to the apartment.

She leaned back against the door staring into the darkness. Her heart was beating hard, her breath coming in harsh gasps. She felt hot and weak and aching. All because he had touched her with his hands, with his mouth.

It's going to happen sometime. Why not with me?

And she wanted it with him. She had never felt like this with anyone else before.

But she had never felt so weak and powerless before, either. The whole world around her was chaos, and she could only survive if she felt strong and able to handle that chaos. At that moment, she felt she couldn't handle anything.

A kind of wild chemistry.

Why had it happened? Maybe she could have resisted an ordinary attraction, but not one that was shaking her to her core.

She dropped down on the couch and huddled there.
She could feel the soft material of the couch against her
body.

Naked and moving.

How would it feel to be naked with him above her,
in her?

Her stomach clenched, and she bit her lower lip as her
whole body tensed.

Crazy. Intense. Feverish.

But it wasn't going to go away. She knew that now.

She had to have it. She had to have *him*.

She lay there for hours until the intense storm of
feeling passed.

No, not really passed. Just faded into the background.
She knew it would come back. As soon as the thought
of him returned.

But at least she could think. She wasn't as mindless
as she had been when John had been touching her.

She got up and went to the window. It was going to
happen. She was going to have sex with John Gallo.
Accept it. No big deal. Most of the girls in her class at
school had been screwing around for the last couple of
years. Chastity had little value on the streets or in the
projects.

It was a big deal to her. She would *not* be like her
mother. This was her life, her body. She didn't want to
have to trust anyone with either.

Only herself. She had to be in control.

And she had almost lost that control tonight. Whenever

she was near John, that control shattered. So she had to be prepared.

She had to be safe.

She slowly turned away from the window and went to the bathroom. She opened the cabinet under the sink and took out her mother's pretty pink patent box. There were four discs still in the box. Her mother usually got a six-month prescription for birth-control pills.

Eve stared down at the discs with the circle of tiny pills. She had never thought of birth control because she had been sure that she would not need it for a long time. When her life was on track, when it was convenient. But she knew that Sandra's pills worked for her mother and let her be in control of the situation. Control. Nothing was more important than being able to be in control of this insanely volatile emotional roller-coaster ride. Yet it felt strange and a little frightening to realize what she was going to do.

But she had to be safe.

She took one of the discs and put the rest back into Sandra's box.

Now she was in control. She didn't have to rely on anyone but herself. She could take what she wanted.

And the excitement was already starting to build within her.

John Gallo's Chevy had just pulled up across the street from the restaurant.

Her heart was pounding. He was there, soon she'd be with him.

Eve drew a deep breath and threw her towel on the counter. "I'm out of here, Teresa. Mr. Kimble said I could leave early."

Teresa nodded as she saw the tan Chevy. "Maybe you're not as serious as I thought. If anyone could jar you out of it, it would be him. Have a good time." She slid a second glance at the car across the street. "And I think you will."

Eve was barely hearing her as she headed for the door. John Gallo was getting out of the car. He stopped as he saw her crossing the street toward him.

His eyes narrowed. "This is . . . different. You didn't call the cops on me for harassment. I think that might be a good sign."

"Stop thinking." She got in the passenger seat. "Just get me out of here."

He smiled. "Right away." He got back in the car and started the engine. "Home?"

"No." Her hands were clenched tightly together on her lap. "I don't want it to happen in the apartment. I don't want to think of you there."

"Happen?" His gaze was on her face, and he pursed his lips in a silent whistle. "Oh, yes, this is going to be very unusual. Why?"

"What difference does it make? Why are you surprised? You've been telling me all the reasons that I should let you screw me. Maybe you convinced me."

"It makes a difference."

"You're right, I want it. I want you. I don't know why I do or why it has to be you, but that's the way it is." She looked straight ahead. "Last night I . . . hurt when

I thought about you. Why should I feel this way when I can do something about it?"

"No reason at all." His hand reached out and rested on her thigh.

She could feel her muscles tense beneath his touch. His hand felt heavy, warm, through the thin denim of her jeans.

"You like this?" His hand was rubbing sensuously back and forth. "Yes, I can feel that you do."

She couldn't breathe. She reached out and put her hand above his knee.

His muscles became rock hard beneath her hand.

"No, you can't play the same game." He took her hand off him. "Not while I'm driving."

"Then stop driving."

"As soon as I can. Where?"

"Anywhere. I don't care."

"I do." His hand was moving between her legs. "I've been thinking about it. No motel. There's a reservoir off the highway. We can find a place."

"You must have been sure that I'd end up giving in."

"I've been hoping." His fingers were closing, pulling, gently pinching. "And I thought my chances were good. Chemistry."

Chemistry.

Her breasts were swelling, her body was tensing, burning, opening. She was leaning back, her head moving back and forth as his hand . . .

"Get there," she said through her teeth. "Find that place."

"We're almost there." He was going down a bumpy

country road. "It won't be long." He muttered, "It had better not be. I'm going crazy." He pulled down a side road, then they were suddenly off the road and completely surrounded by trees and brush. He jammed on the brakes. "Come on." He grabbed a red plaid blanket from the backseat and opened the driver's door. Then he was around the car and opening her door. "Quick."

She was already out of the car. "Where?"

He was spreading the plaid blanket on the grass at the side of the road. "Is it okay? It's clean and private. No one comes here . . ." He was pulling off his shirt, his movements frantic. "If you don't like it, I'll find another place later. I can't—"

"It's fine." She was unbuttoning her shirt. "I don't care." She just wanted him to touch her again. In the way he had only minutes before, as he had last night. She unfastened her bra and threw it aside.

He was naked. She could see the gleam of his flesh in the moonlight. How had he been so quick?

"I'll help, Eve. Lie down."

She was on the soft wool blanket. He was pulling at her jeans. Then they were off, and he was with her on the blanket. She gasped as she felt the hardness of him against her.

"Shh, you'll like it." His hand was moving in and out. She cried out, her back arching off the blanket.

"See, nothing but pleasure." His mouth was on her breast, nibbling, sucking. "Sweet . . ."

Not sweet. Maddening. Insane . . .

His mouth on her breasts, his hand between her legs, probing.

He lifted his head, his breath coming in gasps. "I can't take much more. I'll take more time later. But could I—" He was over her, moving between her legs. "Don't say no, Eve. Please, don't—" He stopped, closing his eyes. "Wait. I knew I'd go crazy. It will be just a second. I've got to protect you."

"No." She was pulling herself up to meet him. "Do it!"

"The hell I will. I promised you that—"

"It's okay. I'm safe. I took care of it." She was glaring up at him. "Now do it!"

He plunged deep!

Pain. Only for a moment.

Fullness. Friction. Movement.

Yes.

She was moaning, meeting him thrust for thrust.

Deep. Deeper.

His hands were cupping her buttocks, lifting her to every thrust.

"That's right," his voice was ragged. "Give it to me. Burn me . . ."

She was the one who was burning. Every tactile surface of her body seemed hot and sensitized. Her nipples, the flesh of her stomach brushing against his, the soles of her feet that were pressed into the blanket.

Then he was moving harder, deeper. "Eve, I can't hold off any . . ."

She couldn't, either. Her teeth bit into her lower lip as she felt the rising.

Madness. It was all madness . . .

It was only seconds later that her back arched off the blanket, her arms sliding around him to pull her to him.

He cried out and collapsed on top of her.

"You screamed." He was gasping for breath as he lifted his head. "Did I hurt you?"

She'd screamed? She didn't remember making a sound. But then she hadn't been thinking, only feeling. "You didn't hurt me."

"You're sure? I've never had a virgin. You were . . . tight."

"Yes, I was." She was gasping, too. "But it was okay. Did it bother you?"

"Hell, no." He flexed within her at the memory. "It was fantastic." Then he was getting off her and lying beside her. "But I should have been more careful. I thought about doing it, then it was gone, swept away."

Everything had been swept away but the act itself, Eve thought.

And it was still here. The urgency was gone, but her body was still tingling, warm, vibrantly alive. No one had told her that the after-effect would be like this.

John was pulling her close again, cuddling her in his arms. "Thank you," he said softly. "It was good, the best, Eve."

"Yes, it was." She rubbed her cheek in the hollow of his shoulder. "I don't see how it could be better. Do you?"

He was silent. "Don't be hasty. There's always a way to make anything better. Let me think about it."

She nodded. "I'm willing to listen. You know best . . . for now."

He chuckled. "But you think that may be temporary?" He smoothed her hair. "You may be right." He was silent. "You're sure that you're protected?"

"I'm sure. I wasn't going to go into this unless I knew I was safe."

"And you didn't trust me to do it. I meant it, Eve. I wasn't going to let you run any risk."

"It's my body. I take care of it." She lifted herself on one elbow and looked down at him. "This way I don't have to trust you. Isn't that what you really wanted? No strings. That's what you said."

"Yes, that's what I said." His finger traced the curve of her upper lip. "But I've been known to be unreasonable now and then. Maybe I'm hurt that you didn't trust me."

"I don't think so." She frowned. "But it's too dark to see your face. I can't tell if you're— Where are you going?" she asked, startled, as he jumped to his feet and was heading back to the car. "What are you doing?"

"You don't like it dark? Let there be light." He flipped on the headlights.

She inhaled sharply as she was illuminated in the intensity of the headlights. She scrambled to her knees, staring at his dark shadow near the car. "I wasn't expecting that."

"Sometimes the unexpected is exciting."

"I feel . . . naked. Somehow, I didn't before." She had only been aware of textures, scents, sensation.

"I like you naked."

"I'm too thin."

"You're perfect."

"Liar. Why did you turn on the lights?"

"I felt your burn. I wanted to see it." He was coming toward her out of the shadow. Lord, he was beautiful.

Olive skin that looked darker in contrast to the clear light. Muscular stomach and thighs. And the expression on his face . . . Full lips, white teeth, and glittering dark eyes that were sensuality itself. "*While* I was feeling it." He fell to his knees in front of her. His fingers tangled in her red-brown hair, and he tilted her head back. "The light is turning your skin golden as if it was sunlight." He bent his head, and his lips enveloped her nipple. "Do you feel the heat, Eve?"

"Yes." It was happening again. This time the sensation was so erotic that the intensity was almost painful. Her nails dug into his shoulders. "What are you going to do?"

He was kneeling there, ready, tense. Both of them caught in the brilliant spotlight. She had a sudden hazy memory of the moment in the hospital the first night she'd met him.

Ready to perform . . .

"It's what you're going to do." He lifted his head and moved her legs on either side of his hips. Then he was raising her, bringing her to him. He whispered. "Let me feel the heat. Come burn me, Eve . . ."

CHAPTER

5

It was almost dawn when they left the reservoir.

"You're quiet." John shot her a glance. "Are you having second thoughts?"

"Why?" She looked at him. "It would be a little late, wouldn't it?" She didn't know how many times they'd come together in ways that she hadn't even known existed. "And it was my choice."

"I could have left you alone."

"You said it was going to happen sometime, and it might as well be you. You were right." She gazed out the window. "You were right about a lot of things."

"What things?"

"Chemistry. You said it didn't happen very often like this. I don't see how it could. Too intense. But that's good in a way. Because it can't happen like this very often. I'm not going to have to worry about being pulled into another . . . situation like this. Once you go away, I'll be able to go back to the way things were."

"Will you?"

"Yes, and so will you. That's what we both want. That way this won't hurt us, it won't interfere."

He didn't speak for a moment. "You have it all worked out."

"You exploded into my life like an atom bomb. I had to find a way to make sure that I wouldn't be destroyed by it. How do you expect me to behave?" She looked him in the eye. "You're the one who was hunting me, telling me how we deserved it. Well, you convinced me. As long as we don't hurt anyone else or ourselves, then this could be a good thing. I'm going to make sure that we don't."

"I guess I wasn't sure how you'd react."

"Did you think that I was going to give you some kind of guilt trip? That I was going to beg you to tell me you loved me?" She shook her head. "That isn't what this is about. I don't even know what love is all about." She shrugged. "I don't even know if there is such a thing. I've never seen it. There's a lot of talk, but it seems to go away pretty fast; and then there's a lot of arguing. Maybe it's only something in the movies. What do you think?"

"I think maybe there could be a lot of different kinds of love. And there are people we're supposed to love and people we do love. I couldn't stand my mom and dad. I love my uncle. As for the movie kind of love . . ." He smiled. "I'm a guy. Sometimes we think with our dicks." He met her gaze. "There were a few moments back there that if you'd asked me, I would have said I loved you."

And there were a few moments that he had been the giver of a pleasure so intense that she had loved everything about him, his body, his skill, the way he had made her feel part of him. She had wanted to keep him with her forever. "But I didn't ask you. I promise I'll never ask you."

"I suppose I should feel relieved. I guess I do." He glanced back at the road leading to the reservoir. "Sure I do. You've just made me a little dizzy. You're right, this is what's going to work for us." He paused. "As often as possible. When?"

"Tonight." She looked at him. "Every night. Until we decide we don't want it anymore."

"That's not going to happen."

"It might." But it didn't seem possible to Eve, either. She had thought she was satiated when they had left the reservoir, but she could feel a stirring as she gazed at him. She knew his body so well now. It was a beautiful body, sleek and tough and strong. He could lift her, move her, hold her, with no effort. Yet he didn't make her feel helpless. She'd learned she could stop him with a touch, make him shudder just by a movement. She hadn't realized she'd have that power. He'd always been so dominant and forceful that it had amazed her that she didn't have to take power, it had been given.

He pulled up in front of the development. "You'll only have a few hours to sleep. Are you going to go to school today?"

"Of course." She got out of the car. "School is

important. I told you, I can't let this hurt me." She started across the street. "It probably won't be like this every night."

"No?" She heard the car pull away from the curb. "Don't count on it."

She couldn't count on anything, she thought as she unlocked the door of the apartment. Everything was new territory. She just had to keep on with her usual routine and try to keep her head straight.

Shower, first. Then set the alarm.

Even the drops of warm water falling on her body felt different. Her breasts were taut, and there was a tiny mark. A bruise? Strange. She hadn't been aware of any roughness. But at times they'd been like two wild animals. She remembered his mouth . . . It could have happened then.

Don't think about it. Her breasts were swelling, and she was feeling her body tingling, readying. All it had taken was the memory, and the heat was returning.

She wanted him again.

She leaned her forehead against the wall of the shower. It was all crazy and mysterious and sometimes a little frightening. If this was what sex was like, what would it have been if there had been love between them?

But she understood love even less, and its potential could be even more dangerous. Hadn't both she and John agreed that it could be deceptive and was to be avoided? She didn't know enough about John Gallo even to explore the possibilities. Yet when they had been talking, she had felt a curious sadness.

No, she did not love him. She would *not* love him. The only thing of which she could be both certain and secure was that she loved his body.

That would be enough.

"I like the reservoir better." Eve turned over in bed and gazed at the sheets of rain pounding the window. "I felt strange coming here."

"I couldn't control the weather." John drew her closer. "And this isn't a bad motel. It's clean and not seedy. I made sure of that."

"It just made me think of—" She broke off and pushed away from him. "I have to go to the bathroom." She swung her legs to the floor and stood up. "I'll be back."

"You sound like Schwarzenegger in *The Terminator*." He put his arm behind his head, watching her as she went toward the bathroom. "Though you don't look anything like him."

"Thank heavens." She closed the bathroom door. A few minutes later she was washing her face and hands and stopped to stare into the mirror. She was naked, her cheeks were flushed and her hair tousled, her body ripe and glowing. She looked like she'd been doing exactly what she had been doing.

She turned and went back into the motel room but didn't go right back to bed. She went over to the picture window and drew back the curtains and looked out onto the parking lot. "I can't see anything. It's raining rivers . . ."

"What's wrong?" John asked quietly. "Did I do something you didn't like?"

"No." She always loved everything he did to her. Even though she had been a little uneasy when they'd come there, it hadn't changed her response. She was wondering if anything could. For the past three weeks, they had been together every night and every other spare moment they could steal. Those hours had been as sensual and hazy as a harem dream. She had only been aware of touch and scent and coming together. Her body had become so attuned to his that all he had to do was look at her, hold out his hand, touch her hair, and it started. "It was kind of . . . exotic. Where did you learn to do all that?"

"That's a question you shouldn't ask." He stood up and walked toward her. "I figured if I liked sex, I should do it well. And I didn't wait until I was sixteen like you to start." He grinned. "I was trying to avoid coming home as much as I could, and I had to have something to keep me busy." He pushed her hair aside and pressed his lips to the back of her neck. "And then I found the *Kama Sutra*."

She shivered and whispered, "I think you wrote the *Kama Sutra*."

"At any rate, I thought you were ready for a little distraction. You were acting pretty stiff when I mentioned the motel." He slipped his arm around her waist. "You're never stiff. You bend." He delicately licked her ear. "You open . . ."

"And I did. Again and again."

"Yes." He went still. "But not right now." He pushed

her away from him. "I think we'll have a little down-time." He crossed the room to his duffel on the floor. "I brought you a present."

"What?" She stared at him in astonishment. "Why?"

"Because I wanted to do it. You must have noticed that's all the reason I need." He reached in the duffel and brought out a tissue-wrapped object. "My uncle brought it back from Japan years and years ago. He meant to give it to his girlfriend, but she jilted him. So he gave it to me and told me to make a kite of it. I never got around to it." He tore off the tissue and unfurled a length of gold silk. "I was thinking how pretty it would be against your hair."

She put out a tentative finger and touched the silk. "It's beautiful, but it's not a scarf, John."

"It is if I say it is." He draped it over her hair. "Beautiful. Sun on fire." Then he arranged the rest of the cloth over her shoulders and breasts. "There, you look like a harem girl."

She smiled. "That's odd. I was just thinking that these past weeks have been like a harem dream."

"Is that good?"

"It's . . . erotic." She slipped the length of gold off her hair to pool around her shoulders. "Thank you. But it's not really my style. I'm too . . ." She remembered Teresa's description. "Serious."

"I like serious." He was drawing her over to the easy chair in front of the window. "But I like erotic better." He dropped down in the chair. "It's a good thing it's raining so hard that no one can make out anything through this glass. The office would be getting complaints about those shameless nude people in 2A." He reached up a hand to pull her down on his lap.

Instead, she dropped down on the carpet in front of the chair and linked her arms around her knees. "Why did your uncle's girl jilt him?"

"Another guy. He was overseas a lot on missions. He didn't blame her."

"But you did."

"Yeah, I wanted to kill her. But I was only twelve, so that would have been difficult." He leaned forward and began to rub her shoulders beneath the silk. "And I got over it. Why were you stiff tonight?"

She was silent. "Motels remind me—Sandra spends a lot of time at hotels and motels."

He cursed softly. "Why didn't you say no? I knew you didn't want to have me come to your apartment. You've made that clear. But I'd have found somewhere else."

"Because I'm not Sandra, and I've got to get over letting things like that bother me." She was silent a moment, then said jerkily, "She's not really a prostitute, you know. She just likes to have a good time and is willing to be paid for it. I think she has a good heart. When I was little, she acted as if she cared about me . . . when she wasn't stoned."

"How kind. And did you care about her?"

"Yes, she was pretty and she laughed a lot. Later things changed . . ." She shook her head. "I was confused, then I guess *I* changed. She stayed the same." She was gazing out at the rain. "You said you couldn't stand your parents. Was it always like that, or did it come later?"

"Always. They never wanted a kid. I was in their way. When I got too much in their way, I ended up with burning cigarettes being put out on my back. My father particularly liked that form of discipline."

"That's terrible."

"I thought so, too. I tried to push him down the steps once. I didn't do it right, and he only fell against the wall. He beat the hell out of me. After that, I just tried to stay away. Unless my uncle was home from overseas. Uncle Ted took the heat off." He smiled. "Unintentional pun."

How could he joke? "I can see why you'd love your uncle."

"I was lucky. If I hadn't had him around, I would have ended up in reform school. I've always been pretty wild, but he taught me to channel the violence. Thanks to him, I'm going to have a good life."

"In the Army."

"Only a means to an end." His hands slipped down and began to slowly rub her breasts beneath the silk. She gasped. It was unbearably erotic to feel the rough warmth of his palms alternating with the cool texture of the silk against her nipples. "I'm always going after the big score."

The sensation was causing her to lean her head back against him and arch beneath his hands. "Is that . . . what you're after now?"

"With your cooperation." He tore the silk away from her and tossed it aside. "And I believe I'm going to get it." He lifted her onto his lap and made the adjustment. "Aren't I?"

She groaned, and her nails bit into his shoulders as

he started to move. She couldn't breathe. Fullness. Heat. The sensation was building quickly to an indescribable pitch.

She closed her eyes and let it take her over the top.

"Eve."

She was being shaken.

Then lips were on her nipple.

She knew those lips, that tongue . . .

She opened her eyes to see him above her in bed. He was dressed already.

"It's time we left," John said. "You said that you wanted to be back by five." He used his teeth in a last teasing kiss and lifted his head. "Now or never."

She sat up and shook her head to clear it of sleep. "I must have been sleeping hard."

"It was the rain." He smiled. "And other things." He pulled her from the bed and sent her to the bathroom with a slap on her derriere. "Ten minutes."

She was out in seven and carefully packed the silk wrap in her bag. "Thank you again for this."

"Oh, I enjoyed it."

She remembered the feel of the silk against her breasts. "So did I." She moved toward the door. "Let's go."

The rain had stopped, but it was still misty as they reached the car.

She cast a look back at the motel.

"It wasn't so bad, was it?" John asked as he intercepted her glance. "It's just a place. We made what we wanted of it."

And what they had made was a wild and unforget-table sensual memory. "Not bad at all." She got into the passenger seat. "But I still like the reservoir better. Maybe it won't rain tonight."

He got into the car. "It had better not. I want it right. We don't have that much time left."

She stiffened, her gaze flying to his face. "How long? When do you have to report for basic training?"

"Four days." He started the car. "We both knew it was coming."

Yes, but she must have blocked out the approach of the inevitable ending. "Where are they sending you?"

"I'm not sure. I signed up in Milwaukee, so I have to go back there. They'll probably send me to a camp in Wisconsin." He frowned. "I don't want to talk about it. I don't want to think about it."

"But you are thinking about it, or you wouldn't have mentioned it." She drew her sweater closer to her body. "And we should think about it. It's going to take a little time to get used to the idea. It feels . . . different than it did when we first talked about it."

"Then you think about it," he said roughly. "Tear it apart and tell yourself how smart and practical we're be-ing. All I can think about right now is that next week I'm not going to be making love to you."

"It isn't making love."

"Whatever. Screwing you. Any word you want to use. It's the same result." He was silent a moment. "What if it *is* making love? Neither of us knows what that's like. What if this is it?"

"Just because it seems different? It has to be because we just know each other better."

"Maybe." His hands were tightening on the steering wheel. "Yeah, but it does feel different. And I don't like it."

She didn't know how she would feel after he was gone, either. Her body had become so accustomed to him that he seemed part of her. "We have four days."

"Big deal." Then he grimaced. "I'm acting like a kid. Like I said, I didn't expect to feel like this." He looked at her. "Chemistry is supposed to wear away. It didn't do it. We need more time."

"Well, we don't have it."

He was silent. "Maybe you could come with me and stay near the camp."

She stared at him in disbelief. "So I could put my life on hold and make myself available to you? Hell, no."

"Okay, I know I was out of line. I'm not thinking too clear."

She wasn't thinking clearly, either. For an instant, she had actually considered it. No, not considered. There wasn't anything that resembled cool consideration in the way she was feeling. "And I'd be interfering in your life, too. I won't do that, and I won't give up my plans to follow you around and be your private whore." She was shaking. "Someday you'd leave me, and I'd end up somewhere in another development like the one where I grew up. That's not for me. We do what we said we'd do. It's over when you get on that plane and go off to basic training."

He muttered a curse and didn't speak for a long moment. Finally, he said quietly, "Okay. I know I'm not being fair. I'm reaching out and grabbing what I want. I told you once that you couldn't trust me if I wanted something bad enough." He glanced away from her. "I'm even tempted to try to persuade you to do what I want. I might be able to do it. I have those four days, and I have some pretty potent weapons on my side. You love what we do together as much as I do. It could be enough to tip the balance."

"No way."

"Don't challenge me." He smiled recklessly. "I'm trying to overcome my darker side. I know you're right." He parked in front of the development. "It's just hard for me to care."

She got out of the car. "I care enough for both of us."

"Tonight?"

She should say no. He was behaving with a volatility that made her uneasy, and her response was equally unsettling.

"I'll make it special for you," he said softly.

She could feel the melting begin. Special? He meant erotic, wild, and possibly wicked. And he always kept his promises. Why should she cheat herself? "Tonight." She started across the street. "Four more days."

Eve sat up in bed and brushed her hair out of her eyes. "What time is your flight?"

"We've got time." He pulled her back over him. "Ten tonight."

"An hour before I get off work." She glanced at the clock on the nightstand. "It's three now."

"We've got time," he repeated. "You don't have to be at work until six. I'm packed and ready to go."

She stopped arguing. She didn't want him to leave. Their coming together in the motel room had been hot and frantic, and yet the hunger was still there.

She lay against him, feeling the male hardness and strength of him. She was breathing hard, and she could hear his heartbeat pounding beneath her ear.

His hands were moving over her body. "I know every curve and crevice of you," he whispered. "I've memorized every single part of you. I know your smell, your taste, your texture. If I were blind, I'd be able to recognize you."

And she'd be able to recognize him, she thought. But she wasn't sure that she wanted to remember John Gallo once he passed out of her life. The experience had been too intense, and the emotions she had felt had been confusing. Not only passion, but there had been surprising moments when there had been tenderness.

"They'll probably send me somewhere else after basic training, but I might be able to come back here for a week or so." He was stroking her hair. "I'll call and let you know."

"And after you're away for a while, you might decide that it's better to keep your distance. I won't expect anything from you."

"Because you don't want me to expect anything, either." He tangled his fingers in her hair and lifted her head to meet her eyes. "I've got the message. But I'm not sure that I'm going to pay any attention to it. Are you afraid of me, Eve?"

She was afraid. Afraid of the sex, which was a stronger drug than anything Sandra took, afraid of the way she was beginning to reach out to him in ways that weren't sexual. She liked to watch him, liked his flashes of wry humor, even his silences. "I think we've gone too far."

"Maybe. But that's not going to stop me." He was kissing her, rolling her over on the bed. "Tell me that two minutes from now."

She wasn't able to talk at all after that two minutes. All she could do was to move with him and try to keep from screaming with pleasure. This time she felt totally powerless. He was controlling the pleasure, demanding the response.

And she was giving it to him, giving whatever he asked. She couldn't help herself.

It was only later, when she lay panting and shaking from the aftereffect of that storm, that she realized what that helplessness meant. He had made her feel weak, and that was the true danger.

And it was good that John Gallo was leaving that night.

It was eleven thirty, Eve realized as she climbed the steps to the apartment. John would have been in the air over an hour and a half. It had been strange not to see his Chevy parked in front of the restaurant when she'd left work. Stranger still to come straight home instead of going with John to the reservoir.

Don't think of the reservoir and what we did there.

She had kept busy and had been fine all evening. She had allowed herself no time to remember all the erotic games they'd played in the motel this afternoon. Only they hadn't been games. Everything she'd done with John had been done with searing intensity.

She unlocked the apartment door and went inside. She turned on the light and kicked off her shoes. Empty as usual. Her mother hadn't been home at all that week. She'd shower and go to bed. She hadn't gotten much sleep in the last month, and she might be able to doze off.

Maybe.

She didn't feel sleepy. Every nerve was keyed, and the effort to keep from thinking about John Gallo was added stress. Homework? She'd gotten behind in that, too, but there was nothing urgent. She'd get back in the routine now that she had no distractions.

Distractions?

That was a tame word for John Gallo. Oh, yes, he had distracted her and seduced her and taught her a hundred ways to enjoy her body . . . and his.

But that last time at the motel had revealed that pleasure could be as much a trap as the one she was trying to escape. He was too good, and he had warned her that he would do anything to get what he wanted.

Right now he wanted her.

It might change with time and distance, but that might be too late if he persuaded her to do what he wanted. Even now she could feel her body flush, ready, as she remembered what he had done this—

The doorbell rang, startling her.

No one came to the door at that time of night.

Unless her mother had lost her key again. She misplaced it at least once or twice every few months.

She slid back the viewer in the door. "Again, Sandra? We're keeping that locksmith—"

It wasn't Sandra.

John Gallo.

Eve slid back the bolt and threw open the door. "What's wrong? Why are you—"

She was crushed against him, his mouth on hers, hard, frantic.

And she was frantic, too. Her arms slid around him, and she was making sounds deep in her throat. "Why?" she gasped. "I thought you were gone. Why are—"

"This is why." His voice was guttural; his hands ripping open the buttons of her shirt. "I was sitting at that gate at the airport, and I couldn't get you out of my mind. I had to have you one more time." He was tearing off her bra, his lips on her breast. "Don't say no, Eve."

No? She was as wild as he was. The shock of his appearance had sent her hurtling back into the sensual storm she always experienced when she was with him. She could scarcely breathe. Her hands were running up and down his back, bringing him closer as his tongue sent sensation after sensation through her. "The plane . . ."

"I can catch one at three. I'll still be there on time." He'd backed her against the kitchen table and was pulling down her jeans. "I don't give a damn . . ."

And she didn't either. "The couch . . ."

He wasn't paying any attention to her. She didn't know if he even heard her. He'd lifted her onto the kitchen table, and he was suddenly over her, in her, with one movement. She inhaled sharply. Fullness.

Hardness all around her. The table against her buttocks, his belly pressing down on hers, the stroking . . .

The stroking!

His breath was harsh, his chest rising and falling against her with every thrust. "I knew you . . . wouldn't want it here. This is your space, and you don't want me in it." Another deep thrust. "You don't want to . . . remember me here. You don't want to remember me at all, do you?" He sank deep and rotated. "Do you?"

She gasped as her hands clutched wildly at his shoulders. "It's not—" She shuddered as the pace quickened. "You told me—"

"I said a lot of things, didn't I?" His face above her was flushed, fierce, completely sensual. "But all I can think about right now is that you have—to—remember me. I won't let you forget me. Every time you look around you, you're going to remember me here, doing this to you." He suddenly slid back off the table, taking her with him.

Her legs instinctively curled around his hips.

He was walking, pausing to stroke, then walking again.

Then they were on the couch. "Do you know how many times I thought about doing it with you here?" he whispered. "You liked the reservoir because it was neutral territory, and I'd give you anything you

wanted. But toward the end I didn't want neutral."
He was moving fast, hard. "I wanted this. Because I
won't—be—forgotten, Eve."

Wildness. Hunger. Heat.

Madness.

She had to have more.

Arching, clasping, taking . . .

And then there was no more to take.

It was beyond . . .

She screamed.

He was still moving. "That's right." He was gasping,
"Again, Eve. You can do it. I'll just do this . . ." His eyes
were glittering, wild. "More . . ."

Again.

"I want to make you—but I can't—wait." The tempo
grew harder, more intense. "Can't—" He groaned, his
spine arched, his head thrown back, his face a mask of
pleasure so intense it looked like pain. "Eve!"

He collapsed on top of her.

She didn't want it to stop. On and on and on . . . She
clasped him to her with all her strength, as she tried to
get her breath.

He lifted his head and kissed her lingeringly.
"Beautiful . . ."

"You always say that. I'm not . . ."

"You are. Like a flame . . ." He kissed her breast.
"And you feel like a flame curling around me. When I
was at that gate, I kept thinking of the way you felt. I
thought I'd go crazy if I didn't have you one more time."

"You did go crazy." And so had she. All he'd had to

do was explode through that door, and she had been ready for him. Ready? She'd been wild for him. Everything she'd been telling herself about how good a thing it was that they were separating had vanished the minute he'd touched her. Which meant that everything she had told herself was true. "And you're going to miss that second flight if you don't leave soon. It's after midnight."

"I won't miss it." His tongue traced her lower lip. "I want to stay, but I've done what I had to do." He got to his feet. "I have to go shower. Stay here. I want to see you like this when I come back." He vanished into the bathroom.

She didn't know if she could have moved if she'd wanted to. Every muscle felt limp, and she was lying there in a warm haze. He'd said he was going. There was no reason to stir right now. She didn't have to think or worry. Everything was the same as it had been that afternoon. This had just been a wild, unexpected epilogue.

She heard the shower. He would be gone soon. The wrenching pain she was feeling was all part of the confusion their togetherness had begun to foster lately. She would be fine. It would go away when he went away.

He came out of the shower ten minutes later. "Good." He smiled. "You stayed there. I wasn't sure if you'd do anything I told you to do. Resistance should be kicking in about now."

"I didn't want to move." She met his gaze. "And you're leaving. Maybe I wanted to please you."

"You did." He dropped to his knees in front of the

couch. "And I pleased you, didn't I?" He put his palm on her belly. "It's a wonder. I was so hot I could only think about myself and how fast I could have you." He traced the outline of her navel. "I'm lucky you didn't kick me out."

"You knew that wouldn't happen. And you said you'd been wanting it to be here. So I don't think it was as mindless as you say."

He was silent. "Oh, I was mindless. The other was just instinct." He bent and kissed her nipple. "I've got to get out of here, or I'll have to have you again. I can't miss another plane." His teeth tugged gently at her earlobe. "I've got to do what I promised my uncle I'd do. I won't mess up my chance."

"No, that would be a mistake."

"So that may mean I won't be able to get back here for a while. And you won't come to me."

"No."

"But I *will* come back, Eve." He lifted her up and put his cheek against her belly. It felt rough and hard against her bare flesh. "And you *will* remember me. Say it."

"You'd be hard to forget."

"That's not good enough." He lifted his head, and his eyes were glittering, burning, as they held her own. "Tell me. You'll remember everything we did, everything we are together. No matter how long. You won't forget me."

She couldn't pull her gaze away. His intensity was overpowering and hypnotic, enveloping her, binding her.

"Tell me," he said softly. "You know it's the truth.

You're part of me. You'll always be with me. You'll remember."

How could she help it? No matter how their paths parted or intertwined, he'd been the first in so many ways, and the power of his personality had stunned and beguiled her. Even at that moment, she couldn't imagine the days or years to come without him.

"I'll remember you," she whispered.

"That didn't hurt, did it?" He smiled brilliantly. His arms closed tighter, and he kissed her. "The only thing that will hurt will be the waiting." Then he put her back on the couch and got to his feet. "And I'll cut that down to as little as possible."

"I'm not going to wait for you. That's a trap, too. And you won't want to wait for me after you've been gone for a while."

"I didn't think I would, either. But things are changing. I'll have to see." He moved toward the door. "But one thing I do know. I've never felt like this about anyone before you. I'm not sure that I'll ever feel like this again. I want to reach out and grab and hold on." He opened the door. "But that's my nature. Good-bye, Eve."

"Good-bye, John."

He was standing framed in the doorway as he had been framed by the elevator doors that first night. He was the same, yet not the same. Muscular thighs outlined in denim jeans, same face that was hard yet beautiful in its sensuality. But now she knew that body, that face, in a thousand different positions and expressions. She knew his toughness, his bluntness, his seductiveness, the bitterness that he seldom spoke about, the driving passion that could be as explosive as a lightning flash.

He wanted her to remember him?

This was how she'd remember John Gallo.

CHAPTER

6

*T*he water. Stay out of the water. The current was so strong it would carry her away and over the falls.

Eve's breath was coming in harsh pants that hurt her chest as she scrambled up the bank and into the brush.

Run.

A bullet took the bark off the oak next to her.

Close.

How could he see in this thick brush?

She heard the splashing in the river behind her. He wasn't afraid of the current. Could the devil be afraid of anything?

"Eve!"

It was John Gallo. He caught up with her and grabbed her hand. "This way."

"No!" She tried to pull away.

"Trust me." He was gazing down at her, and he

looked as desperate as she felt. His face was some-
how . . . different. John's face, yet not the John she
knew. "I'll find her. I won't let you die. Trust me."

"Why should I? When have we ever trusted each
other?" She jerked her hand away and started to run
again.

A moment later, another bullet grazed her hair, then
embedded itself in the ground in front of her.

And she heard the sound of running footsteps behind
her. Her heart was beating so hard it was jumping out
of her chest. Find a way, or she was going to die.

Trust me.

Never.

Pain, high in her back . . .

She hadn't heard that bullet.

Death?

Eve jerked upright on the couch, her eyes wildly
searching the darkness.

Her pulse was racing, but the palms of her hands were
cold. It took a minute for her to realize that she was not
still in that deadly brush.

A dream?

But it had seemed so real. John Gallo had been gone
nearly three weeks, but he had also seemed so real. Al-
though it was a John Gallo she had never known. If
she was going to dream about John, why wouldn't it be
sensual, sexual, and not a horrible, deadly chase that
had ended her life. That was what her time with John
had been all about. Sex, passion, and mindless pleasure

that had ended with a desperate intensity that had almost frightened her.

And perhaps that was why she had dreamed of John as the pursuer, the enemy, just exaggerated and translated into a life-and-death struggle.

And all this soul-searching was crap over a simple nightmare. She swung her feet to the floor and got up and went to the bathroom. She drank a glass of water, then went back to the couch.

Go back to sleep. It was only a dream. She was doing fine. She was back in her routine of work and school and keeping herself so busy that she barely thought of John. It was as if that period was also a dream. It was probably good that she had experienced that passion then and not later. She could put it behind her and concentrate on work.

And that was crap, too. She was giving herself excuses, and there had been nothing calculated about what she'd done.

But it was over now, and she was doing just fine.

"You don't look so good." Teresa was gazing at Eve critically. "You got the flu or somethin'?"

"Maybe." She finished the to-go order and set it on the warming shelf. "It's going around."

"Well, you're white as that paper bag. Don't breathe on me. I've had enough bugs this year."

"I'll stay away." She wished Teresa would be quiet. Her head was pounding, and she was fighting against throwing up. The smell of frying hamburgers was making her stomach churn.

"You should go home. You gonna have to ride the bus?"

"How else?"

"I thought maybe John might be back in town. He's been gone a couple months, hasn't he? Have you heard from him?"

"No. I didn't expect to hear from him."

"Hot and heavy, then good-bye?" Teresa made a face. "Yeah, that's the way it goes. But it can be worth it."

"Maybe."

"He had a real thing for you. I couldn't get him to pay any attention to— Where are you going?"

Sick. So sick.

She barely made it to the bathroom before she threw up.

And then threw up again.

Lord, she felt awful.

She sank down to the floor beside the toilet.

She'd get up again soon, but she wasn't sure her legs would hold her right now.

"Eve?"

Teresa.

"I'm okay. Go back to work."

"You're not okay." She opened the door of the enclosure. "Can I get you a wet towel or something?"

"No, just leave me—" She scrambled over the toilet again and threw up. "I'll be okay."

"Yeah, sure." Teresa was wetting a paper towel at the

sink. "Like my roommate, Linda, was okay. You think I don't know the signs. How far along are you? Almost two months? Three?"

"What are you talking about?"

"I'm talking about that gorgeous son of a bitch who didn't protect you." She laid the towel on Eve's forehead. "You're only a kid. He should have—" She broke off as she saw Eve's expression. "What did you expect? Anyone could see that you were so hot for each other, you were dizzy with it. You should have come to me. I'd have helped you."

"You think I'm . . . pregnant?"

"The timing's right. My roommate started getting morning sickness at about three months." She frowned. "Aren't you? Haven't you missed your periods?"

"I'm not always regular. I thought the pills might have—" She closed her eyes. "I *can't* be pregnant." She could feel the panic rising. She had not permitted herself to even think of the possibility. "I was on the pill."

Teresa was dabbing at her forehead. "Nothing is fool-proof."

"My mother never got pregnant, and she's been on them for years."

"I don't know. Maybe you're not pregnant," Teresa said. "But I'd go to a doctor and find out." She paused. "And then maybe call John Gallo and see if he'll help you out. He should pay if he's going to play."

"Pay?"

"You're sixteen. You can't handle this. I can take

you to Linda's doctor. If you're not too far along, an abortion is easy. She only had to stay home two days after hers."

Abortion.

The word struck her like a blow. The shocks were coming at her too fast, too horribly.

She shook her head, hard. "I'm not pregnant. You're wrong. It's a mistake."

"It always is." Teresa patted her shoulder. "Look, you go on home. I'll explain to Mr. Kimble."

Eve looked at her with alarm.

"No, not that you're pregnant. He might get rid of you. Bosses don't like to deal with women's problems." She helped her to her feet. "You have the flu, remember? Stay here. I'll go get your purse."

Stay here? She felt so weak that she didn't know if she'd even be able to get to the bus stop. Nausea, shock, horror were all attacking her, bringing her down. She hung on to the basin to keep upright.

"It's okay." Teresa was back and handing Eve's purse to her and helping her toward the door. "Get going."

"I will." She stopped to look back at Teresa. Even through the haze of shock and panic, she realized that the girl had been kinder than Eve could have expected. "Thank you."

Teresa shrugged. "We've got to stick together. I could be in the same fix myself someday. The only thing you can trust a guy for is to give you a good time. The rest is up to us." She gave her a gentle push. "Get on home. Crackers used to settle Linda's stomach."

Eve wished she'd stop comparing her to her room-mate. Maybe she wasn't in the same condition. Maybe Teresa was wrong.

But she had the panicky feeling that she was right.

Sandra came home three hours after Eve arrived at the apartment.

"Eve?" She frowned as she peered into the dimness. "What are you doing home? And, why are you sitting in the dark, honey?"

"I don't feel well." She felt like an animal with a mortal wound huddled in a cave, not able to face the light. "Go to bed, Sandra."

"Maybe I could get you something? Need an aspirin?"

"No, it's my stomach. Go to bed."

"Okay, you be sure and call me if you need anything." Sandra drifted toward the bedroom. "It must be bad. I can't remember the last time you missed work."

"It's bad." Terrible. The worst thing that could have happened to her.

Then Sandra was gone, disappearing into her pretty pink bedroom.

Relief. Eve didn't know if she could have contended with Sandra tonight. She was alternating between the shakes and that terrible nausea. And the realization of what a terrible, irresponsible fool she had been. That's right, reach out and grab what you want. Forget all your plans for making something of yourself, a few weeks of sex were worth anything, weren't they? Oh, Lord, how could she have run the risk?

And she was sick again.

She jumped to her feet and ran into the bathroom and retched. She no longer had anything in her stomach, and it made it all the more painful.

"Here, honey." Sandra was handing her a cloth. "Rinse out your mouth and wash your face. You'll feel better." She turned. "I'll get you a soda. Sometimes it helps."

It seemed she was being forced to accept help from another unlikely source. First, Teresa. Now, Sandra. "I can get it."

"I know you can. But let me do it."

What had gotten into Sandra? The last thing Eve wanted was to have Sandra fussing over her.

She'd get bored soon. Just drink the soda, and she'd go away. Eve washed her mouth and face and went back into the living room.

"Sit down," Sandra said as she handed her the can of soda. "Drink it slow, honey."

"You can go to bed now, Sandra."

"I know I can. I could leave you alone." Sandra sat down. "But I don't want to do that." She folded her hands nervously on her lap. "Maybe I leave you alone too much. But you never seem to need me. Even when you were little, you were so strong, stronger than me." She paused. "I'm not a good mother to you, Eve. My folks kicked me out when I got pregnant, and having a kid was just too much for me."

"It's all right. I never did need you. I could take care of myself."

"But can you do it now? I remember how I felt when—" She drew a deep breath and her hands clasped even tighter. "You're going to have a baby, aren't you?"

Shock. She had not expected Sandra to be observant enough to jump to that conclusion. "Why do you think that?"

"You're sick. You're never sick." She paused. "And last week I noticed one of my birth-control discs was missing. You took it, didn't you?"

She nodded slowly.

"That was my prescription, Eve. It might not have been strong enough for you. Or maybe it won't work unless you take it for a couple weeks first. I've been on them so long that I don't remember. If you'd come and asked me, I'd have told you it might not work well for you."

But she would never have gone to Sandra. Dear God, she had thought by not trusting John, she was protecting herself in the best possible way. Eve closed her eyes, and whispered, "You've been taking them all these years. I thought I'd be safe."

"Are you going to have a baby, Eve?" Sandra repeated.

Eve wanted to deny it. She wanted to deny it to Sandra and herself and the whole world. But she had to accept it, deal with it. She couldn't hide in the dark forever. She said jerkily, "Yes, I . . . think so."

"Oh, honey." Tears were glittering in Sandra's eyes. "I was hoping I was wrong. That handsome young man who helped me?"

"Yes."

"How does he feel about it? Does he want to marry you?"

"Marry? He doesn't care for me that way. Because I'm pregnant? It wasn't that kind of— He doesn't know. I won't tell him. He's gone away. Chances are that I may not see him again."

"Then you're alone," Sandra said. "The way I was when I had you."

She nodded jerkily. "Yes, isn't it funny?" She added the bitter words that had so upset her, "Like mother, like daughter."

Sandra reached out a tentative hand and touched Eve's arm. "I can help you. I'll take you to that Planned Parenthood Clinic tomorrow and sign all the papers. You don't have to have this baby."

Abortion. It was everyone's first thought.

"My folks wouldn't sign the permission, and I was only fifteen. They said I had to take responsibility for my sins. I was so scared . . . I don't want you to be scared like that, Eve."

She was scared right now. But not of having the child itself. It was giving up all her dreams of digging herself out of this slum. The fear of repeating all the mistakes of her mother and everyone around them.

And she had already started that cycle.

She had been so confident that if she was careful and worked hard, she could have it all.

She had not been careful enough, and it might destroy her.

Unless she destroyed the child she and John Gallo

had created from that passion that had seemed worth
any risk.

No.

The rejection was so strong that she felt almost ill
again.

"Eve?" Sandra's gaze was on her face. "It's the only
thing to do, honey. Believe me, I know how hard it is to
raise a kid. It drains you . . ." She added quickly, "Not
that you weren't a sweet little baby. But toting you and
picking you up from charity day-care centers. Working
for minimum wage just to eat. It never seemed to stop.
Everyone needs a little fun in their life."

And that scared fifteen-year-old girl maybe more than
others. Eve had never realized how vulnerable Sandra
had been all those years of Eve's childhood. "I'll think
about it, Sandra."

"You do that." She stood up. "We'll talk about it
in the morning. I'll be ready to go with you." She
headed for the bedroom. "Then maybe we'll stop and
have lunch. If you have enough money. I'm broke
again. Money just seems to run right through my fingers."

On dope. But Sandra hadn't seemed to be on anything that night. Or if she had, it hadn't been obvious.
She had been sincere and gentle, and if Eve hadn't been
so upset, she would have been touched.

She was touched, she realized. Admit it. She was only
trying to harden her heart to Sandra because she'd been
hurt so many times before. Strange, she didn't usually admit that Sandra could hurt her, even to herself.
Maybe she felt a kinship because of the baby she was

carrying. But how could that be when the child wasn't even real to her yet?

She wouldn't tear this feeling apart and examine it. She had needed someone, and Sandra had been there. It hadn't happened for years. Maybe that had been partly her fault. She had withdrawn from Sandra when she had realized that she couldn't trust her to be there for her. How long ago? She couldn't remember.

And she didn't want to think about Sandra just then. It was time she stopped sitting in the dark and feeling sorry for herself. She had to make a choice whether to give up and let life run over her as it had Sandra or fight back.

There was no choice. She would rather step in front of a train than let herself be beaten down by what had happened to her. She had to find a way to cope.

All right, sit still. Let herself get over the shock and pain of what had happened to her first.

No. Nothing had "happened" to her. She couldn't blame anyone, not even fate. She had been so dizzy with the need for him that she hadn't been thinking clearly and coolly as she usually did. She had done this herself by lust and stupidity and overconfidence. Accept it and go on.

And try desperately to find a way out of this web that was about to smother her.

Eve had already showered and dressed the next morning by the time Sandra wandered into the living room.

"Not sick? You must have slept. You look better than me." Sandra yawned. "But then I never was a morning person."

"There's orange juice in the fridge," Eve said. "No bacon. But you can make toast. No, I'll make it while you get dressed."

"You're in a hurry." Sandra looked at her. "Those Planned Parenthood offices don't open until after nine, Eve. We've got time."

"I'm not going to have an abortion." She put bread in the toaster. "But I still need you to go to school with me and see the guidance counselor."

"Eve, you don't know what it's like to have to take care of a baby. You need to—"

"No, I don't know. But I may find out." She got out the orange juice. "Or maybe not. I haven't decided if I'm going to put the baby up for adoption. It might be better for both of us. If I don't see a way out for us, I won't bring the baby into the same situation that trapped both of us, Sandra."

"That could work," Sandra said. "But it would be hard for you. Look what kind of mess Rosa Desprando is going through. She should have given up Manuel."

"That's what her father says." She set the orange juice on the table. "But I'm not Rosa, and I'll make up my own mind. I'm going to get through this."

"An abortion would—"

"No, Sandra. I may not be practical, but I can't do it. I'm not going to make a kid pay for my mistake."

Sandra sat down at the table. "So what am I supposed to do?"

"I'm going to drop out of school. I won't be ashamed for the other kids to know, but it's not practical for me to try to get through when I'll be big as a house. But I want to start working on my GED right away. Then by the time I have the baby, I'll have my GED and can try to get into college."

"You're still going to try to go to college?" Sandra was shaking her head. "It's just not possible, Eve."

"Watch me. It's possible. Come with me to the guidance counselor, and we'll get a jump start on that GED. I have a straight-A average, and they'll probably look on me as a lost lamb. If I go in there alone, they'd turn the social workers loose on me." She met Sandra's eyes. "I need you. Will you help me?"

Sandra nodded. "Of course, honey. Just let me have breakfast and shower, then we'll go."

"Try to hurry." She turned away. "I have a lot to do today. Before we go to school, I want to go to a doctor and make sure I'm not doing all of this for nothing. Though that would be too lucky."

"You have it all planned out."

"I have to have a plan. It's the only way we can survive."

"We?"

"My baby and me." She glanced back over her shoulder. "And maybe you, Sandra. If you want to go through this with me."

"You want me?"

She told the truth that she had stopped admitting to herself years ago. "I've always wanted you."

Sandra smiled brilliantly. "Then you've got me." She stood up. "And I'll dress real quick. Do you think I should wear my new pink dress? I do love it. Or maybe the navy blue one would make me look more serious."

"The pink one," Eve said. "Be yourself. To hell with being serious. There's going to be enough of that in our lives."

After she finished with the guidance counselor, she left her mother at the apartment and took a bus to the restaurant. She went directly to the office.

George Kimble looked up at her entrance. "You're looking pretty good. Teresa said you were sick. Flu?"

"I feel okay." She drew a deep breath. "But it's not flu. I'm pregnant."

"So?" He looked her up and down. "You don't look far along. Are you resigning?"

"No. I'm asking for more hours. I just quit school, and I need the work."

"And I don't need someone who gets sick all the time and has to go home. You put me in a bad spot last night."

"It won't happen again."

He leaned back in his chair and shook his head. "Who was it? That kid who kept coming in here and picking you up?"

"Yes."

"Won't he help you out?"

"I'm not asking."

He wearily shook his head. "You kids. You could have the whole world at your feet, and you throw it away. I like you, Eve. I thought you had your head in the right place."

"I guess I didn't. I do now. Will you give me those hours?"

"It's not good business. I couldn't rely on you."

"You can rely on me." She put her hands on the desk and leaned toward him. "I want a twelve-hour shift. I'll be here every day, without fail. If someone else doesn't show up, I'll work a double. I'll be the most valuable employee you have, Mr. Kimble. Yes, I may get sick, but I won't let it interfere. I'll be here. Most of the time, it doesn't last during the entire pregnancy. I'll work through it."

"So you say."

"Look at me." She held his eyes. "I made a mistake, but I'm not going to let it hold me down. I'll be working on my GED, but having a baby isn't cheap, and I need that money. Afterward, I'm going to hold you to your word about working around my hours while I go to college. I'm not asking for charity. You're going to get your money's worth, more than your money's worth. Now do I get my twelve-hour shift?"

He didn't speak for a moment. "You get it. Show up tomorrow at 1 P.M." He looked down at the papers on his desk. "Now get out of here."

She turned to go.

"Eve."

She looked back at him.

"If you think I'm going to be soft on you, forget it. I'm going to work your ass off."

She nodded and walked out of the office.

It had been easier than she'd thought it would be. But that didn't mean that Mr. Kimble wouldn't toss her out if she didn't follow through.

She would follow through.

"You okay?" Teresa asked, her gaze on the office door. "Did he fire you?"

"No. He gave me extra hours. I start tomorrow."

"Really? Then do you want to see Linda's doctor?"

"No, I'm going to have the baby." She turned toward the door. "It's going to be all right, Teresa."

"Yeah, sure."

She couldn't convince Teresa when she had to work everything out for herself. "I have to leave now. The doctor gave me all kinds of vitamins and stuff to pick up from the drugstore." She opened the door. "I've got to have everything set up before I start working full-time. See you tomorrow."

She started toward the bus stop down the block. Then she stopped. It was ten blocks from here to the housing development. The doctor had said she needed exercise. It would save money if she walked it whenever possible. She was going to need every penny. Sandra had said she'd get a job, but she couldn't count on her promises. She had to keep on relying only on herself as she'd always done.

She turned and started down Peachtree Street. Every step was a confirmation that this was the route she had to go. She had to build her strength if she was going to keep to the schedule she'd set for herself. She had to build her strength to keep the baby strong. She had to find ways to do both. Challenge herself to get through this and come out with all the prizes.

Very grand, she thought ruefully. The only prize she was after was to get home and hope that Sandra was still there and had not flitted off as she usually did.

A small prize, a small step, but she would take it. She would work on the giant steps later.

SIX MONTHS LATER

"There's a man downstairs who wants to talk to you," Rosa said when Eve opened the door. "I left him on my bench in the yard. Nice man. He said he'd come upstairs, but he has a bad back."

"Who is he?" Eve asked. She didn't really have time to talk to anyone. She had to finish this paper for her English class before she left for work. "Salesman?"

"I don't think so." She frowned. "He doesn't have that slick look. I didn't get his name. He sort of reminds me of someone."

"That's a help." She came out on the landing and started down the steps. "Look, Rosa, you were supposed to be studying with me this morning and not sitting with the baby on that bench."

"But he needs the sunshine."

"And you need your GED. And you're going to get it. I want you here tomorrow morning."

"Okay." She made a face. "You didn't used to be so bossy."

"Yes, I was. I just didn't have time to concentrate on it." She called back to her, "Now I make the time."

Rosa leaned over the railing. "Your baby is going to come out of you cracking a whip."

She grinned as she opened the front door. "I'll take the chance. That will be two of us to nag you."

She was still smiling as she turned to the man sitting on the bench. "Hello, I'm Eve Duncan. What can—" She inhaled sharply.

He sort of reminds me of someone.

He was a thin man in his late forties or early fifties, with thinning gray-brown hair and olive skin and dark eyes.

John Gallo's eyes.

"How do you do? I'm Ted Danner." The man got to his feet with an effort. "I'm sorry to make you come down. I just couldn't face those flights of stairs. John may have told you that I have back problems."

"You're his uncle Ted." She moistened her lips, trying to recover from the shock. "Yes, he said you injured it while you were in the service."

"I thought he'd tell you about me. We're very close." He smiled gently. "He's like my own son. He's a good boy."

"Why are you here?"

"He asked me to come."

Another shock. "What?"

"Well, actually, he asked me to keep an eye on you when he left for basic. He said that I shouldn't approach you, that you'd resent it."

"But you're here."

"I tried to keep myself from coming. But I had to talk to you." He looked at the front of her maternity smock. "I saw you on the street three weeks ago, and I was . . . surprised. How far are you along?"

"Eight months."

"And it's John's child?"

"No, it's my child."

"But John fathered him?"

She nodded. "But you don't have to worry. I'm not going to claim him as the father." She paused. "I prefer he not know. You should agree to that. John said you were eager that he have a career in the military. A baby would just get in his way." Her lips tightened. "Don't tell him."

Ted Danner shook his head. "You poor child. You're so alone."

"The hell I am. I'm doing fine. Don't tell him."

"I don't have a choice at the moment. I can't write to him. I don't know where he is."

She stared at him, stunned. "What?"

"Right after basic and Ranger school, he was sent overseas. I heard from him from Tokyo right after he arrived, then nothing."

"That doesn't make sense. You have to be able to trace him. You're military yourself."

"Unless he volunteered for a special mission. John's

smart and ambitious, and that would be a way for him to rise through the ranks."

"Just what you'd do," she said dully.

"That's what I've been telling myself." He shook his head. "It's different when it's someone else doing it." His voice was husky. "I love that boy."

She could see that he did. His eyes were moist, and his last words had been unsteady. "But you don't know anything for certain. He could be fine."

Ted nodded. "I've dropped from the radar any number of times, and here I am with nothing but a bad back. I've been doing a lot of praying lately." He stood up. "I thought you should know in case you wanted to do a little praying, too."

She was so stunned that she didn't know how she felt. It was hard for her to believe that the John Gallo she had known could be in any danger. "I'm sure that he'll be all right."

Ted Danner nodded. "I thought you should know. But don't worry too much. It wouldn't be good for you." He started down the walk toward the gate. "If I can do anything for you, let me know. It's the least I can do. John would want me to stand by you."

"You have your own problems. Your nephew would want you to take care of yourself."

"You're a good girl, Eve," he said quietly. "I can see why John cared about you."

She watched him walk stiffly down the street. Poor guy, he was really worried, and John was obviously all he had. But he was jumping the gun. She couldn't believe that John Gallo was dead just because he was temporarily missing. He was so young and strong and tough. Men like him weren't easily killed. She refused to think that it could happen to him.

Or was it fear that was keeping her from acknowledging that his uncle might have reason to panic? She had still not come to terms with how she felt about John. Just when she had convinced herself that it was purely sexual emotion, his uncle had shown her a love for him that must somehow have been deserved. He had seen his torment as a child and lived with him, been a companion.

She had never seen that torment. He had not let her get that close.

But he had been close enough to give her this child in her body.

Perhaps, even though she couldn't believe he was truly in danger, she should pray for the father of her child.

CHAPTER

7

Dammit, not in the middle of the night!
But why not? Babies didn't pay any attention to the clock. Just make it as inconvenient as possible for the mother.

Eve turned away from the commode, and called, "Sandra, I've got to get to the hospital. My water just broke."

"Not in the middle of the night!"

"My thought exactly." She turned to the closet. "I'll get my suitcase, and you run downstairs and wake Mr. Milari. He promised he'd take me to the hospital in his taxi no matter what time. You may have to persuade him. I'm sure he was hoping it wouldn't be at four in the morning."

Sandra yawned as she stumbled out of the bedroom. "I'll convince him." She headed for the door. "Call the doctor."

"I will." The pains were beginning, and she took a

deep breath. "After I deliver, call Mr. Kimble and let him know. Tell him I'll only be out seven days like I promised."

"For heaven's sakes, you worked up to the last minute. He can't expect you to jump right back, and—"

"Yes, he can. And I will."

Sandra stopped at the door. "You haven't told me whether you're going to put the kid up for adoption. I should let the people at the hospital know."

"They'll know when I do." She had been wrestling with that decision for months. She should probably give the baby up. It would be better for Eve and for the baby. All the odds were against you when you were sixteen and had a kid to raise. Look at what had happened to Sandra. But ever since the first movement, the child had become real to her. It was her baby, her child. "Let's just get me there."

"You're back with us." The plump, freckled young woman was smiling down at Eve. She was wearing a badge . . . MARGE TORAN, LPN. "You had us worried when you blacked out just as the baby was coming. Though it was a really long, difficult delivery. Heaven really wanted to keep that child."

The nurse was smiling, Eve realized hazily. That must mean everything was all right. Medical people didn't go around grinning if they had to give you bad news. "My baby?" she whispered.

"You have a little girl," the nurse said softly. "A beautiful little girl. Is that what you wanted?"

Eve shook her head. "I didn't think about it." She had deliberately kept herself from thinking about the sex of the child. She had been afraid that she would grow even closer to her baby and not be able to make that crucial decision. "Does she have . . . everything? Toes, eyes . . ."

"All the right number of everything. She's perfect."

"That's good. I tried to make sure she'd be healthy. It will give her a better . . . chance." Was she making sense? She felt as if she was drifting away. "And if she's a girl, she'll need every . . ."

Another girl. Sandra. Eve. And now this little girl Eve had brought into the world. A chain. Would her daughter give birth at sixteen in some run-down slum? Did the chain have to go on and on?

"Would you like me to bring her to you?" Nurse Toran asked. "We're cleaning her up, but you'll be able to see her soon."

She shouldn't see her. She should tell the nurse her daughter needed a better place, a better life, a better mother.

"You rest." The nurse was at the door. "I'll bring her as quick as I can."

Then she was gone.

Eve closed her eyes. Don't go to sleep. They're going to bring her. She was going to get to see her little girl.

"Eve."

She opened her eyes to see Sandra beside the bed. "Hi."

"It's a girl," Sandra said.

"I know. The nurse told me. Thanks for staying with me, Sandra."

"I wanted to do it. I remember how lonely I felt when I woke up after I had you."

The chain again. But this was a different link in the chain. A less cruel link.

"Have you seen her?"

"Not yet." Sandra smiled. "You get the first glimpse." She took Eve's hand. "But they let me in to see you. You look good, kind of glowing."

"Plain old perspiration. She gave me a hard time."

"What do you expect? She's your daughter."

"And your granddaughter."

Sandra's eyes widened in mock horror. "Eve, I'm much too young to be a grandmother. Grandmothers have gray hair and wrinkles."

"Then you'll set a new trend."

Sandra's smile faded. "You're going to keep her."

She shook her head. "I know I shouldn't do it. She deserves more."

Sandra nodded. "It wouldn't be smart."

"Here she is." Nurse Toran was coming through the door carrying a pink-wrapped bundle. "She's magic. She doesn't look like a newborn at all. And I know newborns aren't supposed to see well or smile, but I swear she smiled at me. She seems to be glad to be here." She put the baby in the curve of Eve's arm. "Though that may change. She's going to be hungry soon." She folded the soft pink blanket away from the baby. "Say hello to your mama, cutie."

So tiny, Eve thought. So delicate.

And then she looked down at the baby's face.

And her little girl smiled at her.

"Oh, my God," she whispered.

And it was not a curse.

A cap of wispy red-brown hair framed that tiny face. Dark eyes stared up at Eve, curious, alert, full of joy. Reaching out for everything that life held.

"What did I tell you?" the nurse said softly. "Magic."

"Yes." Eve's arm tightened on the baby. "I never dreamed . . . May I keep her with me?"

"For a little while. Then you'll have to sleep." Nurse Toran headed for the door. "But both of you seem pretty happy right now."

Happy? That wasn't the word. Eve felt as if her entire being was opening, beginning to shine, with a kind of luminous radiance. A radiance that was coming from the child she was holding.

"She's beautiful, Eve," Sandra said.

"Yes." Eve couldn't look away from her little girl. "I know every mother thinks her child is special, but she is special, isn't she? Even the nurse could see it."

"So pretty." Sandra took a step nearer. "And look at the way she's looking at me." She put a gentle finger on the baby's hand. "She likes me, Eve."

"I think she loves the whole world." Eve touched the satin of the baby's cheek. "It makes you want to make sure that she keeps on loving it, that nothing ever hurts her." Her lips brushed the baby's head. "Don't you worry. I'm here. I'll keep you safe."

"Eve."

"I know. But she's magic, Sandra. And she knows no one could ever love her like I do." She said softly, "Don't you, baby? It's sort of like a golden river flowing back and forth between us that will never end."

"You're going to keep her."

"I want to keep her. I feel as if my heart will break if I lose her. I don't know if I'm strong enough to give her up." She could feel the tears sting her eyes as she pressed her cheek against that silky head. "But I'll think about it. I'll give myself a little time."

Sandra shook her head. "Well, while you're thinking, you'd better give her a name. You can't keep calling her baby."

A name.

"I never thought of names." For the same reason she hadn't wanted to know the sex of the baby. She looked down at the little girl. "What about it?" she asked her. "I don't want to just pull a name out of a hat. We should decide it between us. I want to share everything with you."

"She's a newborn." Sandra chuckled. "She can't decide anything yet."

"But she's magic." Her little girl was looking up at her, and Eve was getting lost in that gaze that seemed to be reaching out, asking, holding. "Give her a chance. Look at her. Isn't she beautiful? And she has a beautiful soul. I know it."

"A name," Sandra prompted.

Beautiful child. Beautiful soul. Eve thought for a moment, then said softly, "Her name is Bonnie."

"You're breast-feeding her," Sandra noticed when she walked into Eve's hospital room the next morning. "I suppose that means the decision is made?"

Eve nodded and tucked the blanket around Bonnie, who had drifted off to sleep. "I thought a long time about it. I didn't sleep last night. I was afraid that I was just being selfish. She deserves better than that from me."

"But you're still keeping her."

"Yes." Eve gazed down at the baby, who had made a tiny sound. Are you dreaming, sweetheart? I hope they're wonderful dreams. "Because I realized something." Her glance shifted to Sandra. "All my life, I thought the only thing I wanted was to pull myself out of the gutter and have a clean, decent life. That was going to be my destiny." She added simply, "But I was wrong. I was born for only one thing. To love and take care of my little girl. None of the rest matters. I'll break the chain, but it will be for her. Everything that was going to be for me, will be for her. For my Bonnie."

Sandra was silent a moment. "It's going to be so hard, Eve."

Eve nodded. "I'll need help. I have to work and go to school. I was going to ask Rosa to move in with me, but I'd rather have you." She paused. "But I can't have anyone on drugs around Bonnie. You were great while I was pregnant. You only took off three times during those months. But you have to be completely clean now. One time, and I'll have to keep her away from you."

"For heaven's sake, Eve, a few little sniffs don't do anyone—" She broke off as she met Eve's gaze. "I know I'm lying to myself. I always knew. I wouldn't hurt her, Eve."

"I can't take the chance."

Sandra hesitated. "You'd really trust me to take care of her?"

Eve nodded. "I'll be scared to death until you prove yourself to me. I'll be calling every fifteen minutes."

"Mr. Kimble wouldn't like that." Sandra smiled. "So I guess I'd better put your mind at rest. She'll be safe with me. After all, I took care of you, didn't I?"

"Yes," Eve said. "And you were younger than I am. You were a very brave girl, Sandra."

Sandra blinked. "You think so? I never thought about it. I just did what I had to do. You can't be brave if you're scared all the time."

"Sure you can." She paused. "But I don't want to saddle you with my child, Sandra. That's not fair. Unless it's what you want, too. Do you?"

Sandra didn't answer for a moment. "I'm lonely sometimes, you know. You're so strong, Eve. For a long time you haven't needed me. I kind of liked helping you out lately. It made me feel important."

"You are important." She looked down at Bonnie. "And you could be very important to her. She's going to need all the help we can give her. We'll keep all the ugliness away from her. She's got to have a good life, Sandra. If we work together, we can give it to her."

"You truly need my help?"

"Of course, I do."

Sandra came closer and looked down at the sleeping Bonnie. "Look at her." She touched Bonnie's red-brown curls. "She's got hair like mine. She's going to be real pretty. You're right, you do need my help. You never did take any pains to look nice. I'll have to show her all the little tricks. I think her hair is going to be curly." She added absently, "I don't remember John Gallo having curly hair."

The comment came as a little shock to Eve. Bonnie had seemed to be so completely Eve's own that she had not thought of John Gallo having any part of her. Or perhaps she had blocked out any connection. That was more likely. "He didn't. It was thick and a little wavy, but not curly." Her gaze ran over Bonnie's features. Her skin was a little more olive than Eve's, dark eyes, but they might fade to Eve's hazel. She didn't have that faint indentation in the chin that John had. No, she was definitely more Eve's child than John Gallo's. Except for the beauty that everyone had instantly noticed. No one could deny that John had stunning good looks and, in spite of his telling Eve that she was beautiful, she knew it wasn't true.

But Eve would not think of her daughter as an extension of either one of them. She was an entity in her own right. She was Bonnie.

"Then are you going to help me with my little girl?"

"I think I have to do it, don't you?" Sandra smiled gently down at Bonnie. "You all are claiming she's magic, and naturally she wouldn't have it any other way. I knew that first minute that she took a liking to me."

"What a sweet little girl. She looks like a ray of sunshine in that yellow dress."

Eve turned around to see Ted Danner coming down the street toward her, his gaze on Bonnie sitting up in her stroller. "Let's see, she must be five months?"

"Six." Eve bent down and adjusted Bonnie's visor. "But she's small for her age." She added quickly, "Though she's very healthy."

"I can tell." He was smiling as he bent down and chucked Bonnie under the chin. "And a happy child. That's important. John would have been proud of her."

"She's happy. She loves her rides in the stroller."

"I know." He paused. "I've been watching you for the last week as you took her for walks. I guess I was trying to work up the nerve to talk to you."

"Why? Because you thought I'd resent your meeting Bonnie?" She frowned. "Look, Mr. Danner, I have no bad feelings toward you. John loved you and thought you were the kindest man alive. It wasn't right for him to draw you into what was between the two of us, but it was only kindness that led you to do it." She paused. "You haven't heard anything about John yet? It's been so long."

"Longer for me than for you." He looked down at

Bonnie. "You've been very busy. And John must seem like a dream to you now."

"Sometimes. You have to understand. We didn't really know each other."

"He thought he knew you. He talked a lot about you. He said he'd never met anyone before who moved him as you did." His gaze shifted to Bonnie. "And he gave you this wonderful child."

"I assure you that it wasn't his intention. Neither of us wanted this to happen. It just did." She paused. "I won't try to convince you not to tell John about Bonnie. I'll have to face it sometime."

"No, you won't." His eyes were suddenly glittering with moisture. "You're not going to have to worry about my John any longer. That's why I had to gather my courage before I faced you. I got this notification last month." He fumbled in his pocket and brought out a crumpled piece of paper. "He's dead. He was lost off the coast of North Korea a few weeks after he arrived there. The remains were discovered in an inlet five weeks ago. They say the dental records are indisputable proof. The Army is very sorry about my loss. They'll probably send me a damn medal." His voice was suddenly bitter. "His loss. He was only nineteen years old. His life was hell from the minute he was born. They shouldn't have let him die before he had a chance to live."

"Dead?" she whispered. It came as a complete shock. She had rejected the possibility of John Gallo's death, but it was there before her. "They're sure?"

"Read the notification."

She took the crumpled paper and scanned it. All very official. All very sad. But, as Ted Danner had said, it didn't tell the real tragedy of the death of that strong, young man who had just started to live. Memories of John Gallo were suddenly bombarding her. John at the hospital, John carrying Sandra up the stairs, John moving over her in bed. Always strong, always dominant, always vibrant and complicated, with a presence that could be either restrained or explosive. He had been in her life for such a short time, and yet he'd had more impact than anyone she'd ever met. And John Gallo was no longer alive? She was suddenly feeling a terrible sense of loss. She handed the notification back to him. "I'm so sorry, Mr. Danner."

"So am I." He stuffed the paper back in his pocket. "I promised him I'd keep an eye on you. Would you mind if I still do it? It would make me feel I'm doing something for him. I won't get in your way."

"I don't mind." She reached out and touched his shoulder. "Maybe you could come to dinner some night. I'm a lousy cook, but my mother is pretty good."

He shook his head. "No, I wouldn't impose. You have your life to lead." He smiled with an effort and gently brushed his hand on Bonnie's cheek. "She has the look of him, doesn't she? She's going to be pretty as a picture."

"Yes, she is." If he wanted to see John in Bonnie, she wouldn't disillusion him. "And I'm grateful every day that I have her."

He nodded. "I'll leave you. I just wanted to let you know about John. You and I were the only ones who really cared about him. I guess I wanted to share." He started down the street. "Good-bye, Eve. Take care of that little girl."

"I will." She stood and watched him slowly walk away. She could feel her throat tighten. He wasn't an old man, but between his injuries and sorrow, he appeared that way.

Bonnie gave a cry, and Eve saw that she had dropped the pink rabbit toy that Sandra had given her. She automatically picked it up and handed it back to her. Bonnie was immediately happy. It didn't take much to make a baby happy, particularly Bonnie. Her daughter had the sunniest disposition on the planet. "Come on, Bonnie, let's go back. I don't feel like walking anymore."

But she stopped when she reached the green bench outside the front door that she always considered Rosa's bench. "Maybe we'll get a little more sun before we go back inside." She sat down on the bench and turned Bonnie's stroller to face her. "It's not fair to cut your outdoor time short just because I'm upset."

And she was upset. She had told herself a thousand times that her relationship with John had been based entirely on the physical, but that didn't seem to matter anymore. A part of her life had vanished from the earth. She couldn't ignore it. She didn't want to ignore it. Not when she was gazing at her daughter's smiling face.

No, Bonnie wasn't smiling now. She was staring gravely at Eve as if sensing that her mother was troubled.

Eve had noticed before that Bonnie appeared to be attuned to her every mood. Imagination? Maybe. But Eve
knew she had that connection with Bonnie, so why
shouldn't her daughter have that same bond?

"He's gone, Bonnie," Eve said softly. "He was your
father, and I don't even know what to tell you about
him. I didn't know him that well myself. But everyone should know something about the people who
brought them into the world. I don't know anything
about my father. Sandra didn't want to talk about him.
I think he hurt her. Your father didn't hurt me." No, he
had disturbed her, aroused her, and taught her about
some of the most beautiful, heady moments a woman
could know. "I know he was hurt himself. Though he
wouldn't talk much about it. But what I do know is that
he was strong, and beautiful like you, and he never lied
to me. Those are all good things."

Bonnie was clutching her rabbit, but her gaze was
fixed on Eve's face.

"You don't understand any of this." Eve could feel
the tears rise to her eyes. "Sometimes, I don't either,
but we should try. If I tell you about our time together,
maybe I'll understand it, too." She wiped her eyes on
the back of her hand. "Though most of it I'll have to
skip because it's X-rated." She laughed shakily. "And
that's a shame because that's the part where you came
on the scene, and that's the best part of the story." She
leaned forward and kissed Bonnie's cheek. "The very
best part."

Then she leaned back on the bench. "I guess I should

start at the beginning. I met your father on a hot summer night right here, very close to where we're sitting now. He came to my rescue like some hero out of the storybooks I'll be reading you when you get a little older. His name was John Gallo . . ."

CHAPTER

8

Eve." It was Catherine knocking on the door. "Answer me. We have to talk. You're making me feel guilty as hell. I did what I thought best. How the hell did I know you were going to go into a tailspin like this?"

Guilty? Catherine should not feel guilty because Eve had responded like an idiot. No, like that sixteen-year-old girl she had been when she'd given birth to Bonnie. She had run into her room and tried to hide in the darkness, in the only safe haven she'd ever known. For heaven's sake, she was a mature woman who had gone through hell and returned. She could handle anything that came her way.

Except the accusation that Catherine had made. Because if Catherine was right, then her whole life and everything she believed was upside down.

But Catherine was wrong. She had to be wrong.

"Eve."

"Coming." Eve got heavily to her feet and moved toward the door. It was fully dark, and she flipped on the light as she unlocked the door. "Sorry. I didn't mean to upset you. I was a little . . . surprised." She grimaced. "Understatement."

Catherine came into the room and closed the door. "Why do you think I hesitated to talk to you? I knew it wasn't going to be a welcome development." She went over to the kitchen. "Let me get you a cup of coffee. I could use one, too."

"Stop coddling me, Catherine. As I said, I haven't thought about John Gallo since Bonnie was born. It was just a shock having you bring up his name in connection with her death." She paused. "Even though I knew it had to be a mistake."

"It's no mistake."

"John Gallo was killed while he was in the Army."

Catherine shook her head. "No, he was still alive at least six months ago."

"Catherine, I saw the official death notification."

"And since when does that guarantee anything? I've been in the CIA for years, and most of the time nothing ends up what I think it's going to be. It's a twisted world, Eve."

"John Gallo was nineteen, and he wasn't a CIA agent. He was just a kid right out of basic who was in the wrong place at the wrong time."

"A very lethal kid. A month after he was in basic training, they tapped him for Ranger training. That's what he was doing in Asia. He was a natural. He'd not only been trained by his uncle, but he had an aptitude that was remarkable." She paused. "That was why they sent him to North Korea on a special mission. A hush-hush assignment that was very politically incorrect. He and two other Rangers parachuted into the country to spy on a fledgling nuclear facility. Strictly against the diplomatic policy at the time. The government had promised North Korea that they would not violate their borders in any way. They had orders to bring back photos and any other information they could gather."

"Where he died."

"No, where he was betrayed and captured by the North Koreans. The other two Rangers were killed, and he was thrown into prison. He was there for six years before he managed to escape."

"And the government covered it up?" Eve shook her head dazedly. "No, that didn't happen. It's too bizarre. That notification nearly broke his uncle."

"It's true nevertheless."

"It has to be someone else. You've got the wrong information. How did you dig this up anyway?"

"I called in favors. I checked every agency and source I had available, then I made Venable check all of his. Someone did a massive cover-up of everything concerning John Gallo. Even though I was able to break through the curtain, I barely managed to skim the tip of the iceberg." She paused. "But he was out of that North Korean prison before Bonnie was kidnapped. And he was seen in Atlanta about that time."

"No." Her voice was shaking. "He didn't know anything about Bonnie. He would have no reason to hurt her."

"But would he have had reason to hurt you? That's what a lot of family killings are all about."

"He would have had to hate me. He didn't hate me."

"How do you know how his mind was twisted in that prison? He was tortured, solitary confinement, starvation. Six years of that kind of treatment could unbalance anyone. He was in a mental hospital in Tokyo for months after he escaped."

She closed her eyes. "Dear God, you're scaring me, Catherine."

"Why? I didn't go to all this trouble just to hand you a name and go on my way. We can find him. I'll find him for you, Eve."

"I don't want it to be him." She opened her eyes. "I've always thought Bonnie's killer was some faceless monster. That's easier to accept than his being someone I know." She made a helpless gesture. "Know? Someone I went to bed with. Someone who gave me my Bonnie." She shook her head in wonder. "And then took her away? How can I believe that?"

"I didn't say it was a sure bet," Catherine said. "I said that it was a strong possibility."

"It's one I can't cope with." Her voice was shaking. "I swore I'd always protect Bonnie, and it was terrible when she was taken. It was my duty to make sure she was safe and I failed her. But if it was someone I knew, then it's even worse. Maybe I could have sensed it, done something to—"

"You're not thinking straight," Catherine said. "You didn't even know he was alive."

"I still can't accept that he is." She ran her fingers through her hair. "You're right. I'm not able to put anything in perspective right now. I have to think . . ."

"First, you have to believe me when I say that everything I've told you is true. I wouldn't have brought all of this down on you if I hadn't been certain." Catherine handed her a cup of coffee. "Then you have to tell me what you want me to do about it."

"I believe that you think it's true." Eve lifted the cup to her lips. "But the investigation surrounding Bonnie was extensive. I told them who Bonnie's father was. Wouldn't they have found out that John Gallo wasn't dead?"

"I'm sure they checked. I told you, massive cover-up. The Army didn't want anyone to know John Gallo was alive."

"Why?"

She shook her head. "I haven't found that out yet. It had to be something more than an illicit special ops mission if they were willing to protect him from a high-profile murder investigation."

She shivered. "They suspected he might have killed Bonnie and they'd still protect him? A man who would kill a child? No one would do anything that horrible."

"I've seen dirtier cover-ups."

Anger was suddenly searing through Eve. "No you haven't," she said fiercely. "There's nothing more horrible than Bonnie's death or the man who caused it."

"Sorry. You're right." She studied Eve's face. "You're

ready to go out and kill someone yourself. That's good. I'd rather have you on the warpath than in pain. Now drink your coffee, and let's find a way to get to the bottom of this."

She took a swallow of coffee. It was hot and strong and helped to relieve the chill. "You say John Gallo was seen here in Atlanta about the time Bonnie was kidnapped. How do you know?"

"There was a written notation in one of the Army Intelligence files on Gallo by an informant who mentioned that Gallo was here during that period."

"And who was this witness?"

"Paul Black."

Eve stiffened. "What?"

Catherine nodded. "The man your friend Montalvo told you was a prime suspect in your daughter's murder. He gave you three names. Two didn't pan out, and you were preparing to go after the third. Paul Black."

Shock after shock. "And he was testifying against John Gallo? What was their connection?"

Catherine shrugged. "Another blank. But I'll find out."

"No, I'll find out." Eve took another drink of coffee and put the cup down with a click on the bar. "Because I'm going after Gallo and making him tell me everything that happened when he came to Atlanta that month." Her eyes narrowed on Catherine's face. "And you knew that would be my reaction. You wouldn't leave me up in the air for long. You've got an idea where John Gallo is right now?"

Catherine nodded. "I should know very soon. I

squeezed someone in Army Intelligence, and he's going to see if he can give me a lead. It's a Colonel Queen, and he didn't like it one bit that I'd managed to unearth all of this." She hesitated. "But are you sure that you want to do this yourself? Is it going to be difficult for you? I wasn't sure how you felt about John Gallo."

Neither was Eve. It had always been a complex relationship and, now that she knew there might be a possibility of his involvement in Bonnie's death, that complexity had deadly overtones. "Do you mean am I going to be sentimental about dealing with him? It was sex all the way. He kept me dizzy the entire time we were together." She smiled coldly. "No, I won't hesitate just because I was a teenage kid who couldn't control her hormones. And if I find out he killed my Bonnie, I'll cut his heart out."

Catherine blinked. "Well, that certainly defines the situation. It's hard for me to picture you like that. I've never had that experience."

Eve knew that to be true. Catherine was the widow of a May-December marriage. She had been seventeen when she married her sixty-two-year-old mentor. "I can't picture myself like that any longer, either. That girl doesn't exist anymore."

"I just hope that Joe realizes that she doesn't," Catherine said.

Joe.

Eve had been so whiplashed by her feelings about Catherine's news, which had blown her away, that she had not thought of how it would affect Joe. She could only hope it wouldn't be a springboard to more tension between them. Catherine was right; she had never spoken to Joe about John Gallo because he was already far in her past when she and Joe had met. Their love affair had become a passionate relationship that had gone on for years, with no other interest for either of them.

Except for Bonnie. She had always been there between them.

And John Gallo was Bonnie's father.

"You're going to tell Joe about Gallo?" Catherine asked.

"Of course I am. How could I do anything else? Joe has been searching for Bonnie as long as I have."

"Just inquiring." Catherine paused. "Would you like me to tell Joe? After all, I'm the one who opened this can of worms."

"I'll do it."

"But you don't want to do it." Catherine's shrewd gaze was fixed on Eve's expression. "I'm going to go and break the news to him. You'll have enough aftershocks from that quarter to deal with once you pull yourself together."

"I'm okay now."

"You're angry at the moment. That's keeping all the other emotions at bay." She headed for the door. "You can't stay mad forever."

"Yes, I can. If I find out that Gallo had anything to do with Bonnie's death."

She smiled. "I know how you feel. Hold on to it. You may need it." She opened the door. "I'll check with Venable and see if he's heard anything, then go and talk to Joe."

The door closed behind her.

Hold on to it. Hold on to the anger. She would have no problem doing that. She had thought she was done with John Gallo, but he had erupted back in her life in the most painful way possible.

All right, sit here and think back. Try to find any reason why John would commit such a terrible crime.

How could she do that when she didn't really know him?

She had to know something that would make this madness clear. Catherine had said that there were precedents for a father killing his child. Eve knew that to be true from her own professional experiences.

Start at that point and analyze.

Joe was standing on the top step of the porch, gazing out at the lake, when Catherine went in search of him.

"Hello, Catherine." He turned to face her. "Venable wants you to call him. He couldn't reach you."

"I'll call him back later."

"Do that." He met her eyes. "Now what's the story with Eve?"

Catherine should have known that Joe would sense something. Joe Quinn had the sharpest instincts and the keenest intelligence of anyone she had ever met. She had worked with any number of CIA agents over the years, and she would have jettisoned them in a heartbeat for a partner like Joe.

And perhaps not only in the field.

She remembered the first time she had become aware

that she was attracted to Joe. They had been down by the lake, and a storm had been coming up. The wind had been blowing his brown hair, and his tea-colored eyes were glittering recklessly. She had looked at him and thought he was like the storm, full of danger and power and yet with the maturity to be able to leash his lightning. She had not been conscious of being physically aware of a man since her husband had died, and it had come as a shock.

But she had rejected the thought immediately. Eve was her friend, and she wouldn't violate that trust. Besides, she had known from the instant she had met him here at the cottage weeks ago that there was only one partner he would accept in his life.

Eve was his center. Catherine would be content to be his friend as well as Eve's, and she had already started to lay the foundation.

"Why do you think there's a story?" She came over and stood beside him at the rail. "What a suspicious man you are, Joe."

"Body language. I saw the two of you standing here on the porch over an hour ago. Pure tension. I was tempted to come and interrupt you, but I decided Eve wouldn't like me barging in if I wasn't invited to begin with. So I've been waiting. I don't have to tell you that I wasn't waiting patiently. It's not one of my virtues." He smiled recklessly. "Hell, I'm much better at the barging part, followed immediately by investigation and disposal."

"I remember." And her latest memory was of Joe in the Ivanova marshes in Russia, aiming at a gas tank and blowing up the car that was pursuing them. Damn, he had been good. Hell, he had been magnificent. "But you restrained yourself this time. Could it be that you're acquiring diplomacy?"

"No way." His smile faded. "I just know Eve. We have to walk very carefully around each other every now and then."

"When it concerns Bonnie."

He looked out at the lake. "Bonnie rules our lives. The moment she was taken, she stopped being Eve's daughter and became her obsession."

"I know that. Can you blame her?"

"No, but I did after a while. God knows we did our best to find her. I couldn't see why she wouldn't let go. I loved her, I ached for her pain, but I needed for that pain to stop." He glanced down at her. "I've never told anyone that before. But you guessed, didn't you?"

She nodded. "I care about Eve. I'm concerned about her happiness. You make her happy, Joe."

He shrugged. "Sometimes."

"Do you still resent her fixation on Bonnie?"

"Resent isn't the right word. There are times when I love Bonnie and want to find her as much as Eve. But I never knew her, so it's harder for me. I want Eve as well as Bonnie to be at peace and it's like a constant open wound. So I hurt, and I get tired and angry." He grimaced. "But it comes and goes. Other times, I try not to trigger anything that might upset the balance."

"Like not barging in where Eve doesn't want you? In this case, you don't know that's true."

"Don't I?" He smiled tightly. "Then tell me I'm wrong, Catherine. Then tell me why we're here talking about Eve and Bonnie. Tell me why you turned your phone off so that even Venable couldn't reach you. You're a professional, Catherine. You'd have to have a pretty good reason. And then, instead of calling him back immediately, you decided to stay out here and chat with me. Am I that fascinating?"

Yes, he was. The combination of tough spirit and brilliant brain was totally fascinating. "I suppose you'll do. But no, that's not the reason I'm out here."

He leaned back against the rail and crossed his arms across his chest. "So I repeat, what's the story, Catherine?"

"Catherine's gone," Joe said when he came into the cottage thirty minutes later. "She said to tell you that she'd call you."

His voice was quiet, too quiet. Eve's gaze flew to his face.

No expression. That wasn't good.

"She told me she'd get back to me as soon as possible." Eve turned to the kitchen bar. "We still have steak from the barbecue. Would you like a sandwich?" Cripes, that was a dumb thing to ask. It just went to show how nervous she was feeling. This was Joe. She had nothing to be nervous about. Just try to get him to open up about it. She turned back to face him. "Catherine told you about John Gallo. How do you feel about it?"

"Initial reaction? Relief. A chance to get the son of a bitch who killed Bonnie."

She was feeling relief, too, that his initial reaction had been so uncomplicated. "Yes, he could be the one."

"Second reaction. I bristled. You didn't want to talk to me about it, or you wouldn't have sent Catherine."

"I didn't send her. I was going to do it."

"But you didn't want to do it."

She wasn't going to deny it. "I felt awkward, and I had to come to terms with it myself. She said she understood."

"Yes, Catherine would understand. The two of you are a lot alike. But you didn't think I'd understand. Third reaction. Curiosity and a touch of suspicion. Why not, Eve? Why would the possibility of John Gallo being Bonnie's murderer make you not trust me after all these years?"

"I do trust you. What are you talking about? I've never trusted anyone as I do you."

"Not even John Gallo?"

She gazed at him in disbelief. "I never trusted him. That wasn't what our relationship was all about."

"And what was it about?"

"Just sex."

"And that's supposed to fill me with confidence? You'd never have a sexual relationship with someone you didn't trust."

She didn't answer. What could she say? The Eve Joe knew wasn't the one who had been with Gallo.

But Joe's gaze was on her face, and he could always read her. "Or could you?"

"Evidently I could when I was sixteen." She drew a

deep breath. "But that doesn't matter. That's not what this is about, is it? John Gallo may have killed Bonnie. I have to find him."

"We have to find him. Together." He met her gaze. "Nothing has changed. Or has it?"

"What the hell do you mean?" Her hands clenched into fists at her sides. "Do you think I wanted him to come back into my life? I thought I was going to be going after Paul Black and now John's back and there's some connection. And you're acting weird as hell and as if you're blaming me for—"

"I feel weird as hell." He had taken three steps, and he reached out and grabbed her shoulders. "And I'm not blaming you for anything. I'm just trying to keep control while I sort this out. You didn't expect this? What do you think about me? Bonnie is still everything to you. What about her father?"

"What about him? He may be a monster, he may be my daughter's murderer." She shrugged off his grip and took a step back. "Do you think that I'm thinking about anything but that?"

Joe stared at her for a moment and shook his head. "No, I'm being an ass." He turned and dropped down on the couch. "She's the only one who is really important to you. The rest of us are just hovering on the sidelines." He held up his hand as she opened her lips to protest. "You can't help it. We both know it's true. I accept it. Gallo's appearance on the scene just threw me for a loop. I've become accustomed to playing second fiddle to Bonnie. I won't do it for anyone else."

"It's not true." But it was clear that his reaction had

been as volatile as Catherine had predicted. "You're always front and center. Dammit, I love you, Joe Quinn."

He didn't respond directly. "Why does Catherine think that Gallo could be the killer?"

"Insanity. He had very bad treatment from the North Koreans, and she said it might have twisted him."

"It's possible. What else?"

"There have been many cases where a father has gone off his rocker and killed members of the family, including children."

"And?"

"The fact that he was seen here in the city the month of Bonnie's disappearance and made no attempt to contact me." She said quickly, "But that isn't an automatic red flag. His uncle may not have even told him about Bonnie after he escaped. It's possible he wouldn't have wanted to upset him if he was already subpar mentally as well as physically. As for not contacting me, seven years had passed, and our relationship was very brief."

"But productive. Anything else?"

"I've been going over anything about John that I knew and might have a bearing. He could be very violent. He told me once that he enjoyed it."

"So do I on occasion."

"His background might have contributed to making him unstable. He was abused as a child. Many serial killers have that in common."

"Are we considering him a serial killer? As far as we know, Bonnie may have been his only victim."

"I don't know what he's become. I'm confused and angry and just trying to make some sense out of this."

She added, "That's all I know right now. Is the third degree over?"

He nodded. "I had to know everything you know." He took out his phone. "Because I'm not going to wait for Catherine. I'm calling Venable back myself, then FBI at Langley to see if I can pull some information out of them."

"Catherine will get back to us soon."

"No doubt. But I'd rather do it on my own." He gazed at her as he dialed Venable's number. "One way or the other, I want this over. And I'm not trusting Catherine to keep me in the loop."

"What are you talking about? Catherine and you are so much alike that you could almost finish each other's sentences. You're two warriors looking for a battle. I'm the one who could be left out in the cold."

"Not this time. Catherine is your friend and trying to pay a debt. She knows this is going to be difficult for you, and she'll try to make it easier."

"By leaving you out?"

He nodded, his lips tightening. "It's already starting. I can see it coming. But it's not going to happen. I'm going to find John Gallo or Paul Black or both and find which one killed Bonnie." He began to speak into the phone. "Venable. Joe Quinn. We have some talking to do, and I want straight answers."

Eve stood listening for a moment, then turned and went out on the porch. She didn't know if Joe would be able to get what he wanted from Venable, but she was willing to step back and let him try.

Not that she had any choice. Joe in this mood was

not pliable. He would travel his own path through hell or high water.

Was he right about her trying to close him out? Joe knew her so well that he sometimes knew what she was thinking before she was aware of it. From the moment she had heard about John Gallo, she had felt a shock and rejection. If John was the murderer, then Eve had brought him into their lives. She was directly responsible for all the hell and torment Joe had experienced in the past years of searching for Bonnie and her killer. She had no right to expose him to more danger because of a man who was part of her past before Joe had come into her life.

She gazed out at the moonlight on the lake. Beautiful and clean and safe. Just like her life with Joe. But the waters were placid, and her relationship with Joe seldom was. Comfortable at times, but the undercurrents of passion and turbulence were always just under the surface.

So different from what she had known with John Gallo. Joe didn't know that girl, and she couldn't explain her to him. By the time she had met Joe, she had experienced childbirth, motherhood, and the most terrible tragedy a woman could survive. It had burned out all traces of that girl she had been.

Burn.

"You burn, Eve."

She should have forgotten those words John had spoken. Why hadn't she? She was sure that he had only the most fleeting memories of her.

Unless Catherine was right, and he had twisted their relationship into the beginning of a horror story.

And, if that had happened, she could not let Joe be caught up in that horror story.

Eve received a call from Catherine an hour later.

"I heard from Venable," Catherine said. "He's been able to confirm the story about John Gallo's being alive. He has a source who says that Gallo's records were buried so deep that no one could dig them up in the next hundred years." She paused. "And that at one time there was a contract put out on him."

"By whom?"

"Military."

"My God, the same people who sent him into North Korea put out a contract on him because of what he found."

"That's the way it looks."

"What the hell happened to him there?"

"It's what happened after he got out of that prison that we've got to know about. I got my call from Nate Queen at Army Intelligence, and I'm hoping that he'll prove Venable wrong about how deep we have to dig to find out where Gallo is right now."

"What did he tell you?"

"The word is that Gallo moves around a lot but that he may be located in Utah."

"Where?"

"Somewhere in the mountains."

"That's damn vague."

"It's more than we had an hour ago."

"What about Paul Black?"

"No mention of him other than that one statement. Not in connection with Gallo."

"It's crazy. Paul Black was a suspect himself, and yet it seems as if he's a witness against John. Then you tell me that Black faded away in the investigation as if he'd never existed?"

"That's what I'm telling you. I'm still probing."

"Then I need to be doing some probing myself. I'll call Luis Montalvo and see what else I can find out about Paul Black. He gave me the name as a possible suspect. He may know more than what was in the original report he gave me."

"Montalvo?"

"Montalvo used to be an arms dealer in Colombia. I did a forensic reconstruction job for him, and in return he hired investigators to try to find leads to Bonnie's killer."

"It sounds like a devil's bargain. Can you trust him?"

"Sometimes our association is a bit strained, but, yes, I can trust him."

"Then by all means probe to your heart's content." She paused. "How is Joe?"

"How do you think? You're the one who insisted on talking to—" She wasn't being fair. Catherine had been trying to take away the burden from her. She was just so on edge about Joe's reaction that sharpness had come out of nowhere. "And I'm grateful. But Joe didn't particularly appreciate it."

"I noticed. After I laid everything out for him, he got

very quiet. It was clear I wasn't wanted, so I made my exit." She paused. "But I don't believe he was quiet with you, was he?"

"That's the way it started. It didn't stay that way. Before it was over, he was on the phone with Venable getting his own update and making sure that he wasn't being closed out."

"Smart. Joe has great instincts."

"I don't want to close him out."

"But you're going to do it. It's only a matter of time. He could see it coming, and so could I."

She didn't deny it. "I can't risk Joe. Not this time. Not with John Gallo."

"Because he was close to you, and you have some idea that closeness may have put all this madness into motion? That closeness is the very reason Joe will see that he's involved. He's taking this very personally. I knew he would."

"Well, I'm taking this personally, too. How the hell could I help it? Bonnie's my daughter, and John Gallo was my—"

"Lover?" Catherine asked softly.

"No, we weren't lovers. That implies an emotion other than sexual. We were two kids whose hormones were so charged we couldn't control them."

"And that's all?"

"He was a lot of firsts. He was my first sexual experience, the first who taught my body pleasure, the first for whom I was willing to postpone my ambitions and enjoy the moment." She paused. "And the first and only man to give me a child."

Catherine gave a low whistle. "That's a pretty impressive list. Do me a favor and don't go over that list with Joe."

"But it all has one common denominator. Sex. I have so much more with Joe."

"But he's a guy. He may have a brilliant mind, but I'd bet sex is as important to him as it was to that kid, John Gallo. Particularly a possessive man like Joe, who is absolutely nuts about you. Those 'firsts' may blow him away."

Eve wasn't going to argue. Joe was mature and sophisticated on most planes, but their relationship had a potential for moving him toward much more basic responses. "Just find John Gallo. Maybe we'll be able to get to him before Joe goes into high gear and tries to wrap it up himself."

"As soon as I hear myself." Catherine hung up the phone.

CHAPTER

9

"I need more information about Paul Black," Eve said as soon as Montalvo picked up the phone. "You said you'd try to find out more about him after we crossed the other two suspects off our list."

"Ah, you're back on the hunt? I was wondering how long you'd be able to resist temptation."

"There was no question that I was resisting anything. I've just been busy."

"And Joe Quinn had nothing to do with your hiatus?" His voice lowered silkily. "I'd never keep you from trying to find Bonnie. I'd be there by your side. I know what it is to lose someone."

Yes, the skull that Eve had done the forensic reconstruction on had been Montalvo's wife. That loss had been one of the things that had bound them together. "Joe isn't keeping me from trying to find Bonnie. He always helps me." She changed the subject. "When I got the initial reports, you told me that Paul Black was off the radar, and you didn't know where he'd disappeared. What else do you know about him? Why was he on your list?"

"He was in jail in Atlanta on a DUI charge and told another inmate, Larry Shipman, he'd kidnapped and killed Bonnie Duncan. He was still drunk at the time, and when he sobered up, he told Shipman that if he told anyone, he'd cut his throat. Shipman wasn't going to run a risk when he didn't give a damn about anything but himself. Years later, when my investigators got hold of him, a nice amount of cash persuaded him he should care after all."

"But was he telling the truth?"

"We won't know until we find Black. Shipman believed him."

"Did Shipman know anything else about Black? Can we go back and ask him questions?"

"I'm afraid not."

"Why not?"

"Six months after Shipman talked to my investigators, he was sent to prison on a drug charge."

"Then we'll go to the prison."

"And two months after he was locked up, he was found dead in the prison laundry. Presumably an inmate decided he didn't like him. They never found out which one." He paused. "Cut Shipman's throat."

"Cut his throat?" She made the connection. "Paul Black's threat. But it had to be coincidence. That was years later."

"But it was only a few months after he turned

informer. A curious coincidence. It interested me when I heard about it, but you were looking in another direction. Besides, Paul Black was still not to be found no matter how hard we tried."

The timing had probably been no more than coincidence. The idea that Black had been hovering over Shipman all those years waiting for him to break his silence was far-fetched . . . and totally chilling.

"What's Paul Black's background?"

"He was orphaned at three and grew up in Macon, Georgia, in a church orphanage. He got a construction job at seventeen and went to Athens, Georgia. He got in trouble almost immediately and spent time in jail for robbery. After he was paroled, he worked as a fry cook, then was arrested again when he almost killed another cook with a butcher knife. Paroled again two years later and disappeared for a while. Next appearance was in the county jail when he talked to Shipman."

"Do we have a picture of him?"

"Yes, I'll send you his mug shot when we hang up. Pretty ordinary-looking guy. Any other questions?"

"No idea where he is?"

"Not a clue."

"Another question. Did you ever hear of him working with anyone?"

A silence. "And that's an odd question. Did you?"

"I need an answer, Montalvo."

"As far as I know, he was a lone wolf. Obviously, he couldn't even get along with the people he worked with."

"Was he ever in the service?"

"No."

"And he disappeared right after he told Shipman he'd killed Bonnie."

"That's right." He paused. "You're very intense. How far along are you on this hunt, Eve?"

"Not far enough. Thanks, Montalvo."

"I'm dismissed? But I don't want to be dismissed. I'll keep on looking for information about Black until I find enough that will make you want to take me along for the ride. It sounds as if there's something intriguing in the wind."

And Montalvo will do it, she thought. She'd be lucky if he didn't show up on her doorstep anyway. Montalvo was completely unpredictable. "Good-bye, Montalvo."

"Good-bye, Eve. I'll be in touch." He hung up.

She was afraid he would be in touch. Again, if she moved fast enough, she might avoid Montalvo's interference. She heard a ping and accessed the photo Montalvo had sent her.

The mug shot of Paul Black was not flattering. In the photo, he appeared to be in his late twenties, with dark, crew-cut hair and eyes that could be either brown or gray. His nose was long, and his mouth was wide and full. As Montalvo had said, very ordinary.

She put her phone away and stood for a moment looking out at the water.

Peaceful, soothing to the soul. She'd stay a moment, drink it in, and let it bring her that same peace. There was nothing serene about her own soul tonight. She was too lost in disturbing memories and intense worry about the future.

All of which were swirling around her like a tornado.

John Gallo was out there somewhere. Who was he now? What had he become during these many years? She could not imagine him a murderer.

Not even when she had seen how violent he could be?

But she could also be violent. She had found out that truth in the years of hunting Bonnie's killer. There was no question at all in her mind that if she found that John Gallo was the murderer of her daughter, she'd kill him without a single qualm. Bonnie deserved her revenge.

She could feel the anger begin to sear through her and took a deep breath. So much for serenity and the search for peace. There would be no peace for her anytime soon.

It would be better not to think at all.

She would just try to be patient and wait for Catherine's call.

"You're never patient, Mama."

Bonnie.

Eve looked over at the little girl sitting with her back against the porch rail. Dressed in jeans and the Bugs Bunny T-shirt she'd been wearing the last time Eve had seen her, curly red hair shining in the moonlight. She felt the same rush of love she always felt when Bonnie came to her.

"That's not true. I've been patient for a long time. Since I lost you, baby."

Bonnie's face lit with her luminous smile. "But you didn't lose me, did you, Mama? I'm always here."

Eve had thought she had lost her forever and had been spiraling downward toward death herself when she had begun to dream of Bonnie about a year after her disappearance. At least, for a long time, she had told herself it was a dream when her little girl came to her, talked to her, brought her healing and comforting. It was only recently that she had accepted that Bonnie was no dream. "I hate to tell you, but the fact that you're a ghost has a few disadvantages."

Bonnie chuckled. "What disadvantages? You know I'll always be with you."

"Whenever you want to be. You don't come nearly enough. You dictate all the rules." She made an impatient gesture as Bonnie opened her lips. "And now you'll say it wouldn't be good for me. That I have to live my life. You always do."

"Then I don't have to say it." She leaned back and gazed up at the night sky. "Aren't the stars pretty? You used to sing me a song about a star."

"Yes, I did." Her throat was suddenly tight, and she had to clear it. "But you liked the song about all the pretty little horses more."

She nodded. "But I like the one about the star, too. It's nice being able to look at the stars with you."

"Then come more often."

"You need to be alone with Joe. You belong with him right now." She smiled. "I try not to come too often when Joe is around. He tries to accept me, but I make him uneasy."

Eve couldn't deny that was true. It was only recently that Joe had started to be able to see her daughter, and

he was not comfortable with it. Joe was a complete re-
alist, and the concept of Bonnie as a spirit battered
against every bit of training and instinct. Well, Eve had
been the same way at first, telling herself that Bonnie
was only a dream or a hallucination. But after years
she had accepted that, by some grace of God, Bonnie
was permitted to come to her. If that made her crazy,
then so be it. "It may be different once we've found you
and the man who killed you, baby."

"Maybe. But it's you and Joe who are important. I
shouldn't matter this much to either of you."

Eve shook her head. "Stop preaching at me. I've
heard this before."

Bonnie's smile faded. "But I have to keep saying it.
Particularly now. I'm getting . . . I'm afraid for you."

Eve stiffened. "Why did you come tonight? Is it be-
cause of Paul Black?"

"Partly. But there's so much else . . ."

"Is it . . . John Gallo? He's your father, Bonnie."

"I know." Bonnie looked back up at the stars. "I al-
ways knew . . ."

"What do you mean?"

"So much pain . . . so much rage."

She felt a chill go through her. "Bonnie, what are you
saying?"

Bonnie shook her head. "I just want you to take care.
It's all coming . . . I'm going to go now."

"Yes, scare me to death, then go off to Never-Never
Land."

"I'd take you with me if I could. Look at the stars,
Mama."

"You just don't want me to see you go."

"It hurts you."

Eve raised her eyes to the starlit sky. "What happens in Never-Never Land, Bonnie?"

"All good things."

"I'm glad. I want everything good for you, baby."

Bonnie didn't answer, and Eve knew that she was gone.

But Eve didn't look back at the step on which Bonnie had been sitting.

She kept her gaze on the stars and thought about Bonnie and Never-Never Land.

MAZKAL, UTAH

"Nate Queen is coming up the drive," Bill Hanks said as he put down his phone. "He said you were expecting him?"

"For a long time." John Gallo gazed down at the chessboard. "No one is with him?"

Hanks shook his head. "And Brian did the usual search at the gates. He's clean."

"As clean as he can be. I'm sure he has some dirty tricks up his sleeve." Gallo moved his queen. "Checkmate." He got up from the game table. "Bring him in as soon as he gets here."

He moved over to stand in front of the floor-to-ceiling windows overlooking the Rocky Mountains. He'd bought the ranch because of that view.

And the fact that he could not be approached without

knowing about it at least twenty minutes in advance. He'd ordered that Nate Queen pass through the first barricade without a challenge, but no one got past the gates without being searched.

"You're completely paranoid, do you know that?" Queen asked irritably from the door. "And I didn't appreciate the body search."

"You should expect paranoia." Gallo turned to face him. "I have a mental problem. Haven't you heard?"

"Oh, I've heard," Queen said as he came into the study. "You've caused me nothing but problems. And you're going to cause me more, aren't you?"

"Probably."

"I didn't have to come here. You could have talked to me on the phone."

"But then I wouldn't have been able to see your expression. You've lied to me before, Queen. I needed to know that I had a chance to catch you in one if you tried it again."

"Paranoia," Queen repeated. "I didn't tell Catherine Ling anything. I've just been setting her up for a regretful refusal. She's stirring up too much shit for me to totally ignore her. It seems Eve Duncan is a good friend, and she's trying to help her."

"I found out that much for myself. How close is Catherine Ling coming?"

Queen hesitated. "Close. But we'll take care of it."

"I might have to take care of it myself."

"No!" Queen said. "Stay away from her. She's CIA."

Gallo smiled. "Do you think that would make a difference to me?" He could see the anger and frustration in Queen's face. But there was also the fear. Gallo made sure that the fear was always there. It was easy. All he had to do was look at them and let them see. "All your tight little agencies and bureaus with all their rules. They make me sick."

"You're already sick." He was silent a moment, gathering his arguments. "Look, you do anything to a CIA agent, and it will be twice as hard for me to protect you."

"Do you protect me, Queen? It's rather like a wolf protecting a sheep, isn't it?"

"You're no sheep," Queen said roughly. "And I've protected you for years, and you know it. You made sure of that."

"Now how could I intimidate a powerful colonel with Army Intelligence?" He tilted his head, pretending to think. "Maybe because it gave you the opportunity to position yourselves outside my lair to wait for me to make a mistake?"

"That's a possibility," Queen said. "I'd like nothing better than to bring you down, Gallo." He was clearly trying to overcome his anger. "Be reasonable. Let me handle this. You don't want the CIA on your ass."

Gallo shrugged. "Why do you say that? I don't care, Queen."

Queen shook his head. "I can see that you don't. That's why you should have been exterminated years ago."

"A lot of people agree with you. I assure you that it's not from lack of trying. From the moment I was born until your appearance in my life."

"Let me handle it," Queen repeated. "Leave Catherine Ling and Eve Duncan alone."

"I'll think about it." He turned back to the window. "You may go now, Queen."

"May? You arrogant bastard."

"I can afford to be arrogant. You're on my turf."

"You'd be arrogant anyway, you crazy, murdering, son of a bitch." The door slammed behind him.

Should he go after him, Gallo wondered idly. It wasn't good to let Queen's fear of him dissipate when it took very little to reinforce it.

No, it wasn't necessary, and he wasn't in the mood. He could deal with Queen at any time. Queen might have thought it was pure arrogance when he'd dismissed him so summarily, but he did have some thinking to do.

He gazed out at the mountains. He must think clearly and carefully and not let emotion get in the way. Queen might think he was a cold-blooded killer to be extermi- nated, but the emotion was definitely there. He did not feel cold.

He was eager.

For the prospect of the deaths and torment that might come? That would be Queen's interpretation.

Or eager for something else?

Either way, it was not a decision to be taken lightly.

"What are you doing?" Joe was standing behind Eve in the porch doorway. "You look like you're communing with the moon."

"Maybe I would if I thought it would do any good. I was only getting some air." She turned and came toward him. "I just finished talking to Montalvo."

"I was about to call him myself."

Which only showed Eve Joe's sense of urgency. Montalvo and Joe were on guarded terms most of the time. She could see that tension now. "Now you don't have to do it."

"Did Montalvo offer to come and help you?" he asked. "It wouldn't surprise me."

She didn't answer directly. "I don't need anything but information from Montalvo. He couldn't give me much." She handed him her telephone. "A photo of Paul Black. Montalvo still hasn't been able to get a lead on his current whereabouts."

Joe glanced at the photo. "I'll give it to Venable in case he doesn't have it yet."

"And there's nothing in Black's report that indicates he ever had a partner or even an associate. He was never in the service, and how that report from him on John Gallo ever got into Agency files is a mystery."

"It seems everything about John Gallo is a mystery." He handed her back the phone. "Except to you, Eve."

She stiffened. "How can you say that? The John Gallo I knew doesn't exist any longer. Any more than the girl I was back then exists."

"That's right, you told me that, didn't you." He turned. "I admit I'm very interested to meet John Gallo."

And she hadn't told him that Catherine might have a possible location on him. Her decision had evidently been made. "He may not be Bonnie's killer. Catherine wasn't sure."

He went back into the house. "I'll still be interested to meet him."

Should she stay out here and wait for Catherine's call or go in and go to bed?

She hesitated before following Joe inside. She'd let him have a little time to himself, then she had to talk to him. She was going to make him more angry and resentful before this was over, but she didn't want the strain to go on right now. She wanted to be close to him and try to make him understand.

Make him understand that sixteen-year-old Eve? He'd already told her that he couldn't comprehend her motives because that girl wasn't the same person he knew.

Then talk to him, make him understand.

Joe was already in bed by the time she came into the bedroom. He was naked as usual, the sheet flung carelessly over his body.

"No call from Catherine?" he asked.

She shook her head and went into the bathroom. "I'm not waiting up for it."

He was still lying in bed, his arm beneath his head, when she came out a few minutes later. His muscles were tense, his face without expression. "But you wanted to wait up for it, didn't you? You just thought it would be more diplomatic to soothe the savage."

"When have you known me to be diplomatic? Particularly with you. Our lives are based on being painfully up-front with each other." She got into bed. "And you're not a savage . . . most of the time."

"You see, you know me very well," he said mockingly. "All my moods, faults, and virtues. You know what I am and what I can be."

"Not necessarily. If you're claiming to be predictable, it's far from the truth. You change, you surprise me."

"Do I?" He paused. "But not as much as you surprise me. This one threw me into the stratosphere."

"It wasn't a surprise that I deliberately sprang on you. I was just as shocked as you were. Probably more."

"And you're straining at the leash to go on the hunt again." He was staring into the darkness. "And I'm the leash, aren't I? You want to break free and go find Paul Black . . . and Gallo."

"I don't regard you as some kind of restraint, Joe. You've always helped me." Be honest. "It's just that this time I'd feel more guilt if anything happened to you." She wearily shook her head. "Or maybe not. I always worry that I'm going to get you killed when I'm the only one who should be putting her life on the line. Perhaps this time it just seems different."

"Because of Gallo."

"Yes. And because it could have been my mistake that caused Bonnie to be killed if I linked myself with a monster. You don't blame me any more than I blame myself for being such an idiot."

"I don't blame you. I have no right. I was no saint when I was a kid. Hell, I'm no saint now. That's not why I'm so damn upset."

"Then why?"

"I'm jealous."

"What?"

"Oh, not of Gallo," he added grimly. "Though that may come. I'm jealous of the fact that there's part of you I don't know, that I might never know. I hadn't thought about it before. When I met you, I knew I loved you almost from the very first. I couldn't do anything about it because you were in agony about losing Bonnie, and you stayed that way for years. All I could do was stand by and be your friend. Then I got my chance, and I took it."

"Thank God."

"But because there was so much history between us, it blurred everything else. You were the complete package by the time I met you. I couldn't imagine you any differently."

"A very broken package." She cuddled closer to him. "You helped put me back together. As I said, by that time, that other girl didn't exist."

"She has to exist. She's part of you." He added flatly, "And I don't know her. I *have* to know her."

Because Joe's love was as possessive as it was passionate. Even Catherine had recognized that about him.

"What do you want to know?"

"I can't demand, you have to offer. And you're not willing to do that right now. Because I wasn't part of your world, you don't think I'd be able to relate."

"And could you? You were a rich kid. You went to Harvard, for heaven's sake. Do you want me to tell you about the stink of the projects, the graffiti on the walls? How it felt to be a teenage female and afraid of when I'd be targeted next? How I was afraid I'd never break free of them? As a cop, you've seen them, but you haven't lived them."

Silence. "And John Gallo has."

"Yes, he told me that the project where he grew up was worse than the one where I lived."

"So you became soul mates."

"Our souls had nothing to do with it. Do you want me to tell you that we were drawn to each other because we were both slum kids? I can't do that." She was saying exactly what Catherine had warned her against. She couldn't help it. She wouldn't be anything but honest with Joe. "We were both loners. The only reason we came together was chemistry. And the reason we separated was that both of us realized that chemistry could ruin any chance of our climbing out of the dung heaps where we were born." She was silent, then said, "Is there anything else you want to know?"

"Hell, yes. Every single detail, but I'm not going to ask because that would probably drive me crazier than not knowing. *Damn* chemistry."

She suddenly started to chuckle. "Joe, don't damn something that we value so highly. Chemistry may not have brought you and me together originally, but it's helped to keep us together and strong for years. Do you think that anything I had with that kid, John Gallo, could have had the same kind of endurance and staying power?"

"I've no idea. But you're not going to find out." He was suddenly on his knees on the bed. "And I find I'm becoming annoyed at being thought of as the steady, boring stallion in the barn." He threw the sheet that covered them on the floor. "Endurance? Staying power?"

She inhaled sharply as she gazed at him. She always

loved the look of Joe naked. Beautifully muscular shoulders and thighs, tight buttocks and belly. He looked completely at home with his nudity, like Adam in the garden, or a sultan in his harem. Joe was a magnificent lover, innovative, passionate, sometimes teasing, sometimes wicked. In those moments, he was completely sexual, completely devoted to the act itself. Yet tonight there was something else . . .

His expression. His eyes were glittering recklessly as his hand reached out and cupped her breast. "Shall I show you endurance, Eve?"

Her heart was suddenly pounding beneath his hand. "I don't know. Should I be worried?"

"Not you." His mouth was suddenly on her nipple, drawing strongly. "You can take me." His lips moved down to her belly. "You can match me. We just have to go to the next level." He moved over her, cupped her buttocks in his two hands and sank deep. "Like this."

The fever was starting. No, it was here, rising. She was moving, arching against him, trying to take more.

"That's right." His tone was guttural. His words came hard and fast with every thrust. "Give—me—everything."

Harder.

Madness.

Deeper.

It couldn't be deeper, but it was.

Her entire body was on fire. The sensitive nerves beneath her skin were causing the flesh to swell, become part of the act itself.

He was shifting her back and forth and rotating, each movement taking, building, peaking.

"Now," he whispered in her ear. "Now, Eve."

He drove deeper.

She arched. Her teeth bit into her lower lip as her entire body convulsed. "Joe!"

Pleasure. Intense. Explosive. Mind-blowing.

She was panting, clinging desperately to him, as the room whirled around her. Over. Dear heaven, it had been more intense than she could—

But it wasn't over.

Her gaze flew up to his face. "You didn't . . ."

"No." His mouth was tense, but full and sensual. Everything about him held that same extreme sexual tension. He lowered his head and kissed her, his tongue teasing hers, then outlining her lower lip. He whispered, "Endurance."

And he started to move again.

Skilled, teasing, alternating hard and gentle.

Her climax had been so intense, it wasn't possible that she could climb to that peak again.

But it was happening. Joe was bringing her with him, using every sexual skill in his arsenal.

And it happened again.

"Endurance?" Joe asked as he looked down at her. "Not such a bad trait, is it?"

And he started to move once more.

The entire night became a sensual dream of arousal and satisfying that arousal. It was hours later that the passion ebbed enough for her to roll over and put her head in the hollow of his shoulder. It was her favorite place, but tonight even that position seemed to lack a certain security. "Were you . . . angry?"

"Did I seem angry?"

"I don't—I guess not. It was just . . . fierce."

"You didn't enjoy it?"

"Of course I did. Don't be an ass. You were . . . extraordinary."

"Then I'll have to do it more often until it becomes ordinary." He kissed her temple. "And then we'll go on to the next level."

"There can't be a next level."

"Yes, there is. We'll find it." His tone was absolutely positive as he got out of bed and strode toward the bathroom. "Maybe I can't ever know what made up the psyche of that sixteen-year-old girl, but I can make sure that our chemistry comes out way ahead of anything you knew back then."

"It always did, Joe."

"Maybe." He stood there in the doorway, naked, confident, handsome, totally mature. Joe, who had been her salvation and her love. Joe, who could raise her to the realm of complete eroticism.

He smiled. "But I'm an overachiever. I think we'll stretch our limits."

He disappeared into the bathroom.

She lay there, her gaze on the door. Her body felt flushed, lazy, yet her muscles had an underlying tingle that wouldn't leave her. It was as if they were waiting for the next touch, the next—

Her cell phone rang on the bedside table.

She reached over to get it.

Catherine.

"Sorry to call you in the middle of the night, but I thought you'd want to know as soon as I did. I just talked to Nate Queen."

"And?"

"Nothing. He says he can't find any more information than he gave me before. Bullshit. He knows something. He's stalling."

"So what are you doing?"

"I'm going to keep after him. What else? And if I don't get answers, I'm going to zero in on him in person. I won't let him weasel out on getting us what we need."

Joe had come back into the room and was staring at Eve. "Catherine?"

Eve nodded, before saying to Catherine, "You thought he'd be able to tell us. What changed?"

"How do I know? His superiors stomped on him? He got panicky? I don't know much about him. Queen wasn't my original contact. I'd done a favor for Dan Murphy, an agent on the lower rungs at Army Intelligence, and I tapped him for help. He was willing at first, but he just handed me off to Nate Queen like a hot potato when I brought up Gallo. I'll call you back when I know more. What did you find out from Montalvo?"

"Not much. As far as anyone knew, he never worked with a partner and was never in the service."

"That's a start. Elimination can be valuable, too. Bye." Catherine hung up.

"Am I to be told what Catherine found out?" Joe asked quietly.

"Zero. Nate Queen, with Army Intelligence, thought he might be able to find John Gallo. He just told Catherine he was mistaken. She thinks someone got to him. She's going after him."

His lips tightened. "Maybe she needs help."

"Believe me, she can handle him."

"You're probably right. It appears half the Intelligence community owes Catherine a favor, and the other half is wary of her." He got into bed. "And she's collecting all of their debts in your cause, Eve."

"I told her she didn't owe me anything. Catherine doesn't listen to anything she doesn't want to hear."

"Single-minded? Is that the pot calling the kettle black?"

Catherine and she were alike in so many ways and also had a multitude of differences. "Whatever. This time, I'll take what she's offering."

"Naturally." He had not pulled her close. He was lying on his own side of the bed. "That goes without saying." He was gazing into the darkness. "She's offering you Bonnie."

Catherine called her back at ten the next morning. "Still no luck with Queen. He's not taking my calls. I did find out that he wasn't at headquarters. He was out in the field."

"Where?"

"I couldn't find out. He's supposed to be back this afternoon and I'm going to fly up to INSCOM and ask him."

Eve chuckled. "And Joe was wondering if you were going to need his help with Queen."

"I might call him if I can't get the bastard to talk. Joe and I could play good cop–bad cop. We'd be a good team. Is he at the precinct today?"

"Yes, it's a wonder he keeps a job the way I constantly pull him away from it."

"I didn't notice any pulling. Are you working?"

"Not yet. My adopted daughter, Jane, just called me from London, and we talked for a while."

"But I bet not about Gallo."

"No. Why would I worry her? She'd want to jump on a plane and come here. This is my problem." She added, "But I'll be working soon. I'm expecting a skull from Austin, Texas, today. A little boy they found buried in the woods near the freeway."

"I'm glad you have something to keep you occupied. Otherwise, you'd be a basket case. I'll try to give you a heads-up as soon as I corner Queen." She hung up.

Eve pressed the disconnect. Nice of Catherine to be concerned about Eve's mental health, but she would be a nervous wreck whether or not she was working. It was all a matter of degree.

It was after ten. The FedEx truck should be bringing the skull from Texas. She got a cup of coffee and went out on the porch to wait for it. It was a sunny day and the lake was reflecting the incredible blue of the sky. It would be good to sit here and enjoy until she had to start work.

Her cell phone rang.

Catherine again?

She checked the caller ID.

She stiffened.

It was not Catherine.

CHAPTER

10

A **number she didn't recognize.**
Unknown number.

Why get so tense? It could be a marketing or sales firm.

She punched the button. "Eve Duncan."

"You sound very curt and businesslike. But then you always were a no-nonsense woman . . . in some areas."

The breath left her body. She closed her eyes, struggling for control.

John Gallo.

"I can almost feel your shock." His voice was mocking. "But I don't understand. The moment you decided to stir up the pot, you must have known that I'd have to contact you. I couldn't just let you fade into the great beyond. Though God knows I did try."

"John?" she whispered. She tried to pull herself

together. "You're damn right I'm shocked. I didn't even know you were still alive until yesterday."

"Really? Then it was all due to Catherine Ling that I have this excuse for our rapprochement? I thought you'd stumbled across something that led you toward me and were just using her. I must thank her when we meet. And here I was so annoyed with her."

"She's my friend. She knows how much I want to find my daughter's killer."

"Our daughter," John corrected.

Shock rippled through her. "No, Bonnie was mine and always will be mine. You had nothing to do with her." She paused. "Unless you were the one who murdered her. Catherine thinks it might be you."

"What do you think?"

"I don't know. It might be true."

"And what would you do if you found that it was?"

"I'd kill you."

"Interesting."

"Is it? I'm glad you find the prospect entertaining. I mean it, John."

"I know you do. That's why it's interesting. You've developed the killer instinct. Whenever I thought about you, I thought of you as strong, driven, the huntress, yet never violent. What did you think about me?"

"You were out of my life; and then I thought you were dead. I didn't think of you."

"Yes, you did. You may have pushed it into the background, but the memory was always there, wasn't it?"

"No, my life was too full to remember a kid who dropped into it, screwed me, then disappeared."

"I had years of fullness, too, and of emptiness, and of darkness, and of a haze somewhere in between. But I always remembered you, Eve. You were something to hold on to in the darkness." He chuckled. "And in the haze you could be anything I wanted you to be. I must tell you about that period in my life."

"I don't want you to tell me anything. Except the truth about Bonnie. Did you kill her?"

"Would you believe me if I told you that I didn't?"

"I might."

"No, you wouldn't. You never trusted me even when we were . . . close."

"You were here in Atlanta the month she disappeared. I know that much. Do you deny it?"

"I don't deny it."

Silence.

"Is that all you're going to say?"

"I didn't phone you to answer questions. Phones are so impersonal, and impersonal is something we've never been with each other."

"If you won't answer questions about yourself, what about Paul Black? What's your connection with him?"

"I know him. He's part of my darkness."

"Dammit, don't give me double-talk. Black confessed to his cellmate that he killed Bonnie. Catherine also said he had some connection with you. What connection?"

He ignored the question. "I want to see you."

"What?"

"I thought talking to you might be enough, but I've

changed my mind. It's been very . . . provocative. I've decided that there has to be final resolution. I know who you are, what you've become, but I have to reach out and touch it."

"No, you don't. You have to tell me if you killed my Bonnie."

"We've already discussed the absence of my credibility."

"Answer me."

Silence. "No, I did not. Do you believe me?"

She didn't answer.

"You see, if I'd answered yes, you would have believed me. But denial is always the problem. Should I say I killed her?"

"I want the truth."

"You always did. I want to see you, Eve."

"So you can kill me, too?"

"Why should I?"

"Because I'm after you. I'll find you. I'll find out if you killed Bonnie. If you're a murderer, that would be reason enough to kill me."

"Good reasoning. And, add to that the fact that you've already said that you'd kill me if you thought I'd killed Bonnie, it should make me very lethal-minded."

"You're taking all of this very lightly."

"No, I'm not." The mockery was suddenly gone from his tone. "If I were, I'd be handling this in an entirely different manner. I'd disappear where you couldn't find me. I'd find a way to rid myself of Catherine Ling in a manner of which you would not approve. But I found myself unwilling to do either. So the only other alternative is to come to terms with you."

"After all these years?"

"A good many things got in the way. Not the least was Bonnie's death."

"If you didn't kill her, why didn't you contact me? I know she didn't mean anything to you, but she was your daughter. Surely even you couldn't be callous enough to ignore the fact that she'd been kidnapped."

"I didn't ignore it." He paused. "When can I see you?"

"When you're willing to come into an ATLPD precinct and make a full disclosure. There's no way I'd risk meeting you one-on-one."

"But of course you'll do it. Do you think I don't know how desperate you are? I've watched and followed your path for years. You've risked your life on much slimmer leads."

"I'll just wait until Catherine finds a safer way for me to contact you."

"Like Nate Queen? He'll never give her what she wants. He knows better."

"How did you know she was dealing with Queen?"

"Why, I own him, Eve."

"You pay him?"

"No, he pays me, and there are other elements to our arrangement. Fear does equally well. Actually, it's sometimes more efficient."

"He's a government agent. Why should he be afraid of you?"

"Because I want him to be. Queen will not only not

help you, but, if I choose, he'll protect me from you. I'd really hate to ask him to do that. Will you come?"

"I've given you my answer."

"But it's not the one I want to hear," he said. "Change your mind. I'll let you know later where to meet me. In a public place, if you like. Though we won't stay there." He chuckled. "Doesn't that sound ominous? One hand is stroking you; the other is holding the knife. Though, as I recall, you never had an objection to that method of doing things. You liked it soft, and you liked it rough."

"Stop recalling," she said through clenched teeth. "Forget everything that happened between us. None of it matters. It's as if it never took place."

"I can't forget, and neither can you. What we were is the basis of what we are now. I'll try not to be blatant about it, but I'm not going to ignore it."

"I am." She was silent a moment. "If I do come, will you talk to me? Will you tell me what I want to know?"

"You're actually expecting me not to lie to you?"

"You never lied to me before."

"You see, you can't ignore our history, either. I could have changed. I *have* changed."

"Will you tell me what I want to know?"

"I'll tell you some things you want to know. I don't promise to confess all to you."

"Confess." She jumped on the word. "Do you mean confess that you killed Bonnie?"

"Confess is just a word. Though it does bring up thoughts of courtrooms and church confessionals. I suppose I might indulge myself by cleansing my soul of a few sins. Do you know, I don't believe I'd mind using you in that way. Very odd. I haven't felt the need of sharing my sins in a very long time, perhaps never. Don't you find that unusual?"

"There's only one confession I want to hear from you."

"Then step into my web. No one ever said that I was without guile. There's no telling what secrets I may tell you." He chuckled. "Though don't tell Queen I said that. He doesn't like the idea of my telling secrets. He may lose his sense of judgment and decide you're a threat, too."

"Evidently, you're the threat."

"I've never said that I wasn't one. But I've always been honest about it. I even warned you, Eve."

Yes, that was true. And she had ignored it and gone headlong into an affair with him. What an idiot she had been.

"You're thinking that you would never make that mistake today," John said. "You never know. My phoning you is probably a mistake, but I couldn't resist. Every now and then, I have a lapse and just go for it."

"Why? There's an excuse for acting without thinking when we were that young, but all that's behind us. We have responsibilities and knowledge of the consequences. We don't have the right to 'go for it.'"

"I have the right to take whatever I can take. It's an integral part of my personality. One of my personalities anyway. Queen will tell you that I probably have several swirling about, causing turmoil to him and everyone else."

"What are you talking about?"

"Ask him. He'll be delighted to tell you about all my little foibles. He thinks I'm crazy."

Eve felt a chill. "And are you?"

He was silent a moment. "Yes, occasionally." He added mockingly, "But don't let that keep you from renewing our acquaintance. Look upon it as a challenge. I'll be in touch." He hung up.

A challenge? Eve was shaking as she pressed the disconnect. This wasn't the kind of challenge she needed or wanted. The entire conversation with John Gallo had been disturbing. Disturbing and frightening. His voice had been the same, and yet the intonations of mockery had been different. She had found herself trying to anticipate what he was going to say, but it had been like talking to a stranger.

For God's sake, he was a stranger. What was she thinking?

She wasn't thinking at all. Emotion had taken over.

Then throw it out and start thinking like the woman you've become and not the girl you were.

She drew a deep breath. What had she learned from that call?

Not much. He had admitted he had been in Atlanta at the time of Bonnie's kidnapping. He had said he had not done it, but the underlying mockery had made everything he'd said suspect. Nate Queen and Army Intelligence evidently knew everything about him, but the odds were that Catherine wouldn't be able to get anything out of them.

And he'd said that he was unbalanced at times. There had been no mockery in those words.

Crazy. It would take a man who was unbalanced to kill a helpless child, his own flesh and blood.

Bonnie.

The pain was always there, but the possibility of John Gallo's being her killer had brought the agony alive again.

The agony and the bitterness.

He might well have killed her if he'd been gripped in a fit of insanity. If he had not killed her, then he could know who did.

Damn him.

All these years he had been alive, standing on the sidelines, watching her pain. What kind of monster had he become? If Catherine had not been able to unearth this connection, would he have continued to stand back and monitor the hell Eve was going through?

No way. She knew about Gallo now. There would be no more of his standing in the shadows like a vampire drinking in her pain and loss. She'd jerk him into the sunlight and burn him alive if she found he'd killed Bonnie.

She pulled out her phone and dialed Catherine. "I just talked to John Gallo on my cell. You're going to find it hard as hell to find out anything from Nate Queen. Gallo says he owns him. I believe him."

"Shit."

"But Gallo wants me to meet with him. Somewhere public."

"Why?"

"I don't know. I can't be sure. He says he wants to 'resolve' our relationship. It sounds like some kind of whim." She paused. "He admitted he wasn't stable."

"Then you stay away from him. We'll set up a trap."

"I'll think about it."

"Think about it? You just said he was crazy. That's the only way to handle it."

"What if he gets spooked? He said his other choice was just to disappear. Evidently, he's damn good at that. No one knew he was alive all these years."

"You're thinking about meeting him."

"He may have killed Bonnie. Or he may know who did. It's possible he could tell me where to find Paul Black. I'd lose all of that if I blow this chance."

"That's not all you could lose if you meet Gallo. He felt safe before. You're a threat to him now that you know he could have killed Bonnie."

"I can't blow it," Eve repeated.

"Stay where you are. I'm coming back to the cottage."

"Catherine to the rescue? I didn't say that I'm meeting him. He didn't even set up a place yet."

"I know you. I'm tempted to call Joe and tell him to—"

"No!" No threat to Joe. The hint that John Gallo was unbalanced had made the danger even more clear. If Eve was going to take a chance, it would not be with Joe's life. "Joe can't be involved, Catherine. I'd keep you out of it, too, but there's a chance that you'll be able to find out more from Nate Queen. We need all the help we can get. I'm having trouble getting anything but double talk from Gallo."

"Then it's a waste. Stay away from him."

She wanted to stay away from him. It wasn't possible. "I'll try to keep in contact with you."

"I'm on my way." Catherine hung up.

Definitely Catherine to the rescue, Eve thought. Well, she would deal with her friend when she arrived. Catherine was at her rental house in Louisville, Kentucky. That meant that it would take her at least four or five hours to reach the cottage. Unless she took a helicopter. Eve wouldn't rule out that possibility.

At any rate, she'd better marshal her arguments and start making plans to avoid Catherine's machinations.

The FedEx truck was coming down the lake road to the cottage.

First things, first. She'd set up the skull that the Austin PD had sent her and start the initial measurements. There was no reason to neglect her job because her personal life was suddenly in such chaos.

"You have my package?" She came down the steps as the truck stopped. "I'll take it. I have to sign for it, as usual?"

"Yep." The uniformed driver bent down and grabbed the box. The next minute he'd jumped down and was holding the clipboard out to her.

She took the pen and scrawled her name. "Thank you." Her finger was tingling, and she absently rubbed it against her pants as she handed him back the clipboard and pen. "Always right on time."

"Not this time. Long overdue." He raised his head and looked her straight in the face.

She froze with shock.

John Gallo. Different, so different. Yet unmistakable.

"It's okay," he said quietly. "Don't be scared. It's nothing, really."

Darkness.

Eve wasn't answering her phone. It was going straight to voice mail.

Not good.

Catherine frowned as she pressed the disconnect. There was a possibility that Eve might be ignoring her call to avoid an argument. But that wasn't like Eve. She had no problem with confrontation.

She tried to call again. Same result.

Okay, bite the bullet. Eve might not be pleased with her, but Catherine wasn't going to go against instinct. It had saved her neck too many times to ignore it. She dialed Joe Quinn.

"Catherine," she said when he answered. "Are you at the precinct?"

"Yes."

"Do me a favor. Call Eve. See if she answers. I need to know if she's just not answering my calls."

"And why would she do that?"

"Because I'm pushy, and she doesn't want to be pushed. Just do it. Okay?"

Joe hung up.

He called back two minutes later. "What the hell is happening?"

"She didn't answer?"

"I called three times." His voice was harsh. "Voice mail. Why were you pushing her?"

"I'm in my car on the way to the lake cottage. But it will be several hours before I get there. Go home and check to make sure everything is okay."

"Why shouldn't it be?" he asked. "Dammit, answer me, Catherine."

"John Gallo called Eve. He wanted to arrange a meeting."

Joe muttered an oath. "And, of course, she was going to do it."

"You know Eve. The chances are good. She thinks she should handle this herself."

"I know. And she wouldn't listen to you. She won't listen to me, either. What else did Gallo tell her?"

"That Nate Queen won't tell her anything. He said they have an arrangement. No, he said he owned Queen."

"Yes, and that would be the only excuse she'd need. I'm getting in my car now. I should be home in thirty minutes. I'll call you from there." He hung up.

The deed was done. If nothing was wrong, then Eve was going to be very upset with her. Catherine sighed as she hung up the phone. At least she hadn't told Joe the most frightening thing about Gallo's call. No use worrying him unless necessary. Now all she could do was wait for Joe's call.

The call came forty minutes later.

"She's not here," he said curtly. "The Jeep was still in the driveway. The house was left unlocked. A half-full coffee cup was on the front porch railing."

"No note?"

"Nothing."

"Shit."

"My sentiments. If she went somewhere to meet Gallo, she would have used her own transportation. And she wouldn't have left the house unlocked. We always use the alarm."

"You think that Gallo decided he didn't want to wait to set up a meeting?"

"Don't you?"

"Yes." She hesitated. "There's something else you should know. Gallo admitted to Eve that he was unbalanced."

There was a silence, then an eruption of oaths. "My God, and she was going to meet him anyway? No wonder you were on your way back down here. You should have called me right away." He added roughly, "Oh, I know why you didn't. You two have this bond, and everyone else is on the outside. But if anything has happened to her, I'll break your neck, Catherine."

"And I won't blame you. But you'd do better to think of breaking Gallo's neck as soon as we find him."

"And that will be damn soon. Are you somewhere near a city?"

"Knoxville, Tennessee, is about thirty miles from here."

"Go to the airport. I'm renting a plane, and I'll pick you up."

"And where are we going?"

"You tell me. Can you locate Nate Queen?"

"He should be back in his office at INSCOM Fort Belvoir, Virginia, by now. But he also has a condo in Alexandria. Should I call him?"

"No, we're going to pay him a visit. There's too much wiggle room on the phone. He's going to talk. I'll know everything he knows about John Gallo within an hour after I have him. I'm going to pin him down so tight he won't be able to breathe. As a matter of fact, that's an even better idea." His tone was savage. "Gallo thinks he owns Nate Queen? He just yielded possession. I'm the one who's going to own Queen from now on."

SAN FRANCISCO INTERNATIONAL AIRPORT

The gate area was crowded, and Paul Black was barely able to get a seat at Gate 2.

He would rather have been at Gate 1. From where he was sitting, he could see a little girl of seven or eight standing next to a flight attendant. She was a pretty, brown-haired little girl, her hair pulled back in a blue ribbon. Her face was eager, her eyes shining.

A first flight?

She was probably one of the thousands of unaccompanied minors who flew every month entrusted to the airlines' flight attendants. The flight attendant seemed to be in her early twenties and was chatting with the man next to her.

While the little girl was going toward the doughnut stand in the center of the gate area.

It would not be easy, but it would be possible, he thought.

Train stations, bus stations, airports were all prime areas to make contact. Airports were a little harder, but that only made it more interesting. He usually preferred bus stations in European and Asian countries, but he couldn't be choosy at the moment. He hadn't had a kill in over a week.

The little girl had her doughnut and was coming back toward the flight attendant.

The woman barely glanced at the little girl when she sat down next to her.

Maybe it would be easier than he thought.

The mind-set of the people at travel centers was always different. Sometimes the travelers were nervous, excited, unhappy, but there was always a chance that their altered perception would lead them more easily to do things they wouldn't ordinarily do.

He had read once that Andrei Chikatilo, the Soviet serial killer who had been convicted of killing at least fifty-three women and children, had made a habit of contacting his prey at train stations. It was a wonder the fool had not been caught before. Personally, Black preferred to be unpredictable. It was the only safe method and, combined with his clever acquisition of Queen as a protector, it had worked wonderfully well for him. He had stopped counting at sixty-two kills and, though he had occasionally skirted capture, he had never been really in danger.

Paul Black glanced up at the clock. He had forty minutes before he boarded the flight. Time to spend them doing something he'd enjoy. He took out his cell and dialed Nate Queen.

"I'm coming after you, Queen," he said softly. "I just thought I'd let you anticipate a little."

"Black?" Queen's voice was hoarse. "What are you talking about? Why? Haven't I protected you? Let's talk."

The bastard was scared shitless, Black thought. Good. Fear was power. It was as heady as straight vodka. "I don't like to talk. That's what's made our relationship work so well. You give me an assignment, and I do it. I give you a bill, and you pay it." He paused. "Benkman didn't like to talk, either. He just wanted to kill me and walk away. You shouldn't have sent him, Queen."

"Why would I want to kill you? You're valuable to me."

"I think you're playing both ends against the middle. You don't care how faithful an employee I've been over the years." His voice was mocking. "No gold watch. Just a bomb under the terrace. So I must have been more valuable to you dead than alive."

"It wasn't me." Queen's voice was panicky. "Maybe Gallo did it on his own. He doesn't tell me everything."

"It doesn't matter. I'll get to you both."

"Look, we can work this out. You need me as much as I need you. They would have executed you years ago if I hadn't protected you. You know that's true."

"And the reason you protected me is that you know the minute they catch me, I'll tell everyone how you've constantly stolen evidence and whisked me away from the local police. In how many countries? At least a dozen." Turn the screw. "And I'll give details to the media. Ugly details horrify the media. You're so comfortable in your cushy job, just waiting to retire and tap all the money you've stolen and go to some Caribbean island. That dream would be blasted to hell. They'll start a witch hunt."

"Maybe I made a mistake," Queen said. "I admit I was getting nervous. I needed someone who would just do the kills I assigned, then go undercover until we needed him."

"Oh, someone who didn't like his job?"

He hesitated. "I may have thought that you were out of control."

"I am. You've never been able to control me."

The little girl at Gate 1 was wandering away from the flight attendant again. Black felt tension grip him. It was too tempting. The challenge, the possibility . . . the hunger.

"Give me another chance," Queen said.

He jerked his attention away from the girl. "Why now? Why did you send Benkman now?"

"I told you that—" Queen stopped. "Gallo is becoming difficult. I'm tired of dealing with him. I needed a sacrificial lamb."

Black burst out laughing. "And I was your lamb? What fools you are. You should have let me kill him when I wanted to do it."

"We had our doubts whether you could do it. He's as nasty a piece of work as you are."

Black's smile vanished. "I could do it."

"Then maybe we could deal. You forget my lack of judgment. And I turn you loose on Gallo for a very substantial sum. Look on it as a challenge."

The challenge was the little girl at Gate 1. Gallo would only be an amusement in comparison. "How much?"

"Double the last job."

"You really are finding him difficult. Or me a threat."

"A little of both," Queen said. "I want information from him before he dies. I need a ledger he's been holding."

"How do you know I won't take it?"

"You wouldn't be interested. Blackmail requires a certain effort and restraint. You only want one thing from us."

Freedom to keep doing what he loved best.

Queen knew him better than he'd thought.

"I might be interested. I've always hated Gallo's guts." He added, "As long as you understand, you won't get another chance with me. Where is Gallo?"

"Mazkal, Utah." He paused. "Where are you?"

"San Francisco."

"Very close."

"I'm close to you, too. Only a few hours away."

"But you'd get nothing by killing me."

"Except satisfaction."

"Be reasonable."

"But all the FBI profilers say that men of my persuasion are seldom reasonable."

The flight attendant at Gate 1 was leaning on the departure gate desk and talking to the gate agent.

The little girl was standing several yards away looking out the huge window at the planes.

"Black, change your mind."

"I may. Or I may not. If you're not dead in the next
twelve hours, then you'll know that I've decided to forgive you and gone after Gallo instead." He hung up.

He leaned back in his seat, his gaze on the little girl.
Such shining brown hair, such a pretty little girl.

Her flight wasn't due to board for another fifty-five
minutes. That was enough time to lure her out of the
airport.

If the flight attendant was as careless and self-
centered as she appeared.

If the little girl was as innocent and eager as he
judged.

If Black could use all his skill and cleverness to
persuade her to come with him.

It would be difficult. It would be a challenge . . .

So should he accept that challenge? Should he forget
her and get on his flight to Washington? Or should he
catch a later flight to Utah?

Let the little girl decide.

He got to his feet and strolled casually toward the
window.

If it proved too awkward or dangerous a task to take
what he wanted, then he'd return to his own gate and
continue to Washington.

If he was able to lure the little girl from the airport,
then he'd come back after he'd sated himself and take
the flight to Utah.

He stopped a good five feet from the child and gazed

out the window, ignoring her. Never too close at the start. In the crowded airport, it would be better to use words rather than actions. And they must be the right words. But he would have no problem. He was an expert, a master, at this game.

Queen or Gallo?

Sweet little girl, you choose who is to die.

CHAPTER

11

Y**ou're probably going to be very angry with me,** Eve."

John's voice. John Gallo's dark eyes looking down at her.

She was lying on a couch. Red drapes at the window. Where were they? A motel . . . ?

"It may help to know that I made sure that you wouldn't have so much as a headache."

Not a motel.

She was jarred wide-awake.

She sat bolt upright on the couch. "What the hell!"

"It's fine," John said quietly. "It may not have been the diplomatic way to go about it, but you're so surrounded by people who would have gotten in my way that I decided this was the safest way to handle it."

She had a sudden memory of the numbing sensation

as she'd handled the pen. "A knockout sedative in that pen? No, it wasn't diplomatic. How the hell could it be?" She looked around the huge room. A study. Walk-in stone fireplace, book-lined walls, four floor-to-ceiling windows. "And where the hell am I?"

"My place in Utah. It seemed to be the safest place for a get-together?"

"Utah? You knocked me out and bundled me off to Utah? You *are* crazy."

"I told you." He smiled. "And you're not scared. How refreshing."

"You want someone to be afraid of you? It won't be me. Go screw yourself."

"I don't particularly want it. It just happens. So I use it." He leaned back in his chair. "Now be quiet so that I can look at you. When I was masquerading as your friendly FedEx deliveryman, I was trying hard to make sure that you wouldn't look at me. Which meant I couldn't really look at you."

She glared at him. "You had plenty of time to look at me while you were bringing me here. How many hundreds of miles?"

"But you were unconscious all the way here on the plane, and there was no spirit to be seen. What I remembered most about you wasn't on the surface. I want to see if it's still there. Just give me a moment."

She drew a deep breath and tried to rein in the anger. She needed a moment of recovery, too. Shock and anger had blurred everything in their wake. She had reacted as she would have done if he had been the John

Gallo she had known at sixteen. He was not that boy. He was a man and one of whom she had to be wary. But she'd be damned if she would be afraid of him.

Though perhaps there was a reason why he inspired fear, she thought as she studied him. There was a chilling quietness, watchfulness, about him that she didn't recognize as a quality in the boy she had known. His stunning good looks had survived the years, same olive skin, dark piercing eyes, slight indentation in his chin. Faint lines at the corners of his eyes told of time in the sun, a thin strand of white streaked the dark hair above his temple. His lips were the same except for a curve that was faintly reckless. Yes, he looked older, harder; the edge that she remembered had become dagger sharp. He weighed less, still muscular, but spare, whip-lean.

Her gaze shifted up to meet his eyes. "As you can see, I'm not the same person. Comparisons are impossible. We start new, John."

"On the contrary, everything I saw in you is still there . . . and more." He tilted his head. "You had wonderful potential, and I didn't even recognize it. I was so dizzy about what was between us that I was blind to anything else."

"Potential? Don't be patronizing to me, John."

He smiled. "I wouldn't think of it. You were always able to intimidate me."

"Bullshit. Why?"

"Because you always knew what you wanted and could stay the course. I had problems in that direction."

He stood up and went over to the desk and picked up a silver carafe. "Coffee? I thought you'd probably need a shot of caffeine after you came back to me."

"How do I know that there's not another knockout drop in it?"

He smiled. "Because I have no reason. I had to get you here with a minimum of trouble from outsiders. So I put a trace of the fluid on the pen. Now there are no outsiders, and I'm willing to put up with any trouble I get from you." His smile faded. "God knows, I deserve it." He poured coffee into two cups. "You still take it black?"

"Yes." How had he remembered that little detail?

"I do, too, these days. A strong dose of caffeine and a glass or two of wine are the only jolts I allow myself."

"I don't care about your taste in coffee. Why have you brought me here, John?"

"I thought I'd made that clear."

"Resolution? Nothing needs to be resolved between us but the question of whether you killed my daughter."

"Perhaps not for you." He gave her a cup. "But you're saner than I am. I need more structure." He sat back down. "Structure is important when you're tottering on the brink."

"Brink of what?"

"Fill in the blank." He lifted the other cup to his lips. "I've fallen into any number of abysses in my life. Some of them were hard to climb out of."

"Am I supposed to feel sorry for you?"

"No, you've had your own falls." He leaned back

wearily in the chair. "Who would have guessed, Eve? We tried so hard to avoid being trapped, yet it happened to both of us. Terrible traps."

"Mine wasn't terrible," she said curtly. "Bonnie is—was the highlight of my life and always will be."

"You're telling me you didn't feel trapped when you found you were pregnant?"

"No, I felt stupid and angry with myself, but I always knew that I could find a solution. Afterward, there was no question of traps or anything else that wasn't founded in love." She gazed directly in his eyes. "Bonnie was all love. She bridged gaps. She made me try to understand myself and everyone around me. Do you realize what a wonderful gift that can be?"

"And you've never regretted having her even after all the pain you've experienced?"

"Regret? She *lived*. She lit up my world."

He looked down into the coffee in his cup. "And then she was taken away from you."

"Was it you, John?"

He lifted his gaze. "No."

She was believing him, she realized incredulously. No, she mustn't trust him. "Then you know who did it?"

"Maybe."

"Don't *tell* me that." Her voice was shaking. "You have to know something. You have to tell me."

"I'll think about it." He sat up straight in the chair. "Though it would probably be better if I just sent you back to your police detective. Did you tell him about me?"

"Of course."

He gave her a shrewd glance. "Not everything."

"Details? No, he wouldn't be interested."

"I bet he would."

"How did you know about Joe?"

"I know everything about you, Eve." He finished his coffee. "One of Nate Queen's principal duties was to compile and update dossiers on you. I know about your lover, your work, and your adopted daughter, Jane MacGuire." He smiled. "She's a very good artist. You'll recognize one of her paintings on the wall as you go down the hall."

She tried to hide her shock. She had naturally assumed Jane was not involved at all with John Gallo. "Why would you want to go to a gallery to buy her painting?"

"Curiosity? I'm very inquisitive. It's my nature, and while I was in prison, it was developed into a fine art form. She's very beautiful. She resembles you. I found that odd since you're not related."

"Coincidence. But you didn't talk to her? Ask her questions?"

He shook his head. "I just stayed in the background and watched and listened." He paused. "Just as I did with you."

"Why?" Her voice vibrated with intensity. "Were you ashamed? Was it guilt?"

"There's always guilt." He stood up. "We're all flawed, some more than others." He smiled down at her. "And I'm the most flawed man you'll probably ever run across. I was starting down that path when we came together, and I went into overdrive after I left you." He headed for the door. "Bill Hanks will take you to your room. I've confiscated your phone, and you'll find the house phones won't work without a code inserted."

"I want my phone. I need to call Joe Quinn. I won't have him worried. You can monitor the call if you like."

"Oh, yes, Joe Quinn." He glanced back over his shoulder. "I'm very interested in that relationship. I think I need to explore it."

"And does that mean I can't call him?"

"It might complicate things. You can join me for dinner in an hour, and we'll talk some more. Or you can stay in your room, and I'll come to you."

Another stone wall.

"Who is this Bill Hanks?"

"He's my head of security, companion, chess partner, whatever. His job description is 'as designated.'" He stopped at the door. "But he's very loyal. You'll not be able to convince him to help you leave until I give the order to let you go."

"I'll find a way when I'm ready." She stared him in the eye. "And that's not yet. You haven't answered any of my questions."

"I answered the important one. You're just not sure you believe me."

"The only way I can start to do that is to know more about you. I didn't have spies, peering behind bushes and invading my daughter's gallery shows. We have to be even."

"You always insisted on that." He opened the door. "I'll answer everything I can. Feel free to ask Bill anything you like. I'll tell him that he's not to feel he has to protect me. It goes with the territory with him. He's been with me a long time."

She hesitated. "In Korea?"

"Only the last part of my stay in that fine hotel. That's why I trust him. He avoided the final indignity." He smiled. "He's not crazy like me."

She stared at the door as it closed behind him. She was as confused and frustrated as she'd been when wakened a little while ago. She had to know *more,* dammit. He was holding out bits of information like carrots before a donkey.

But he had said that it had not been he who had killed her Bonnie. It might be foolish to follow her instincts and believe him, but it was happening.

And she was profoundly grateful. That would have been the ultimate horror.

But he might still have been involved in some way. She had to find out. She had to know what he knew.

"Ms. Duncan?" A short, stocky man was standing in the doorway. He was fiftyish, with short sandy hair and pale blue eyes. "I'm Bill Hanks." His smile was warm and broad. "May I take you to your room? John said you'd like to freshen up."

Eve got to her feet. No dizziness. No aftereffects from the sedative. John had spoken the truth. "Thank you. How courteous of him. After a kidnapping, it's always nice to have TLC."

Hanks chuckled. "I imagine it's difficult to compare kidnappings, but this one is top-grade. John insisted that we do it right. It wasn't easy. We knew from Queen's reports that you were expecting the FedEx skull, but

FedEx is a very efficient company. It was dicey stealing that truck from the lot when John decided he wanted to move quickly."

"Queen was monitoring my activities that closely?"

"If he hadn't been, John wouldn't have been pleased. Queen doesn't like to displease John." He stepped aside and gestured for her to precede him into the hall. "It usually has repercussions."

"What kind of repercussions?"

"Unpleasant," Hanks said vaguely.

So Hanks wasn't going to be entirely frank with her after all. She'd have to push until she hit a wall, then keep on pushing.

Hanks indicated a painting on the wall. "John said you'd want to see the painting. It's pretty good, isn't it?"

And it was definitely one of Jane's. Though she recognized the brushstrokes and technique, it wasn't a painting with which Eve was familiar. It was a forest wreathed thickly in mists, and it was both mysterious and terribly lonely. "Very good."

"She called it *Lost*," Hanks said. "John said that she got it right." He was leading her down the shining cherrywood-paneled hall. "I think he would have bought it even if it hadn't been painted by your daughter. He said you adopted her when she was ten?"

"Or she adopted me. We've never been entirely sure how it came about."

"She's very young to be so successful."

"Yes." She added deliberately, "But it's not Jane I want to talk about." She glanced around the hall. "This is quite a place. Luxurious. John Gallo has money now?"

Hanks nodded. "He always says that money has more power than an AK-47. He made sure that he was stocked with that particular ammunition."

"And how did he get it?"

"He made the U.S. government pay generously for his six years in prison. Then he took the money and did a tour of gambling casinos around the world and ran up his cash reserve into the stratosphere by counting cards."

She frowned. "How did he do that?"

"Card counting? He taught himself in prison. He was always smart, and he had a lot of time on his hands. It kept his brain sharp. It was real bad there." He paused. "And it was one of the ways he kept himself from hanging himself in that cell."

She could picture his desperation, the searching for anything to occupy the mind and replace the horror surrounding him. "I see."

"No, you don't," Hanks said baldly. "You can't. I was only in that place for five months before John took me with him when he escaped. I'll never forget it. The smell, the heat, the pain. I still wake up in a sweat. And John was in there six years."

She was silent, trying to understand the scope of that horror. "He told me . . . he's crazy. Is it true?"

Hanks didn't answer directly. "Aren't there times when we're all a little crazy?"

"You're dodging. He said you might try to protect him."

"He has . . . moments. Uncontrollable fits of rage that's like nothing I've ever seen. John said that those fits are like those he's read about in histories of the Vikings. Berserker. They don't come as often these days."

"And Queen and Army Intelligence know about them, too?"

"Yes; in the beginning, they encouraged them."

Her eyes widened. "Why would they do that?"

"They aided his performance." He stopped before a bedroom door and turned to face her. "After he got out of prison, they were still trying to use him. They sent him out on missions that involved assassination or extraction of personnel from hostage situations." His lips twisted. "He was very good at it. Picture Rambo on speed. And that berserker bullet could cause him to go into almost superhuman overdrive."

"They knew he had mental problems, and they still sent him out?"

"John thought they probably wanted to get him killed with the least amount of trouble. He didn't care. It didn't matter if he lived or died. During that period, right after he escaped Korea, he had a bloodlust that wouldn't stop. All he wanted was the opportunity to vent it."

Bloodlust. Berserker. And that period right after he'd gotten out of prison was when Bonnie had been taken.

"I can see you drawing into yourself," Hanks said quietly. "You wanted to know. He told me to tell you."

"When did he stop working for them?"

"After a couple years. Maybe he worked it out of his system. Or maybe he managed to heal himself. They sure weren't going to do it for him."

"But he evidently still has a connection with them."

"Yes, but now the tables are turned. They don't use John, he uses them."

"And why do they allow it?"

He shrugged. "That you'll have to ask him. I've never discussed it with John. There are some things I'd rather not know. It's safer for me. If I had to guess, I'd say he knows where a few very dangerous bodies are buried. At any rate, Queen jumps when John snaps his fingers." He opened the door. "If you need anything, give me a call."

"How? I don't know your blasted codes."

He smiled. "I won't be far. John said that I was to take care of you."

"And keep me from escaping?"

His smile faded. "It will only be for a little while. I think you're safe."

"Think? What if I'm not?"

Hanks didn't answer.

"John said you were loyal. That covers criminal activities? Why? Does he pay you that well?"

"He took me out of that prison. He didn't have to do it. I had a shattered leg and a fever. He had to carry me a good portion of the way to the coast. He would have been safer on his own." He nodded slowly. "Yeah, I'm loyal."

That couldn't be more obvious. John had clearly bought that loyalty in a way that would ensure that it was unbreakable.

"Any more questions?" Bill was smiling again. "Last chance."

"One more." She met his gaze, bracing herself. "Were you in Atlanta with John that month before my daughter was taken?"

He shook his head. "I was still in a hospital in Tokyo. They practically had to rebuild my leg. I didn't hook up with him until almost a year later."

"But you knew about her?"

"No, John never spoke about her or you until later. I never even knew he had a kid. The first I heard of your Bonnie was years later, when he was pressuring Queen to keep a dossier on you."

"You weren't curious?"

"John sets limits, and I don't step across the line. You might follow my example."

Her lips twisted. "Or he might go berserk?"

He turned away. "It hasn't happened for a long time. That doesn't mean it can't happen." He was moving down the hall. "The dining room is back the way we came and to the right. John has a great cook he hired away from a casino in Las Vegas. Those clothes on the bed are a loan from her. You're a little thinner than she is, but they should come close."

Eve glanced at the worn jeans and oversized black sweatshirt with MIRAGE CASINO emblazoned in white. "They should be okay. Thank her for me."

"Thank her yourself. Judy's not shy about making her presence known. But she makes terrific Mexican fajitas." He slanted her a smile. "And she's very loyal to John, too."

"Did he break her out of prison, too? I thought you said he hired her from a casino."

"He did. But there are all kinds of prisons, aren't there? She had a three-year-old and an abusive husband. John sent the husband packing and brought Judy and the kid here where she couldn't be bothered."

Eve stood in the doorway and watched him disappear down the hall. Bill Hanks had been a treasure trove of information, but he had not alleviated her uneasiness. John Gallo might have become a man who deserved gratitude and loyalty in some quarters, but he was also an assassin and a man prone to violent fits of passion. She was still feeling the chill that had shaken her when Hanks had told her of those berserker episodes.

Get over it. She had told Gallo she would not be afraid of him. She had to work her way through any fear and get to the truth.

She turned, closed the door, and glanced around her. Comfortable, even elegant room, oak furniture, black watch plaid coverlet on the king bed, a bouquet of intricate brown twigs in a gold vase on the carved chest. The décor had Western elements, but it was definitely not a designer room. It appeared too strong, too individual. She glanced at the plaid coverlet on the bed.

A red plaid blanket on the grass of the reservoir.

Too John Gallo.

She looked away and went to the wide window across the room. The sun was going down behind the mountains, and the terrain was spectacular. The red of the rock spiked with the verdant fir and pines made it appear that the scenery she was looking at was on some exotic and distant planet. It came as a slight shock to see that there were wrought-iron gates barricading the house from the wildness of the terrain beyond.

Barricades. She would have thought that John would shun any kind of enclosure after that Korean prison. But the wrought iron was open and airy. Maybe that was a compromise he'd had to make. But why was the house barricaded at all? Who was he trying to keep out?

She turned away and headed for the door across the room that presumably led to a bathroom. She needed to shower and to think. She had been caught up with John Gallo, but there were other problems to consider. Even if Catherine had not told Joe about Gallo's phone call, he would know that something had happened to her. She would never have just gone off and let Joe worry.

And what about Catherine? She had been joking about Catherine to the rescue, but Catherine would instinctively move to help her.

Dammit, Gallo had caused her a monumental headache by acting with such arrogant recklessness. And that headache had nothing to do with the knockout drops he'd given her. She had to find a way to contact Joe and make sure he knew that she was safe and avoid any overt action.

Fat chance. Joe never avoided any action if there was a chance he could take the game. He was already on edge, and this idiotic move of Gallo's would be the spur. And how could she convince him she was safe when she wasn't sure herself? Bringing her to this place had not been rational, and it was clear even Gallo's friend wasn't certain that he had come all the way back from that period of madness.

And if he hadn't, then she'd deal with it. Gallo was her problem and no one else's.

She couldn't let that madness hurt Joe.

The room looked more like a library than a dining room, Eve thought as she paused in the arched doorway. The walls were lined with as many bookshelves as the study had been. A fireplace trimmed in copper added to the ambience.

"Hurry and sit down." John Gallo rose to his feet from his chair at the head of the table. "Judy has been fretting about her fajitas getting cold. She's a perfectionist about temperature."

"Judy?" Oh yes, Hanks had mentioned John's cook. "Heaven forbid I disturb any of your employees. She obviously rules the roost."

"Food is important." He seated Eve, then sat down again. "I found that out while I was in prison. It's amazing how deprivation fine-tunes one's appreciation of things we generally take for granted."

"Deprivation?" The question had just tumbled out. She had not meant to ask him any questions about that period.

"I was a skeleton when I got out." He shrugged. "But I managed to keep muscle tone. I exercised for hours every day to make sure that I'd be ready to act when I got the chance."

"Evidently that chance came." She looked around the room. "I like this room. It has a sort of subtle richness. It's the kind of place where you'd want to linger and talk."

His gaze followed hers to the bookshelves lining the room and she was surprised to see pride and affection in his expression. "I like it, too. I made the entire house into a haven. When I knew you, I had no use for havens, but that changed."

"You must like books. I don't remember that about you. I can't recall you ever mentioning it."

He chuckled. "Not surprising. We didn't do much talking, did we?"

"No." She veered immediately away from that implied intimacy. "And I didn't know much about you in any area."

"At the time, I was more interested in physical than mental exercises." He held up his hand as he saw her expression. "I'm not talking about sex. I always had too much energy, and my uncle Ted managed to channel it by teaching me everything he had learned in the Rangers."

She nodded. "Rick Larazo. I remember you saying something about it."

His brows rose. "You have a good memory."

And she didn't want him to know that more was coming back to her all the time. She picked up her water glass. "It comes and goes. What about the books?"

"Another form of starvation. It actually was more intense because after a while, physical hunger diminishes. The mind doesn't give up so easily. I stole a Bible, a book of verses, and a copy of *The Encyclopedia of Mythology* from the effects of one of the prisoners who died in my cell. They weren't enough, but I was able to hone my memory and managed to develop other outlets."

"Like card counting?"

"One of the more profitable. There were others that were more abstract, but I—" He broke off as a small, thin woman in jeans and a denim shirt came into the room. "You're late, Judy. Here I've been bragging about your—"

"I'm never late." She plopped the two huge covered dishes down on the table. "I had to wait until you got in here to start cooking. If you'd been in here on time, I might have had a head start, but how—" She stopped and tilted her head, studying Eve. "I've seen your photo before. And you're sure no movie star like he sometimes brings here. No offense. These days movie stars don't have to be glamour queens, but you don't look—"

"Judy Clark, Eve Duncan," John said. "And Eve is a star in her own realm."

"Skulls." Judy snapped her fingers. "You do something with skulls."

"Reconstruction," Eve said. "Definitely no glamour."

Judy nodded. "But solid work, good work. I have a six-year-old little girl myself. I don't know what I'd do if my Cara disappeared. I remember thinking that it probably made those parents feel better that they at least know, Ms. Duncan."

"Eve. Mr. Hanks told me you had a daughter. She's six now?"

"Yep." Judy's face lit up with a smile. "She's real pretty. Not like me. And smart as a whip. She's in the kitchen now, helping me. Would you like to meet her? I'm trying to get her to be more social-like. She's kind of shy."

An abusive husband, Hanks had said. That usually translated also to abuse toward the children. "I'd like that very much."

"Then I'll have her bring in some of the sauces when I bring in the tortillas."

"I want to thank you for lending me these clothes. It's very kind of you."

"No problem. They're not fancy but, like I said, you don't look fancy yourself. They suit you just like they do me. Though I'd think John would—" She stopped. "I'll go get the tortillas. I'm letting the food get cold." She disappeared through the side doorway.

"Movie stars?" Eve asked Gallo.

"Not often. I was curious."

"Another form of starvation?"

"No, as I said, curiosity. I wanted to sample, not devour." He lifted the lid, and steam ballooned off the fajitas. "Like I do these fajitas."

"You should have waited." Judy had appeared with two covered plates. She was trailed by a little girl with sandy brown hair and huge brown eyes with extravagantly long lashes, who carried a tray of condiments. "You're too impatient. I keep telling you, John."

"Life's too short." John met Judy's gaze. "Isn't it?"

An indefinable expression flitted across her face.

"Yeah, I guess maybe you're right." She set the covered plates on the table. "Which is why you should enjoy the hell out of my fajitas. Eat." She pushed the little girl forward. "Cara, this is Ms. Duncan. She's a friend of John's. Say hello, honey."

Cara stared at her gravely. "Hello. You're wearing Mama's shirt."

"She was kind enough to lend it to me. I'm glad to meet you, Cara."

Cara nodded. "I wanted to see you. Mama said you were better than the movie star." A smile suddenly broke the gravity of her expression as she turned to John. "How is she better, John?"

"In all sorts of ways." John smiled back at the little girl. "I'll explain later. It would take too long."

"Come along, Cara." Judy gave the child a gentle shove toward the kitchen. "I'll let you help load the dishwasher and then off to bed you go. Say good night."

Cara looked over her shoulder. "Good night, Ms. Duncan. Good night, John."

"Good night, Cara," Eve said.

Then the door swung shut behind mother and daughter.

Eve smiled as she gazed after them. "Sweet child. So solemn. And Judy's . . . unusual."

"They broke the mold. Or she broke it. That's more likely."

"Not the ordinary employer-employee relationship."

"I don't do employer well. I just have people who work with me. I don't have time for any other crap."

He handed her the steaming plate and the plate of tortillas. "Like I told Judy. Life's too short. What were we talking about before she came in?"

Eve had to think for a minute. "Books?"

He nodded. "After I escaped and got some semblance of a mind back, I started collecting and reading. I like having books around me."

"You'd get along with Catherine's son, Luke. He has a passion for books, too." She unwrapped the tortillas. "And for the same reason."

"I didn't know she had a child. How old?"

"Luke is eleven." She looked at him. "I'm surprised you don't have a dossier on Catherine, too. She was the one who Nate Queen was dealing with."

"Oh, I do. But I guess he didn't think her personal life would be of any interest to me." He picked up his fork, and added casually, "Or maybe he was protecting her."

She was abruptly jarred. The conversation had not been ordinary by any means, but it had possessed an odd, almost comfortable, familiarity. That last remark was not at all comfortable. "Why should he think her child should be protected from you?"

He warily looked up. "I said the wrong thing."

"Did you? Nate Queen knows more about you than I do. Why should a child be threatened?"

"He shouldn't be threatened." His lips twisted. "But Nate Queen thinks I'm capable of any atrocity. I can't blame him. I don't have a great track record."

"Against children?"

"No," he said quietly. "I've never hurt a child to my knowledge."

"You'd either know or not know."

"I hope you're right. I'd never do it deliberately." He shook his head. "But there were missions when I was so messed up, I didn't know what was going on. Sometimes I even blacked out, sometimes for days at a time. I just obeyed orders and got the job done."

"And what if a child was in the way?"

"I don't remember any—" He broke off. "What do you want me to say? Dammit, I *can't* be sure. Maybe I don't want to remember." His eyes were glittering in his taut face, and the words spat like bullets. "You want to know for certain? Ask Queen if I ever murdered a kid. I'm sure he's kept a tally going of all the sins I committed during those missions. But that's all they did. They kept records. They didn't try to stop me." He stopped and drew a breath, obviously struggling for control. "But that's not what you really want to know. You want to know about Bonnie. I don't believe I've ever had one of those blackouts except on a mission. I'd remember Bonnie."

"Why? You've never told me why you were in Atlanta. How did you even know you had a daughter?"

"I'll get to it." He looked away from her. "Eat your dinner. Judy will come stomping back in here and yell at both of us."

"I don't care."

"But I do." He looked back at her. "And you're in my world now. My world, my people. I'll give you what you want, Eve. But it will be in my own time. This isn't easy for me, either."

She had known her questioning had been painful

for him, but she had not been able to stop herself once she'd started. "Then, dammit, why did you bring me here?"

"I told you why."

"Resolution? Bullshit."

"Maybe for you." His smile was slightly self-mocking. "But when you're a touch unstable like me, it's important."

"When can we talk about Bonnie?"

"Soon." He poured her a glass of wine. "But now we'll talk about other things. Tell me about Joe Quinn, Eve."

"I love him," she said tersely. "He's strong and straight and everything I could want. I don't need phony movie stars to pamper my ego like you, John."

He made a face. "That evidently stuck in your head. I admit sometimes I do have to reach to keep amused." He added soberly, "I'm not on the attack about your lover. Life is rough and can be lonely. I'm glad that you found someone to make you happy. I've tried, but it never happens with me."

She had not expected that response, and it caught her off guard. She went back to the original subject. "When can we talk about Bonnie?"

"Tell me about your reconstructions. How does it feel when you're doing the sculpting? What kind of technique do you use to get such accuracy?"

She didn't answer.

He smiled and lifted his glass to her. "My world, Eve," he said softly.

And no amount of persuasion was going to move him until he wanted to be moved. But she couldn't just abandon the subject. Go along with him. She'd come back to Bonnie later. She picked up her fork. "Forensic reconstruction isn't exactly light dinner conversation."

He followed through immediately. "Neither is stealing from corpses, prison, and starvation. In comparison I think you're on the sunny side." He handed her the glass of wine. "So tell me about your skulls."

CHAPTER

12

Colonel Nate Queen lived in an impressive condo in the trendy area of Alexandria, Virginia, outside Washington, D.C.

"Nice address," Joe said. "You wouldn't think the military would pay this well."

"Private funds? Do you want me to go in and get him?" Catherine asked Joe, as they drew up before the building. "He'll be surprised to see me, but he won't go for the jugular."

"Are you trying to protect me, Catherine?" Joe asked. "Or don't you want me to take out one of your prize contacts?"

"Both." She grinned at him. "You're such a gentle soul that I wouldn't want Queen to think that he'd have a chance with you. That could be fatal." She got out of the car. "But you don't seem amenable. Suppose I take out the lock, then disable the alarm while you go up and start the discussion with Queen. Good cop–bad cop?"

"Queen will probably be too savvy for that. We'll see how it goes." Joe moved toward the front door.

Catherine was able to unlock the door for him a few minutes later. "Give me a minute." She went around the side of the building, traced the alarm wire, and disabled it.

When she came back around to the front, Joe had already gone inside and disappeared. It didn't surprise her. She was right behind him, moving silently through the foyer and up the stairs.

She heard a curse, then a solid thump from one of the bedrooms on the second floor.

Silence was clearly no longer necessary.

She took the rest of the steps two at a time and reached the open door of the bedroom seconds later.

Nate Queen was naked, on the floor beside the bed, and Joe was straddling him, his hands around Queen's throat. A stream of obscenities was issuing from Queen's mouth.

"Shut up," Joe said between his teeth. "I'm not ready for you to talk yet. You're not saying the words I want to hear."

Joe was mad as hell. Time to enter the scenario before Joe's grip on Queen's throat proved lethal. Catherine turned on the overhead light. "Let him up, Joe. We wouldn't want him to catch cold." Her gaze wandered farther down on Queen's naked body. "Or suffer a serious inferiority complex." She picked up a brown robe from the chair and dropped it down on Queen's face. "Move very carefully, Queen. My friend's not in a good mood."

"Or don't." Joe released Queen and got off him. "I'd just as soon that you didn't." He glanced at Catherine. "He gave me a few problems. He was awake. You'd think he was expecting us."

"Not you. Do you think I'd be scared of you?" Queen jerked the robe off his face and sat up. His heavy-jowled face was flushed with rage as he glared at Catherine. "What is this, bitch? Since when do you bring your scum to—"

"Careful," Catherine said. "He brought me. I'm just here to try to keep you alive long enough to get the information we need. It's not going to be easy for me. I'm almost as angry with you as he is."

"We're wasting time." Joe dug his hand in Queen's hair and pulled him toward the chair a few feet away. When Queen began to struggle, he punched him in the stomach, then heaved him into the chair. "John Gallo. Tell me where he is. Now."

Queen's expression changed, became wary. "Catherine, I told you that I couldn't help you out. My source folded on me."

"I heard what you told me," Catherine said. "I didn't believe you then. I sure as hell don't believe you now. You're dirty, Queen. You're working hand in glove with Gallo. Talk."

"Go screw yourself."

Joe's hand was suddenly on his throat, his thumbs on the carotid muscles. "Be respectful, Queen. You're not going to die yet, but you'll hurt. I'm really good at pain."

Queen's face was turning beet red, and his eyes were bulging. "Catherine, stop him from—"

"Let him breathe, Joe. At least for a minute or so."

"What are you doing to me?" Queen gasped. "You're a government agent, Catherine. We're on the same side."

"I'm not on your side," Catherine said. "You lied to me. I want to know where Gallo took Eve Duncan."

"Eve Duncan?" Queen moistened his lips. "I don't know anything about her. Or Gallo."

"Gallo knows a lot about you. He told Eve that he owned you."

"That son of a bitch." Queen's expression turned ugly. "Crazy, arrogant bastard. Someday, I'm going to find a way to cut his heart out."

"Stand in line," Joe said. "The problem may be moot. Where's Eve Duncan?"

"I told you, I don't know anything about—" His head snapped back as Joe's fist crashed into his jaw. "Shit." He shook his head to clear it. "He never mentioned Eve Duncan. You were the one who was causing problems, Catherine. I thought he might go after you."

"And you didn't warn me?"

"I tried to convince him to leave you to me." He was gazing at Joe. "How could I know he'd go after her? It was Catherine who was stirring up the trouble. Catherine can take care of herself."

"Where is John Gallo?"

He shook his head. "I can't talk about him. I'd lose my job in a heartbeat."

Joe leaned forward, his face close to Queen's. "Do you know what you'll lose if you don't talk?" he said softly. "I'll cut off your dick and stuff it where the sun doesn't shine."

"Joe, don't bother your head with little things," Catherine said, straight-faced. "I have a friend in Hong Kong who taught me much more sophisticated methods to get what we need."

"Don't get involved in this, Catherine," Queen said. "Gallo is our problem. We'll deal with him."

"You didn't deal with him," Joe said. "Now it's up to us."

"Where is he?" Catherine asked softly.

"I don't think he'll hurt her."

"But you don't know."

"He's been interested enough to insist we give him reports on her." He added quickly, "But he never made a move."

"Until now," Joe bit out. "You said he was crazy. What made you think he wouldn't be volatile as hell?"

"Our psych people think that he's keeping it under control these days. Though they say he has signs of dissociative identity disorder—a split personality." He stared at Catherine accusingly. "Why couldn't you leave it alone?"

"Where is he, Queen? You mentioned Utah. A lie?"

He shook his head. "I was thinking about turning you loose on him. I thought maybe I could convince my superiors to let you at him. I'm sick to death of Gallo."

"Where in Utah?"

Queen didn't answer.

"You *will* tell me, Queen," Joe said softly. "You'll tell me where he is, how to get to him, and everything else you know. You'll either tell me now or later. You'll be a lot clearer and more coherent if you choose now."

Queen glanced at Catherine. "Stop him, or I'll make things so hot for you that the CIA will throw your ass out so fast your head will spin."

"Eve's my friend, Queen." She held his gaze. "You made a mistake. Correct it, and you'll get out of this without too much damage. Where is Gallo?"

His glance shifted from her face to Joe's. Then he looked away. "Oh, what the hell. What do I care? I'm not going to take any more punishment to protect that bastard. Gallo has a place in Mazkal, Utah. A big compound in the mountains. If he has Eve Duncan, he probably took her there. I'll give you the address, but it's guarded as tight as Fort Knox. You're not going to get in."

"I want to know everything you can tell me about access," Catherine said. "We'll get in."

"And you're going to tell Gallo that I told you?"

He was afraid, Catherine realized. Queen wasn't a coward. Gallo must be formidable. The knowledge was making her uneasy. "It may not be necessary."

"No, you can't kill him," Queen said. "He has to stay alive. We're safe as long as he's alive."

"Meaning your branch of Army Intelligence?" Joe asked. "Then you may all start having to live on the edge." He took a step back from Queen. "I want an address, a map, and anything else I can use against Gallo." He picked up the robe on the floor and threw it to Queen. "Start moving."

"I have to go to my office downstairs." Queen shrugged into his robe. "I have a map we made of his compound about a year ago. At least what we knew about it. He's a secretive bastard."

"Now why would you want to go to that trouble?" Catherine said. "Planning a raid? Or were you going for extermination." She followed him as he left the bedroom. "I'd say a raid. Gallo must have something on you. You'd want to get in and make sure the evidence wasn't left carelessly about if something unforeseen happened to him." She glanced over her shoulder. Joe was going through the drawers on the nightstand. Smart move. Queen might want to keep anything of importance close to him. She followed Queen down the stairs. "What does he have on you?"

"Screw you. I'm giving you what you want. That's all you'll get from me." He turned on the light in the office. "I can still get out of this if I work it right. And who knows, Gallo may kill you."

"You can always hope." She watched him go over to the desk and unlock the drawers. "But you'd better hope Eve is still alive when we get there. Otherwise, Joe is going to explode, and no one may come out alive. He'll go nuts."

"Another one?" Queen asked sourly. "I'm used to dealing with nutsos after Gallo."

"Are you? Why deal with Gallo? Why not just lock him up and throw away the key?" She tilted her head.

"Oh, that's right; you did that, didn't you? But the North Koreans decided to keep that key."

"He volunteered," Queen said defensively. "He was a Ranger. He knew that going in on that mission was dangerous. He made the choice."

"He was there for a long time. You couldn't arrange a trade?"

"It wouldn't have been wise. If we'd acknowledged Gallo, then we'd have had to make awkward explanations."

"My God."

"Horrified?" His lip curled. "Why? You know how it works. You do what you have to do to get the job done."

Yes, Catherine knew, but this was nasty beyond belief. "But he escaped. Did you at least help?"

He didn't answer. "I have the map here." He pulled out a folded paper and pushed it across the desk. "And a few possible scenarios that we thought might work to take him down."

"Did you help him escape?" she repeated.

"It would have been too risky." He scowled. "He made out all right. After he reached the coast, he was picked up and taken to Tokyo. He had good medical attention."

"What kind of shape was he in?"

"Why are you asking? Why do you care? He's your target."

"You said he was crazy. If he's crazy, he's a threat to Eve. I have to know how crazy . . . and why. What will trigger him?"

"He was half-starved. He was in solitary for the first

two years. He was tortured. No permanent physical damage that the doctors could tell."

"Physical. Mental?"

"Hallucinations. Periods of total withdrawal. Nightmares. Episodes of uncontrollable rage. After six months, we convinced the doctors that he was well enough to be released into our custody."

"Why would you want to do that? Why not leave him in the hospital?"

"It wouldn't have been smart."

"Why not?"

"When he was delusional, he was . . . indiscreet. He raved like a lunatic. We couldn't afford for the Koreans to know about his mission. Washington would have been embarrassed."

"So you took him away from medical care. What did you do with him?"

"We put him back doing the work he'd been trained to do. He was a Ranger."

"As ill and irrational as you say he was?"

"He performed very well. We were surprised."

She was studying his expression. "You sent him out to get killed," she said softly. "He was an inconvenience, and you wanted him out of your path. Suicide missions."

"Ridiculous. He survived them, didn't he?"

She just looked at him.

"See how sympathetic you are when he has his knife to your throat," Queen said bitterly. "Or when you find Eve Duncan in a gully in those mountains."

"I'm not sympathetic." She crossed the room and

stuffed the map in her pocket. "I just get sick to my stomach with all of us sometimes."

"Do you have it?" Joe was standing behind her.

"Yes. I was about to get rid of him."

Queen stiffened.

"No, I'm not going to kill you." Catherine came around the desk. "As you said, it wouldn't be smart. We've all got to be practical and smart, don't we? Though I'd love to take you out. I have a hunch you caved too easily and are using us to do your dirty work. But I'll resist the temptation. Just can't let you cause us any trouble." She reached in her pocket and pulled out a hypodermic. "Fight me, and you'll end up with air in your bloodstream and a possible embolism. Otherwise, it's fourteen hours of sleep."

"Don't do this."

"Take your choice." She plunged the needle into his neck.

Two seconds later, Queen collapsed on the desk.

"You came prepared," Joe said.

"I usually am. My teacher, Hu Chang, always preferred potions to brute force." She looked down at Queen. "Though I might have preferred to use pain instead. Queen is a slimeball. What they did to Gallo was very ugly."

"Ask me if I care. Gallo has Eve."

She nodded. "And we have fourteen hours before we have to worry about Army Intelligence." She turned toward the door. "And a few hours will be taken up just getting to Utah. We'd better get moving. On the way to meet you, I contacted the pilot I used when we flew to

Russia. I thought we might need him. You remember Dorsey?"

He nodded. "How quick can he get here?"

"He was in Miami. He should be at Reagan National Airport by the time we drive there. Once we're on the plane, we'll look over Queen's map and suggested plans of entry and see which one we think will work."

"He caved quicker than I thought he would." Joe's tone was disappointed. "Too bad."

"He wanted to get away from dealing with Gallo." She moved toward the door. "And he was willing to get in hot water with his superiors to do it. They're handling Gallo with kid gloves. He's definitely got the upper hand. They're not about to help us."

"They don't have to help us." He opened the door of the car. "They just have to stay out of our way."

Someone was in the room.

Eve woke, her heart pounding, her gaze wildly searching the darkness.

"It's okay," John Gallo said. "You're safe. It's just me."

She could see him, only a dark shadow, sitting on the big chair by the window.

She drew a long breath and sat up in bed. "And that's supposed to give me a sense of security? What are you doing here?"

"Nothing carnal. Though it's natural that you should think of that. It was the bedrock of what we were together."

"Not anymore."

"I'm not as sure as you are. I still feel a stirring when I look at you. I don't know if it's memory or imagining how it would be now. But that's not why I'm here."

"I'm going to turn on the lamp."

"No, don't. The darkness is easier for me." He paused. "I'm naturally defensive, and I need to close everything out but what I'm going to say. Or I won't say it. Ask me about Bonnie."

Her every muscle stiffened. "Did you kill her?"

"I did not."

"Then what were you doing in Atlanta that month?"

"I wanted to see her."

"You knew about her? Your uncle Ted told you about Bonnie?"

"No, he died while I was in prison. If he wrote me, I never got the letters. I wish I could have been with him at the end. I loved him."

"There wouldn't have been letters. The Army reported you dead."

"I know. It was an exaggeration, but not much of one."

"How did you know about Bonnie?" she repeated. "How did you know I'd had your child?"

"I didn't know. I wasn't sure." He leaned back in the chair. "God, I'm sorry, Eve. I promised I'd protect you."

"I didn't let you. I was too full of my own independence and made a stupid mistake." She paused. "But it wasn't a mistake. Bonnie was . . . If I hadn't given life to her, that would have been the mistake. She was the happiest, most loving little girl I've ever known."

"But it wasn't easy for you."

"What difference does that make? She was here. I

had her with me for seven years. Do you know what a miracle that is?"

"Shit." He was suddenly across the room and kneeling on the floor by the bed. "No, I don't know anything about miracles. Or maybe I do." His voice was muffled against the bed. "Maybe you were a miracle, Eve. I was lost and you gave me . . . something. Yeah, it was sex, but I think maybe it was leading somewhere else. We were just afraid to follow it. So we lost it."

"And now it's too late."

"Is it? I guess it is. But it's not finished. I don't know if it will ever be finished. Not now. Not after Bonnie."

"John, you didn't even know Bonnie."

"Didn't I?" He laid his cheek on her hand lying on the bed. "After I was caught and thrown into that prison, it was like being smothered alive. I reached out and tried to think of anything that would take me out of there. I thought of my uncle and the good times we had. And I thought of you, Eve. Sexual daydreams? Sure, some of them. But not all of them. Sometimes it was like being in a cool, clean lake. Everything around me was hot and dirty and full of pain. But you were none of those things." He was silent for a long moment. "But as time passed, it got worse. They did things to me that made me—I couldn't hold on to Uncle Ted or you. I think I knew I was dying."

"John . . ."

"I'm not trying to make you feel sorry for me. I just have to tell you this. And you have to know it all. It was about three years after I was captured that I started to dream about Bonnie."

She froze in shock.

"You don't believe me. How could you? Okay, I dreamed about a little girl, red curly hair, hazel eyes. She was a toddler in the first dream. Happy, smiling . . . It made me feel . . . I don't know. But I could hold on to her. I didn't drift away. She saved me."

"How . . . often did you have that dream?" she asked unevenly.

"Every night, I think. Sometimes I didn't know whether it was night or day. I'd just close my eyes, and she'd be there. She seemed to get older . . . and she'd talk to me."

"About what?"

He shook his head. "Just things. Once she was starting school and was excited. Sometimes she'd sing me songs that she'd learned. One song she liked a lot. Something about all the pretty little horses. Other times she'd just sit and smile at me. I think she knew when I was too bad off to talk to her."

"All the Pretty Little Horses"? How often had Eve sung that song to Bonnie? Dear God, she had sung it to her the night before Bonnie was taken. She asked unsteadily, "And she told you her name was Bonnie?"

"No, after a while I just knew." He paused. "Just as I knew she was a part of you. And of me."

"Are you lying to me, John?" Her voice was shaking. "If you are, may you burn in hell."

"I was burning in hell. I knew I was going crazy.

The only thing that kept me sane was that little kid who sang and smiled and never once asked me one question about where I was or what was happening to me. Because she knew that I could never answer her."

She closed her eyes to keep back the tears. "When did the dreams stop?"

"About a month after I reached Tokyo. I was still in the hospital fighting fever and raving with delusions. Then she wasn't there any longer. I tried to tell myself that she was just part of the craziness. But I knew she was real. I'd heard of weird stuff happening in wartime. Wives visiting husbands at the front, telling them things . . . stuff like that. Astral projection they call it. But it wasn't like that. She was there, she was real. She was . . . mine. I got scared. I had to make sure that she wasn't a delusion, too. Because that would mean that I was truly insane. After they released me, I went back to Atlanta. You'd moved from the old housing development to a house on Morningside."

"Yes, I wanted Bonnie out of the projects."

"It was a pretty house, old, but pink geraniums were hanging from the front porch. I stayed across the street and watched until she came home from school. She was wearing a gold plaid top and jeans and some kind of sparkly fairy barrette to hold back her hair. You came out to the bus stop to meet her, and you took her hand. You smiled down at her, and I knew that you both were going to be all right. You were going to college, your mother was straightened out, and you loved that kid. You were going to have everything you ever wanted. You certainly didn't need me. I was sick and half-crazy, and I'd have been more of a burden than the child I'd given you."

"No, I didn't need you," she said unevenly. "But I wouldn't have sent you away."

"Pity?" He shook his head. "I couldn't have taken it. Besides, I had a place to go. Queen and his buddies had a dozen jobs waiting for me overseas." He added bitterly, "I was in demand. So I left Atlanta and didn't come back to the U.S. for over three years. You know what happened during those three years. She was kidnapped about a month after I saw her and I didn't even know until I'd returned to the country. Do you know how often I've wished that I'd gone up to you that day at Morningside? Maybe I could have done something, stopped it."

Eve could feel his pain, deep, ragged, vibrating in the darkness. "She disappeared right before our eyes," Eve said unsteadily. "One minute she was there, the next she was gone. Lost in the crowd at that park. Could you have done more than Sandra or me?"

"I don't know. Life's funny. Sometimes you move a piece, and everything changes. It's a question that has haunted me."

"It haunts all of us. It took me a long time, but now I accept that it's the man who killed her who is to blame, not me." Her hand reached out and gently touched his hair. "And not you, John."

"I haven't reached that point yet. I didn't protect you. I didn't protect her. That leaves me zero for two." He caught her hand and held it tightly. "When I came back and found out about Bonnie, it blew me away. I was still balanced on the edge and it threw me down into the pit. When I fought my way out, it still took me a long time to come back." His hand tightened. "I wanted to kill someone, but there wasn't anyone to kill. So I went looking."

"So did I."

"I know. You'd think one of us would have been able to find him in all these years." He paused. "But I think I'm coming close, Eve. I promise I'll get him for you."

She tensed. "Who? Tell me who."

"So that I can get you killed, too?" He shook his head. "I'm a great destroyer, Eve. But I'm not going to destroy you. I've done enough to you."

"Who is it? Black?"

His lips were warm as he brushed them against her palm, then gently put her hand back on the bed. "You took care of our Bonnie all those years." He got to his feet. "Let me do this for her now."

"The hell I will."

"Now that's the Eve I remember." He turned and moved toward the door. "The burn . . ."

He wasn't going to tell her. He was just going to leave her in turmoil and bewilderment. But there was one thing she had to know. "John."

He stopped as he opened the door, a dark shadow outlined by the lights from the hall.

"Did you . . ." She stopped, then went on. "I know you said that your dreams of Bonnie stopped in that Tokyo hospital. But later . . ." She had to get it out. "Did you ever . . . dream of Bonnie after she was taken?"

Silence. He stood there, his head bent.

"John."

"Yes," he said hoarsely.

The door shut behind him.

She closed her eyes as the tears slowly started to run down her cheeks.

Magical, the nurse had told Eve when she'd brought Bonnie to her at the hospital. And Eve had always known that Bonnie was special. She had not known how special until that moment. So many questions. How had Bonnie managed to reach out to save the father she had never known? She had never mentioned any dreams to Eve. Was that contact with him on a separate level? Had Bonnie even realized it herself in her daily life with Eve?

And Bonnie was still a presence in his life, still standing guard over John Gallo as she did with Eve.

She had reached out, comforting, loving, saving.

And Eve had never known it was happening.

"Bonnie," she whispered. "Why, baby?"

She huddled there, remembering John's words, his voice, the pain that had surrounded him and reached out and enveloped her. In the darkness, she had not been able to see a single expression, but she had known every emotion he was feeling and believed every word he spoke was true. It had created a bond with him enormously stronger than any she had known when she was that sixteen-year-old fighting her way out of the projects.

And that bond was Bonnie.

Catherine and Joe got out of their rental car in the foothills halfway up the mountain and Catherine spread the map on the hood of the vehicle.

"We can bypass this checkpoint." Catherine pointed to the square box drawn on the map. "If we go around the mountain route above the house. We'll still have to chance the guard just inside the gate, but it's better than having to do both." She traced the box to the side entrance. "Then we can get in here if we can disable the alarm."

Joe looked up at the huge redwood-and-glass house perched on the side of the mountain. "What time is it?"

"Four thirty-five. Queen won't wake up and be in a position to bother us for another three hours." She added, "Unless someone goes to his place looking for him. That's always a possibility." She was frowning down at the map. "I can take out the video cameras indicated on the map. But Queen wasn't sure the map was entirely accurate. If Gallo is as smart as they think he is, then he'd have some cameras well hidden. I wish we had time to do our own search." She held up her hand. "I know we don't. We have to get in and find Eve."

"If she's there. If Queen guessed right about Gallo's bringing her here." Joe was looking at the upper floor of the house. "Two bedrooms on the main floor near the garage area. They're small, maybe servants' quarters. Four bedrooms on the top level. Eve will probably be in one of them." I hope, Joe thought desperately. Who knew what the crazy son of a bitch would do with her? The clock was ticking, and he needed to find her. "Once we get inside, I'll take the bedrooms on the upper level. You check out the ones near the garage."

Catherine nodded. "And keep cool, Joe. I know

you're mad as hell. But Eve won't thank us if we kill Gallo when she thinks she can get information out of him."

"Ask me if I care." He was moving up the mountain. "I'll be careful because I want to keep Eve alive, but there's no way I'll stay cool. Gallo is going down."

The buzzer went off on the security pad on the nightstand in Gallo's bedroom.

South slope.

He reached over and activated the video camera. No picture.

His phone rang.

"I've got it, Hanks," he said when he picked up. "Any other alarms?"

"Not yet. Two cameras on the south slope have been disabled. They missed this one. We should have a visual when the courtyard C2 picks them up. They're pretty good, and I figure that they'll get C1 and take it out. But C2 is impossible to detect unless you know where to look. Shall I get a team to head up the slope and intercept?"

He thought about it. It could be that Queen had gotten impatient and was trying for a strike. But there was another possibility. "No, let them reach the courtyard. I'll make a decision then." He hung up and quickly dressed.

The buzzer sounded again. C2 camera.

He pressed the video. Two figures, dark clothes, moving swiftly. He zeroed in on them.

A woman, dark hair pulled back, slightly exotic features.

A man, tall, brown hair, dark eyes. He'd seen photos of that face. Joe Quinn.

The woman must be Catherine Ling.

Hanks phoned. "They're right on top of you. What do we do? Take them out?"

Dammit, I'm backed in a corner, Gallo thought. He couldn't risk Joe Quinn getting killed, and he couldn't even guarantee to control the situation once Quinn erupted on the scene.

"No, don't touch them. I'll call you back."

He had known that it might come to this when he had taken Eve, but he'd considered it worth it. What the hell. It might have been necessary anyway. The circle was closing.

He had to move fast. Quinn and Catherine Ling had gotten around most of the alarms with incredible speed and accuracy. They'd be in the house in no time.

He snatched the backpack he always kept ready from the closet and moved down the hall toward the guest room.

Eve sat up as he threw open the door. Her eyes were wide in her pale face. "What is it?"

"It's your Joe Quinn being superhero," he said. "I'd heard he was smart. I didn't realize he'd be able to move this fast."

"What do you mean? Where is he?"

"Pounding on the gates." He was crossing the room toward the bed. "I'll either have to kill him or bow out. I'm going to let him have the castle."

Her hands clenched on the cover. "I'm not going with you."

"I'm not asking you to come. I think we've said what had to be said." He reached in his pocket and handed her a key. "Milwaukee, Wisconsin. Queen may get desperate and aggressive once they realize I've gone. You may need ammunition."

She gazed at the key in her palm. "I don't understand."

"Blackmail." He turned and moved toward the door. "He'll understand even if you don't. If you don't need to use the leverage, save it for me. Believe me, I can use it." He reached in his pocket, pulled out her phone, and handed it to her. "Your property. You might try to intercept your Joe Quinn. I'll try to call Hanks off, but if they come together, there might be damage."

He moved quickly down the hall and down the stairs.

"John!" Eve had followed him and was standing at the top of the stairs. She was wearing one of Judy's sweatshirts, her red-brown hair was rumpled, her expression intense. She looked almost as young as she'd been when he'd first met her. "Dammit, I'm not going to let you go without telling me about Paul Black. Where is he? *Talk* to me."

"Sorry. No more time. You'll have to be satisfied." He opened the door to the basement and ran down the stairs.

She called after him. "How can you say that? I'm *not* satisfied." He went around the corner of the landing, and she was lost to view.

Check to see how close Quinn was to gaining entrance.

John punched the video button on the panel by the exit door that accessed the passage to the outside. He couldn't see Joe Quinn, but Catherine Ling was almost directly beneath the camera. She was working quickly to disable the house alarm. The expression on that beautiful, exotic face was intent, totally focused.

Suddenly she stopped and looked up.

He inhaled sharply.

She knew he was watching her.

What the hell? He knew she couldn't see that camera, but she still knew. Incredible instincts. Catherine Ling was remarkable. He'd be interested to explore those instincts.

Not now. No time.

He keyed in the exit code for the door, and it swung open. The next moment, he was closing and locking it behind him.

He pulled out his phone as he moved down the ramp that led to the outside passage.

CHAPTER

13

I think they know we're here." Catherine turned as Joe came around the side of the house. She clipped the final wire on the alarm. "We should get the hell out of this courtyard."

"Are you sure?"

"Yes." She shook her head. "No. But I'd lay odds I'm right."

"You go. Take the mountain road back down to the car. I'm going in."

"The alarms are off." Catherine moved toward the French doors across the veranda. "Divide and conquer. You take the kitchen door. Be careful."

"I'm not going to barge in with guns blazing," Joe said sarcastically. "And I'm not leaving here without Eve." He added curtly, "But I don't need you. Get out of here."

Catherine was bent over the locks on the French doors. "Shut up, Joe. I'm busy. I'll see you inside."

Joe didn't argue. He shrugged and hurried around the side of the house toward the kitchen door.

Catherine didn't like this.

It was too quiet.

Queen's map and plans had said there were no courtyard guards, but she had still expected it to be harder. Queen had been too wary of Gallo and Intelligence's own chance of infiltrating the compound. If it was this easy, why hadn't they tried their luck before?

The French doors swung open.

Darkness.

She drew her gun and threw herself into the room and to the side.

She waited.

Nothing.

But she could hear someone in the hall.

"Joe?" Eve's voice. "Joe, it's okay. He's not here."

Catherine rose to her feet. "Eve!"

Eve threw the door open. "John didn't mention you, Catherine. Are you okay? Where's Joe?"

"Here." Joe was standing in the doorway, a gun in his hand. "Where's Gallo?"

"I don't know. Gone. He knew you were coming." She moved across the room toward him. "How did you find out where I was?"

"Queen." His gaze was narrowed, moving around the hall. "Gone? You're certain?"

"He told me that he was leaving. He gave me back my phone and said to try to intercept you. I tried, but

I guess you had your phone off. He didn't want you hurt."

"I bet he didn't," Joe said bitterly. "And did he hurt you, Eve?"

She shook her head. "No, I was a little scared and uneasy at the beginning, but I'm—"

Joe had pulled her close and kissed her hard. "Thank God."

"He didn't mean to hurt me, Joe."

"The hell he didn't." Joe let her go. "He's nuts. Ask Queen."

"John's not crazy." She made a face. "Though he might deny that himself. Emotionally disturbed on some subjects? Yes. But he's not insane."

"He evidently managed to convince you," Joe said. "Let's see if he can convince me when I catch up with the bastard. We didn't see any vehicles leave the garage. How did he get away?"

She shook her head. "When he came to my room to tell me he was leaving, he had a backpack."

"And how long ago was that?" Catherine asked.

"Fifteen minutes? I'm not sure. I'd followed him when he was going downstairs and ran back upstairs to throw on some clothes. Then I came down to see if I could open the doors and try to locate you."

"And intercept me," Joe said tightly.

She looked at him. "Yes. Even if he wasn't here, he has guards on the property who might hurt you."

"Bill Hanks, head of his security," Catherine said. "Five others on the team. Besides the guards at the two checkpoints."

"Queen, again?" Eve asked.

Catherine nodded. "I think he was planning a major assault. He's not fond of John Gallo."

"John's not fond of him, either."

"You said you followed him downstairs. Where did he go?"

Eve pointed to the door at the end of the hall. "I think it leads to the basement."

Joe turned and headed for the door. "Stay with her, Catherine."

Eve sat down on the bottom step. "I'm fine. You don't have to guard me, Catherine. Go with him."

"It's easier to do what he says than to argue with him." Catherine smiled. "Unless I have a reason to argue. I don't right now. I'll just let Joe work off some of that steam and let you fill me in while he's not around."

Eve nodded. "I can tell that his steam is scalding hot." She frowned. "Dammit, it didn't have to be this bad. I tried to get John to let me contact Joe and tell him I was all right."

"I'm not sure that would have done much good. Joe would still have gone on the warpath."

"But you might not have had to come with him. I'm sorry, Catherine. I didn't intend to involve anyone but myself. John pulled the rug out from under me."

"Well, I am involved. I started all of this by trying to solve all your problems. You should sock me."

"I'll think about it." Eve grinned. "But I don't believe that an—"

"What are you doing sitting on the steps?" Judy was

coming down the hall, dressed in a navy robe and furry blue slippers. "For goodness' sake, you look like an orphan sitting there, Eve. Come along to the kitchen. I've made coffee and I have doughnuts. They're store bought, but they're pretty good." She turned to Catherine. "Who are you?"

"Catherine Ling. And you are?"

"Judy Clark," Eve said. "She cooks for John Gallo." She looked at Judy. "John's left the property, Judy. You don't have to wait on his guests any longer."

"Yes, I do. John just called me and told me to take care of you." She turned and moved down the hall. "So come on. I've told Bill Hanks to come to the house. John wants me to smooth the way and make sure there's no trouble."

"Why would he do that?" Catherine asked as she caught up with the cook.

"How do I know?" Judy said. "He doesn't usually mind causing his share of trouble. I just take orders." She opened the door to reveal a pristine, clean, bright kitchen. "Sit down. There's another one of you, isn't there?"

"Joe went down in the basement to see if he could track Gallo."

"John is long gone now. Pour your own coffee. I'll go after this Joe. I don't want him bumping into Hanks when I'm not around." She turned, and her furry slippers flopped as she hurried back down the hall.

"A character?" Catherine asked Eve.

"Maybe. But I think I like her." She poured coffee into two cups. "And evidently John trusts her."

"Then are we sure that she's not doping the coffee?"

"Trust you to think of that." She lifted her cup to her lips. "Though, as a matter of fact, getting doped was how I got here. John thought he would avoid complications."

"Gallo doped you?" Catherine looked at the cup in front of her. "Then I think I'll pass on this."

Eve couldn't blame her. "Then go make a pot of your own. But Judy will probably go on the attack for messing around her kitchen."

Catherine studied her. "You appear to be very at home here. Comfortable."

"Not comfortable. I'm just not afraid." She looked at Catherine over the rim of her cup. "John never intended to hurt me, Catherine. And he wouldn't have left if he'd wanted to hurt you or Joe. He was trying to avoid trouble."

"Then he shouldn't have kidnapped you and brought you here. Not a good way to avoid problems."

"I'm not defending him. He was arrogant and completely wrong."

"Then why does it sound that way?"

Because Eve was more confused and divided than she'd ever been in her life. She took a swallow of coffee. "He didn't kill Bonnie, Catherine."

"Because he told you he didn't? Queen thinks he's a split personality."

"From what I've heard about him, Queen may be a monster himself."

"I won't disagree with you. But he's one of the monsters I deal with every day. Gallo is apparently a different breed." Catherine picked up her cup. "Maybe I'll chance this stuff. It doesn't seem to have hurt you."

"I was the official food taster?"

She grinned. "Well, you were going to do it anyway." She sipped the coffee. "And maybe the dope is in the store-bought doughnuts."

Eve smiled back at her. "Then we'll skip them." Lord, she was glad that Catherine had come with Joe. She needed her to lighten the tension gripping her as she waited for the confrontation with Joe. "John didn't kill her, Catherine. I know it."

"You couldn't know it unless he'd prove it. Did he?"

A wild story about a little girl who sang songs to him in prison. "All the Pretty Little Horses." A wild story she believed with all her heart. "No, he didn't prove anything."

"You were very emotionally attached to him as a teenager. Could that have influenced you?"

"I keep telling you, it was no love affair." But it had turned into a love story for both of them. Though not for each other. A love story about Bonnie. "He didn't do it." She finished her coffee. "He's trying to find out who did kill her."

Catherine stared at her. "He told you that? Queen said he was very clever. Eve, he'd realize that was the most persuasive thing he could say that would make you believe he wasn't her killer. You'd identify with him immediately."

And Eve knew that was true. It didn't make any difference. "I believe him."

Catherine shook her head. "Look at it objectively

from my point of view, Joe's point of view. Gallo finds out that we're on his trail. He has a choice of going deeper undercover, killing you and everyone connected with you, or convincing you that he's not really the bad guy as you've been told. The first two choices are messy and would interfere with this nice life he's built for himself. So he looks for a way to get you away to himself and go for option three."

"He didn't kill her." Eve saw the impatience on Catherine's face, and added, "I know you think I'm being unreasonable. You're right. Reason has nothing to do with this. But he loved Bonnie, and he would never murder her."

"He couldn't have loved her. He didn't know her."

Eve couldn't explain without seeming even more irrational than Catherine thought her to be. She could only repeat. "He didn't kill her. If it will make you feel better, I'm not going to let him off with just accepting that as fact. There are so many things about this I don't understand, but I think he's way ahead of me in the search for Bonnie's murderer. I believe he knows who did kill her, and I'm going after him and make him tell me who it is."

"Or make him confess that he did it himself." She was frowning down at the coffee in her cup. "I don't like the setup, Eve. He swoops down and takes you away and hypnotizes you into thinking you have some kind of joint mission. The odds of his being able to do that are damn slim. He has to be a spellbinder. I knew when I was talking to Queen that Gallo was bigger than life.

Yeah, I was feeling sorry that he was a victim, but I don't feel sorry for him now."

"I'm not going to try to convince you." She stood up. "I'm going after Joe. I'm getting worried. He should have been back by now."

"Wait. I'll go with you."

"Finish your coffee." Eve was already at the door. "Judy said there was no way he could catch up with Gallo."

"She doesn't know Joe." She joined Eve as she reached the hall. "I wouldn't want him after me. He's a driven—" She broke off as Judy opened the basement door.

Joe was not with her.

Eve stiffened. "You didn't find him down there, Judy?"

She shook her head. "He found a hatchet among the tools down there and broke the lock on the exit door. There's a passage that leads underneath the courtyard and down the mountain. John always left a vehicle in the trees about a quarter mile down the path. Your Joe Quinn is somewhere in the passage or already on the mountain path." She paused. "I had to call Bill Hanks to go after him."

Eve's heart skipped a beat. "Why? You said John told you to make sure there was no conflict between them. You're putting them in a hunt-and-chase position. That's asking for trouble."

Judy shrugged. "He was going after John. I couldn't run the risk of him catching him. I told Hanks to try to be careful. But nothing is going to happen to John." She looked Eve straight in the eye. "You have your priorities, I have mine. Too bad if your Joe Quinn gets hurt. If he'd stayed here, he would have been fine."

It was all very simple for Judy, Eve realized. If John Gallo was threatened, then Judy would cause the sky to fall to get him out of trouble. She wouldn't care who else was hurt. Eve started for the basement door. "You get on the phone and get Hanks off Joe's trail."

"Where you going?" Judy asked warily.

"I'm going to find Joe. If you want to obey John's orders to keep me safe, you'd better make sure Hanks backs off because I'm going to be with Joe."

"No." Judy took an impulsive step toward her. "You can't get in—"

"But she can," Catherine said softly. She gave Judy a look that stopped her in her tracks. "And you'd better back off, too, and do what she says." She was following Eve down the basement stairs. "Then you can go to your cozy little kitchen, have one of your dandy 'store-bought' doughnuts, and wait for the flak to settle."

Tire tracks.

Joe dropped to his knees and examined the marks to the side of the trail. Fresh tracks. The driver was in a hurry. He had peeled onto the road. Heavy truck or van, probably an off-road vehicle.

How fresh? He listened, tuning out the night sounds. The sound of an engine, faint but . . .

Yes.

And that driver had to be John Gallo.

He felt a rush of fierce satisfaction.

He jumped to his feet and scrambled up on the shoulder of the slope, drawing his gun. Damn I wish I had my rifle. But his Beretta had a fairly long range for a handgun. It might be enough if he could get close enough to shoot out one of the back tires.

He ran to the top of the incline.

A Jeep Cherokee, descending the twisting mountain road, was coming into view around the curve a short distance below him. Not short enough for Joe. Gallo would have to come around the next curve at an angle closer to where Joe stood for him to use the Beretta.

That meant Joe had to get at least fifty feet down the mountain to reach that next twisting level of the road.

He threw himself off road. He skidded down the loosely packed rocks of the slope, falling, picking himself up, and skidding again.

Twenty feet.

He slipped and rolled down the incline until he was stopped by some low shrubs.

He caught his breath and jumped up.

Ten more feet.

Not as slippery as the incline above. No falls.

He was there.

And Gallo was coming around the curve only twenty feet below him!

He *had* him.

Go slow. He had maybe a minute until Gallo was out of sight again. The shot had to be right. He aimed carefully at the right-rear tire.

He started to squeeze the trigger.

Pain.

His arm jerked as a bullet tore through his forearm!

Shit.

Not from Gallo.

The shot had come from above.

Rage tore through him as he saw Gallo disappear around the curve.

Another shot. Grazing his ear. He had to get out from the middle of the road and into the pine trees on the slope.

He glanced up the mountain as he dove into the trees.

Two men. One short, thin, the other taller and burly. They were separating, fading into the trees on the slope, and coming down the mountain after him.

Good.

He was bleeding. He took off his shirt, tore it in two, and wrapped one piece tightly around his forearm. Now forget it and go on the hunt.

Where was the bastard? Hanks wondered. He knew he'd hit him with that first bullet.

Hanks's phone vibrated.

"He's disappeared," Brock whispered. "Dammit, Hanks, I've searched this slope, and he's not here. Did you see him? Maybe he's unconscious or something and fell off the slope."

"No, keep looking." He was uneasy. Quinn was more than they'd bargained for. He'd been seconds away from putting a bullet into Gallo's Jeep, and now they couldn't locate him. "I saw him go into those trees, and he's wounded. He can't be moving fast."

"All I can say is that I haven't seen him, I haven't heard him and I'm damn spooked about— Shit!"

Hanks stiffened. "Brock? Are you—"

The sound of metal on shale. Brock's phone dropping? He didn't know, but he'd better get over there.

Fast.

When he reached him, Brock was lying crumpled on the ground.

Dead? No time to check. Hanks moved into the trees, his gaze searching the darkness.

"Quinn," he called. "This isn't necessary. We don't want to kill you. We had orders to stop you, and we did it. Give up, and we'll talk. That's all I—"

Quinn dropped down from the trees, knocking him to the ground.

Hanks struggled desperately beneath Quinn's weight, trying to position his gun to fire.

"No way." Quinn's left arm was around his neck, jerking his head back. "Now we'll talk." His voice was low, fierce. "Tell me where Gallo was heading."

"I don't know."

"That's not the answer I want to hear. I'll give you thirty seconds, then I'll break your neck."

"I don't know. John never told—"

"Fifteen seconds." Joe jerked Hanks's head back farther and angled it. "I'm pissed. Can you tell? I'm not—"

"Let him go, Joe." Eve Duncan came into his line of sight. "You don't want to do this."

"The hell I don't."

"Then I don't want you to do this," she said. "Everything is crazy, but I don't want more violence added to the pot." She suddenly saw the bloody shirt wrapped around Joe's arm. "And you're hurt, dammit."

"Let him go." Catherine stepped out of the shadows, her gun aimed at Hanks. "I'll take care of it. He won't be a problem."

Joe hesitated, then reluctantly released Hanks's neck. "He's already been a problem." He got off Hanks. "I would have been able to stop Gallo if he hadn't interfered. I had that Jeep in my sights."

"And John's Jeep might have gone off the road and tumbled down to the valley," Hanks said as he sat up and scooted quickly away from Joe.

"I was aiming at the right tire. Gallo could have controlled the Jeep if he didn't lose his head. I didn't want him dead . . . yet." He turned to Catherine. "You said you'd take care of him. Get him out of my sight. My arm's hurting like hell, and I want to make him hurt, too."

Catherine gestured with the gun. "Move, Hanks. I need to get you away from here."

Hanks didn't move. "Did you kill Brock, Quinn?"

"Brock?" Joe gave him a cold glance. "He's the other one with you? No, I had to work quickly, and I didn't want to shoot and give away my position. He'll be waking up soon."

Hanks felt a rush of relief. He had had an idea that they had barely tapped the skilled savagery in Quinn, and they'd been lucky. Damn lucky. "Then I want to take him back with me."

"You're pushing your luck, Hanks," Joe said. "Get out of here."

Eve was standing next to Quinn. "You should be the one getting out of here. I need to take a look at that wound as soon as we get back to the house."

Joe nodded absently, his gaze still on Hanks. "Don't let him go anywhere until I can talk to him, Catherine. He might know where Gallo was going."

"I don't have any idea," Hanks said roughly. "Do you think John would tell me? Not likely. Not that I'd tell you if he did."

"Go," Catherine said. "You're being stupid, and I'm through with dealing with stupid, macho men tonight."

Hanks hesitated, then strode up the path.

"How bad is it?" Eve asked, as Catherine and Hanks disappeared in the trees.

"I could function," Joe said. "Probably not too bad."

But he wasn't sure, Eve thought, and she'd seen Joe close out pain and focus efficiently many times before. It was part of the discipline and experience of his SEAL training.

And the instinct of the warrior in battle. "Is it still bleeding?"

He impatiently shook his head. "Stop fussing. I need to get back to the house and search it. We may be able to find something there that will lead us to Gallo."

"I'm not fussing." She felt a ripple of irritation that overcame the concern and worry she had been feeling. "By all means, let's go back and search. I want to find Gallo as much as you do."

He shook his head. "No you don't."

"You listen to me, Joe," Eve said fiercely. "No one wants to talk to Gallo more than I do. I know nothing about Paul Black, and John seems to be the only one who can tell me anything about him. I might have had a chance of persuading him to talk to me, but you put him on the run. Do you think I won't do anything on earth to find him and make him tell me everything he knows? Bill Hanks isn't going to be able to help. He as much as told me when I first met him that John didn't often confide in him. And Hanks preferred not to know."

"He could have been lying."

"I don't believe he was." She took his elbow and nudged him forward. "You and Catherine are both working and analyzing this as if it were an objective problem. Well, I'm not objective. So you do your thing, and I'll do mine. But don't expect me to approve when you go running down a mountain and get yourself shot and then—" She drew a deep breath. "To hell with it. Let's get back to the house and take care of your arm."

Jacobs was scared, Nate Queen realized, as he held the phone a few inches away and listened to the spate of curses and questions. He should have expected it. Thomas Jacobs always fell apart when the going got tough. Queen sometimes wondered why he still kept Jacobs on as a minor partner instead of ridding himself of the coward. But Jacobs had been with him a long time, even at the initial recruitment of Gallo. He knew more than was comfortable for Queen. Besides, he was willing to set up all the little deals with which Queen didn't want to bother.

"I know all that," Queen said. "I didn't handle it well. But are you telling me you would have been able to handle Catherine Ling and Quinn? They were nasty as hell, and there was no way I was going to end up dead."

"Of course not. But there should have been a way to stop them."

"It's done. I only told them what I had to tell them."

"You said you gave them the map." Jacobs paused. "What are the chances they'll get into the compound?"

"I wouldn't bet against them. They disabled my security system, and it's fairly sophisticated. They're both tops in their fields, and they work well together. After they get in, it's a different proposition. They'll have to deal with Gallo."

"But you said Quinn is lethal. That could be a problem. We can't afford to have Gallo dead before we get our hands on the ledger."

"I'm sending a team to Utah to move into the compound if we hear Gallo has been killed."

"It may not even be in the compound. Gallo warned us it would go straight to the *Washington Post* if you moved against him. It may be in a damn lawyer's office somewhere. You blundered big-time, Queen."

The prick. He was getting pissed. "How was I to know that he'd go after Eve Duncan after all these years? He kept talking about Ling. Who the hell could tell what he was thinking? Ling is CIA. Duncan was no threat."

"Then why did he take her?" Jacobs was silent, thinking. "Was it to frighten her into keeping silent that he was still alive and might be a suspect? Or was it something else? As you say, he's unstable. Who knows what's going on in his head?"

"Frighten? Gallo doesn't bluff. She may be dead by the time Quinn gets to her. Serve the bastard right."

"And if she is dead, we'll have to do a cleanup for Gallo. You'd better hope that she's still alive. So what do we do?"

"We find out what's going on in the compound. Who's our man on the payroll there?"

"Lon Davarak. He's a perimeter guard. It's as close as we could get to Gallo. Hanks is damn careful of the guards for the house."

"Then call Davarak and get him to scout around and see if he can find out what the hell is happening." He was silent again. "Eve Duncan . . ."

"What are you thinking?"

"He had a kid with Eve Duncan. When he made no attempt to approach her after Korea, we assumed that she was nothing to him, just a good lay. Even the reports on her he demanded could have been just to protect himself." He paused again. "But we know he's emotionally disturbed. What if those emotions are focused on Eve Duncan? It could be an Achilles' heel."

"I don't think so. He's not vulnerable in that way. He's cold as ice."

"You have no imagination. We have to accept that Gallo's temperament can change like a weather vane and take advantage of it."

"And how are we supposed to do that?"

"Why, if Gallo hasn't already cut her throat, we might do well to look deeper into the possibility of Eve Duncan."

Judy was in the study, emptying the contents of desk drawers into boxes, when Eve and Joe came into the house.

"What are you doing?" Joe asked.

"What I've been told to do." Judy glanced at his blood-soaked arm. "Got yourself hurt, didn't you? It wasn't Hanks's fault. He was only protecting John."

"Where are Catherine and Hanks?" Eve asked.

"In the living room. She tried to stop me from packing up, but I told her she'd have to shoot me. I do my job, and Gallo told me he wanted these out of the house before those military guys decided they'd come calling." She straightened her gaze on Joe's arm as she added grudgingly, "But I guess I could bandage that up for you first. There's a first-aid kit in the kitchen cabinet."

"I'm going to do it." Eve's eyes were on the boxes. "Why doesn't he want Queen to see those records?"

"We'll see for ourselves," Joe said. "And the only

thing in which I'm interested is Gallo's name and address."

"The only names and addresses you'd find are banks and account numbers," Judy said. "John spread his funds in banks all around the world. He said that as long as Queen and his buddies didn't know where it was, they couldn't find a way to confiscate it." She looked him in the eye. "I'll let you take a look if you don't believe me. I don't think you'd tell Queen anything about the banks. You want John, not the money." She turned away. "I've got to finish up here. John said that if they found out that he'd gone on the run, Queen would move in quick." She glanced at Eve. "And to tell you that you should watch out for them."

"*I'll* watch out for them," Joe said grimly. "And John Gallo."

"Come into the kitchen and let me clean that arm," Eve said. "You can go through those boxes after I make sure that wound's taken care of." She suddenly turned back to Judy. "You talk as if John's been preparing to go on the run for a long time. Why? And why now?"

She shrugged. "I just know that he told me right after I came to work for him that there was a good chance that it would happen. He told me what to do. I'm doing it." Her lips tightened. "He told me to take care of Hanks, too. If you hadn't gone running after John, this would never have happened. Are you going to have Hanks thrown in jail?"

"Maybe. It depends on what he can tell me."

Judy shook her head. "He's a good man. You shouldn't

have—" She stopped and opened another drawer. "Talk to him, Eve. It's your responsibility. This wouldn't have happened if you hadn't come here."

"She hardly had a choice," Joe said dryly.

"I don't know anything about that," Judy said. "But John didn't hurt her, did he? Everything's okay."

"Come on, Joe." Eve knew she'd better get him out of there before Judy's simplistic approach to the situation made it infinitely worse. "And a wounded arm isn't exactly okay, Judy," she said as she drew Joe out of the room.

"The place seems to be reeking of Gallo's fans," Joe said sarcastically. "Everything he does is just fine as long as no one is dead."

Eve pushed him down in a kitchen chair. "You didn't hear that from me. I'm a Joe Quinn fan."

"Are you?" He watched her unwind the bloody shirt from around his arm. "That's nice."

"Are you being sarcastic?" She examined the wound. "It's a flesh wound, but it's not pretty. I'll clean it up as best I can, but I want a doctor to give you an antibiotic." She went to the sink, filled a bowl of water, then searched for and found the first-aid kit. "We'll get out of here as soon as we can and find a hospital."

"After I take a look at the documents in those boxes," Joe said. "Though I'm not sure it will do me any good. Gallo's cook-slash-majordomo was being very careless about throwing everything in those drawers into the to-go stacks. No selectivity. She may have been telling the truth." His gaze was on Eve's fingers as she carefully washed the wound. "But money is important to most people. Maybe I can use those records as bait for Gallo."

She opened the first-aid kit. "No."

His gaze lifted to her face. "You object?"

"I'm just telling you it wouldn't work. It would hurt him, but it wouldn't bring him back."

His eyes narrowed. "How do you know? Have you become an expert on Gallo in such a short time?"

"He has a purpose. He wouldn't let himself be distracted." She put antiseptic on the wound and flinched as he inhaled sharply. "Sorry."

"It doesn't matter." His gaze was on her face. "What purpose, Eve?"

She was silent as she began to wrap the wound.

"Eve."

"You won't believe me any more than Catherine did."

"What purpose?"

"He's trying to find Bonnie's killer," she said quietly.

Joe began to curse beneath his breath. "He gave you that bull, and you—"

"There are two cars coming up the mountain." Catherine was standing in the doorway. "Hanks got a call on his phone from one of the perimeter guards, and I let him take it. Hanks thinks it may be MI. He said Gallo warned him to expect a call from Army Intelligence if anything disrupted the status quo." Her lips twisted. "I think we may constitute a disruption. They may not know Gallo has flown the coop, but they must know we're here and are using it as an excuse to invade the property."

"Queen."

Catherine nodded. "That's my bet. He's sent out the troops." She looked at Joe. "So what do we do? Stand our ground and take whatever they want to throw at us? Or take off and avoid the confrontation until we're on our own turf?"

"How much time do we have?" Joe asked.

"Hanks says ten minutes." She paused. "He said Gallo told him it wouldn't be pretty. There would be interrogations. He gave him orders to take off and have everyone at the compound spread to the four winds."

Joe thought about it. "Where is Hanks now?"

"Living room. I left him tied up." She paused. "I talked to him, Joe. I believe him when he said he wasn't trying to kill you. He was just trying to do his job and protect Gallo."

"He may know where Gallo is."

She shook her head. "He might, but I don't think so."

Joe glanced at Eve. "Do you know where he is?"

Her eyes widened. "No, I do *not*."

He shrugged. "It was a possibility." He pushed back the chair. "Let Hanks go. Tell him to get the hell out of here and take Judy and anyone else in the house with him. We'll take that passage back down the mountain and circle down to where we parked the car." He stood up. "You get Eve down the mountain, Catherine. I'm going to go take a quick look at those records in the library, and I'll follow."

"Right." Catherine turned on her heel and hurried out of the kitchen.

Eve hesitated. She didn't want to leave him. Joe was

on edge and still in battle mode. There had already been one violent encounter tonight, and she wanted him away and safe.

"Get going, Eve." Joe didn't look at her as he strode out of the kitchen. Anger, frustration, and tension were in every line of his body. And who could blame him?

And she could do nothing about it now but trust that he'd control the impulse to let loose an emotional flood.

She turned and moved out of the kitchen in search of Catherine.

CHAPTER

14

"The place is deserted, Colonel Queen," Lieutenant Sagalin said. "The house was lit up like a Christmas tree. Hot coffee in the kitchen, the office looked like a tornado had hit it. But no one is around."

"No sign of Gallo? Or Eve Duncan?"

"A woman's jeans and shirt in the bathroom of one of the upper bedrooms. Gallo's clothes were in his bedroom. Our informant said that Gallo took off before Catherine Ling and Joe Quinn got here."

Queen's hand tightened on the phone. What the hell? He hadn't expected Gallo to go on the run. If anything, he'd expected his men to find Quinn's and Ling's bodies, along with Eve Duncan's in the house. Why had Gallo run?

Paul Black? Black had had time to get there from San Francisco. Queen knew how terrifying he could be. Yes, that might be it. Perhaps Gallo wasn't as invulnerable as

Queen had thought. He felt a rush of relief. Black had made his choice, and that choice wasn't Queen.

And if Gallo had gone on the run, there was no chance that he would have left the ledger at the house. He would have taken it with him. He could only hope that Black was on Gallo's trail.

"What do we do now?"

It was probably too late to do more than cover all the bases. "Go to the library and take every file you find and load the computers in your vans and bring them back here."

"Anything else?"

Queen had a sudden memory of Gallo sitting in that luxurious library, taunting him. He'd acted like some kind of snooty English lord of the manor instead of the vicious, murdering bastard Queen knew him to be. And Queen had been forced to listen and choke on his fury.

But the situation had changed, and that meant the rules had changed. Screw Gallo.

"Burn the damn house down to the ground."

Joe, Eve, and Catherine had reached their car and were on their way down the mountain when Catherine looked up at the rearview mirror. "My God."

Eve glanced at the mirror, then quickly over her shoulder. Gallo's beautiful mountain house was burning, the flames licking the surrounding trees and leaping for the sky. "Why?" she whispered. "It was such a lovely house."

"Frustration," Joe said. "Revenge. It was evident that Queen hates Gallo."

Yet it seemed strange to Eve that Gallo, who had been the clear victim of Army Intelligence, would be so hated. "They wanted to hurt him. I wonder what they would have done if they'd found Hanks or Judy in that house."

"Queen isn't stupid. He'd be careful of any move that might draw attention."

Eve shook her head. "And that fire doesn't draw attention?"

"They'd find a way to do it so that it looked like an accident," Catherine said. "It's not difficult."

And Catherine would be adept in those methods of destruction, Eve knew.

"You're upset." Joe's gaze was on her face. "It's just a house, Eve."

"No, it was a home. I think it meant something to John. He told me he'd had it for ten years. How would you feel if someone burned down the lake cottage?"

"Mad as hell."

"And I'd be sad."

"And you think Gallo would feel as you do. You're identifying with him."

She shrugged. "I think it would mean something to him. I think he's been hurt enough."

"You'll forgive me if I'm a little lacking in sympathy. I went through hell imagining everything he could be doing to you. I can't identify with him at all."

That was very clear. The entire situation was complicated and barbed with emotion on both their sides.

"I'm not saying it wasn't wrong of him to do what he did. I'm saying that what he went through may have contributed to his making the mistake." She changed the subject. "Where's the plane waiting, Catherine?"

"At a private airport about thirty miles from here," Catherine said. "You should be back in Georgia in about four hours."

"That's good." She leaned back in the seat, her gaze once more on the flaming ruin in the rearview mirror. So much ugliness and destruction. It was beginning to touch everyone and everything around her. Tonight, Joe had been wounded, and it might have been horribly more serious.

And it had been her fault that he had been hurt. He had come to the rescue as he always did, as he would always do. Because Eve would not stop, could not stop, as long as Bonnie and her killer were out there.

And someday Joe's selfless giving would end tragically. It was only a matter of time.

She could feel the tears sting her eyes as her every emotion vibrated in rejection of that thought.

No.

She couldn't let it happen.

Paul Black stood on the north slope and gazed at the flaming fury of the burning house.

Pity. It had been a nice house, and now Black would have no chance to go in and search it. It appeared that Queen, as usual, had been ruled by his emotions and not his head when he'd given the order to put it to the torch.

It annoyed him that Queen was getting in his way even before the hunt had begun.

He leaned back against a tree and watched Queen's errand boys get into their trucks and start down the mountain. He was no longer in any hurry. He had missed Gallo but had watched all the other people pour out of the house. He had license numbers and photos of all of them. He'd e-mail them to Queen and have him identify them. Then he'd carefully choose who was to receive his attention.

Find a mate, find a cub, find a bait so succulent it was impossible to resist. There was always a way to trap the prey. Like the prey Black had just devoured. Pretty little Daniele, who had followed him from the airport as if he was the Pied Piper once he'd offered her the right bait.

The flames were burning hotter now. He felt as if he could feel them from where he watched. He liked fire. Everyone spoke of the fires of hell, and he had always thought he would have no problem there. If there was a hell, he was sure he would become the archdemon and rule it. If there was no hell, perhaps a man like him could live forever. Sometimes after a kill like tonight's he felt as if he could take enough lives that they would give him the power he needed to carry on.

He should go soon. There would be police and firemen coming to put out the fire. But perhaps he would take a few more minutes to enjoy it. As he stared at the yellow-orange flames, he thought he could see the faces of all the prey he had taken through his life like a giant kaleidoscope, moving in and out in a blurring haze. He could not make out all the distinctive faces, but he recognized the Samoan teenager he had gutted only last week. And of course, little Daniele from the airport. She was still fresh in his memory.

But the power she had given him was already fading, and the hunger was beginning anew. He needed a new kill, a strong kill.

Gallo?

Yes, Gallo would be strong.

Or perhaps, if Black was lucky, the road to Gallo would be paved with a river of blood.

"How about a coffee?" Catherine asked Eve as she unbuckled her seat belt after the plane had gained altitude. "I could use one. The adrenaline has seeped out of me, and I need a replacement."

"No, thanks." Eve was looking out the window. "I might try to sleep."

"Whatever." Catherine moved down the aisle to the coffee bar in the front of the plane. She had just poured coffee into the Styrofoam cup when Joe came out of the cockpit. She handed him the cup and reached for another for herself. "You don't look like you want to sleep, either. How's the arm?"

"Throbbing." His gaze went to Eve. "She okay?"

"She's very quiet, Joe." Catherine poured herself coffee. "But I can't blame her. We're not on her wavelength right now. All she would get would be an argument, and after what she's been through, that's not what she needs."

"He has her hypnotized," he said grimly.

"No one hypnotizes Eve," Catherine said flatly. "But I agree he must be clever as hell. He's managed to tap into the one passion that could blind her to everything else."

"Bonnie?" His lips tightened. "But maybe there could be another passion just as strong. She told me that she was different when she knew Gallo."

Jealousy. Catherine had been afraid that demon would raise its head. Joe was one of the most confident men she had ever met, but an all-consuming passion like the one he had for Eve would have primitive roots. "But she's grown up; that girl doesn't exist any longer. No, it's only Bonnie you have to worry about."

"Only Bonnie." Joe lifted his cup to his lips. "That's like saying only a Cat 5 tornado." He leaned back against the cockpit door. "And if he's using Bonnie, then I need to move fast. I have to find him before he contacts Eve again."

"Maybe he won't contact her. He left her when he knew we were coming."

"Which was the smartest thing he could have done. He put himself in the position of avoiding confrontation and hurting people she loved. Now, by running away, he's also lost his home, friends, and way of life. And Eve is feeling sorry for him, dammit. How the hell can I fight that?"

She smiled. "You'll manage. You're already thinking about it. What are you going to do?"

"Go after Hanks. I had to let him go, but he'll be easier to find than Gallo. I've just been on the phone with a friend in the Bureau and asked him to e-mail me a dossier and any records of Hanks's relationship with a John Gallo."

"Hanks said he didn't know where Gallo is."

"Even if it's true, he's been with Gallo for years. I might be able to trace, connect, and reach a possible destination."

"I'd think Judy Clark would be a better source."

"Then you go in that direction. She's very loyal and fierce about Gallo. I'd rather deal with Hanks."

Catherine smiled and nodded. "A regular pepper pot."

"He seems to have a way with the ladies," Joe said dryly.

"Judy didn't impress me as being able to be swayed by charm. Neither is Eve. It could be they're seeing something there that we can't."

He finished his coffee and threw the cup in the waste container. "You'll have to tell me whether they're right when you meet him." He started down the aisle toward Eve.

Catherine watched him sit down beside Eve and fasten his seat belt. Eve smiled slightly, then looked back out the window, where the purple clouds were being touched with the gold of dawn.

Yes, Eve was definitely quiet and a little remote, Catherine thought. Eve was thinking, weighing, and feeling very much alone.

That could be dangerous.

When they reached Atlanta, Catherine walked Eve and Joe to their rental car before getting back on the jet to be flown home to Kentucky. She fell back with Eve as Joe went around the car to get into the driver's seat.

"If you need me, call me," she said quietly. "I'm here for you no matter what. I may argue with you, but in the end I'll do whatever you want me to do. That's what friends are all about. Don't close me out."

"I know you and Joe want the best for me."

"You're thinking of us as a team. We worked together because it was necessary." She made a face. "And because a lot of the time we think alike. But we're not joined at the hip. Remember that, Eve."

"I will." She opened the passenger door. "Have a good trip home, Catherine."

"I'll be placing a few calls to Venable and seeing if I can get a handle on where to find Hanks and Judy Clark." She gave Eve a hug and looked at Joe as he started the car. "Take care of that arm, Joe."

"Right, say hello to Luke for me."

"If I can tear him away from the *Lost Cities of the Ancient World*. Since he found that book, he's been glued to it." She stepped back. "I think he may be planning on finding a couple of them. Luke is so independent, it wouldn't surprise me if he got a plan together and took off on his own. But I'm going to work at it and make sure he includes me in that expedition. That may be my chance at bonding." She turned back to the plane. "I'll call you if I find out anything from Venable."

Eve watched her as Catherine climbed the steps and boarded. Then she glanced at Joe. "She's already in work mode again."

Joe shrugged. "She's CIA. And she has a personal interest. I'm glad to have her on board."

She smiled faintly. "Because you think alike."

"Yeah." He drove out of the airport lot onto the street. "With some exceptions. She's more inclined to giving the benefit of the doubt."

He was talking about John Gallo.

She didn't answer. It was difficult defending John, and she was too tired and drained to make the attempt.

She turned away and watched the skyscrapers and domes of the great city flow by the window.

"Why don't you take a nap?" Joe asked Eve as he unlocked the door of the cottage. "You didn't sleep on the plane at all."

"I tried." Eve looked at the blue-and-white notice she'd taken off the door. "FedEx tried to deliver my skull from Texas. I'll have to call them and tell them to redeliver." It seemed such a long time ago when she'd waited out on the porch for that delivery. She put the notice on the kitchen bar. "You didn't stop at a hospital to have that wound looked at."

"I'll do it on the way to the precinct."

"You're going in to work?"

His brows lifted. "I do have a job."

She gave him the ghost of a smile. "When I don't interfere with it."

"You could hardly help it in this case, could you? I'll shower and change and be out of here." He went past her down the hall.

She went back out on the porch and sat down on the swing. She would try to sleep in a little while, but she was too wired right now. She would sit here and let the peace of this familiar, beautiful place sink in and quiet her spirit.

Had Gallo gotten in the habit of going back to his place in the mountains for the same reason? To heal wounds and quiet his soul after the storms of life? But he no longer had a place to go for sanctuary now.

And she was identifying with him again. She mustn't do that if she was to get what she wanted from him. Joe thought Gallo was the enemy, and perhaps that was true. But not for the reason that Joe feared.

She set the swing gently rocking, watching the morning breeze stir the tops of the trees.

Help me, Bonnie. I don't know what to do. Everything is more of a mystery than I dreamed. I believed him, but is it true? If it's not a lie, did you come to love him? And if you loved him, does that mean I have to help him? You healed his wounds and kept him sane. Is that what you want from me?

No answer.

No sudden wonderful, loving vision of her daughter to give her any of those answers.

Of course not.

Bonnie never came on demand, dammit. That would be too easy.

So work it out for yourself, Eve thought. That's what life is all about. No easy answers.

"What are you thinking?" Joe stood in the doorway, looking at her. "You're frowning."

She forced a smile. "I was thinking that there are no easy answers. And that I was ready for a lightning bolt to flash down and illuminate all the darkness."

"But that would be an easy answer." Joe moved over to the swing and stood looking down at her. "Did I ever tell you how beautiful you look with the sunlight on you?"

"You're blind. I've got to have circles under my eyes, and my hair looks like a haystack."

"It doesn't matter. You glow from inside out. And then the sun touches you, and it shows how your eyes shimmer with life and every character line."

"Those are called wrinkles, Joe."

"Those are called beautiful." He bent down and gently brushed her lips. "Trust me."

Lord, she loved him. She pulled him down and held him close. "Why are you saying this? Why now?"

"Because I looked at you, and I remembered that, no matter how many problems we have, it would be worse being apart," he said gruffly. "I can't be easy. It's not my nature. But it's my nature to love you." He kissed her quick and hard and released her. "That's all. Remember that when I'm being a surly son of a bitch and out to hold on to you through hell and high water." He turned and ran down the porch steps. "Go to bed and try to get at least a little sleep before you call FedEx to bring back that skull. You don't need to dive into work without any rest. I'll call you later and bring home dinner."

She watched him get into the car and back out of the driveway.

No, he'd never be easy. Joe was brilliant, complicated, and wary. He made friends with extreme caution and kept them forever. Dear God, how lucky she'd been that he loved her and wanted to keep her in that same golden circle.

Joe's car turned the curve in the road and disappeared from view.

As a golden circle could be broken, as a life could so easily be lost.

Joe . . .

The key John had given her. Why hadn't she told Joe and Catherine about it? At first, it had slipped her mind, but later it had been a conscious decision. But why had she made that decision?

She took out the cell phone that John Gallo had handed back to her in that bedroom. He had said that it was to communicate with Joe, but had he really meant that to be the purpose? She had come to realize that nothing about John was clear and absolutely straightforward. He had abandoned her to Joe and Catherine tonight, but wasn't that the best way to avoid the complications he had been trying to skirt?

And then he had given her back her phone. Had he also given her a choice?

She slowly scrolled back to John Gallo's call the first day that he had phoned her.

Choice?

She wasn't prepared to make that choice yet. She was tired and emotionally drained. She had to give herself time to think and make sure she wasn't going to stampede herself into doing something as impulsive as that sixteen-year-old kid she had been might have done.

She started to put the phone back in her pocket, then stopped and dialed the number of FedEx. She would have the skull delivered as soon as possible and start work.

Doing the reconstruction would remind her of who she was and how far she had come from that girl in the Peabody Housing Development.

Joe didn't come home until almost midnight. He'd called her late in the afternoon and told her he was going to have to work late on a murder case in Vinings.

He quietly slipped into bed. "Awake?" he whispered.

"Yes." She yawned and cuddled closer. "I was working."

"I saw the reconstruction on your worktable. I told you to take a nap."

"I wanted to work. I didn't do much. Only started the measurements."

"Have you named him yet?"

"Dale."

"Do you want to talk about him?" His hand was stroking her hair.

"Dale?"

"John Gallo."

"No. Unless you want me to talk about him."

He didn't answer for a moment. "Not right now. But we're going to have to do it. You're behaving . . . I don't know." He pulled her tighter. "But I don't like it."

She didn't like it, either. She didn't like the fact that she had worked for hours trying to block thoughts of Gallo and Paul Black out of her mind and hadn't succeeded. She didn't like that she felt a tension building whenever Joe mentioned Gallo's name.

He kissed her and nestled her head into the hollow of his shoulder. "We'll work it out. Go to sleep."

She closed her eyes, feeling the pounding of his heart beneath her ear. Life. She brushed her lips against his warm, smooth skin. She wanted to feel the textures, breathe the scents of him. She wanted to cherish this moment.

Because she could feel the choice approaching.

She got up with Joe and had coffee with him before he left for work. Then she started working on the reconstruction of the little boy. More measurements. Concentrate. They all had to be correct.

But she couldn't concentrate. By eleven she knew there was no way she could block the decision any longer.

She shook her head as she gazed at the skull on the easel. "I'm sorry, Dale," she said softly. "It's not that you're not important. But you'll have to wait a little longer."

She took out her phone and walked out on the porch. Choice.

He had handed her the phone and must have realized what that meant.

She rolled back the calls and brought up the number from where he'd called her.

She pressed the button for return call.

It rang once, twice.

On the third ring, Gallo picked up.

"Is Joe Quinn standing at your shoulder?"

"No." She had to gather her thoughts. She hadn't been sure that he would answer. "I can't involve Joe any more in this. He was shot last night."

Silence. "I know. Hanks called and reported after he left the compound. I didn't want that to happen. Is Quinn okay?"

"Yes. But it did happen. He was hurt. He could have been killed. This is your responsibility. Make it right. Tell me where to find Paul Black."

He chuckled. "You're using guilt to get your own way? That's very ruthless, Eve."

"I'll use whatever I have to use. I have to find Bonnie's killer. I won't have Joe sacrificed on the altar of my obsession."

"Yet you can't give up the hunt."

"No, and that's my guilt."

He was silent. "We're a fine pair, aren't we, Eve?"

"Tell me," she said. "You said you didn't want to destroy me. But can't you see? I'm destroying myself and Joe. I have to find him. I have to find *her*."

"You won't let me do it for you?"

"I have to know. I have to be certain."

"And you can't trust me."

"I don't know you. I've never known you. How can I trust you?" She paused. "But I know that, in spite of what you said, you wanted to leave the door open for me. You wouldn't have given me back my phone. You wouldn't have answered the call."

"My door is always open for you, Eve."

"And you gave me that key. How did you know I wouldn't turn it over to Queen?"

"I had to take the chance. I knew Queen would take advantage of what I'd done to make his move. You had to be protected. Has he contacted you yet?"

"No."

"He will. He didn't find what he wanted at the house, and he'll start exploring possibilities."

"He made me angry." She paused. "He burned your house."

"Hanks told me. Judy managed to get out everything that was valuable from the office."

"Senseless. Queen wanted to hurt you." She paused. "Did he do it?"

"Yes." He didn't speak for a moment. "Stupid. I knew with my head that it was just a shell made out of brick and wood. I knew it could be taken away from me like everything else. I was prepared for it. But I'd never really had a home, even as a kid. I guess I wanted one. Funny. I suppose it sort of crept in when I wasn't looking. Primitive instinct. We're all savages once you tear away the trappings."

"It was a lovely place."

"It's gone. Don't think about it."

"Is that your philosophy? I don't think so. Bonnie is gone. You're still thinking about her."

"That's different."

Yes, everything about Bonnie and her life and death were different and special. "Did Paul Black kill her?"

He didn't answer immediately. "I believe he did."

"Do you know where he is?"

"No, but I know how to bring him to me."

Her hand tightened on the phone until the knuckles turned white. "Then tell me where you are. I have to be with you."

He didn't speak.

"I'm not going to plead with you. But I swear I'll give that key to Queen. Maybe he knows something about Black that he didn't tell Catherine. And I'll let Queen use me as bait to try to get you. I don't think you'd want me to do that."

"You'd be crazy to deal with him," John said roughly. "Your just having that key will tell him that you know too much. That was your insurance policy."

"He's an Army Intelligence agent. He might have you targeted, but I'm a private citizen. He'd have a difficult time trying to harass me."

"I'm not talking about harassment." His breath expelled with exasperation. "I'll say you're not pleading. Back off, Eve. This isn't a good move."

"I can't back off. Tell me how to reach you." She had to persuade him. "I have a right, John. No one has a better right than I do to catch that bastard. You know it, and I know it. Isn't that the real reason you made contact with me? You say we're all savages. Maybe that primitive instinct told you that this was something we had to do together."

He was still silent, and Eve wasn't sure that she'd made an impact.

Then he said, "Take the Delta flight to Milwaukee this afternoon. When you get in, call me, and I'll come and get you. Queen will probably have someone following you. He won't stop you because he'll hope you're leading him to me."

"And I will be."

"I'll take care of that when you get here. Be careful." He hung up.

It was done.

Eve hung up and stared out at the lake.

"We're going to find you, Bonnie," she whispered. "This is the time, isn't it? This is how you wanted it." Why was that certainty growing within her? She could be fooling herself because she wanted it so much, and the search had gone on so long. She was taking a chance on John Gallo. Joe and Catherine were right that he was the ultimate wild card.

And she had taken a chance on him once before, and it had changed her life. He had given her Bonnie.

Stop questioning. The decision was made.

She got to her feet and moved toward the door. She would make her airline reservations, write a note to Joe, and try to get a couple hours' sleep.

She went to her worktable and covered the reconstruction she'd started on Dale. "Just a little interruption," she whispered. "You've waited a long time. Wait just a little longer." He was her job, her duty. This was the part of her life that had been born when she had lost

Bonnie. But she had to return to the time before she had become the woman who had brought all those other children home until she could come back and do that duty.

If she came back.

Was that why she was having this feeling of destiny, the conviction that Bonnie was guiding her? Was she going to die and join Bonnie? Did Bonnie know that this time Eve would not come back to Joe?

The prospect held no fear for Eve. Joe would be safe. Joe and Jane would have each other.

And she would have Bonnie.

"Eve Duncan just boarded a flight for Milwaukee," Queen told Jacobs when he hung up the phone. "I've told one of our people in the Chicago office to get over to Milwaukee and make sure she's under surveillance."

"Why Milwaukee?" Jacobs asked. "Quinn wasn't with her?"

"No, he's at ATLPD headquarters." Queen smiled unpleasantly. "I think she's given him the slip. Maybe Quinn was wrong about Gallo taking Eve Duncan. It could be that she decided to renew old times. They must have been a hot item when they were younger."

"You believe she's gone to join Gallo again?" Jacobs repeated, "Why Milwaukee?"

"Gallo grew up in Milwaukee. He knows it like the back of his hand. He'd feel comfortable there." He paused. "Maybe enough to find a hiding place for the ledger."

"And you believe Duncan is joining him because they're having an affair?"

"Women seem to find him attractive. He's had several mistresses over the years. Even a couple movie actresses. Why else?"

"I researched her when Gallo requested the files on her. She's not the kind of woman who'd abandon her career and a stable relationship to jump into bed with a man she hasn't seen in years."

"She was willing to do it when she was sixteen. Maybe she still has a yen for him." He shrugged. "At any rate, we should explore it. I doubt if Gallo feels the same way, but if there's a chance, we'll grab it."

"There's another possibility." He paused. "Paul Black."

Queen shook his head. "I don't think Black has surfaced yet. He had me e-mail him some information about Gallo's employees, and I sent him current info about Eve Duncan as well, including the fact that she's on her way to Milwaukee."

"Why pull Black into it?"

"Why not? The hunted pursuing the hunter. Better he go after Gallo than me. I knew I shouldn't have tried to hand Black over to Gallo. It boomeranged, and it could have been fatal. But I handled it damn well."

"So you say," Jacobs said. "But you've been prone to impulsive behavior of late. You didn't have to burn down Gallo's place. It will make him difficult to negotiate with if that becomes necessary."

Bastard. Jacobs hadn't had to deal with Gallo all

these years. He hadn't realized what bullshit Queen had had to take from him. "It won't be necessary. I'll find him, and I'll find the ledger. The woman may be the answer." He turned and moved toward the door. "She's going to find Gallo a little too hot to handle."

The note was propped up on the coffeemaker on the counter.

Joe had expected it. He had tried to phone home twice before he'd gotten into his car and driven home. He tore open the envelope and pulled out the sheet of paper.

> *Joe,*
>
> *I'm with John Gallo. He can lead me to Black. You know why I didn't tell you before. It's time I assumed full responsibility. God knows, I've leaned on you too long. This isn't your war, and I won't have you be a casualty.*
>
> *I'll be in touch. I love you.*
>
> *Eve*

His hand clenched the paper, then he crushed it into a ball and hurled it onto the counter.

Control the anger . . . and the fear. He had known this could be coming. It had been building for the last few years, and he had been able to fight it off.

He would still fight it off.

But he had to find Eve first.

He pulled out his phone and dialed Eve.

Voice mail.

He called Catherine.

She answered immediately. "Trouble?"

"Why would you think that?"

"Eve was too quiet."

"She's gone to John Gallo. He's convinced her he can take her to Black."

"Then we have to find Gallo. I suppose she's not answering her phone?"

"Voice mail."

Catherine was silent. "Okay, so I track down Judy Clark while you go after Hanks?"

"Can you? How is your son?"

"Luke is fine. I've hired a live-in tutor for him. Sam O'Neill used to work for the CIA, but he retired a few years ago. He was a teacher before he joined the Company, and he decided to go back to it. I figured they'd be a good match. Sam's a nice guy but tough, and they get along. Luke wouldn't know what to do with a cozy, maternal housekeeper." She added, "Luke doesn't need me. After being on his own all these years, he's totally independent. He reads and studies, and sometimes we even have discussions. It's a start." She paused. "I wish he did need me. But that will come." She added brusquely, "I'll call Venable and see what we can pull up on Hanks and Judy Clark."

"And I'll go to the airport and check to see if Eve left her car there. It's not here." He added, "Thanks, Catherine. I need to move fast."

"Do you think I'm doing it for you? It's Eve. Every time I look at my son, I remember that I wouldn't have him with me if it wasn't for her. And you do need to move fast. Gallo has her blinded. Hell, maybe she's right about him, but he scares me. He's unpredictable. Queen could be right about him having a split personality, and there's no one more convincing than someone who believes that he's telling the truth. Let me know if she's taken a flight." She hung up.

Split personality. Possible answer. Eve was not easily fooled. She had great instincts about people and would not be easily dazzled.

But Gallo had dazzled her when she was sixteen.

Don't think about it. Think about the Eve you know now.

The Eve who could be walking into Gallo's trap.

CHAPTER

15

Eve's cell phone rang as soon as she walked off the jetway in Milwaukee.

"Go to the Avis rental pickup," John Gallo said. "A tan Toyota Camry has been rented for you. I'll see you soon." He hung up.

Short and to the point, Eve thought as she moved down the aisle. Evidently, he was taking no chances on their conversation being bugged. Not that she could blame him. His home had been burned to the ground a little more than twenty-four hours ago. But where was she supposed to go after she went to the Avis lot?

And when she got into the Camry, there was no note on the seat to help her. What was she supposed to do. Just sit and wait for—

The GPS.

She activated it. An address was on the bottom of the GPS. Marriott Hotel. Downtown, Milwaukee.

She drove out of the lot.

Marriott Hotel.

It had been to a Marriott that she had gone with John when her mother had been in trouble. Some sort of puckish whimsy?

But John had never had that kind of humor. He had always had a reason for every action.

She glanced at the rearview mirror.

Was she being followed?

"Eve Duncan just pulled up in front of the Marriott, Colonel," Brandell said. "She's going up to the front desk and registering. Shall I follow?"

"Not yet. Any sign of Gallo?"

"No."

"Then park and go inside. Find out what room she's been given."

"How?"

"I don't give a damn. Bribery is usually good." He hung up. He was surrounded by idiots and incompetents.

Brandell called back ten minutes later. "Room 1502."

"Keep watch outside and make sure you know when she leaves the hotel."

Queen hesitated a moment, then dialed another number. "Marriott Hotel. Room 1502."

"How very accommodating of you," Black said.

"Accommodating? I've practically drawn you a picture," Queen said. "Just get me what I need."

"Gallo's head and the ledger," Black said. "I'll

probably have to take out the woman, too. It would be dangerous to leave a witness."

"Then she has to just disappear. She has contacts with the Atlanta PD."

"Disappear. No problem. Do you think that I'd still be free if I wasn't an expert?" he said mockingly. "One can't just leave bodies lying about. Actually, it's rather fitting, isn't it? Her daughter disappeared, and now poor Eve Duncan herself."

"As far as I know, Duncan is still hale and hearty and able to cause me trouble. I don't care what you do to any of them. Just get me what I need. It shouldn't be hard now that I've done your groundwork."

"You don't know anything about it. I may not even choose to use your precious information. I'll have to decide. It's sometimes better to go for a fresh, unexpected approach. It's certainly more enjoyable."

"I'm not interested in what's enjoyable for you."

"You may be very interested at some point, Queen."

Back off. That last remark was aimed at him, and Black's malice might also be changed to include Queen. He didn't want to have to deal with Black until he had done his job and retrieved the ledger. He'd already lined up a hit man to take care of Black after he had no use for him. "All I'm saying is that nothing should get in the way of what's important."

"I thought that was what you meant." Black sounded amused. "I'm certain you wouldn't deliberately be rude." He hung up.

Queen expelled the breath he hadn't realized he was

holding. Everything was in motion. All he had to do was sit back and watch and pick up the spoils.

Black looked down at the pad on which he'd scrawled the room number in Milwaukee.

Eve Duncan's room number.

He remembered her well. How could he forget?

And how well and in what ways did Gallo remember Eve Duncan? Queen had said she'd been with him in the house in the mountains.

Is it time to take your toy from you, Gallo?

He felt a surge of fierce pleasure at the thought. Not only the death of Gallo, but making him watch the death of someone he cared about.

But how to do it in the most pleasurable way for himself?

He thought he knew what path he wanted to take. He reached in his pocket and pulled out another note he had made.

San Cecilia.

Eve took out the plastic key the clerk had given her and pushed it into the slot.

"No, my room."

She stiffened and turned to see John Gallo standing behind her. He was wearing a black shirt and khaki pants and looked dark, lean, and completely casual and confident. "All of this cloak-and-dagger stuff is annoying, John. I feel as if I've joined the CIA like Catherine."

He shook his head. "Nary a cloak or dagger in sight." He nodded at an open door down the hall. "My room. It's safer. I've ordered dinner." He took her carry-on and rolled it down the hall. "You were followed from the airport."

"How do you know?"

"I hired an old friend, Peter Chakon, to watch the Toyota and report to me." He smiled. "Would I let you take a chance on being intercepted on your way here?"

"I don't know what you'd do. Was it one of Queen's people?"

"Maybe." He stepped aside for her to enter the room. "Probably."

She glanced around the room. Typical hotel room, blue synthetic-silk spread on a king-size bed, a desk and chair across the room. A small damask-covered room-service table was pushed against the wall.

"Not as nice as the last Marriott we were in together," John said. "But then there are Marriotts and Marriotts."

She looked at him. "That wasn't a pleasant memory, either."

"I know. But I couldn't resist the temptation to repeat history on some level." He shut the door and gestured to the table. "Sit down and eat. I don't know how long we'll have before we're interrupted."

She sat down in the chair. "You think someone is going to come. Then why are we still here?"

"Because I want to see who it is." He uncovered the plates to reveal sandwiches and soup. "Ham okay?"

She nodded. "You said you were curious. I don't think you're this curious."

He sat down across from her. "It's important that I know who may be knocking on the door."

"Queen." She took a sip of soup. "Who else?"

He didn't answer.

She studied him. "Who else?" she whispered. "Black?"

"It's possible that Queen decided to bring him in on a job that he considered important. I worked very hard at being a thorn in his side to bring that about." He poured coffee into her cup. "At least, I hope he did."

"Bring him in?" Her grip tightened on her spoon. "Stop this. I have to know what you're talking about. Start at the beginning. What do you have on Queen?"

He made a face. "The beginning? I try to avoid thinking of the beginning." He leaned back in his chair. "But I'll try to skirt around the really nasty parts. Korea. Five months after I left Atlanta. Fresh out of Ranger school. I was good and cocky and one of the chosen ones. I met Queen and his subordinate, Jacobs, at a meeting in To-kyo. Queen was a major at that time, and Jacobs was a corporal. Jacobs seemed to be some kind of assistant to Queen. They were officers in Army Intelligence and had requested special assistance from my unit. They said Washington had information that North Korea was buying nuclear raw materials to start their own program. They wanted proof but didn't want to disturb diplomatic relations to get it. So they sent me, Ron Capshaw, and Larry Silak in to find it."

"What kind of proof?"

"A ledger of transactions between the North Koreans and arms dealers of various countries. It was described as a slender leather-bound book and easily portable. The ledger was in the possession of General Tai Sen. He kept it at his country home near Pyongyang. Our orders were to go in and grab the ledger and head for the coast to get picked up. The theft went slick as glass." He grimaced. "But everything went wrong from the time that we stole the ledger. We knew the chances were that we all weren't going to make it to the coast. We hid the ledger and separated and took off on our own."

"And you were caught."

"Capshaw and Silak were shot and killed. I was taken to prison and questioned. They wanted to know what happened to the ledger. I told them that I was only a non-com and that Capshaw as the commanding officer had taken it with him when we separated. I thought they believed me, maybe they did for a while. The Koreans have an almost slavish obedience and respect for their officers." He lifted his cup to his lips. "But General Tai Sen decided they had to be sure when they still couldn't find the ledger." He looked at her and his lips twisted. "And this is where I start to skip a few years, if you don't mind."

She shook her head. No, she didn't want to hear about the years of torture and starvation. It hurt her to think of them. "But you didn't tell them where to find the ledger?"

"No, first I thought I was being a patriot. Then I was angry; and then I just endured." He shook his head as if to clear it. "I told you about escaping and the Tokyo hospital and going to Atlanta."

"Queen visited you in the hospital. He told Joe and Catherine that you were raving and that Army Intelligence was afraid you might give away top secret information."

He shrugged. "I *was* raving at the time. And I was probably even more unbalanced than I was later. I'd completely blocked out most of the things that happened. The only thing I remember about Queen's visits were his questions about the ledger. He kept at me."

"You'd forgotten that, too?"

"It was the one question they kept asking in the prison. I blocked it so thoroughly that there was no way it was going to come back without a hell of a lot of time and therapy. That was why Queen got me dismissed from the hospital. He didn't want me talking to any therapist."

She shook her head. "You must have been in terrible shape."

He nodded. "I didn't work my way through the worst of it for years after Queen sent me off to try to get me killed."

"You knew they were suicide missions?"

"Not at first. I was still in a haze for a long while. I was operating on automatic."

And that automatic had clearly been lethal if it had kept him alive. "You said you came back to the U.S. some years later."

He nodded. "Because I'd become clearheaded enough to realize that I was a target. I started to wonder why Queen was so determined to rid himself of me in a way that wouldn't be questioned. Oh, they were very determined." He paused. "And it all came back to the ledger."

"Which you couldn't remember."

"By that time I'd worked my way through the haze enough to start to remember some details." His lips tightened. "And I'd realized that it probably wasn't dedication to home and country that had driven Queen. Some of the missions they sent me on were a revelation. They appeared to have nothing to do with protecting home and country. Dirty. Queen was definitely dirty. So I decided to go back to Korea and retrieve the ledger."

"That must have been—I'd think that you'd have avoided that place like the plague."

"It wasn't easy. The North Koreans had become even more belligerent, and I was on their most wanted list. I was in a cold sweat most of the time I was there." He paused. "But I found the ledger and I took it to Tokyo and had it translated."

She tilted her head. "No nuclear secrets?"

"Drugs and stolen ancient artifacts. General Tai Sen was a joint partner with Queen. He received the merchandise and saw that it was sent to Tokyo to Queen for distribution and sale. The ledger belonged to the general and listed all the transactions in detail, naming names. The most prominent of which were Queen and Jacobs. The general was trying to cut them out of the business and threatening to send the ledger to their superiors if they caused any trouble."

"So they had to have the ledger."

"And didn't mind throwing me into a hellhole and killing two of my buddies to get it." His hand tightened on his cup. "You might say I was a little angry. If I'd found out a year earlier, I would have set up a prison like the one I called home for all those years and done a few experiments on Queen. Maybe I would have hired a North Korean to help. They know the way it's done."

There was such savagery in his face that Eve inhaled sharply. "But you didn't do it. Why not?"

"I found out Queen's connection to Paul Black."

She stiffened. "What?"

"For years, Paul Black has been engaged as an assassin by Queen. When I left the hospital in Tokyo, they hired Black to follow me and to terminate me at the earliest opportunity." He looked down into his cup. "He must have been following me when I came that day to see you and Bonnie. It had to have been obvious as hell what I was feeling when I was staring at Bonnie and you. It was one of the most powerful moments of my life. From what I've learned about him, Black appears to be very thorough and takes his time. Evidently, he didn't find the right time and place to kill me while I was in Atlanta."

"Bonnie," she whispered.

He shook his head. "Queen sent me to Pakistan, and Black followed me. He attacked at the same time I was dealing with the terrorists Queen had assigned me to get. I didn't even realize that Black wasn't one of them." He smiled tightly. "He didn't find me an easy target. As I told you, I was really crazy during those days. He went after me with a knife, and I took it away from him and stabbed him in the belly. At the time I thought he was dead, but he crawled away."

"To recover and go after Bonnie," she said dully.

"Do you think I haven't thought about that every day since I found out Bonnie had been murdered?" he said harshly. "I'd found after searching through his pockets after I stabbed him that he had a U.S. passport under the name of Paul Black. I was lucky he wasn't traveling under an assumed name. I found out later that was common with him. He was so arrogant he thought no one could touch him. But that was all I knew about him. Nothing more. Maybe I should have tried to find out something else, but it didn't seem to matter to me at the time. Hell, I didn't realize that it would concern anyone but me, and most of the time I didn't give a damn whether I lived or died. I didn't know what a monster the son of a bitch was."

"And when did you find that out?" Eve asked jerkily.

"Drink your coffee," Gallo said. "You're too pale."

"I shouldn't be. I've dealt with monsters before." She took a sip of coffee. It was hot and strong and braced her a little. "But it never does any good. Not when I think about those monsters with Bonnie."

"The time Bonnie was taken was too shortly after I came to Atlanta. Just one month. I tried to see if I could find any connection. God knows I didn't want to find one."

"But you did."

"I was already suspecting Queen of trying to kill me. That led me back to Paul Black. Hired by Queen? Maybe. But what connection to Bonnie's kidnapping? I started to work on finding out much more about Paul Black. I bribed and threatened and stole records. It took me over a year, but I put together his picture. He was born in Metairie, Louisiana, and he was in a mental hospital by the time he was twelve. He'd stabbed one of his classmates. The kid lived, and they released Black a year later. After that, Black was more careful and began to move about the country doing what he liked best."

"Montalvo told me the records show he was born in Macon, Georgia."

"Queen altered the records. He was protecting his pet cobra. It was part of the arrangement they had together. Queen protected, and Black did all his killings." He held her eyes. "But he didn't only do Queen's killings. There are all kinds of indications that he was a serial killer before Queen took him under his wing. Very clever, very bloodthirsty. He liked it, and he wanted to keep on doing it. The only way he could see himself staying alive to appease his appetite was to find someone like Queen, who didn't care what he did as long as he performed well for him. According to all the books and reports I've read, a serial killer of that magnitude has a tremendous ego. He has to be all-powerful."

"The terrible thing is that they usually are," Eve said. "They don't stop. They just keep on killing."

"I must have damaged Black's ego badly when I managed to escape him and stabbed him in the belly. I told you that he had a tremendous opinion of himself. He would have wanted to hurt me. In any way he could."

A little red-haired girl in a Bugs Bunny T-shirt.

Eve nodded slowly. "But why didn't he go after you again?"

He shrugged. "I don't know how he thinks. It might be that ego. He might have felt vulnerable after I almost killed him and convinced himself that he didn't have to murder me to inflict the most hurt. He may not have known she was my daughter. Though it would not surprise me that he'd found that out. But anyone looking at me the day I came to see her would know how much I loved her."

"Are you sure he killed her?"

"Do I have proof? No, and I won't know until I hear it from his lips. But I believe he killed her. I've been tracking him over Asia and half of Europe, and there's no question in my mind that he's killed at least a dozen people in that time." He paused. "Though he's very smart. He's like a phantom, moving in and out and away. I think when the police do come too close, he calls on Queen to help him."

"Then he's just as guilty of those murders as Black."

"Yes." He met her eyes. "But then I'm guilty of them, too."

"What?"

"Oh, I wasn't an accessory, but I wasn't able to stop him. That should qualify."

"That's nuts," she said flatly.

He smiled faintly. "I'm not going to address that statement. It would be redundant."

"In all these years, you haven't gotten close enough to catch him?"

"I got close a couple times but he slipped away." He put his cup back on the saucer. "So I put Queen on the job."

"What?"

"I told him that I'd give him his ledger if they gave me Black. He was pretending that he'd had nothing to do with him. I knew they were using him. It was only a matter of time until he decided that getting the ledger was more important to him than an assassin who probably knew too much about him anyway."

Excitement was beginning to build. "Then you can get Queen to tell us where he is? Or do you know already?"

"I knew a few days ago. I'd traced him on my own to Samoa and was going to go after him myself. But I didn't get the chance. His house was blown up, and his housekeeper and an unknown man were incinerated."

"Then Black could be dead?"

He shook his head. "I doubt it. They're checking the dental records, but the height and bone structure aren't right. I think Queen sent someone to kill Black, and it went wrong. Which for me wasn't all that bad. It meant that Black would be stirred into action against Queen." He inclined his head. "And probably me. I can't imagine Queen not throwing me under the bus at the earliest opportunity. When he burned my place, he was behaving with a recklessness that wasn't characteristic."

"Black will be coming after you."

"He's probably breathing down my neck right now." He looked her in the eye. "Which makes me criminally irresponsible to be here with you."

"You can't be responsible for an act I committed myself." She pushed back her chair. "That's not possible. Now I think it's time I went to my room and took a shower and unpacked. Unless we're going to be leaving here soon?"

"Not soon." He got to his feet. "But it's probably not wise to unpack." He added, "Nor to go to your room. I want you to stay here tonight."

She stiffened, her gaze flying to his face. "Why?"

"In another life, you wouldn't even have to ask."

She felt a rush of heat that surprised her. It was as if her body had memories of him that triggered responses that were purely instinctive. "But that was another life."

"Have you ever considered reincarnation?"

"No." She started for the door. "I'll call you after I shower and we'll discuss—"

"I meant it about staying," he said. "And it wasn't for the most obvious and pleasant reason. I just couldn't resist giving the answer that I—" He shook his head ruefully. "I know that it would only make things more difficult, but I'm finding I don't have much control. I'm reacting instinctively."

As I have been doing, she thought. Evidently, they were both being ambushed by memories. "Then I think it's best to think before you act." She had to be honest. "This is strange for me, too." She changed the subject. "Why do you want me to stay?"

"Because I set you up. And I don't want you to be alone."

"Set me . . . What the hell are you talking about?"

"I told you once that you couldn't trust me. Not if it was something I really wanted." He smiled crookedly. "I really want to get Paul Black."

"Well, so do I. What does that have to do with anything?"

"I was trying to be so damn noble and all that crap. I was going to keep you from being hurt. I was going to try to make up for all I did to you." He shrugged. "But I'm not noble. I'm worse than the kid who screwed you and left you alone and pregnant. You were right to tell me to keep to the plan and get out of your life."

"You're making me sound like a victim. I wasn't one then, and I'm certainly not one now. I made sure I was in control of keeping myself from getting pregnant and I blew it. Now will you stop reminiscing and tell me what you're talking about?"

"Reminiscing? That sounds almost sentimental. Neither one of us was ever that," he said. "And I'm talking about the reason I gave in and brought you here. Insurance. It was clear for whatever reason that Black wasn't eager to confront me. I needed a goad. He figured he'd hurt me before by killing Bonnie. Now he's coming back to revisit the situation, and, lo and behold, you're back in my life." He paused. "As I arranged."

"You're saying I'm bait?" She shook her head. "Don't

flatter yourself. I wouldn't be that passive. If you'd said that was what you intended, do you think that I wouldn't have come? The only difference would have been that we might have gotten together a plan that was mutually agreeable."

He stared at her and smiled slowly. "I thought I remembered everything about you, but some details must have slipped away."

She looked at the door. "You think that Queen or Black will know I'm in Room 1502? No one knows you're here?"

"I made sure that they wouldn't. I bribed the clerk to give you 1502 and set up a signal alarm so that I'd know if anyone entered the room. I went in earlier and mussed up the bed and made it look occupied." He paused. "And I set up a camera to record any visitors."

Her brows rose. "My, you were thorough."

"I'm a good hunter," he said simply. "I've been well trained. Ask Queen."

"I don't want to ask him anything. From what I've heard of him, I'd just as soon not make his acquaintance." She added grimly, "Unless it was to try to throw him into jail." She turned away from the door. "It appears that I stay here." She took her carry-on case and threw it on the bed. "How fast do you think Black will move?"

He shook his head. "I have no idea. But Queen will be pushing hard."

She opened the case and pulled out her toiletries and a change of clothes. She headed for the bathroom. "Then we'll be ready to move, too."

His question stopped her at the bathroom door. "Did you tell Quinn you were coming?"

She didn't look at him. "I wouldn't have left without letting him know what I was doing. Did I give him details? No."

"So we're in this alone."

"Yes." She closed the door behind her.

Alone.

She did feel poignantly alone and vulnerable at that moment. She was used to Joe being there, a presence that was both exciting and comforting. But she was dealing with John Gallo, who was not at all comforting. Exciting? As exciting as falling off a cliff into the darkness. She didn't know what he was going to do next or even whether he was telling her the truth. She was going on instinct and memory, and the latter could have been twisted by the passage of time. And obeying instinct would be skipping through landmines.

She stripped and stepped under the spray.

I wish you were here, Joe.

"Milwaukee," Joe told Catherine when he called her from the airport. "Eve took the two forty flight on Delta."

"And you're on your way."

"I will be in another hour. It's the first flight out. But finding out where she was going is going to be a hell of a lot easier than tracing her once she gets off the plane. What did you find out?"

"Hanks may be in Denver," she said. "He owns a

condo there. I've called the number, but there's no answer."

"And Judy Clark?"

"Judy has a mother, Stella Kamski, in St. Louis. It's
a possibility. Judy lived with her until she was married.
And after Judy's divorce, she moved back in with her
until she went to work for Gallo. Her mother even took
care of her kid for a while. I spoke to the mother, and
she said she hadn't heard from her daughter in months.
She seemed . . . stiff."

"You think she was lying?"

"As I said, I think she's a possibility. Judy Clark may be
with her, or she might know where she is. I'm on my way
there now. She lives in a subdivision in Webster Groves.
It's about a four-hour drive from where I am now."

"Call me if you can get anything out of her."

"You know it." Catherine hung up.

But even if Judy Clark was with her mother, Catherine might not be able to get her to talk. She had been
close-mouthed and obstinately loyal in her encounter
with her. Hell, she might not even know where he was.
It was clear that Gallo was very careful about confiding
anything to anyone.

But there was always a chance, and it was all Catherine could think to do. The chances were pretty slim.

She just hoped Joe would be able to trace Eve when
he reached Milwaukee.

"Why doesn't someone come?" Eve's hand clenched
on the gray drapes as she gazed from the window down

at the lights of the traffic spearing the darkness. "I can't say much for your trap, John."

"I've never seen any bait more eager to spring the teeth shut." He smiled across at her from where he was lying on the bed. "You've not been here more than five or six hours. Are you always this impatient?"

"We're close. I want it over."

"It's like the watched kettle that never boils. Come to bed, and that alarm in 1502 will probably go off in five minutes."

She didn't answer, her gaze fixed on the street.

"Come to bed, Eve," he said quietly. "I'm not going to jump you. If you like, I'll curl up on the floor. I've learned to sleep anywhere."

"I'm not afraid of you." She turned to look at him. "I can take care of myself. That's one of the first things that Joe taught me."

"Good for him. Though, as I remember, you were pretty effective when I knew you."

She nodded. "But Joe says technique always carries the day. I learned that the night you saved little Manuel . . . and me."

"How is Manuel?"

"Well, I hope. I lost track of Rosa and her son. She married and left for San Diego a year after I moved out of the housing development." She shook her head. "It's sad that it's so easy to lose touch with people. They come in and out of your life, then they're gone. A lot of it is my fault. I'm so busy most of the time that I don't make the effort."

"What about your mother?"

She shrugged. "We were fine while Bonnie was alive, but afterward we gradually grew apart. Bonnie was the magic that held us together. But even after Bonnie was taken some of the magic lingered. Sandra never went back on drugs. Just the fact that Bonnie came into our lives and stayed for a little while made an impression that never went away." She gazed at him inquiringly. "Any more questions?"

"There will probably be a few as they occur to me. That curiosity . . ." He reached over and turned out the lamp on the nightstand. The room was plunged into darkness. "You're tired. Come and lie down. I won't touch you. You've convinced me I'd be putty in your hands."

She hesitated, then left the window and moved toward the bed. "I have to admit I do know a lot about putty." She lay down on the far side of the bed and tried to relax. It was difficult. Even though there were several inches between them, it felt strange to be in a bed with a man other than Joe. How many years had it been?

"I know you do. You told me about the forensic process at dinner. Your hands aren't quite the same as they were when you were younger. They were always shaped well, but now they look stronger, knowing." He was silent a few moments. "Are you going to tell Joe about this?"

"Yes. Why not? Nothing is going to happen."

"I have a vivid imagination. I think I'd want you to lie to me."

"Joe would not. Which shows how different you are from him. And how similar Joe and I are."

"Two straight arrows. He doesn't bore you?"

"Joe? Not likely. And he wouldn't bore you either, John. There's a razor-sharp edge to that straight arrow."

"I gathered so from talking to Hanks after their encounter the other night. He told me that Quinn wanted me very badly and to be careful. Should I be careful, Eve?"

"Yes, Joe doesn't trust anything you've told me. He might act before I could stop him."

"Would you protect me from him? I'm touched."

"I'd protect him from himself. He has a conscience, and guilt can be a terrible thing."

He was silent. "I know."

The only sound in the dark room was the resonance of their breathing against the backdrop of the traffic down in the street.

"What are we going to do, Eve?"

"We're going to find Bonnie's murderer."

"No, what about us?"

"There is no us. We put a period to that a long time ago."

"You can't put a period to anything between us," he said quietly. "It might have been possible if you hadn't had Bonnie. But the moment she appeared in our lives, she changed the dynamics. You have to accept and admit that to yourself and to me. Otherwise, we're not going to be able to fight our way through this."

"She was *my* daughter, John."

"That may have been the way you wanted it, but Bonnie evidently didn't agree with you. She came looking for me, Eve. She came into that hot box of filth and pain, and she found me. And I thank God for it every day of my life."

She could feel the tears rise to her eyes as she had when he had first told her that story.

She came looking for me.

That simple sentence was enough to break her heart. The miracle of Bonnie, who had come into both their lives and changed them beyond belief.

"Don't fight me, Eve. I don't want to cause you any trouble. I'm just saying that we have to come to terms with a way of handling it that will make both of us content. Not happy. I don't know if we can get to that level. But content would be good."

"I can't . . . you're out of my life. I have Joe now. He's all I want."

"And my first reaction is to try to change your mind. We were so damn good together that sex seems a natural part of any relationship that we could have." He added before she could speak, "But that's the kid, John Gallo, thinking. I know we can't go back. We've both moved on. Well, you've moved on. I'm still struggling."

She was struggling, too. It seemed so right to have him in the bed next to her. It wasn't right. She loved Joe. But there was that strong bond that wouldn't be banished.

"Okay," he said. "So I can't have sex with you. What's left? We were never friends, but that doesn't mean we can't work on it. I admire the person you've become. You can't say the same about me, but I might provide amusement value. Friendships can be based on a lot of weird things."

"There are things about you I admire," she said jerkily. "You're a survivor, and what you've endured would have broken almost anyone else. You thought you were being tortured to protect your country. I admire your patriotism. Most of the time, I think you're honest with me. That's important, too."

He chuckled. "You had to really dig for that list."

"What do you expect? I don't know you."

"I believe we're going to have to rectify that." He suddenly reached over and touched her cheek. "Don't stiffen up on me. I'm not making a move on you. I just want to show you I can touch you with affection that has nothing to do with sex." He stroked the line of her cheekbone. "Because the affection will always be there. Do you know why?"

"No."

"Because you gave me Bonnie," he said simply. "Because together we created something more wonderful than anything I could accomplish by myself if I live to be a hundred." He felt the moisture of her tears on his fingers. "Hey, I don't want this. I just want you to know that no matter what we have to overcome, it's going to be worth it. I think we have to be together some way, somehow." He added awkwardly, "I think maybe . . . she wants it."

"Bonnie?" Eve whispered.

"I've thought a lot about why she came to me in that prison. She was a part of both of us, Eve. The three of us are bound together. I'll never be able to look at you without feeling that closeness with her. Will you be able to look at me without feeling her love?"

She had been trying to shut out every facet of feeling toward him, but his words were tearing down the walls and revealing the truth. He was right. This wasn't going to go away because it was all about Bonnie. For her, Bonnie had been the center of her being. She was beginning to think that Bonnie had been equally important to John. If that was true, then they had no option but to accept and try to find a way to live with it. She said unevenly, "No, I don't think I will."

"Good." He bent down and kissed her forehead, then was gone again. "I just had to get that much established. I was feeling very much alone. I've always been the outsider."

Alone. Outsider.

Yes, John had always been the outsider as far as Bonnie was concerned. Eve had seen to that. She had never told him, never wanted him to know he had a child. She had chosen to bear the responsibility, but she had also garnered the joy. John Gallo had not been permitted either.

"Go to sleep," John said. "If we have an intruder in Room 1502, the alarm will wake us."

Outsider.

"I'm not sleepy. I wonder if you . . ." She started again. "I wonder if you'd like me to tell you about Bonnie?"

She could feel his sudden stillness. "You don't have to do that. I know it might be painful."

"Some of it, but most of it is pure joy. I think . . . I want to share her with you, John. If that's what you want, too."

"Oh, my God."

She didn't speak for a moment, trying to put her thoughts, her memories together. He had missed so much. Where to start on the story of Bonnie?

The beginning.

"The first time the nurse brought me Bonnie, she said she was magic . . ."

CHAPTER

16

Webster Groves was a pleasant suburb that consisted of a mixture of older homes built in the early nineteenth century and newer homes that appeared sleek but lacked character.

Catherine glanced at her GPS. She should be arriving at Judy Clark's mother's home in a few moments. It was close to eleven at night. She might have gone to bed. Should Catherine ring the bell or phone again? Maybe if she told Mrs. Kamski she was outside, she might agree to let her in and talk to her.

Or maybe she would tell Catherine to go take a flying leap.

She'd ring the bell.

The GPS instructed her to turn left at the next street.

She turned on San Cecilia.

Number 230 was halfway down the block, an older

two-story clapboard house. Catherine might not have to worry about waking anyone. Lights were still streaming from one of the windows on the first floor.

She pulled into the driveway and got out of the car.

She stopped two feet before she reached the front door.

Oh, shit. She knew that sound.

Moaning. Muffled but still audible.

TV?

She rang the bell.

No answer but that muffled cry of pain.

That was no TV.

She tried the knob. The door swung open.

She froze, her gaze on the staircase facing the door.

A gray-haired woman in a pink, flowered robe was lying on her back, wrists and ankles spread wide and tied to the pickets on either side of that staircase. Her mouth was gagged, her eyes wide open.

Blood everywhere. Her throat had been cut. Dead.

Catherine dove to the side, reaching for her gun. She hit the wall switch and plunged the foyer into darkness before rolling to one side.

She listened.

Nothing.

No, the moaning again.

Coming from the dining room across the foyer.

She waited.

A trap?

But a trap for whom?

She waited a minute more.

No sound but the moaning.

She crawled across the foyer, past the obscenely spread body on the stairs.

A woman was lying on the cherry dining-room table.

Her gaze wandered quickly around the room. Two chairs turned over. Nowhere to hide.

She crawled to the right side of the door and took a chance.

She flipped on the dining-room light.

Judy Clark.

Blue robe she had worn when she had first met her. One fuzzy blue slipper still on her foot, the other lying on the floor beside the table.

She had probably lost it while struggling with the monster who had thrown her on the table and pinned her there with a huge butcher knife through her stomach.

Catherine drew a deep breath and slowly stood up.

"It's okay, Judy," she whispered. "I'll get you help. Is whoever did this still in the house?"

Judy was also gagged, but she shook her head. Then the cords of her throat strained as she tried to talk.

"Wait." Catherine quickly called 911 and gave them the address and the situation. She cut the questions short and hung up. "Judy, I can't move you or take out the knife. We'll have to wait for the EMTs." She just hoped the ambulance came in time. The blood on the table wasn't as much as on the stairs, but Catherine couldn't judge the loss or the trauma of the wound. "They'll be here soon."

The woman was still trying desperately to speak.

"I'll fix that." Catherine undid the gag. "Now I'll stay here with you and hold your hand until the ambulance gets here."

"No." Judy's voice was rasping. "Help—find—her." Her eyes were glittering wildly in her parchment-colored face. "Took— Don't let him—"

"Shh." Catherine squeezed her hand. "You said he was gone."

"But—he—took—her."

"Who?"

"Cara."

Oh, dear God. Of course, the little girl. Judy's little girl.

"I'll be right back." She released her hand. "I'll go check."

Judy was shaking her head as Catherine ran out of the room. She climbed over the banister and ran up the steps to the second floor. The doors were all open wide. The second room down the hall was a child's room. Pink princess coverlet on the bed. A Disney clock on the wall.

No little girl.

Shit. Shit. Shit.

She quickly checked the other bedrooms.

No little girl. No Cara.

She drew a deep breath.

Damn him.

Then she ran out of the room and a moment later was in the dining room.

"Gone." The tears were running down Judy's face. "Cara."

Catherine took her hand again. "We'll find her. Do you know who took her?"

She shook her head. "We went to bed—early. Then he was just—there. We didn't even know him." The tears were flowing harder. "Mama."

"I'm sorry." What else could she say? There weren't words to express the horror Judy had gone through and was still experiencing. Catherine knew the panic of losing a child to a monster. "I'll help you find your child."

"I think . . . I'm dying. What if—I die? No one may ever find her."

"I told you, I'll find her."

"Promise me." Judy's gaze was desperately holding Catherine's. "Promise—"

"I promise." She only hoped she could find the child alive. "But she'll need you after she comes home. You've got to be quiet and do everything you can to get well."

"Needs me . . ." Judy's eyes closed. "I'll . . . try . . ."

Catherine heard the sound of sirens in the distance.

Lord, let them get here in time.

Catherine called Joe and filled him in from the waiting room at the hospital.

"Could you get a description?"

"I didn't try yet. Neither did the police. She's in

surgery. She may not make it, Joe. Whoever did this wanted to leave her enough alive to send a message. But he didn't give a damn what kind of damage he did with that butcher knife."

"Son of a bitch."

"That's what I say. He took the kid, Joe. Anyone who would do what he did to those two women would think nothing of torturing and murdering a kid."

"And you're mad as hell."

"I keep thinking of Luke and how I felt when my son was taken."

"You have a copy of the photo of Paul Black that Eve gave us. Can you show it to her as soon as possible?"

"I'll have to find a way to get in to see her. The only reason the police didn't take me in for questioning was that I'm CIA. They may still do it if they get enough heat. The murder of Judy Clark's mom was ugly and senseless, and that scares people."

"Let me know."

"Any leads on Eve?"

"Not yet." He hung up.

Catherine sat back down and sipped her coffee.

Joe had been curt and on edge, and who could blame him?

The violence was escalating by the minute, and it all seemed to be heading toward Eve.

What if it wasn't Paul Black who had committed these atrocities? It could be someone else that Queen had hired.

And what would she do if she found out from Judy that it was Black? The taking of Cara Clark opened a whole new avenue of threat. Why was the child taken and not murdered? Why had Judy been left alive to tell them? The kidnapping would be a weapon that might be impossible to overcome. She knew the helplessness and fear that could cripple you when you thought that your action could result in the killing of the helpless.

And that action had not been aimed at Judy Clark. She was almost certain that Eve was the target. Eve would do anything that she had to do to save a child.

And so would Catherine. Give her the chance, and she'd cut the bastard's throat. She felt a surge of sheer savagery at the thought.

Keep cool. She would sit and drink her coffee and wait for news on Judy Clark. If she lived, then Catherine would show her Black's photo and get an ID.

And plan what she would do to the son of a bitch who could perpetrate a hideous act like this.

"Wake up."

Eve opened her eyes to see Gallo's face above her. He smelled of soap, and his hair was wet as if he'd just stepped out of a shower.

He smiled. "I just called room service for breakfast. I thought you'd want to shower and brush your teeth before they get here."

"I do." She glanced at her watch. Seven thirty. She wasn't surprised she'd slept so late. She had talked about Bonnie far into the night. And even after the words had ceased to flow, she hadn't been able to sleep. She had lain beside Gallo in the darkness, answering an occasional question, suddenly remembering something she had forgotten to tell him. It had been a strange and supremely intimate night. By releasing all those memories of Bonnie, she had created a cocoon of togetherness for which she had not bargained. She had always clung to those memories, shutting everyone else out. Now they no longer belonged only to her.

She sat up and swung her feet to the floor. "Maybe I wasn't followed. It could be your trap is a dud, John."

"I admit that I expected the situation to move a little faster." He met her gaze. "But I'm glad it didn't. Thank you, Eve."

She pulled her gaze away. That overpowering intimacy again, the feeling of being part of him. "It doesn't mean anything more than that I felt you shouldn't be cheated of something I treasure." She moistened her lips. "I have a tendency to be selfish about Bonnie. While she was alive, she was everything to me. After she was gone, I still couldn't let her go."

"That's pretty clear. You've been searching for her killer since the day she was taken."

"No, I mean I couldn't talk about her, not even about the good times. I held the memories close as if I was afraid of losing those, too." She looked away from him. "I guess it was time I stopped being afraid and realized that sharing only makes them richer. So maybe I have something to thank you for, too, John."

"You've not talked to Quinn about Bonnie?"

"Of course." How could she explain? "But he didn't know her, couldn't love her. He only knew her as a cause of sorrow and danger to me. And I couldn't tell him all the things that might have brought him closer to her." She smiled as she got to her feet and headed for the bathroom. "But maybe I can now."

He chuckled. "So a night in bed with me is going to bring you closer to Quinn?"

"Yes."

His smile faded. "I hope it does if that's what you want. I want you to have everything you want, Eve. But you have to know that there's no going back after last night." He held up his hand as she opened her lips. "Don't say it. I'd like to think that I could replace Quinn, but I wouldn't even try. You have someone who can give you stability, and that's something I know nothing about. I'd never take that away from you." He grimaced. "But he can't take away the closeness we have together, either. And neither can we, Eve. We're joined in a way that's . . . remarkable. You know it, and so do I." He turned away. "I don't know what it means or how we're going to resolve the situation. But it had to be said."

And she would probably not have faced the finality of that realization at this time, she thought as she closed the bathroom door behind her. She was having enough difficulty sorting out her emotions where Gallo was concerned. Passion? No, both of them were keeping the passion that had been the core of their former relationship at bay. It was memory and Bonnie that had formed the new bond.

And, great heavens, what a strong bond it was proving to be.

"Your phone has been ringing," John said as she came out of the bathroom thirty minutes later. "Four times. Someone is very persistent."

She moved over to the nightstand where she had left her phone on vibrate. She frowned as she looked at the ID.

"Quinn?"

"No." Joe had called her only the one time yesterday, and when she hadn't answered, had not called again. "It's Catherine Ling."

"I caught sight of her for a moment at the compound, and I've read her dossier. She's . . . unusual."

"Unique," Eve said absently. She hadn't intended to answer Catherine, either. It had been possible Catherine might feel obligated to act for Joe.

The cell began to ring again.

"She's not taking no for an answer."

And Catherine would not be so urgent unless there was good reason.

Eve answered. "Hello, Catherine."

"It's about time," Catherine said. "I told you that I was on your side no matter if I thought you were being led down the garden path."

"Why are you calling?"

"Because I thought you needed to be warned that some heavy stuff was coming your way." She paused. "Are you with Gallo?"

"Yes."

"Has he been with you since before nine last evening?"

"Yes."

"Then it couldn't have been him. Put your phone on speaker. He should probably hear this."

Eve flipped the SPEAKER button. "Go ahead."

"I'm at St. Louis County Hospital. Judy Clark just came out of surgery."

Gallo stiffened. "What the hell?"

"Stab wound to the abdomen. She's in ICU now. She may make it, but they're still not sure, and I couldn't wait to try to get an ID from her. Black isn't going to wait for long to get in touch with you."

"My God," Eve whispered. "Black?"

"That's my guess. I can't confirm." She added bluntly, "I thought there was a possibility it might be you, Gallo."

"She's my friend," he said through his teeth.

"Is she? I don't know if you're capable of having friends. You haven't shown any sign of thinking about anyone but yourself. At any rate, your friends seem to end up—" She stopped. "That's not important right now. I'm just pissed because I'm feeling helpless."

"Catherine, how did you find out about Judy?" Eve asked.

"I found them when I was tracking you down and went to her mother's house in St. Louis." Catherine's words were now coming tersely. "Her mother's throat was cut. Judy Clark was pinned to the table with a butcher knife.

I think he left her alive on purpose. He wanted her to send a message. He took her little girl."

"Cara?" John said.

"Cara Clark, six years old. I told the police, and they searched the neighborhood. They always search the neighborhoods first. As if they're going to find the kid wandering around when I told them that he— They did the same thing when my Luke disappeared."

"No sign of her?" John asked.

"I told you. Judy said he took her. Or maybe I didn't." She added wearily, "She was still conscious, and she made me promise . . . I'm not behaving very professionally, am I? When I was checking her bedroom, it brought back too many memories. Those bastards always target the kids." She drew a deep breath. "And this time he's doing something else. This son of a bitch is targeting you, Eve. He wants to have a weapon, and he can't be sure that Gallo would respond to a threat, but anyone who has researched you would know that you would be vulnerable. He may be trying to get at Gallo through you."

"You're wrong," John said. "If it's Black, he'd know that he could strike at me that way."

"I don't know what's between the two of you, and I don't care. All I care about is that little girl and Eve. You've got something he wants. Give it to him. But we have to get that little girl away from him first. Eve, tell me where you are. I'm coming to join you."

"No, Catherine."

"Don't tell me no," she said fiercely. "And don't try

to close me out. I have a hunch that everything that happened here is going to play out with you and Gallo. Judy Clark made me promise to find her little girl, and I'm going to do it. I just hope I find her alive. You're so busy trying to protect Joe and me and the whole damn world that you're forgetting we have a stake in this. I'll let you deal with Joe on your own, but you're not going to stand in my way. Tell me where you are. Joe said you flew to Milwaukee. Are you still there?"

She should hang up and try to keep Catherine out of it, Eve thought. But Catherine was already deeply involved because Eve had made that attempt. Now that a child was at risk, there would be no way to keep her on the sidelines.

And Eve wasn't sure she had the right to do it. Everyone should do everything they could to bring that child home. "I'm in Milwaukee. Marriott. Room 1505."

"But we may not stay here," John said.

"Then let me know as soon as you leave." Catherine hung up.

"She's a tiger," John said.

"More than you know." Eve shoved her phone in her pocket. "And there wasn't a chance in hell of keeping her out of it now." She was stunned, the full impact of Catherine's words hitting home. "It takes a lot to shock her or blow her cool. The attack on Judy and her mother must have been hideous."

John didn't answer.

Eve glanced at him and stiffened with shock. His expression had changed, hardened. His eyes were glittering and wild in his taut face. But it wasn't only his expression, but the aura of sheer rage that surrounded him. She had never seen anything like it in her life. She took an involuntary step back. "John?"

He whirled away from her. "Don't talk to me." His voice was hoarse, almost guttural. "Give me a minute."

She watched him walk to the window and stand with his back to her. The line of his spine was almost painfully stiff, as if he was striving not to let loose that rage.

Berserk.

She remembered Hanks's words describing John Gallo when he lost control. This had to be what he had meant. The rage was being contained, but just the intensity of the emotion and the violence hovering on the brink were frightening. She could imagine how terrifying he would be if he did lose control.

He didn't speak for a few minutes. "I'm sorry." His back was still turned to her, and his words were halting. "I didn't want you to see me like this. I told you that I wasn't always stable. I get . . . angry."

An understatement. "I can see that you do."

"Judy has been with me for three years. I like her. I didn't think that she'd be hurt if I gave her a job. I should have been more careful."

"How could you know that Black would target her? You said that you had been chasing Black for years. There was no way you could know that he would appear in your life with no warning. Queen had to have been the one who triggered all of this. Stop kicking yourself and put the blame where it belongs."

"Oh, I'm willing to share the blame." He turned

around to face her. His face was still pale; but the wildness was only a shadow, not a living presence. "It's time I put an end to Queen. He's not going to be of use to me any longer. He's brought me Paul Black and all the ugliness that means. He had to have given the info about Judy's mother to Black. I'm going to have to pull Queen into the circle."

Total ruthlessness and ferocity.

"Ugly." He was reading her expression. "Yes, I am. I tried to tell you. I've worked through some of it, but I'll never get rid of all the hate. I'm twisted, Eve."

She smiled sadly. "So am I." She added, "And I'll have no problem with your hating Black or anyone protecting him. Not if Paul Black killed Bonnie. Now stop all these melodramatics and tell me why we're moving."

A slight smile touched his lips, and suddenly the last trace of menace vanished. "Trust you to deflate me."

"I told you that I wasn't afraid of you, John. Though I can see why you might intimidate. It's a civilized world, and you apparently forget that occasionally."

"I'll try to remember around you." His smile disappeared. "It's no use our staying here and trying to trap Black. He's not going to spring it. He's going to set a trap of his own."

"With Judy's daughter, Cara." Eve nodded. "And that bloody carnage in St. Louis was to prove he was serious." She felt sick as she thought of the monstrous brutality that Black had committed just to prove there were no limits to what he would do. That little girl . . . "He'll contact you."

"Without the shadow of a doubt." He turned and picked up his duffel and put it on the bed. "Get your things together. We're not going to wait around for Black to move on us. We're out of here. Then we'll work on turning the situation around."

"Right." Eve had already unzipped her carryall. "Can we get out of here without being seen? You said I was followed."

He nodded curtly. "Service elevator. End of the hall. It leads to the kitchen, and we can go out the employees' entrance."

He had thought of every contingency, Eve thought. But he hadn't thought of Black ignoring the obvious trap and going his own way. The realization sent a chill through her.

"We'll get him, Eve." John was reading her expression. "He's smart, but he's not invulnerable."

Yet he had killed her little girl years ago and had since killed and killed again and no one had been able to stop him. "He seems to be—" She broke off and picked up her case. "Of course he's not invulnerable."

She headed for the door. "Let's go. I'll have to call Catherine soon and tell her that we've left the hotel. I suppose you do know where we're going?"

"Yes." He opened the door for her. "We're going back to my childhood, Eve."

"Son of a bitch." Queen's hand tightened on the phone. "Did you have to cause such a stir, Black? Taking that kid was a bad move. People get upset about children.

Do what you like on your own, but this is my job you're doing."

"Then find a way to take the heat off me," Black said mockingly. "Why are you so upset? You've done it before. Plant some evidence, find a convenient witness to give a false description. Judy Clark will probably die anyway, and that will make it safer. I decided I needed the little girl."

"Don't kill her. There's too much publicity already."

"Don't tell me what to do. You want your ledger. I'm going to get it for you." He added softly, "Cover me just like you've always done, and everything will be fine." He hung up.

Queen cursed beneath his breath. Cover the homicidal son of a bitch? How was he supposed to do that when Black was becoming more reckless all the time? He'd planned for this to be Black's final job for him, but the bastard was going to ruin him if he couldn't find a way to control him.

And if he killed the kid, Queen hoped to hell he hid her body so that no one would ever find it.

Whining asshole.

Black pocketed his phone and turned to the little girl sitting on the chair across the room. She had tousled sandy blond hair and was wearing a pink Cinderella nightshirt. Her feet were bare and dangling a few inches from the floor. She was one of the quiet ones. Her big brown eyes wide and frightened as a doe before the final shot of the hunter.

They were all different. That was what made the child-kills such an exquisite pleasure.

"Did you hear me tell him that your mother was going to die? She wasn't quite dead when I took you from the house." He smiled. "But you saw what I did to her, didn't you?"

She nodded, her eyes filling with tears.

"You mustn't cry. I don't like it. If you cry, I'll do the same thing to you that I did to your mother and grandmother."

"I won't cry." Her voice was almost a sob as she frantically tried to stop. "Please don't hurt me."

"You have eyes like a deer, like Bambi. Did your mother ever let you see the DVD about Bambi, Cara?"

"Yes."

"And do you remember how the hunter killed Bambi's mother?"

The tears were beginning to roll down the child's cheeks. "It was sad."

"But that's what hunters do, they hunt the pretty deer. I've decided that's what I'm going to do with you. I'm going to turn you loose in the forest, and we'll play hunter and deer." He got up and strolled across the space separating them. "I'm a very good hunter, Cara." He reached out and touched her tear-wet cheek. "You're going to have to be very clever, very fast to get away from me. I'm afraid that you won't be able to do it. I'll catch you and kill you and skin you."

"Please. I'll be good." She was sobbing. "Don't hurt me."

"But you're not a good girl. I told you not to cry."

"I'll stop. I'll stop."

"Too late." His hand dropped away. "But we won't play that game for a while. We're going on a little car trip." He took her arm and led her toward the door. "And then I may need you to talk to someone on the phone. You'll do that for me, won't you?"

"I'll do anything you say. I promise. I'll be so good."

Those pretty doe's eyes swimming in tears, gazing frantically up at him. It had been a brilliant idea to go for the hunt. He could hardly wait.

He smiled down at her. "Yes, in the end you'll be very good for me."

Eve gazed in bewilderment at the huge bus terminal in the middle of the city.

"This is returning to your childhood?"

"In a manner of speaking." John took her arm and nudged her through the crowd to the front entrance. "When I was a kid, this was where the housing project that I grew up in was located. Several years after I left, they tore it down and sold the property to a developer. They made it into a bus depot." He shrugged. "I was just as happy. I hated the place."

"The Bricks," she murmured. "You said everyone called it the Bricks."

His brows rose. "You remember that? I'm surprised."

"So am I." The memory had come out of nowhere. "I guess I remember more than I thought about that time."

Then she recalled something else. "I had to gather all my memories of you together once when Bonnie was a baby. I suppose they kind of stuck."

"Really? And why did you do that?"

"Your uncle had just told me that you were dead. I thought I should tell Bonnie a little about her father." She grimaced. "It was a crazy idea. She was only eight months old. She couldn't have understood any of it. But I remember her looking at me as if she did."

"Maybe she did," John said quietly. "You told me the nurse said she was magic. Maybe that was how she was able to come to me in that prison. You gave her the key."

Eve was once more aware of the wave of intimacy that seemed to be a recurring theme. She looked away from him. "I don't know. All I wanted to do was not let her go through life without knowing something about the man who gave her life. All the rest is a mystery. I'm still having trouble with understanding what you told me." She changed the subject. "Why are we here? I'm sure it's not some sentimental journey to the past."

"No." He nodded at the wall of lockers across the terminal station. "When I was looking for a place to hide Queen's ledger, I thought of this spot. I have only ugly memories of this site, and I thought I'd add another bit of ugliness to the place. Why dirty up any other area?" He held out his hand. "The key I gave you?"

She reached in her bag and located it. "The ledger is here?"

He took the key and his pace quickened. "Yes.

Locker 57. Come on, let's retrieve it and get the hell out of here."

She watched him unlock the locker. "It still bothers you? Even though the place was torn down years ago?"

"There's nothing more vivid than childhood memories." He pulled out a leather briefcase, checked inside, and slammed the door of the locker. "Yeah, it bothers me."

That had been a stupid question. A father who had put his cigarettes out on his son's back? That was not a memory that would vanish with time. "But you had your uncle Ted."

He nodded. "And that saved me." He took her elbow. "Let's go. I've got what I came for. This place suffocates me."

She didn't speak until they were in the car and driving away from the bus station. "Then why didn't you find another place for the ledger? It hurts you. It's not worth it."

He shrugged. "Maybe it's a form of self-flagellation. It could be I feel the need to punish myself for all my sins." He paused. "Or perhaps just for one particular sin."

"What sin?"

"I'm not going to use you as a confessor, Eve." He nodded at the briefcase he'd put on the floor of the passenger seat. "Take a look at the ledger. I want you to be able to identify it if it becomes necessary."

She undid the briefcase and pulled out a thin, cloth-wrapped brown leather volume. The pages were stiff, brittle, the entries clear, but in a script that must have been Korean. "I wouldn't be able to identify any of these entries."

"There's a mark in green ink at the bottom of the sixth page. The color is very close to the blue of the other entries. You probably wouldn't know it was there if you weren't aware of the difference."

"I see it." She looked at him. "You believe that there's a possibility the ledgers could be switched?"

"It's possible. If I'm not around, I want you to be able to identify it."

"Why wouldn't you—" Then she understood. "You think you might be killed."

"I have every intention of staying alive. Anything can happen. Now take a photo of the ledger and a few of the pages with your camera phone."

She took the photos, then replaced the ledger in the briefcase. "Now what?"

"Now we go up to my cabin about seventy miles north of the city." He smiled faintly. "It's on a lake, and that place has only happy memories for me. My uncle rented it and took me up there several times when he was on leave. When I managed to start making money after I broke with Queen, I bought the cabin and several hundred acres around it."

"And why are we going there?"

"I know the area. Queen does not. Neither does Black. That's enough reason."

"You're going to call Queen and make a deal?"

He didn't speak for a moment. "Yes, I'll call Queen." But he wasn't committing, she realized. She felt a chill as she remembered that rage that had so shocked her. Well, she had been angry with the senseless atrocity, too. What measures would she take to save little Cara Clark?

She would just have to see how the scenario unfolded.

CHAPTER

17

The cabin was small, only a bedroom, living-kitchen combination, and a tiny bathroom.

"Nothing fancy." John put their bags down inside the door. "I don't entertain here. I'll get the broom out of the closet and sweep up after I make a pot of coffee."

"I'll sweep." The place could use it. It didn't appear neglected, but the dust was a fine film on the floor. "How long has it been since you were here?"

"I don't remember. A year?" He was at the cabinet getting down a can of coffee. The vacuum hissed as he opened it. "When I used to come up here with my uncle, he made sure I cleaned the place up before we spent even an hour here. He hated dirt. That was his military training."

"I remember him as being a very kind man. He loved you."

"Yes." He put the coffeepot on the burner. "And I loved him."

She opened the door and swept the dust outside. The clean air rushed in and made the interior smell of pine and earth. She paused a moment to look out at the incredible beauty of the blue lake. "I can see why you liked it as a boy. It's night and day from the stink of the projects. I would have loved it here."

"Sorry. You wouldn't have been invited. It was strictly a man-to-man outing. No girls allowed."

She smiled. "Chauvinist."

He smiled back at her. "Well, maybe we would have let you come. You're not the usual female. You'd have held up your end."

"You're darned right." She put the broom back in the closet. "I was planning on taking Bonnie camping, but I had school and was too busy." Her smile faded. "Sometimes life goes by too fast, doesn't it?"

"Yes."

"And then it's gone."

"Sit down." He got down two cups and was washing them at the sink. "Bonnie didn't miss what she'd never known. You gave her a great life." He set the cup in front of her. "Maybe the next time around, we'll be able to do it all."

"Do you believe there's a next time?"

"Why not? Millions of people believe in reincarnation. I believe in hope. I believe good people like Bonnie and you deserve a second chance." He poured coffee in her cup. "And I believe that even not-so-good people like me might have a chance to work it out."

She could feel her throat tighten with emotion. "I believe in hope, too. I'm still working on everything else." She took a drink of the coffee. "It's difficult when I want so badly to have Bonnie given a second chance. I ask if I'm fooling myself."

He shook his head. "You always were a complete realist. So was I. But in that prison, I found that reality faded and was only as true as I believed it to be. And dreams could be far more authentic than any reality." He lifted his cup. "And they called me mad. But madness can make life bearable, Eve."

"You're not mad, John."

"You haven't seen me fall from grace. Not really. Tell me that after you have." He looked out the window. "The sun is going down. It will start getting chilly. I'll make a fire as soon as I call Queen." He took another swallow of coffee and pushed back his chair. "Which will be right now." He took out his phone and put it on speaker. "Let's get it over with." He dialed the number. "Then we can get the stench off us by taking a walk down by the lake."

Queen answered after the third ring. "Gallo? Where are you?"

"What an absurd question. Do you really think that I would tell you? As I recall, you sicced your dogs on me and burned my place to the ground."

"That was a misunderstanding. I merely wanted to stop you from making a mistake. Taking Eve Duncan could have been a terrible disaster for both of us. You were much too impulsive."

"No more lies." John's voice was terse. "I know what

Black did to Judy Clark and her mother. It's not your style. You called him in to find out where I was. And you let him take the kid."

"I don't know what you're talking about. I told you I'd find him for you."

"And you did, in Samoa. But I think you screwed up, and now he's pulling the strings. But you must have some control of him, or you wouldn't be furnishing him with information."

"This is all guesswork."

"Good guesses, logical guesses. This is the end of the story, Queen. Stop bullshitting me and let's get down to cases. I'm expecting Black to contact me at any time and offer to trade Cara Clark for your ledger."

He was silent. "I had nothing to do with him taking the kid. You know that Black can't be controlled."

"But you made a deal to put him on my trail."

Another silence. "I didn't like to be at your beck and call. I want that ledger. You've been holding it over my head too long. You should have expected it."

"Oh, I did. But I didn't expect him to murder and take a six-year-old to do it. You know as well as I do that he'll kill that little girl. You've got to stop him."

"I told him not to do it. I said it would be a mistake."

"That's not strong enough. You brought him down on Judy Clark's family. Now you've got to do what you can to stop the damage."

"You should have given me the ledger. None of this would have happened."

"You want the ledger? I have it with me now. It's within reach of my hand. But the moment Black kills that little girl, it will go to the *Washington Post,* and they'll spread it all over their paper. It won't be long until you'll be toted off to a federal prison."

"Wait. Give the ledger to Black. That would solve everything."

"He'll still kill the kid. No, you have to stop him. I want you to come personally and meet with him. I don't care what you do to convince him, but do it."

"I'll call him and try to—"

"Meet him. Face-to-face. Are you frightened, Queen? Is Black too much for you?"

"I'm not scared." Queen hesitated. "You'll give me the ledger?"

"When this is over, I won't give a damn about the ledger. But if Black kills that kid, then I'll blow you out of the water, Queen. Get here and get here fast. I want you to run interference and get me that kid."

"I could try to do it," Queen said cautiously. "Though it would be better to—"

"Catch the first flight to Milwaukee. I'm sending you a photo of the ledger so that you'll know I have it in my immediate possession."

"It's reasonable that you'd give me the ledger," Queen said thoughtfully. "After all, you'll find a way to get Black, and that's what you've always wanted."

"Very reasonable. Now get your ass here as soon as possible." He hung up.

"He's going to come," Eve said.

John nodded. "Why not? It's so 'reasonable.'" He stood up. "Let's go for that walk. I need to cool down."

But he didn't seem nearly as angry as he had after

he'd heard about the attack on Judy Clark and her family. He was tense, not on the edge of explosion.

She fell into step with him as he strode down the lake path. "Will Queen be able to do anything with Black?"

"I doubt it. Black doesn't pay any attention to anything but what he wants to do. But Queen may be able to run interference or cause a distraction."

"That's why you wanted him here?"

"No, I wanted him here because we're coming to the end of the road, and I wanted him where I could reach out and take him."

Her gaze flew to his face. "You're going to kill him?"

"You don't think he deserves it? Let's go over the list. He sent me into that prison and let me rot there. Suicide missions. Protecting Black from being caught and tried for dozens of murders. He gave Black the address where he could find Judy Clark and her little girl."

"I'm not arguing that he may deserve it. He's committed terrible crimes, and he seems to have no conscience." She looked out at the lake. "I'd just rather he be used to save Cara Clark if possible."

"I'll try to let him have his chance . . . first."

But he would not change his mind about Queen's death, she realized. And she was not sure she wanted him to. Queen was not the same brand of monster as Paul Black, but he was a monster just the same. "So we just wait for a call from Paul Black. I'd have thought he'd have contacted us already."

"Black is unpredictable. He enjoys dragging out his kills. He's probably enjoying himself right now."

"You think he's killed that little girl already?"

"If he decided it's worth it to him to get Queen's ledger, then he'll keep her alive . . . until he gets it."

And after that she was dead and thrown away like his other victims.

Like Bonnie.

"We've got to get her away from him."

"Yes." He had reached into his pocket to pull out his phone. He looked up a number and dialed.

"Who are you calling?"

"St. Louis County Hospital. I want to check on Judy. It would be nice if we could be sure that little girl will still have a mother if we can save her."

Eve listened as he talked to the hospital authorities. When he hung up, she asked, "She's still alive?"

He nodded. "But they wouldn't give me any details. Hospitals are careful who they give information to these days. If there's any chance to live, Judy will grab it. She's always been a fighter."

"And she'll want to live for her daughter. She made Catherine promise to save her."

John nodded. "Completely unfair to your friend, but that's how the ruthless maternal streak works. You'd understand and empathize."

"Absolutely." She glanced at him. "And it is ruthless. I may be able to think rationally about Queen, but Paul Black is a different matter. I have to find Bonnie, and I have to kill her murderer. There's no question about it." She looked back at the lake and suddenly shivered. The water looked cold, the entire forest appeared silent and without warmth or life. Was it because she was thinking of death? Or was it some kind of harbinger of things to come?

"Are you cold?"

"A little." She turned back to the cabin. "The sun is down. It's time we went back."

"You go on." He leaned back against a tall pine. "I'll stay here for a while. I'll watch you until you get inside the cabin."

She didn't argue. She had an uneasy feeling that . . . it was almost as if she was being watched. But there could be no one watching in this very private sanctuary.

She glanced back over her shoulder to see John still leaning against the tree beside the lake. His gaze was on her, but there was a remoteness about him that was as chilling as everything surrounding him.

She was glad to get inside the cabin and slam the door. Imagination. They were getting close to Bonnie's murderer, and Eve's nerves were raw and on edge. It was no wonder that she wasn't thinking with any degree of clarity.

The remedy was to get her mind working on a real problem and solution.

Catherine. She still had to call Catherine.

She reached for her phone and quickly dialed.

"I'm in Milwaukee. I just got off the plane from St. Louis," Catherine said when she picked up the call. "Where are you? Still at the Marriott?"

"No, we're at a cabin in the woods about seventy miles from the city." She paused. "Queen should be on his way to Milwaukee. John told him that he'd give him a ledger he desperately wants if he could get Black to release Cara Clark."

"Fat chance. I saw what he did to that kid's mother and grandmother. He likes what he does. I can't see him giving up another kill because Queen wants him to do it."

"Neither does John. But he's hoping for a distraction."

"And I'm thinking Queen will go for a double cross," Catherine said. "But we might be able to use that, too."

"Listen, Catherine, I know you have a stake in finding Black, too. But you can't kill him until I can talk to him. I have to be certain he killed Bonnie. I have to know what happened and where I can find her."

"It's going to be hard to remember that when I think about that kid, Cara, watching what Black did to her mother. But I promise I won't do anything that will hurt you, Eve. How is Queen arriving? Military or commercial?"

"I don't know."

"I'm thinking commercial. He's crooked, and he tries to keep MI from knowing anything about his less legal moves. I believe I'll stick around here at the airport and see if I can spot Queen."

"And then what?"

"I'll play it by ear." She paused. "I just called the hospital. Judy Clark is out of ICU. They think she'll make it."

"Wonderful. John called and inquired, but they wouldn't tell him anything."

"It's a murder case. They probably weren't sure that

he wasn't checking to see if he had to go to the hospital and finish the job. It's a cynical world."

"And you were just as doubtful about him."

"Not anymore. Not about this murder. But that doesn't mean I'm convinced he's one of the good guys. A good guy doesn't dope you and lug you to his lair in Utah." She went on before Eve could answer. "I'll call you if I find out anything interesting. Have you talked to Joe?"

"No."

"Neither have I lately. He called once, and I ignored it, so that I wouldn't have to lie to him. But you *will* hear from him. Joe isn't going to let you fall off the face of the earth. Particularly since he knows Black is surfacing."

"I'm hoping that it will all be over before—"

"Don't fool yourself." Catherine hung up.

Eve wasn't about to deceive herself that she had anything but the smallest chance of keeping Joe away from the danger to come. Yet she had to take that chance. Her world was chaos, and she had to keep Joe away from it.

She went to the window and gazed out. It was nearly dark, and John was a dark shadow against the paler gray shadow of the lake. He was very still. His head lifted, as if he was listening.

What was he hearing?

Sounds of the forest?

Voices?

Did you hear voices, John Gallo?

And she must still doubt his sanity if she thought that there was a possibility that he did.

And what voices?

The voices of men you've killed?

Bonnie's voice?

He was straightening, turning away, coming back to the cabin.

She whirled away from the window, feeling a bolt of panic, as if caught intruding. She went to the stove and put on the coffeepot.

But the question stayed with her.

Bonnie's voice?

Catherine dialed Venable as soon as she hung up from Eve. "I have to know when Queen is arriving in Milwaukee," she said curtly. "He's probably on commercial. Can you get it for me right away?"

"Your wish is my command," Venable said sarcastically. "You do know that the St. Louis police have been making inquiries about you? They want to know if you might have turned rogue."

"It was Paul Black. But Queen is up to his eyebrows in this shit. I have to get that kid away from Black. Can you get me the info on Queen?"

"I'll get it. Anything else?"

"Equipment. Active-infrared night-vision glasses. Guns. I couldn't take mine on the plane." She had another thought. "The latest version of Celltec our people have managed to develop. Deliver it to me at the Milwaukee airport right away."

"And how do you know I have contacts in Milwaukee?"

"You have contacts everywhere."

He swore beneath his breath. "You'll have them." He hung up.

And he would deliver as promised. Venable didn't like the idea of the kid being taken. He wasn't a bad guy if his duty didn't get in the way of his sense of right and wrong. Duty always won hands down in that case. She had learned that through bitter experience.

But he'd come through this time.

She turned and headed for the bar in the terminal to wait for Venable to call her back.

"He's on Delta 105 and should be arriving at eight fifteen," Venable said. "Did you get your equipment?"

"Delivered thirty minutes ago. Very prompt, Venable."

"Thank you. I always like to please you. It was hard as hell to get my hands on that Celltec." He paused. "Be careful, Catherine."

"Queen should be no problem."

"He can recognize you. You're very memorable."

"I'll stay out of his sight. That's why you got me the latest version of Celltec. I can tap into any of his calls from halfway across the airport."

"See that you do." He hung up.

Catherine checked her watch. Thirty minutes before Queen's flight arrival. Time to position herself and get ready.

And hope Queen called Paul Black as soon as he

reached the terminal. Otherwise it might get very dicey if she had to follow him to another location.

Paul Black was refusing to answer his phone, dammit.

The bastard always tries to dominate me, Queen thought. He could imagine Black sitting there smiling as he let the phone ring.

Queen stopped at the baggage claim and dialed again.

That time it rang four times, but Black finally answered.

"I told you I was handling this," Black said. "I don't want you whining at me about the kid. We're getting along just fine, aren't we, Cara? She understands the rules now."

"I'm not going to argue with you about her any longer. There's so much publicity that you can't let her live. It would be too awkward. Just be sure that she totally disappears. Where are you?"

"Just outside Milwaukee."

"Gallo and Duncan aren't at the Marriott any longer."

"I didn't believe they'd stay there for long. But I have you to tell me where they are, don't I? Why do you think I answered your call?"

"You didn't answer the first call," Queen said sourly.

"Where are they?"

"I don't know. I have to find out. Gallo knows about what happened in St. Louis. He thinks you're going to try to use the kid."

"Because he's a very smart man. Is Duncan still with him?"

"Yes."

"Then that will make it easier. She reportedly has a soft heart where children are concerned."

"And a very hard heart where you're concerned. She's sure you killed her daughter."

"Is she? Then that will be a double reason for her to lose her perspective when we start negotiating."

Queen hesitated. "Gallo is pressuring me to become involved. He wants me to persuade you to give up Cara Clark."

Black laughed. "Good God. He doesn't realize what he's asking, does he? He believes I'll listen to you?"

Queen could feel anger flush his cheeks with heat at the sheer arrogance of the words. "He knows I hire you. It would be natural to think that you have respect for my opinion."

Black ignored his answer. "And what did you tell him? That you have no influence on me?"

"No, I thought that we might find a way to trap him. I just arrived at the Milwaukee airport, and I hoped we could work together to get the ledger." He paused. "You do remember that the ledger is the primary goal in this exercise, Black. Everything else is of minor importance."

"He'll give me the ledger to keep me from killing the little girl."

And Gallo would have no more trust in Black's restraint than Queen did. They both knew his word was without value. "You make the first contact, then let's discuss it. I can find a way to lead Gallo and Duncan to you. Then we need to get the job done quickly."

Black was silent. "I'll consider it." He added, "I'm not sure that I want to get out quickly. I promised myself some fine hunting. Cara would be disappointed."

Queen stifled his impatience. Black had to be handled carefully or Queen would never get his hands on the ledger. "Just get me the ledger, and you can do all the hunting you want to do. But you'll have more time to play with the kid if we take care of Gallo and Duncan first. And I can help you with them. You can see that, can't you?"

"If you don't get in my way."

"It will be your rules. Just make the contact. I'll be standing by."

"I'll let you know." Black hung up.

Queen felt a surge of fierce satisfaction as he shoved his phone in his pocket. He had made progress. Once Black thought about it, he would probably agree to let Queen become part of his plans. Black was clearly more interested in the processing of his precious kills than anything else. Once involved, Queen could make the move to assume control.

He picked up his carry-on and moved toward the entrance to pick up his rental car.

"There's some canned beef stew in the cupboard," John said as he opened the door. "We might as well eat something."

"I'm not—" But she was hungry, she realized. They hadn't eaten all day. They had even missed the breakfast

John had ordered that morning at the hotel. "Why not? You heat it, and I'll wash some bowls to serve it."

He nodded and headed for the cabinets. "That sounds like a plan."

It was strange yet oddly comfortable working with John to prepare the simple meal. The momentary uneasiness she'd experienced earlier was gradually disappearing. But the curiosity remained, and she yielded to it when they were almost finished eating.

"I was watching you before you came back to the cabin." She didn't look at him as she spooned up the last of the stew in her bowl. "You looked as if you were listening to something. Were you communing with nature?"

"Nothing so spiritual. My uncle taught me to identify the sounds of the forest. He said someday it could keep me alive. I was concentrating and seeing how much I remembered." He was studying her expression. "You looked a little spooked when I came into the cabin. What did you think I was doing?" He nodded slowly. "You're not sure of me. What was your first thought?"

She hesitated and then said honestly, "Voices."

His brows rose. "Schizophrenia?"

"You said you had delusions in the hospital."

"But not lately. I like to believe I'm on the up path."

"Yet you told me the first time you called me that you had moments of instability."

"And I do." He smiled faintly. "Did I really appear to be listening to voices? Who did you suppose was whispering in my ear? An angel or the devil? No, I've never heard either entity singing to me in this forest."

"Nor anywhere else?"

His eyes narrowed on her face. "Why are you being so persistent?"

Say it. Don't back down. "I was wondering if . . . Bonnie."

"You thought that I was imagining I heard Bonnie's voice? A voice from the dead?" He shook his head. "I'm not that crazy, Eve."

"Crazy? I know someone who would argue that with you." She tried to smile. "My friend, Megan, hears voices from the dead, and she's one of the sanest people I know."

"You believe her?"

"Sometimes it's difficult not to believe her. Though I was more skeptical than you in the beginning." She picked up her coffee cup. "But now I believe that there are many things out there that defy understanding or reality itself. You experienced one in that prison when Bonnie came to you."

"What are you getting at?"

"You told me that you'd dreamed of Bonnie even after she was killed. How many times?"

He stiffened. "Not often."

"Did the dreams come when you were in the depths of despair? When you desperately needed someone, something?"

He was silent, then slowly nodded. "Yes."

"And what kind of dreams, John? Was she so real that you felt as if you could reach out and touch her? After they were over, did you feel a sense of peace?"

"God, yes," he said hoarsely. "Bonnie was— Why are you asking me these questions?"

"Why do you think?" She met his gaze. "How do you think I survived after she died?"

"You dreamed of Bonnie?"

"I dreamed, I hallucinated, I had fantasies. I told myself I was doing all of those things in the beginning. I didn't care. I had my daughter again. Then, gradually, I began to believe her when she told me that she was not a dream." She smiled as she lifted her cup to her lips. "So if that's crazy, then you're not alone in your moments of madness, John."

He didn't speak for a moment. "This wasn't easy for you. It leaves you a little vulnerable. Why did you tell me?"

"The same reason that I told you all about Bonnie from the day of her birth. I felt perhaps I owed it to you." She shook her head. "And to let you know that if you begin to think that visits from Bonnie are a sign of craziness, then at least you're not alone in that particular madness. We share it."

"And another experience that draws us together. As I said, if you're trying to distance yourself from me, then it's going to be more difficult."

"I'll worry about that later." She gave him a level glance. "I'm very confused about how I feel about you, John. There are times when I'm suspicious as hell and wonder if you're the best con man on the planet. There are other times when I believe you're as crazy as Joe and Catherine told me and could be a Mr. Hyde waiting to strike. But I have to rely on my instincts where Bonnie is concerned. I believe you loved her."

He inclined his head. "And so you're willing to take a chance on me."

"Yes, because I believe she must love you, too."

His head jerked back as if she'd struck him. "I wasn't expecting that. I don't deserve her to feel anything for me. I wasn't there for her."

"Maybe it doesn't matter to her."

"It has to matter." His voice was suddenly rough. "It matters to me." He pushed back his chair and strode over to the front door and threw it open. He stood framed in the doorway, his legs parted, the moonlight glinting on his dark hair, gazing out into the darkness. "I've had enough talk about Bonnie, and voices, and things that go bump in the night. All I want to think about is getting Paul Black and killing the son of a bitch. Why doesn't he call?"

Eve could see the barely contained violence in every muscle of his body. Yes, it did matter, and the guilt and blame he felt must be a constant thorn. She stood up and started to stack the dishes. "You can't want it any more than I do. But I guess I'm more accustomed to things that go bump in the night than you are." She carried the dishes over to the sink. "I've gotten to expect it."

He glanced back over his shoulder. "Yet you were always the complete realist as a young girl."

"I still am a realist." She smiled. "I just accept that no one can be sure of just what reality is. Your reality may not be mine . . . or Bonnie's." She changed the subject. "I'll wash these dishes, you dry. Okay?"

"Okay." He turned to face her. "I guess you're aware you scared me a little."

"I know. You'll get used to it." She started the water running. "Bonnie will help."

He smiled. "Oh, and what—"

His cell phone rang.

Eve stiffened, her eyes flying to where he was standing.

John was tense, too, but he shrugged as he checked the ID. "I don't recognize it." But he put it on speaker anyway. "Gallo."

"It's been a long time." The voice was deep and faintly mocking. "And we scarcely exchanged anything but a few words. Do you recognize my voice, Gallo?"

"Black?" Gallo asked curtly. "I could hardly forget you since you tried to kill me the first time I saw you. If you hadn't been an incompetent, I would have been a dead man."

"I wasn't prepared for you." The mockery was gone, replaced by venom. "It was Queen's fault that I blundered. He should have told me that you were some kind of freak of nature. I knew I'd gotten my knife in you, but I couldn't stop you. It was his fault that I ended up with my guts spilling out of me. I've never forgiven him for that." He paused. "Nor you, Gallo. It's been a constant twisting fire inside me that I couldn't move on you."

"You moved on me."

"The little Bonnie? Yes, I did, didn't I? And that was very satisfying, but it's not like being able to get at you face-to-face."

"Then why didn't you do it, you son of a bitch?" John asked harshly. "Why not come after me instead of a helpless seven-year-old?"

"One takes pleasure where one can. I was . . . hesitant about confronting you at the time. No one had ever taken me down before. I was faced with the possibility of my own mortality. I found I had to rebuild my confidence. Now, of course, I realize that you were no real threat. I would have killed you years ago if Queen hadn't kept me away from you because he was afraid that ledger would get in the wrong hands."

"Then if I'm no threat, come and get me."

"But there's the question of little Cara Clark. It's not that simple any longer."

"You're using her as an excuse as you did Bonnie. Threaten a kid because you don't have the nerve to go after me. Did Queen tell you that you needed a negoti-ating tool for the ledger?"

"No, the little girl was my idea. I like to deal with children."

Eve's hands closed into fists at her sides at the smug satisfaction in his voice.

"I thought that Cara could possibly be a good bargain-ing chip. You might have expended all your sentiment on your little girl. Such a tragic loss. But you'd recently reestablished a connection with Bonnie's mother, who has a reputation for embracing all lost children. Is she there with you, listening?"

"Yes," Eve said. "Is Cara Clark still alive?"

"Oh, yes. She's right here on my lap. She's a little stiff. She won't cuddle with me. I think that I scare her. What do you think?"

The horror of that little girl being forced that close to Black made her sick. "I think you should let her go."

"That's my intention. But not just yet."

"When?"

"After we get together. Now to business. Gallo, you've been talking with Queen and trying to get him to persuade me to let my pretty Cara go."

"Have I?"

"Yes, and I imagine that you're trying to get him to set a trap for me. Is that true?"

"You mean Queen didn't tell you that, too?"

"No, he probably isn't sure which one he's going to betray. Right now, you're top of the list. You must have realized that you couldn't trust him. Why did you decide to draw him in?"

"Like you, I recognize the end of the game. I want Queen dead. I don't care whether I do it or you have the pleasure."

Black chuckled. "But that's exactly how I feel. We're so much alike, Gallo."

"I'd cut my throat if I thought that was true."

"But Queen tells me that you don't know what is true or not. Think about it. We've both been killers. You under the guise of patriotism and good of the country. While I'm much more frank and totally without self-deception. I enjoy it. Perhaps if you let yourself explore what you really are, then it might surprise you to look into the mirror." He paused. "Because you might see me."

"That's a lie," Eve said. "There's no one like you. There couldn't be. You're a monster."

"You're defending him." Black chuckled. "He's lured you back to him, hasn't he? Would you like me to tell you a few things about him that would make you bolt in panic? You've never seen him when he loses control. It would frighten you. I saw him. I watched him do things that would completely destroy any tender feelings you might have for him. Ask me anything."

"I want to know where Cara Clark is right now and what we can do to get you to release her."

"Oh, very well. I suppose we should get back to the more boring details. Gallo, you want your chance to get the kid . . . and me. I want my chance to get you, Queen, and the ledger."

"If you kill Queen, the ledger won't be of value to you."

"Wrong. I can use the contacts in it, and there's always the North Korean general from whom you stole it. It won't be as useful as if I had it to hold over Queen, but some sacrifices are necessary. Queen sent a totally inept assassin to kill me in Samoa. I regard that as an end to our relationship." He paused. "Queen told me you were at a cabin in the woods. Is it totally private acreage? I believe you'll agree that we can't have any interference."

"It's very private."

"Then we might as well use that site. I like the idea of wild terrain and deep woods. It fits in with my plans.

Naturally, I'll scout the area to make sure that I have every advantage. When I've made a definite decision, I'll contact you again. Give me the directions to the acreage."

Gallo quickly gave him the directions.

"And we're supposed to sit here and wait?" Eve asked.

"No, I don't imagine Gallo will be sitting and waiting. The cabin would be too easy a target. I'll let you know when the game will start." He paused. "But if I see any sign of police or FBI in the area, I won't wait for the game. I'll kill the kid immediately and bury her so deep, you'll never be able to find her."

"I want to talk to her," Eve said. "How do we know that you haven't already killed her?"

"Because I'm not a fool. Come talk to the nice lady, Cara."

"Hello." The child's voice was a wisp of sound. "What should I say? Can you stop him from hurting me?"

"Yes." She hoped she was telling the truth. "It will just take a little while. Don't fight him, Cara."

"He . . . hurt my mama."

"I know, baby. But your mama is going to get well. We just have to get you back to her."

"Her mother survived?" Black was back on the phone. "She must have a great deal of stamina. I was planning on her living long enough to send a message, then fading away. That goes to show you that you can never be certain if you delay the kill. I may have to go back and do it again."

Eve could hear the child sobbing. "Shut up. She doesn't have to hear that."

"But it pleases me. It's always interesting to see how far I can take it before they break. In this case, she's no real challenge. Not like her mother. Judy Clark fought me all the way until I pinned her to the table. So don't tell me not to prod the little darling. I have to stir some life into her." He hung up.

Eve drew a shaky breath. "And how is he going to do that stirring?"

"It's better not to think about it. Maybe if he's eager to get on with the game, he'll get on the move and forget about her."

Eve could only hope he was right. The sound of the little girl's weeping was enough to break her heart.

"He said he'd tell me anything, and I didn't ask anything about Bonnie. All I could think about was Cara." She shook her head. "All these years of hunting, and I didn't ask that question."

"Because you were concerned about life, not death."

She nodded. "And I think I know one answer anyway. All the signs are pointing at Black. I can wait for a little while to be certain."

But not for too long, she thought. All the agony and searching that had torn her life apart was at last coming to an end. Soon she would come face-to-face with the man who had killed her daughter. Soon she would be able to bring Bonnie home. The realization was stunning.

She asked unsteadily, "So what do we do now?"

"We get the tent and sleeping bags from the cellar and leave the cabin as soon as possible. Black is right; it's an easy target. We'll keep on the move while Black does his reconnoitering. We have to keep one step ahead of him until he gets back to us." He strode toward the door in the back of the room. "And while we're doing it, I'll teach you everything I can squeeze into the time we have about how to get around in my woods."

His movements were alert, swift, almost electrified. He was charged by the battle to come.

She realized she was feeling that same sense of vigor and grim anticipation. How could it be otherwise?

The waiting years were almost at an end.

CHAPTER

18

Yes.

Catherine turned off the listening apparatus of the Celltec and carefully adjusted the calibration.

This version of Celltec was fantastic, she thought. The spy equipment had been around a few years, but the CIA had refined and improved it beyond recognition of the first one she had used. The software enabled her not only to tap into Queen's conversation with Black, but latch on to Black's line and transmit a virus into his phone. It amazed her that, even as BlackBerrys and iPhones and other smartphones had become as powerful as many desktop computers still in use, they still lagged so far behind in antivirus technology.

The Celltec system contained malware code that could infect many of the most popular phones. Once implanted in the phone's operating system, the virus could take location info from the phone's GPS chip and continuously relay it back to her Celltec handheld unit. But if Black was using an unfamiliar or unsupported phone, she would be totally out of luck.

Please let him be using one of the smartphones Celltec could access.

Time to see if it worked.

She held her breath as her finger hit the red button.

Come on . . .

The red light came on!

And it was beeping.

And there was a square indicated on a map that had come up on the Celltec.

She *had* him.

And then he vanished from the screen!

Calm down. He had probably only passed out of the cell-tower area. If she drove where she'd seen the last indication, she'd probably pick it up again.

Now what to do with it. Let it lead her to Black right now.

Or wait until he was in a position where he could more easily be taken? Cara's life could be in the balance.

Catherine couldn't judge until she found out what had transpired in that call of Black's to Gallo.

She quickly dialed Eve. "You heard from Black. Did he try to make a trade?"

"He's in the process. He's going to check out the acreage around the cabin and make sure it suits his purpose . . . and is free of traps. How did you know we'd heard from him?"

"I managed to get a fix on his phone when Queen contacted him a little while ago."

"The miracle of technology," Eve said. "A fix. Can you spot his location?"

"There's a good chance. This miracle isn't foolproof. It can go in and out depending on signal dropouts between cell towers. But I think he's on the move."

"John and I are hoping he will be. It may distract him from doing any harm to Judy's daughter."

"I could distract him," Catherine said grimly. "Just give me the chance. I'll cut his heart out."

"Only if you can find him, and you said that it was an iffy proposition."

"So you want me to hold off until I have a clearer focus at him? Okay, I'll do it. But I don't want to put it off too long. You didn't see what he did to Judy and her mother. He liked what he did, and that kid isn't going to be safe until he's dead." She was moving toward her rental car in the parking lot as she spoke. "I'll see you in a couple hours. If Black is heading your way, then I'm going to be right behind him or ahead of him."

"We're not in the cabin any longer. John said we'd be safer moving from site to site in the woods."

"I'll find you. I'm good in the woods. I spent the last three years chasing drug smugglers in the jungles of Colombia." She had reached her car and took out her keys. "Just make sure Gallo is certain who's tracking him before he goes on the attack." She hung up.

The car door swung open before she could unlock it! She ducked to one side, drawing her gun.

"Yes, it's always wise to know who's the enemy," Joe said. "I seem to be included in that number. Get in the car, Catherine."

Oh, shit.

She went around the car and got in the passenger seat. "I don't have to ask who told you I was here. Venable?"

"We've worked together many times before and have an understanding." He added grimly, "And the understanding is that I'll break his neck if he holds out on me about anything connected with Eve. You might take heed of that understanding, Catherine. I'm very close to that point at the moment. I thought I could trust you."

She could see how near Joe was to violence. She had seen that tension before, tension that could erupt in lethal explosiveness. It had just never been aimed at her. "You can trust me. That doesn't mean that I won't do whatever I have to do to help Eve. After St. Louis, I had to be sure that she'd work with me." She met his gaze. "And she wouldn't do it if you're part of the deal. No risk for Joe Quinn. You mean too much to her. We both know that's true."

"Do we? It's hard for me to embrace the concept since I've been feeling like the invisible man."

"Joe."

"Okay, I may know why she's doing it, but it still sucks. It can't go on. I have to be able to be near her, protect her." His hands tightened on the steering wheel. "I want to break something, someone. Hell, I want to smash the entire world."

"Oh, that's going to help."

"Dammit to hell, what do you expect me to—" He stopped and drew a deep breath. "I didn't say I was going to do it."

"Well, that's a relief. At least you're going to limit the damage."

"I'm counting to ten," Joe said. "And then you're going to stop being a smart-ass and tell me where Eve is right now. Then you're going to tell me exactly what's going on."

She thought about it. "The problem still exists. You'll block my ability to take care of Eve if I get you closely involved. She'll shut me out, and she'll shut you out. Solve the problem for me, Joe."

"I don't want to solve—" He stopped. "You tell me where she is, and I promise not to go to her. She doesn't even have to know I'm in the vicinity. I just won't let Black near her. Is that good enough?"

"It's going to bug the hell out of you."

"You've got that right. But I'll do it. The alternative is to choke you until you tell me what I want to know. That's tempting, but I don't think that you'd break, and I'd be wasting my time."

"Heaven forbid you waste your time, Joe." Why was she hesitating? Joe would keep his word, and all her sympathies were with him in this hellish situation. She had hated having to close him out. Other than her husband, she had never worked with a partner, but Joe would have been her first choice. "It may not be too difficult keeping your distance. Eve and Gallo are luring Black up to Gallo's property in the woods."

Joe's gaze was immediately narrowed on her face. "Place. Conditions. Situation. Talk, Catherine."

The lake was still, the wind barely causing ripples on the dark surface.

"See the pretty water, Cara?" Black said as he got out of the car. "It looks deep, doesn't it? I may let you go into the lake later."

"I can't swim," Cara whispered. "Mama was going to teach me."

"That's only a small problem. But I'll have to consider whether I want to do it. Even deep lakes can't always be trusted with treasures like you."

His gaze wandered over the low hills surrounding the lake. Thick shrubs, tall pines, and evergreens, and no sign of habitation except for the small cabin a few miles to the west. Gallo would not have remained in that cabin, so he must be somewhere in the woods.

Did I chase you out into the night, Gallo?

I know about hunting prey in the wild. I've played this game in a good many countries with prey like little Cara. How good are you? Black wondered.

Not good enough. He had gotten smarter, stronger than when Gallo had come close to killing him that day in Pakistan. Black was ready for him now.

He turned back to the car and jerked Cara out of the car by the ropes he'd tied about her wrists. "Come on. I need to find a place for you, then I need to look around." He paused a moment, his gaze on the lake. Still, deep, welcoming. "No, I can't trust you to the lake. There are other places . . ." He reached for his phone. "But now I believe we need to invite some company to this lovely wilderness. Shall I call my good friend, Queen? He was most upset that I took you from your nice safe home. But he's such a practical man. Be very quiet, and I won't be angry with you." He dialed Queen. "I've done as you suggested and called Gallo. Now we only have to set the trap. Where are you?"

"Still in Milwaukee."

"Then get your ass out of there and come up north to the great outdoors. I need your help." He gave him the directions. "You want your ledger, come and get it."

"That's where Gallo and Duncan are?" Queen asked with barely contained eagerness.

"Yes, somewhere in this five hundred or so acres I'm gazing at right now. We may have to go hunting unless you can draw them into a trap. Are you good at hunting, Queen?"

"No, I hire people like you for jobs like that."

"Me, and men like Gallo. It's rather like the hand of fate that you hired both of us so long ago, and now we're all meeting here." He smiled. "I won't object to postponing my hunt if you can think of a way to lure Gallo and Duncan to me. After all, I'm going to have a spirited hunt and chase later. Think very hard on the way here and come up with something brilliant."

"I won't have to think hard. Gallo wants you to die. I just have to offer you to him in a way that he'll think moderately safe. I'm on my way, Black."

"Good-bye, Queen. Safe trip." He hung up.

The first rabbit hurrying toward the trap, he thought

in amusement. Queen would be trying his best to screw Black all the while he tried to snatch the ledger. But he didn't have the expertise to deal with Black and Gallo. They would be out of his league.

He looked down at Cara Clark. She looked pale, even more fragile than she had hours ago when he'd left Milwaukee. It was disappointing. He hoped in the final stages that fear would make her more interesting. "That was a boring conversation. Nothing new. Nothing interesting. But I guess I shouldn't expect it. Do you know who I just talked to?"

She shook her head. "You said . . . Queen."

"That was his name, but not his state of being." He took the rope and started down the trail. "I just talked to a dead man, little Cara. He didn't know it, but he's a dead man."

"I'm becoming attached to your little paradise, Gallo. It has everything that I require," Black said, when Gallo answered the phone. "I believe this place will do quite well."

Black was here!

Eve came out of the shallow cave where Gallo had set up camp, her gaze instinctively flying to the bank of trees surrounding them. Stupid. Just because he was on the property was no sign that he was hovering this close to them. But it might be just what Black would do. He seemed to have no fear.

"I checked out the cabin," Black said. "Have I driven you into the wilds? You're a hardy specimen, but what about your Eve Duncan? It's not kind to expose a lady to such rough country. Tell her to come to me. I'll take care that she doesn't suffer."

"Where should I come, Black?" Eve asked.

"So eager?" Black said. "Maybe she's a fitting mate for you after all, Gallo."

"Tell us how we can get Cara Clark," Gallo said.

"For a start, you have to keep to the proper order. As soon as Queen arrives, I'm going to send him to you to get the ledger. You'll give it to him and send him back to me."

"The hell I will. Once you have the ledger, you'll kill the child."

"You think you'll have no bargaining power? But you will, you know. I'd much rather have you to gut than that ledger. That will be step two. Believe me, I wouldn't risk not being able to draw you to me. Of course, I'll insist you be accompanied by your Eve. After all, she has a vested interest. I can't wait to have a discussion with her. No, I have plans for the little girl that involve you. The only way I would change them is if you get stubborn and don't give Queen the ledger. Then I'd have to do a reversal and kill Cara first. I *will* do that if you spoil the splendid scenario I've developed for Cara's end."

And Eve had no doubt he meant every word he said.

Gallo glanced at Eve and shrugged. "It seems we have no choice at present."

"Where are you now?" Black asked.

"I'm not a fool, Black. Send Queen down the south

path around the lake. I'll come to him somewhere along that stretch. If I see you following him, then Queen will have a long walk for nothing."

"He'll be alone. I'm saving my energy for the big push. But don't make the mistake of trying to follow him back to me. I'll let you know when he arrives here." He hung up.

"Is he lying about keeping Cara alive?" Eve asked.

John shook his head. "There's no way to be sure, but it's consistent with what we know about Black. He wants it all. She'd still be valuable to him if he thought he could use her as bait for a trap."

But John had been right. The choice had been too slim to take a chance on refusing Black.

"He made me feel helpless." She took out her phone. "But we're not helpless. He doesn't know about Catherine. That's an ace in the hole. There has to be a way of getting around this. I'm calling Catherine." She dialed quickly. "She said she might be able to find him with that gadget. Let's give her an opportunity."

Catherine answered almost immediately. "I'm about four miles from the property. Trouble?"

"Black just contacted us. He's sending Queen to pick up the ledger, then he'll have plans later that include John and me. We can't do anything about Queen, but Cara Clark should be safe for a while even after he picks up the ledger. He has plans for her, and they're probably as diabolical as he is. Lord, I hope she'll be safe. But we have to know where Black is on the property fast."

"I'll find him. Don't do anything until I do."

"No promises. Judy's little girl won't stand a chance unless we play this right. Just line up that high-tech phone gadget and locate Black. We'll take it from there."

"I'll call you when I know something." She hung up.

Eve turned to John. "It will give us an edge if she's able to track him. I'm just praying that she can."

John shrugged. "Gadgets can be fluky. I'd rather trust old-fashioned scouting."

"Catherine is smart. We've got to give her a chance."

"If she blows it, and Black catches her, then the kid is dead."

Eve knew that was true, but the actual voicing of it sent panic soaring through her. "She won't blow it. She's a professional. And she cares about that kid, dammit."

John didn't answer as he turned away. "I'm going to scout around the immediate perimeter and make sure we're secure. Stay here and keep your hand on your weapon." He disappeared into the shrubbery.

Eve leaned back against the huge oak tree and stared after him into the darkness. She couldn't blame him for being doubtful. Catherine was only one person, and even the most skilled professional would have difficulty in the situation in which Eve had tossed her. Eve just had to trust her.

But she had problems with trust, and Catherine had only appeared in her life recently.

Before Catherine, she had let only Joe come close to her.

Joe.

A pang of aching loneliness swept through her. She had tried to push thoughts of him away, but they were suddenly all around her. She wanted desperately to see him, touch him. She wouldn't feel such panic if Joe were here. He was a rock, a north star to guide her.

God knows she needed that steady north star in these woods.

Don't be selfish, she thought in disgust. What she needed didn't matter. It was right that she had made sure Joe wouldn't be involved in the madness Black was weaving around them.

But that didn't stop the loneliness.

"Did you pull up the map, Joe?" Catherine asked.

"Yep, I've got it." Joe was squinting at the map he'd accessed on his computer from the county records. "The deed had to be redone when the property was sold a few years ago to Gallo. It should be accurate."

"Print it out. You can hook up the computer to my portable printer on the backseat."

"Right."

"We're about a mile from the property now. I think we'd better ditch the car and start hiking." Catherine pulled onto a side road and drove a mile or so until she found a turnout that would completely hide the car and pulled deep into the brush.

Joe pulled out the map from the printer. "Let's go."

She flicked off the headlights. "And where are we going?"

"I'm checking terrain. There are three areas where Black would be unlikely to set up camp. There's a marsh to the east, high hills on the north tip of the lake, and a stretch to the southwest that was cleared of timber and would be very exposed." He was circling the areas as he spoke. "Anywhere else is a possibility."

"That still leaves a hell of a lot of territory for us to cover." She looked away from him. "We could try to follow Queen back after Gallo hands over the ledger."

"You've been working with Venable too long. Are you willing to risk Cara Clark's life if Black finds out that someone is tagging Queen?"

"Not unless there's no other option." She shrugged. "You're right, my mind-set is different from yours. Let's get going."

She took the Celltec device out of the car and pressed the access button. No light. No red button. "Dammit, I can't get any response. But Eve says he's here some-where. Maybe we're out of cell-tower range."

"Whatever." Joe was moving quickly through the brush. "I'm not going to wait for your gadget to kick in while he could be killing Eve and the kid."

And neither was Catherine. She jammed the Celltec in her pocket and followed him.

"Queen is on his way," Black told Gallo. "Don't keep him waiting. The poor man isn't really equipped any-more for the rough life. He's gotten soft since his early years in the military. Hiring people like us to do his dirty work has sapped his strength."

"But not his greed."

"No, that goes on forever. I'll see you shortly, Gallo." He hung up.

John turned to Eve. "Stay here." He got the ledger from his duffel. "And look sharp."

"I'm going with you." She held up her hand as he opened his lips. "I won't get in your way, but I won't be left behind."

"Have it your way." He turned and moved toward the lake. "But if I go down, you don't stay around and try to save my neck. You take off and do any rescue attempt from long distance."

She didn't answer.

"I mean it, Eve."

"If you go down, you're out of it, and I make my own decisions." She added grimly, "So if you want your way, you'd better not go down, John. Where are we going to intercept Queen?"

"The path winds a good three miles through heavy brush that starts about a half mile from here." He was walking fast, almost trotting. "I'll reconnoiter the area on both sides of the trail to make sure Black hasn't staged an ambush, then wait for Queen to show." He frowned. "And you will get in my way. I'll have to worry about you."

"Then park me somewhere close to the path and come back for me after you make sure the area's clear." She kept pace with him. "That's as far as I'll go, John."

He gave her an exasperated glance but didn't reply.

Five minutes later, they entered into the thick shrubbery that John had mentioned. There was bright moonlight, but the lake path was barely discernible given the overhanging foliage and twisting turns.

John nudged her deeper into the shrubbery. "Don't move."

Then he was gone.

Could she trust him to come back for her? He was being too damn protective.

But John appeared beside her several minutes later. "Come on." He took her arm and was half pushing her down the path. "Queen will be coming around that second curve up ahead in a few minutes. I want to be there ahead of him."

She pulled her arm away and reached in her jacket for her gun. "Then stop protecting me and go get him. I'll be right behind you."

John moved rapidly ahead of her and around the turn.

Her heart was beating hard as she ran after him. Queen might not be as deadly as Black, but he was totally without conscience, and that itself was dangerous.

She stopped short as she came around the turn.

Queen was standing in the center of the path staring warily at John Gallo.

Queen glanced at her as she came into view. "Eve Duncan? I don't believe we've formally met, but I feel as if I know you intimately. You must think she's expendable, or you wouldn't have brought her along, Gallo. Black will kill her, you know. Probably in front of you if he thinks you have a passion for her."

"I know he'll try."

Queen smiled. "I'll bet on him. He's remarkable in his field. Of course, he has one glaring fault. He's unpredictable. His bloodlust is so extreme that it sometimes dominates his reasoning. I've had a few problems with him on that level lately, but I've worked them out."

"Congratulations," Eve said dryly. "Maybe because you're two of a kind."

He shook his head. "He's only a tool. We're nothing alike." He turned back to Gallo. "The ledger."

John reached into his pocket and pulled out the ledger. "Catch." He threw it to Queen. "For all the good it may do you."

"Sour grapes? You mustn't be bitter that I've finally won the prize." Queen pulled out a small pen flashlight and was shining it on the first pages of the ledger. "Okay, no tricks. Not that I'd ever suspect you of trying to cheat me." He tucked the ledger in his jacket. "Now I'd better get back to Black. We wouldn't want him to get nervous. He meant it when he told you he'd kill the kid."

"And will still kill her if no one stops him," Eve said.

"You may try. Black is looking forward to it. He's planned something special." Queen added viciously, "I wish I could be here for the show. I'd like to see you taken down, Gallo. But it's safer for me to take the ledger and ride off into the sunset." He turned and started back down the path. "May you both rot in hell. Good night and good-bye."

He disappeared around the curve of the path.

"It's so tempting," John murmured. "It would only take me thirty seconds to reach him and break his neck."

"Judy's daughter," Eve reminded him.

He reluctantly tore his gaze away and turned on his heel. "It was only a thought." He headed back in the direction of the cave. "We've got to hope that Queen isn't as adept as he thinks about handling Black. Come on, let's go back and wait for Black's next call."

No sign of either a campfire or a lantern.

Joe shinnied down the pine tree to where Catherine waited on the ground. "Nothing."

She nodded. "I didn't think we'd get lucky." She glanced down at the Celltec. "And this thing is giving us zilch." She punched the cell-tower locator button. "It indicates there's possible tower access in the south and east. Maybe we'll get lucky." She started striding through the brush. "I guess we strike out to the south and try there."

Joe moved ahead of her. "Dammit, it took us over an hour to search this quadrant."

She was as bitter and discouraged as he. Time must be running out. She had hoped that they'd be able to get on Black's track right away. "Maybe we can split up and each take—" Her phone rang.

Eve.

"We've just turned over the ledger to Queen. Tell me that you've got Black pinpointed."

"I wish I could," Catherine said. "I'm moving south now. Let me know if Black calls you."

"There's no 'if' about it. He'll call," Eve said. "But we can't control the when. I hope it's not right before he kills Cara. He'd probably enjoy having us on the line when he did it." She paused, then added shakily, "Find him, Catherine. He killed Bonnie and so many others. We can't let him kill anyone else."

"I'll call you as soon as I spot him. Take care, Eve."

"And how is she supposed to take care of herself to-night?" Joe asked savagely, as Catherine hung up the phone. "She'll be so busy trying to save that kid that she won't think of herself. And I'm not there to do it for her."

"John Gallo is there," Catherine said quietly. "She's not alone, Joe."

"No, she's with a man who will bring Black down on her without a second thought. Hell, Gallo may be worse than Black for all we know. Why couldn't we convince her of that?"

There would be no sense in arguing with Joe right now. He wouldn't be able to think logically until he had Eve safe. And Catherine wasn't sure she wanted to argue. There were moments she was as scared as he was at Eve's situation.

She shoved her phone in her pocket and moved forward through the brush. "South, Joe."

"I've got it," Queen said jubilantly as he strode into the camp. He pulled the ledger out of his pocket and waved it. "No trouble at all. He forked it over without batting an eye. Gallo was meek as a church mouse."

"I'm glad you were pleased. I know he gave you a bad time on occasion. It's always good to get your own back, isn't it?" He glanced at Cara sitting a few yards away. "Aren't we happy Mr. Queen got what he wanted?"

Cara was staring at Queen, her eyes wide. "But you said he was—"

"Soon." Black turned back to Queen. "I'm trying to teach our little friend the connection between cause and effect. But she's a bit confused. I believe I'm going to have to demonstrate."

Queen's smile faded. "Well, I'll leave you to your . . . lesson. Now that I've got the ledger, I've no need to stay here any longer. I'd just be in your way."

"That's correct. It's true I don't need you any longer."

"And the remainder of your fee will be deposited in your usual Grand Cayman account. I'll be in touch when I need you again."

Black smiled. "I believe you're taking me for granted. I really don't appreciate your doing that. I've decided I'll do a little freelancing on my own."

Queen stiffened. "As long as you don't get yourself in a situation that I'll have to pull you out of. I can't allow you to be arrested."

"Because I know too much?" He spoke to Cara again. "You see, knowing a great deal can be either a good thing or bad depending on the point of view. You can see that Colonel Queen is breaking into a sweat because he thinks it's a bad thing." He glanced back at Queen. "We're confusing her again. She has so little time that I hate to have that sweet head in a whirl."

"We'll talk later," Queen said curtly. "I'll call you."

"But that would defeat the purpose. I think it has to be settled now." He pulled a pistol from his jacket. "For the good of Cara."

Queen's eyes widened in panic. "What are you doing?

We have a deal. You'd be lost without my help. The police would pick you up in a heartbeat." He was backing away, his hand inching toward his shoulder holster beneath his jacket. "I'll double the fee for your next job for me. Put the gun away."

"I wish I could. I don't like guns. They lack the personal touch. But in this case . . ." He shot Queen in the stomach. "I'll make do."

Queen screamed and clutched his belly.

Black aimed and shot him in both knees.

Queen fell to the ground, groaning with pain.

Black moved leisurely to stand over him. He fired into Queen's chest. "You see, even though the pain is there, it's still only a remote pleasure for me." He added, "So I might as well just end it."

He shot Queen in the head.

He turned to Cara. "Dead man. Just as I told you."

Cara was staring in horror at the remains of Queen's skull, which had been almost entirely blown away. She started to cry.

"I'm getting very tired of all that weeping." He reached down and plucked the ledger from Queen's jacket and stuffed it in his own. "I think it's time we started the hunt."

"Five!"

Joe stood frozen, listening for more shots.

"East," Catherine said tensely. "A little toward the north, but definitely the east."

And there weren't any more shots.

Joe whirled and started at a run toward the eastern quadrant of the property.

"You think it's Black?" Catherine was right behind him.

"Good chance. I'd bet that Queen is no longer with us." He hoped desperately he was right, that none of those bullets had been aimed at Eve or Judy's daughter. "But at least we have a clue to his location. Now, if we can get there before he moves on—"

"And it's east. There's a chance of cell-tower access. We might be able to zero in on him. But we don't have much time. He'll know those shots are a giveaway."

Which meant Black didn't care, that he thought he could afford to let Gallo and Eve know where he was. A trap?

But he didn't know Joe and Catherine were there and tracking him. That could be an advantage.

If there was such a thing in this ugly game.

"East." Eve's head lifted, her gaze flying to the trees. "Those shots came from the east, John."

He nodded and jumped to his feet. "Black." He grabbed his rifle. "Will you stay here?" He answered his question. "No, of course not. Then stay close, dammit."

He took off at a dead run.

"We have to hurry along now," Black told Cara as he jerked her after him up a low hill by the ropes binding her wrists. "Those shots were not only unsatisfying, they were dangerous. But what is life without a challenge? Gallo and Eve will be hot on our trail, so I think that I should make them play the game on my terms. I always have to control the play. Queen didn't realize that, did he? I was right to shoot him, wasn't I?"

Cara was sobbing. "Dead. Ugly."

"Yes, death is ugly. But the art of killing is beautiful. It's power and excitement and everything that life is about." He pulled her the rest of the way to the top of the rise to stand beside him. "And that's what you're going to give me, Cara. Not that shallow little jolt of pleasure I felt with Queen." He pointed to the high hills bordering the north tip of the lake. "Do you know what's behind those hills? A little town, houses, stores, a church. I couldn't touch you there. You'd be safe. You'd like that, wouldn't you? Oh, yes, I can see you would. You're not at all grateful for the kind way I've treated you." He untied her wrists. "Go on, run. The path is clear to the hill, then you'll have to scramble through the brush on your own. Try to get to all the people who will save you from me. They'll even take you to your mother."

She didn't move, frozen. "You're letting me go?"

"Yes." He squatted in front of her, his eyes holding her own. "But I'll be coming after you. If you stop, if you hide, I'll find you and I'll cut you to pieces like I did your grandmother. You remember that, don't you?"

He could see the pulse jumping with terror in her throat.

"Yes," she whispered. "She screamed, but nobody could hear her . . ."

"But everyone will be able to hear you if I catch you." He leaned closer. "Run, little deer . . ."

She gasped and whirled and flew down the path.

Black stood up and watched her run, stumble, fall, and jump to her feet to run again.

He smiled.

The prey had been put to flight.

Now to bring in the other prey to complete the hunt.

He dialed Gallo.

"You sound short of breath. I suppose you heard the sounds of Queen's demise. Are you hurrying toward me in hopes of saving little Cara?"

"You didn't kill her?"

"Not yet. That was only Queen, though Cara was a little upset with all the blood. She started sobbing again. You'd think shock would kick in and stop that nonsense. It was annoying me. So I sent her packing."

Silence. "What are you talking about?"

"I told her that she'd only be safe if she reached the town behind that high hill at the end of the lake."

"There's no town there, you bastard."

"I know, but I had to give her incentive to keep her running. I couldn't have her collapsing and spoiling the hunt." He paused. "Just as I'm giving you incentive to join the hunt. If I track her down, Cara will die. Unless you find her in time. Or unless you kill me. Though I'm betting I'll take you and Eve Duncan out, then be free to finish Cara Clark. Would you like to give me odds?"

"No, you don't have a chance. I'm going to kill you, Black."

"You might if you were the same man you were when

you came close to killing me all those years ago. You had a divine insanity that gave you power. You knew what you were and what you had to do. Now you don't even remember that glory, you're confused and weak." He chuckled. "But I can't talk to you any longer. Cara is almost out of sight, and I have to start the chase. But she's such a little girl I won't have trouble catching up with her." He hung up.

"I'm coming, Cara," he murmured as he started down the path. "I can almost hear your heartbeat. Run . . ."

CHAPTER

19

"Black's made contact," Catherine said curtly as she hung up from talking to Eve. "He's turned Cara loose on the hill at the north tip of the lake, and he's staging some kind of macabre hunt. Eve and Gallo are on their way."

"And so are we." Joe stopped and gazed at the hill looming over the lake. "Black and Cara are approaching the hill from the east. Follow them on that route, and we risk an ambush. We need to climb the hill from the west slope and try to surprise Black."

"But we can't circle the lake and get on the other side of the hill. It would take too much time."

"No, we can't do that." He gave her his gun and ammunition, but kept his knife. "We split up."

"What?"

He moved down the bank and took off his boots and shirt. "I swim across the lake and go up the hill from the west side. You follow Black along the east route. One of us should be able to pick him off."

"Okay, but I'm calling Eve and telling her I'm on my way to join them. I can help them zero in on Black if I can pick up that tower signal." She hesitated. "The lake's pretty wide. I couldn't swim that distance. Can you make it?"

"Come on. I was a SEAL. I live on a lake." He jumped into the lake and gasped. Cold. He started stroking. "Hell yes, I can do it. Get moving, Catherine."

When he glanced over his shoulder, she had disappeared.

Good. No arguments. Just Catherine acting with her usual logic and efficiency. One of them had to stop Black and get the job done.

He swam harder, faster, fighting the cold. Block it out.

He had to get to the other side.

Cara was almost to the top of the hill, Black noticed.

She was out in the open, and the moonlight shone on her like a pale spotlight.

Black could see her scrambling desperately, slipping on the rocks, falling, picking herself up, and running again. The child had more stamina than he had thought she possessed. Perhaps it was only fear that had seemed to paralyze her and made her appear less than she was.

And if Black could see her so well, then she would be clearly visible to Gallo and Eve Duncan if they were anywhere near.

"Perfect bait," he murmured. "You're doing well, Cara. That desperation is enough to wrench the heart. How could they resist?" He moved farther behind the huge boulders. His rifle was loaded and ready. Again, not his preference. He carried other weapons, a pistol, two knives. But a rifle would be safer with Gallo.

Was he still wary of Gallo?

Nonsense. It was just smarter to handle the kill this way. He would take his time and use one of the knives on little Cara later. It would be enough.

That idea would horrify Eve Duncan, he thought with amusement. Come save her, Eve, as you failed to save your own child. Come on, Gallo. Watch the little one struggle and fight for life.

His finger poised over the trigger as he watched the path.

But hurry, I'm getting impatient.

"Oh, God, I see her," Eve said in agony. Poor child. Desperation and panic were in the little girl's every movement. "But where's Black? He has to be here."

"Somewhere close." Gallo's gaze was raking the terrain. "And waiting for us. Don't move. We have cover on the path at this point, but we'll be wide open if we go another thirty yards."

"Dammit, where's Catherine? She said that she could tell us where—"

"Don't curse the bearer of the Celltec." Catherine had suddenly appeared out of the shrubbery to the left of the path. She was dressed in black pants and shirt and looked lean and graceful and totally competent. She caught sight of Cara and inhaled sharply. "Bait. He's staking her out."

"That's obvious." Gallo glanced at her, then looked back at the top of the hill. "You're Catherine Ling. I've heard a good deal about you. Eve thinks you can work minor miracles. I suggest you start."

"You don't have the right to tell me what to do," Catherine said coldly. "It's because of you that Eve is in this mess, and that kid up there is on the verge of getting killed."

"Catherine," Eve said. "Can you locate Black?"

"Yes. I should be in tower range, and I'll bet he's close enough." Catherine pulled out the Celltec. "Come on," she murmured. "Find the bastard . . ." She pressed the button.

The beeper went off immediately, then the small screen lit up with coordinates and squared an area. "Jackpot," Catherine whispered. "The boulders. He's behind the boulders."

Eve's gaze flew to the four huge boulders blocking the path. Steep incline on one side falling to the lake, open terrain on the other, where Cara was climbing. "There's no way to get to him!"

"There's a way," Catherine said slowly. "Just not for us. We have to hang tight."

"What the hell are you talking about?" Gallo said roughly. "You stay here, and I'll go off the path in the shrubs until I run out of cover, then take off after the kid. You give me protective fire until I can grab her and get her behind that stand of trees."

"Too risky," Catherine said. "Hang tight. We'll have a chance if—"

"Gallo!" It was Black shouting. "I'm tired of waiting for you. I know you're out there. Perhaps you need a little encouragement."

A bullet caused the rocks to splinter two feet from where Cara was climbing.

She looked back with panic and frantically tried to climb faster.

"The next bullet will hit her heel. It will probably take her foot off. Do you want to see that, Eve?"

"No," Eve shouted. "Don't shoot her, Black." She turned to Gallo. "You go after her the way you said. I'll go up the path and try to distract him."

"Come on," Black called. "And bring Gallo with you. I was disappointed that I was going to have to use a rifle. This will be much better."

"I'll go slow," Eve said. "I'll talk to him on the way. Get to her, John."

Catherine was cursing. "Dammit, stall. Don't do this."

"No choice," Eve said. "He meant what he said. I'm not going to let him blow off body parts while we watch. Go, John. Once she's safe, we can go after Black."

"Son of a bitch. You're right, no damn choice." John ducked into the shrubbery and was gone.

"Eve, listen to me. I know you're frantic about the kid, but there's another chance to—" She shook her head. "But I don't know if it will be in time."

"If you get a shot, take it, Catherine." Eve started down the path. She shouted. "Hold your fire, I'm coming,

Black. Gallo doesn't think Cara is important enough, but I do. Maybe after you have me, you'll be able to persuade him."

"Oh, yes, I can be very persuasive with your kind of collateral."

"Keep on talking to him, Eve," Catherine said curtly. "Stall. Joe should be here anytime."

"Joe." Eve stopped on the path as shock seared through her. "What are you talking about, Catherine? Joe?"

Eve Duncan had stopped in the middle of the path and was looking back over her shoulder, Black saw, annoyed. What was happening? Was Gallo trying to talk her out of coming?

"I mean it, Gallo," he shouted. "Don't play with me. Maybe I should blow off your lady's foot instead of the kid's. I'm aiming right now."

"But you'll never pull the trigger."

His head jerked around to see the man who'd spoken crouched on the rock behind him. He received a wild mixture of impressions as the man jumped him. Barechested. Barefoot. Brown hair plastered and damp.

Then he was knocked to the ground and the attacker was on top of him and jerking the rifle out of his hand. It went off as he threw it to one side.

Black was cursing as he reached for his knife in his arm holster. "Who the hell are—" But he knew who he was. "Quinn." His knife plunged up at Quinn's abdomen. "Son of a bitch, how did—"

Quinn grabbed his wrist and twisted the knife to one side. "Give it up, Black. I don't want to kill you yet. You have questions to answer."

Black kneed him in the groin and rolled out from underneath him. "I'm not going to die, Quinn. I'm never the one who dies." The edge of his knife tore across Quinn's upper arm. "I'll kill you all."

"The hell you will." Quinn's knife sliced down and entered Black's chest.

Black shrieked.

Quinn sat back on his heels, his breathing hard, harsh. His eyes were glittering wildly in his set face. "Don't die. I was careful. That shouldn't have been fatal. I won't have you dead. I still have a use for you."

Eve tore around the boulder and stopped short.

Joe was sitting beside Black, covered in blood.

Joe's blood?

"Joe?" she whispered. "My God."

"Stay away from him," Joe said. "He's not dead yet, and a viper can kill you with his dying strike."

"To hell with him." She came forward anyway. "All that blood . . ."

"A lot of mine. Most of it is his."

"Where?"

"Arm." He bent over Black. "You stay awake. You keep alive, dammit."

"Oh, I'm alive." Black's voice was hoarse, vicious. His eyes were glaring up at Joe. "She's soft. She won't let you kill me."

"I will kill you. It's only a matter of time." Joe turned to Eve, and said fiercely, "But he can't slip away yet. I won't let him."

"Joe!" Catherine had come around the rocks. Her gaze went immediately to Black. "Good job. But you should have finished him." She glanced back at Joe. "Do you need any help?"

"Not now."

"Then I'm going up the hill and grab that poor kid and bring her down. Eve can take care of you." She turned and disappeared behind the rocks again.

Eve took another step closer to Joe. "Let me—"

"No, I don't need you to take care of me." Joe's eyes were boring into Black's. "All I need is for you to listen while this bastard talks to me. It has to end. We both have to be free. He's going to tell me where he buried Bonnie, or I'll start cutting him to pieces."

"Bonnie . . ." Black was gazing up at him maliciously. "You want to know . . . where Bonnie is? Screw . . . you, Quinn."

"You like making people hurt, don't you? That kid up on the hill. Her mother." Joe put the point of the knife at his throat. "You want pain? I'll show you pain, Black."

"Joe."

He didn't take his gaze from Black. "You've got to know, Eve. He's got to tell you. Where's Bonnie?"

Black spit in his face.

"Where?" Joe didn't move the knife to wipe away the spittle.

"Let me have him." Eve hadn't realized that Gallo

had come and was standing a few yards away. His expression was as grim and savage as Joe's. No, perhaps more savage. "He'll talk to me."

"Gallo." Black's gaze was glittering with ferocity. "I've been waiting a long time for you. Were you so afraid of me that you had to send Quinn to do your dirty work?"

"Shut up, Black." Gallo's voice was almost guttural. "I just came from seeing what you did to Judy's daughter. She's so terrified Catherine couldn't get near her. She's like a wild animal."

"But that was the purpose," Black said. "The hunt wouldn't be nearly as entertaining if she wasn't sufficiently primed."

Joe jabbed him in the throat. Blood ran. Black flinched and began to curse.

"Where did you bury Bonnie?" Joe was ignoring everything around him but his one objective.

"Tell us," Gallo said.

Uneasiness had suddenly supplanted the mockery in Black's gaze as it flew to Eve. "Torture? Aren't you going to stop them?"

"Did you stop when you killed all those children?" Eve said unevenly. "Did you stop when you killed Bonnie? I want to bring my daughter home. Tell me where you buried her after you killed her."

His lip curled. "Bitch. Gallo's bitch. I should have killed you when I had the chance. You and your Bonnie and—" He broke off with a cry as Joe's knife bit down again. "Okay, take him away. I'll talk to you."

"Get off him, Joe," Eve said.

Joe had already swung off Black and moved a few feet away. "Not for long."

Black was staring malevolently at Eve even as he scooted back. "He doesn't like to hear the truth. But you were Gallo's bitch, and now you're that bastard Quinn's bitch. All of this is your fault. I wish I had—no!" Joe had made a motion toward him. He scrambled farther away from him. "You want to know about Bonnie. I'll tell you about her. Such a pretty little girl. Different. I was practically salivating when I first saw her after I followed Gallo to your place. But the job I was being paid for was Gallo. I couldn't move on her."

"But you did move on her later," Gallo said. "Admit it."

"You'd like that wouldn't you?" Black said softly. "You want the bitch to hear it."

"I *have* to hear it," Eve said. "What difference does it make to you. You're probably proud that you did it. Isn't that what you're all about? The killing and savagery and—"

"Yes, I'm proud of my power." He smiled, and his gaze never left Gallo. "And I have no need of Bonnie Duncan's death to add to it. I don't have to take credit for her anymore. Queen isn't alive to pay any longer."

Gallo went rigid. "What are you saying?" he asked hoarsely.

"What do you think I'm saying?" Black asked. "The truth, Gallo. Isn't it time?"

"And what is the truth, Black?" Eve asked.

"I don't know where your Bonnie is buried," Black said. "I didn't kill her."

"Liar!" Gallo said.

"Am I?" He shook his head. "You're not going to be able to convince anyone of that." His gaze darted to Eve. "Don't you want to know who did kill her? I find I can't wait to tell you."

Eve moistened her lips. "Who?"

"Gallo."

Gallo made a low exclamation and lunged forward.

Joe jumped up and stepped in front of him. "Stay where you are. I want to hear this."

"Gallo did it. A fit of madness. One of his blackout periods. Queen said he was always having them." Black's words were coming fast, tipped with venom. "He came back to Atlanta after Pakistan. He killed her."

"No!" Gallo said. "I didn't. I wouldn't."

"You did kill her. Can't you all see it? Look at Gallo's face."

They were looking at Gallo's face, and what Eve saw there stunned her.

Anger. Fear. Torment.

"Shit. Stop!" Gallo's gaze was the only one focused on Black, and he tried to push Joe aside. "His boot. He's going for—"

But Black had already retrieved a dagger from his boot holster and staggered to his feet.

Joe half turned, but it was too late. Black's dagger sank into Joe's back.

Eve screamed.

Joe was staggering back, slowly falling to his knees.

"Oh, God." Eve ran forward and sank to her knees in front of him, trying to hold him. "No." It couldn't be happening. "No, Joe . . ."

Black was running for the rifle on the ground a few yards away. He didn't reach it before Gallo was on him.

Gallo's arm went around his neck, jerking it back. "Say it's a lie, you bastard."

"You did it." He was straining to get the rifle. "You know you—"

Gallo's arm tightened and twisted, breaking Black's neck.

He fell to the ground, dead.

"Eve."

Eve was hardly aware that Gallo had spoken. She was carefully laying Joe on the ground.

Her fingers were checking the pulse on his throat. Alive!

Relief surged through her. But unconscious. Going into shock. The blood pouring from his chest. How long would he stay alive?

"Eve." Gallo was beside her now. "I need to—"

She ignored him as she reached for her phone and called Catherine. "Joe's hurt. We're going to need an air ambulance. I hope he doesn't die before it gets here. Come and help me." She hung up.

"Let me help you, Eve."

She didn't look at him. "You can't help me." She was trying to stop the blood. "I can't even look at you right now. I'll deal with you later."

Pressure. She had to apply pressure. But what if the blade had torn an organ?

"You think I killed her."

"I think Black was telling the truth," she said unevenly.

Gallo was silent for an agonized moment. "So do I."

When she glanced up, he was gone.

It was all a hideous nightmare.

Oh, Joe, why did you come?

I knew it would happen.

Why didn't you let me go?

"Eve." Catherine dropped to her knees beside Joe. "I should have stayed. I shouldn't have left you to go after Cara." She was examining the wound. "It's bad."

"I know," Eve whispered. "I don't know how bad."

"Neither do I. I called for help, but I don't know how long they'll be. We need bandages, blankets. We have to get him warm. He's still wet from the lake."

"He swam the lake?"

"He would have swum the Atlantic to get to you." She took off her jacket and wrapped it around Joe. "I'm going to hike to the cabin and get some supplies. I have to take Cara with me and tuck her in there until the ambulance comes. She's waiting on the path. I would have been here sooner, but I had to coax her into coming with me. She was like a frightened animal. She's sort of shell-shocked, but I was finally able to convince her she was safe now." She jumped to her feet. "I'll be back before you know it."

"I'll know it." She was stripping her own jacket off to help form a makeshift blanket. "Why did you do it, Catherine? Why bring him here?"

"Blame me, if you like, but he wasn't going to have it any other way. I could at least keep an eye on him if he was with me. I did what I thought best." She looked down at Black. "Joe killed him?"

"Gallo."

"Where is Gallo?"

"Gone."

"Why did— You can tell me about it later. I have to get to that cabin."

Eve didn't watch her leave; her gaze was on Joe's face. She lay down beside him, her hand keeping pressure on the wound while she cuddled close to try to share her body heat.

"You're going to be fine, Joe," she whispered. "You can't leave me. You've got to get well and strong and let me tell you how much I love you. No, that's all for me. Get well so that you can live life to the fullest, be what you want, take what you like."

He didn't stir.

Was he growing colder?

Panic was rising, and she held him tighter.

"Live, Joe. Hold on . . ."

ST. JOSEPH'S HOSPITAL

MILWAUKEE, WISCONSIN

"Open your eyes. Coffee," Catherine said.

Eve opened her eyes and straightened in the waiting-room chair. She took the Styrofoam cup. "Thanks."

"Though maybe I shouldn't have bothered you if you

were dozing." Catherine sat down beside Eve. "You've been living in this room for almost two days."

"I wasn't dozing. I just wanted to close everything out for a while." Stark, shining corridors, doctors, nurses, worried family members.

Joe in ICU.

Death hovering, ready to reach out and take him.

"No word yet?" Catherine asked quietly.

Eve shook her head. "Still critical. They don't know whether he's going to live or not." Her hand clenched on the steel arm of the chair. "I know. He can't die, Catherine. Not for me. Not because I won't let my Bonnie go. He's so strong. He should live to be an old, old man. If I hadn't come into his life, he would have."

"We all make choices." Catherine took a drink of her coffee. "Joe chose you. He didn't regret it. The first time I saw you with him, I realized you had something special together. If there were bad times, then he thought the good times balanced them out. That's all anyone can ask."

"No, it isn't," Eve said fiercely. "You can ask for the best, the ultimate, if you care about someone. That's what Joe should have." Then she wearily leaned back against the wall. "But I couldn't give it to him."

"Your coffee is getting cold," Catherine said. "Stop all this emotion and drink it. You need the caffeine if you're going to spend any more time here."

That was like Catherine, Eve thought. Blunt, authoritative, cut to the chase. But on occasion she could be as warm and comforting as a hand-stitched blanket passed down through loving generations. Lord, she was glad she'd had Catherine beside her for the last few days.

She lifted her cup to her lips and tasted it. "It's not cold yet." She asked, "How is Cara?"

"Short-term, fine. No physical damage but a few scratches. I hired a nice motherly woman who had nursing experience to take care of her in a small house near St. Louis County Hospital. Judy Clark is getting better, and Cara will be able to go to see her mother every day. I think that's what she needs." She grimaced. "Long-term, who knows? She's going to have nightmares for the rest of her life thanks to Black."

"Love can do a lot to heal wounds. I'll bet on Judy Clark to bring her through this." She didn't speak for a moment. She took another sip of coffee. "Have the police found John Gallo yet?"

"No, it's as if he disappeared off the face of the earth." She paused before saying, "You haven't spoken about Gallo since the first day we got Joe to the hospital. I didn't know how you were feeling, so I didn't want to push you. Is there anything you didn't tell me? I *will* find him, Eve."

"No, I told you that he as much as confessed to killing Bonnie." She looked down into her cup. "A fit of madness, Black called it. I don't think John even remembered it." Then the rage returned, sweeping reason aside. "But how could he *not* remember? It was Bonnie." She fought to control herself. She was on the edge of spiraling into an emotional tailspin about Joe, and she didn't need thoughts of Gallo to push her over. "I didn't want to believe it. Isn't that stupid?" she said unevenly.

"Yet there have been so many times that I realized he wasn't— For God's sake, he even told me he'd had moments of madness. I just couldn't connect it with Bonnie. Not after I grew to know him better."

"And he managed to con you. I can see how he would be able to do that." Catherine frowned. "But why would Queen bribe Black to take the blame?"

Eve rubbed her eyes, trying to think. It was hard to concentrate on anything but Joe. "Let's see, Gallo was unstable. If he'd found out that he'd killed his own daughter, he might have broken down and gone ballistic. He knew too much, and Queen had to maintain at least minimal control of him. He didn't want Gallo thrown into an asylum, where he'd probably spill everything. So he set up Black as the patsy for John to blame and hunt down. It was safe as long as Queen kept Black just out of John's reach."

"But then there was a glitch, and Black and Gallo were brought into firing range of each other." Catherine nodded. "It makes sense." She glanced at Eve. "And you're angry as hell."

"Yes, and I'll be more angry when I can manage to feel more than token emotions for anything but Joe. I'm pretty much on automatic right now." She took another sip of coffee. "I felt sorry for him. I think I wanted to help him. He made me feel . . . I don't know. Or maybe I can't explain. It all had to do with Bonnie."

"But that's all gone now?"

"I hope it is. I can't be sure. But it doesn't matter if it is or not." Her voice hardened. "The anger is stronger. The sense of outrage is overwhelming.

The bitterness . . . I can't even tell you about that. I'll be able to do what I have to do."

"Forget it. Just focus on Joe. I told you, I'll find Gallo." Her lips tightened. "And if he's as good as Queen said, he may be too much for me to bring him back to you alive. Wouldn't that be just too bad?"

"Yes, it would. You've done enough for me, Catherine. Just find him. That's all I ask." Eve finished the coffee. "Caffeine fix accomplished. Are you satisfied?"

"For the time being. Now what else can I do for you?"

Eve smiled crookedly. "You mean besides killing Gallo and laying him on my doorstep? I meant what I said, Catherine."

"I know you did." She paused. "And have you forgiven me for bringing Joe with me to Gallo's property that night?"

"Don't be idiotic. I knew you couldn't stop him. If you hadn't brought him, he'd have found another way." She added, "And there is something else you can do for me. My daughter, Jane MacGuire, is flying in to Milwaukee in a few hours. Will you pick her up and get her settled? Then bring her here to the hospital."

"I expected her to be here before this."

"I didn't want to tell her about Joe while he was in surgery. She couldn't do anything, and I wanted to give her good news when I told her. But there wasn't good news." Her voice was starting to break, and she had to stop and steady it. "He's still in that damn ICU, and he won't wake up."

"Eve." Catherine's hand gently touched her shoulder. "He has a chance."

"Not a good one. All the doctors think he's going to die. I can tell. They're so damn nice to me."

"Yeah, that's a pretty good indication."

"You think I'm being ridiculous." She sounded that way to herself, too. "Maybe I am. I feel so helpless. They brought in all those specialists, and they can't do anything. Someone should be able to do something. I even called my friend Megan and asked her to send a healer she knows up here. But he's working in Africa right now, and wouldn't be able to break away and get here in time."

"Healer?" Catherine asked warily. "Some kind of witch doctor?"

Eve probably shouldn't have mentioned Megan and the healer. But Megan had confidence in him, and that was enough for Eve. "What the hell do I care? As long as he can save Joe. I'd hire a voodoo priest and furnish him with a snake and a doll." She put her cup down on the coffee table. "I'm going to go to ICU now. They won't let me go inside. They only allow you a short visit every couple hours. But I can stand in the hall and look at Joe through the windows." She got to her feet. "They even try to discourage me from doing that for long periods of time. They say it's not good for me, and they don't want another patient." She headed toward the door. "As if that would matter. But they're the ones who take care of Joe. I don't want to cause any disturbance that might take their focus off him." She paused and looked back over her shoulder. "You'll pick up Jane?"

"Of course I will."

"It's British Airlines—8 P.M."

"Got it." She stood up. "And it would matter if you get so exhausted you break down. It would matter to me. It would matter to Jane. And it would damn well matter to Joe. So don't do it. We'll get through this."

Eve nodded. "I know we will." She didn't know, but she prayed. "Call me if there's any problem with Jane's flight."

She walked down the corridor toward ICU.

Soon she would be able to see Joe again. He'd be pale and drawn, his features appearing as cleanly carved and beautiful as the visage on a tomb. It would scare her to death as it always did to see him like that.

But it scared her more not to see him and to imagine him slipping away with her not by his side.

That was where she should always be. Next to Joe.

If God would let him stay with her. And if Joe still wanted her if he did come back. The memory of that last day at the lake house was suddenly before her. His eyes looking down at her as she sat in the swing.

"I can't be easy. It's not my nature. But it's my nature to love you."

And it was her nature to love Joe.

She had reached the ICU and braced herself as she walked slowly to the glass window.

Please, be better, Joe. Be awake. At least, have more color.

"Hello, Ms. Duncan." The ICU nurse, Karen Norton, was coming out of the ICU unit. "May I get you anything?"

"Yes, permission to go sit with him."

She shook her head. "It's not visiting hours." She

hesitated. "But the doctor said that maybe we should ignore the visiting hours and just let you go to him. Dr. Jarlin wants to talk to you."

She stiffened, her heart leaping. "He's better?"

The nurse shook her head. "I shouldn't have said anything," she said quickly. "Dr. Jarlin will talk to you."

Fear surged through Eve. "You talk to me, dammit. He's worse?"

The nurse was looking at her with that same sympathy and kindness that struck terror into her heart. "Dr. Jarlin will talk to you. I'll call him and tell him that you're concerned." She hurried back toward the nurses' station.

Concerned? She was sick with fear.

Joe was dying, and they weren't going to be able to save him. That was why they were going to let Eve go to him. To say good-bye.

She couldn't say good-bye. He had to stay with her.

She leaned her head on the plate-glass window and closed her eyes. She felt the tears running down her cheeks as the agony flowed through her.

Look at him. Surely she'd be able to know, to sense some change. Maybe they were wrong. Doctors didn't know everything.

She took a deep breath and opened her eyes. She stiffened in shock.

Bonnie.

Bonnie standing by Joe's bed, looking down at him.

Her expression . . . Love. Perfect love.

Why was she here?

The fear became terror.

To take him away, to ease the transition from this life to the next?

"No, Bonnie!"

Bonnie looked across the room at Eve standing behind the glass.

She smiled luminously, but then turned back again to gaze down at Joe with that same expression of love.

Oh God, what did that smile mean?

Could she help him to live?

Or could she only help him to die?

Eve's palms pressed against the cold glass as tension and sorrow tore through her.

"Joe!"

Read on for an excerpt from **Iris Johansen**'s
next book

QUINN

S top me. Find me. Kill me.

Agony tore through him as John Gallo pushed through the brush, the branches scratching his face as he ran.

How long had he been on the run?

Hours? Days?

And why couldn't he stop?

Why couldn't he let the sheriff's men find him, shoot him? He knew these woods so well that it was easy to avoid capture. Whenever they had come near, instinct and self-preservation had kicked into high gear, and he had fled.

And those instincts were so good, he thought bitterly. They had been honed by all the battles, all the killings, all the ugliness of his life. Save yourself so that you can kill again.

But at least he had not stayed to kill his hunters. That was part of the reason why he had not exposed himself. He couldn't trust himself not to kill them. He was too well trained, too expert in the ways of destruction.

And then there was the madness.

There was no telling where that sickness would take him.

He was climbing, he realized. He was climbing the high hill where he'd done his last kill.

Paul Black. He'd broken his neck.

And Joe Quinn. If he was dead, that, too, could be laid at his door.

He broke free of the shrubs and trees and was standing on the edge of the cliff over the lake.

What was he doing there?

One step, and he would plunge over the precipice.

Why not?

Maybe that damnable instinct would not kick in when he hit the lake below.

"It will, you know."

He stiffened, afraid to turn around to see who had spoken.

Madness. It was back, taunting him, torturing him.

"Look at me."

He slowly looked over his shoulder.

A little seven-year-old girl, with curly red-brown hair wearing a Bugs Bunny T-shirt.

The same T-shirt she had worn the day she had died.

The day he might have killed her.

The agony was overwhelming, searing through him, blocking everything but the sight of her and his own guilt.

His daughter, Bonnie . . .

MILWAUKEE AIRPORT
MILWAUKEE, WISCONSIN

"You're Jane MacGuire?"

Jane turned away from the baggage claim carousel to see the woman who had spoken walking toward her. It had to be Catherine Ling, she thought. Her adoptive mother, Eve, had described the CIA agent in detail, but the reality was even more stunning. Catherine Ling was part Asian, part Caucasian, and more exotic and magnetic than any woman Jane had seen except on the movie screen. She appeared to be in her late twenties, tall, graceful, with high cheekbones, huge dark eyes slightly tilted at the corners, olive-gold skin, long dark hair pulled back in a chignon. But it was the aura of power and vitality that surrounded her that was the most impressive. As an artist, Jane's first impulse was to ask her to pose for her. The second was to squeeze every bit of information she could from her. "I'm Jane. You're Catherine Ling? How is Joe?"

"Is that your bag?" Catherine lifted Jane's suitcase off the carousel with easy strength. "Joe was no better when I left the hospital. But as far as I know, he's no worse. Eve doesn't want to leave him, so she asked me to pick you up. I've made reservations for you at a Hyatt near the hospital. We'll check you in, then I'll take you to the hospital."

Jane shook her head. "To hell with that. I'm going to the hospital to be with Eve. I should have been with her ever since Joe was admitted. It's been almost two days. Why the hell didn't she call me before this?"

"You were in London, and there wasn't much you could do. Joe was in surgery for a long time. Eve said she didn't want to talk to you until she could give you good news." She headed toward the exit. "That didn't happen, so she called you anyway. She thought you should be here."

Jane nodded jerkily. "That's what she said. She was so upset that she didn't realize how that sounded. I felt like I was flying to a deathbed." She took her suitcase from Catherine. "She didn't even tell me what happened with Joe, only about his wound. A knife thrust to the back that did serious organ damage." Her lips tightened. "A knife. Whose knife? I don't want to stress Eve out by asking questions. That means you're on the hot seat, Catherine. I want to know everything before I walk into that hospital."

Catherine nodded. "I thought that would be my job." She stopped before a silver Toyota. "Get in. I'll fill you in while I drive you to the hospital." She slipped into the driver's seat. "But I'm going to go through a drive-through McDonald's and get you a cup of coffee."

"You think I'll need the caffeine to get through this?"

Catherine gave her an appraising glance as she started the car. "I think you're probably a cool customer. But you love Eve and Joe. They raised you from the time you were ten. You have a right to be upset and need a little bolstering." She pulled out of the airport parking lot. "And if you don't, I do. You're going to be pissed at me."

"Am I?" Jane stiffened. "Why?"

"I'm partly the reason Joe was hurt."

"Then yes, I'll be pissed at you. I'll want to break your neck. Is Eve angry with you?"

"No, she says no one could have stopped Joe."

Jane slowly nodded. "She's right. No one could ever stop Joe from doing what he wanted to do. I knew that the first time I saw him. But it relieved me. I knew if Joe ever became my friend, it wouldn't be because Eve wanted him to do it. It would be because he wanted it himself. That was important to me. I was a ten-year-old Eve had picked up from the streets because we'd known the moment we'd come together that it was right we stay together. But Joe was a big part of her life even then. I didn't want to have to walk away."

"And you didn't have to do it," Catherine said. "You became a family." She smiled faintly. "A very strange family. Eve Duncan, a famous forensic sculptor, Joe Quinn, a police detective, and you, a kid from the streets."

"We learned to mesh," Jane said. "Eve was no problem. Joe was slower. But we both loved Eve, so we worked at it." She smiled. "And then as we got to know each other, it wasn't work any longer. Funny how love makes everything easier."

"Yeah, funny." Catherine pulled into the McDonald's drive-through. "Do you want anything besides coffee?"

"No."

"Black?"

"Yes."

She studied Catherine as she gave the coffee order. How much love had Catherine had in her life, she wondered. Eve had told her she'd been a street kid like Jane but had grown up in Hong Kong. She'd married a much older man, then been widowed. She had come into Eve's life when she'd asked Eve to help her find her son, who had been kidnapped by a Russian criminal wanting revenge on Catherine. Eve had helped her rescue him, and they had become close friends. There was no doubt in Eve's mind that Catherine adored her son, Luke. But Jane had gotten the impression that, other than Luke, Catherine's life had been her job as a CIA agent.

"You're looking at me as if you're trying to take me apart." Catherine's look was quizzical as she handed Jane her coffee. "Is it your artist's eye, or are you taking aim?"

"Maybe a little of both." Jane met her gaze. "I admit the first thing I thought when I saw you was that I'd like to paint you. But you'll definitely be on my list for extermination if you had anything to do with Joe lying in that hospital. Tell me what happened to him." She looked away, and added, "Let me start you on the path. It was about Bonnie, wasn't it?"

Catherine nodded. "It's not surprising that was your first guess. I imagine you've lived with Eve's obsession for finding Bonnie since you came to her."

"Guess?" Jane took a drink of her coffee. "Finding her daughter's murderer and her daughter's body has guided her life. It's guided all our lives. She's tried for many, many years to bring her Bonnie home." She looked out the window at the passing scene. "And Joe's been with her, trying desperately to understand, to help, to find Bonnie, so that Eve could be at peace. I can't tell you how many times she's come to what she thought was that final resolution and been disappointed. But she never gives up."

Catherine added quietly, "And Joe was getting tired, weary of worrying about her, wanting her to come to terms."

Jane looked back at her. "Yes, how do you know? Joe wouldn't complain."

"Joe and I are a lot alike," Catherine said. "And I had to examine all facets of Eve's problem before I made a move to ask her to help me find my son, Luke. I didn't want to make a mistake."

"Mistake?"

"I promised her I'd pay her back for helping return my son to me," Catherine said. "She wouldn't accept anything, but I couldn't let it go. I knew the only gift she would think worthwhile would be for me to find her daughter's killer." Her lips twisted. "So that was what I had to give her. Whether or not it might destroy the life she had with Joe."

"You found him?" Jane's eyes widened. "You actually found Bonnie's killer?"

"I found two possibilities. Paul Black, who was already on Eve's search list."

"She told me about him."

"But I was betting on a new stallion in the race. One that would be much more troublesome. Naturally, I had to pull him front and center."

"Who?"

Catherine's eyes were fixed on the towers of St. Joseph's Hospital, which had come into view. "John Gallo. He was Bonnie's father."

Jane stiffened. "What? But Eve told me he was dead."

Catherine shook her head. "A cover-up by the military. Eve will explain everything later. I'm just giving you the bare bones. But there was evidence Gallo was in Atlanta the month Bonnie was kidnapped. So I gave Eve all my information and threw in my opinion."

"And she went after John Gallo," Jane whispered.

"And Paul Black," Catherine said. "But she felt terribly guilty about risking Joe again. So she tried to leave him out of it."

"She should have known that wouldn't work," Jane said. She knew how guilty Eve felt about involving Joe, but she could no more stop hunting for Bonnie's killer than Joe could abandon Eve and stop protecting her. Both were facts of life. "Gallo hurt Joe?"

Catherine shook her head. "Paul Black. And Gallo killed Black."

"Good."

"Not so good. Before he died, Black told Eve that Gallo had killed Bonnie."

"And she actually believed the bastard?"

"She told me that she would swear Black was telling

the truth. And Gallo took off and disappeared. Neither the police nor I have been able to find him."

"But what would make him kill his own little girl?"

"He was suffering from bouts of schizophrenia and violent delusions caused by years of mistreatment in a prison in North Korea."

"My God." Jane shook her head. "That must have been a terrible nightmare for Eve. How can you imagine a man who gave you a child could kill it?"

Catherine's lips tightened. "Well, I handed Gallo to her and made her imagine it." She pulled into a parking spot in the lot of St. Joseph's Hospital. "And then I helped Joe try to find him whether Eve wanted him along or not." She turned off the ignition. "Are you still blaming Joe and not me?"

Jane gazed at her a moment. "You're blaming yourself enough. You don't need any help." She got out of the car. "Where can I find her?"

"ICU. The visiting hours are very short, but Eve can watch him through the glass. If she's not in the waiting room, she'll probably be in the hall at ICU."

"Are you coming with me?"

Catherine shook her head. "Eve needs family. I'll check you in at the Hyatt and take your suitcase up to your room. Give me a call when you're ready to leave the hospital."

"Thanks." Jane turned to walk away.

"How did you feel about Bonnie?" Catherine asked suddenly. "I know it's none of my business, but I'm curious. You said that the search for her killer ruled your lives. That must have been difficult for an adopted kid to accept."

Jane shook her head. "I knew what was important to Eve when I came to her. I wasn't her child, I was her friend. That was enough for me. How could I ask for more?"

"Some kids would have been more demanding."

Jane lifted her brows. "You?"

Catherine shook her head. "But then I probably wouldn't have accepted any relationship when I was your age. I was an independent young demon. I suppose I still am."

"Eve is always the exception," Jane said. "You obviously have a close relationship with her now."

Catherine smiled as she started to back out of the parking place. "You're right. You and I are more alike than I would have believed. Eve is the sun we all revolve around."

Jane watched her drive out of the parking lot before she started to walk across the parking lot toward the front entrance. She could feel the tension increase with every step. She was going to Joe, who might well be dying. She was going to Eve, who could lose the man who made her life worth living.

How did she feel about the search for Bonnie? Jane had said all the right things, and they had all been true. What she hadn't told Catherine was the agony she felt when Eve and Joe were put in danger by that search. She could accept it. But she couldn't stop wishing that the search would end.

And she couldn't stop wishing that Eve would release Bonnie.

Or, dear God, that Bonnie would release Eve.

Eve walked slowly down the corridor toward the ICU.

Soon she would be able to see Joe again. He'd be pale and drawn, his features appearing as cleanly carved and beautiful as the visage on a tomb. It would scare her to death as it always did.

But it scared her more not to see him and to imagine him slipping away with her not by his side.

That was where she should always be. Next to Joe.

If God would let him stay with her. And if Joe still wanted her if he did come back. The memory of that last day at the lake house was suddenly before her. His eyes looking down at her as she sat in the swing.

"I can't be easy. It's not my nature. But it's my nature to love you."

And it was her nature to love Joe.

Please be better, Joe. Be awake. At least, have more color.

"Good afternoon, Ms. Duncan." The ICU nurse was coming out of the unit. "May I get you anything?"

"Yes, permission to go sit with him."

She shook her head. "Not yet." She hesitated. "But the doctor said that maybe we should let you go to him soon."

She stiffened, her heart leaping. "He's better."

The nurse shook her head. "I shouldn't have said anything," she said quickly. "Dr. Jarlin will talk to you."

Fear surged through her. "You talk to me, dammit. He's worse?"

The nurse was looking at Eve with that same sympathy and kindness that had struck terror in her heart since she'd brought Joe to the hospital. "Dr. Jarlin will talk to you. I'll call him and tell him that you're concerned." She hurried back toward the nurses' station.

Concerned? She was sick with fear.

Joe was dying, and they weren't going to be able to save him. That was why they were going to let Eve go to him. To say good-bye.

She couldn't say good-bye. He had to stay with her.

She leaned her head on the plate-glass window and closed her eyes. She felt the tears running down her cheeks as the agony flowed through her.

Look at him. Surely she'd be able to know, to sense some change. Maybe they were wrong. Doctors didn't know everything.

She took a deep breath and opened her eyes. She stiffened in shock.

Bonnie.

Through the years she had often had visions and dreams of her daughter. Then she had come to believe they weren't visions at all. It didn't matter. Real or not, having Bonnie come to her had made life worth living and let her come alive in so many ways.

But now something was different.

Bonnie, in her Bugs Bunny T-shirt, her red-brown

*hair shining in the lights of the ICU, as she stood by
Joe's bed, looking down at him.*

Her expression . . . Love. Perfect love.

Why was she here?

The fear became terror.

*To take him away, to ease the transition from this life
to the next?*

"No, Bonnie!"

*Her daughter looked across the room at Eve stand-
ing behind the glass.*

*She smiled luminously. But then turned back again
to gaze down at Joe with that same expression of love.*

*What did that smile mean? Could she help him to
live?*

Or could she only help him to die?

*Eve's palms pressed against the cold glass as tension
and sorrow tore through her.*

"Joe!"

Swirling darkness.

Someone calling.

"Joe!"

Calling him . . .

But he didn't want to leave the darkness. There was
comfort here and yet also a strange excitement and anticipation.

Was this death?

He had never been afraid of it. He wasn't now.

But that voice calling . . .

Eve.

She was hurting, needing him. He should go back.

And there was someone else . . .

Bonnie.

She was there in the darkness. Always before she had been the stranger, the one apart; but now she was close, as familiar to him as Eve, and much of the comfort was coming from her. Did she want him to stay in the darkness?

But he could feel Eve's terror and sadness.

He had to stop them both and try to make Eve happy.

As she made him happy . . .

He had known from the first moment he had seen her all those years ago that he could not be happy if he was not with her.

Strange . . . He had not believed that love could come out of nowhere and stay forever. He had been such a cynical son of a bitch. Smart, young FBI agent, sure of himself and everything around him, ready to take on the world.

He'd been certain the Bonnie Duncan kidnapping wasn't going to be a problem. The local Atlanta police were sure that she was the victim of a serial killer, and the little girl would never show up alive. Sad story, but Joe had worked on other serial killings and had experience in profiling as well. He was well qualified to take on the case. He'd go down to Atlanta and dive in and show the locals how the FBI could handle a case like Bonnie's.

But he wouldn't get involved with the family of the victim no matter how sympathetic he was toward them.

That was always a mistake. It was better to stand apart
so that he could work without emotion. That would be
far more efficient.

Yes, after all, it was just one more case. A few months
in Atlanta, and he'd be coming back to start another job.
There was nothing about this Duncan case in Atlanta
to interfere with his career, certainly nothing to interfere with his life . . .